ale chne 1974

Other Books by Meridel Le Sueur
The Girl
Song for My Time
Women on the Breadlines
Harvest
Rites of Ancient Ripening
Corn Village
Crusaders
North Star Country
Salute to Spring
Annunciation

Books for Children by Meridel Le Sueur
The Mound Builders
Conquistadores
The River Road: A Story of Abraham Lincoln
Chanticleer of Wilderness Road
Sparrow Hawk
Nancy Hanks of Wilderness Road
Little Brother of the Wilderness: The Story of Johnny Appleseed

RIPENING

RIPENING

SELECTED WORK
SECOND EDITION

MERIDEL LeSUEUR

Edited and with an Introduction by Elaine Hedges
and a New Afterword by Meridel Le Sueur

THE FEMINIST PRESS
at The City University of New York
New York

Published 1990 by The Feminist Press at The City University of New York, 311 East 94 Street, New York, N.Y. 10128
Distributed by The Talman Company, 150 Fifth Avenue, New York, N.Y. 10011
Printed in the United States of America on pH-neutral paper by McNaughton & Gunn, Inc.
Second Edition
93 92 91 90 5 4 3 2 1

Library of Congress Cataloging-in-Publication Data

Le Sueur, Meridel.
  Ripening: selected work

  Bibliography: p.
  I. Hedges, Elaine.   II. Title.
PS3523.E79A6   1986   813'.52   86-18308
ISBN 0-935312-41-2 (pbk.)

We gratefully acknowledge the permission to reprint the following copyrighted material:
  "Annunciation," "The Girl," "I Was Marching," "Eroded Woman" and "The Dark of the Time," reprinted by permission of International Publishers Co., Inc. © 1948, 1956, 1966.
  "The Ancient People and the Newly Come," reprinted by permission from *Growing Up in Minnesota: Ten Writers Remember Their Childhoods*, edited by Chester G. Anderson, The University of Minnesota Press, Minneapolis. © 1976 by the University of Minnesota.

This project is supported in part by public funds from the National Endowment for the Arts and from the New York State Council on the Arts.

Cover photograph by Jerome Liebling. Frontispiece photograph by Deborah Le Sueur. Photographs on page 222 (*top right, bottom*) and on page 250 by Jerome Liebling. All other photographs from the personal collection of Meridel Le Sueur.

Text design by Lea Smith.

For the continuous matriarchal root — Hannah Berfield; her daughter, my grandmother, Netty Lucy; her daughter, my mother, Marian Wharton; my daughters, Rachel and Deborah; their daughters, and their daughters, the root cycle turning into view.

ACKNOWLEDGMENTS

In ways that are a tribute to Meridel Le Sueur's belief in the goodness and generosity of people, this book has been a collective, shared undertaking. I wish to thank especially the members of The Feminist Press staff, Laurie Olsen and Carol Ahlum, who, many years ago, made the first visit to St. Paul, Minnesota, to begin collecting copies of Le Sueur's writings; and Paul Lauter and Louis Kampf, who read the first selection of materials and contributed their suggestions and ideas. My debt to Florence Howe is deep: for first proposing that I write about Meridel Le Sueur; and for working with me as I researched material, planned the book's contents and organization, and wrote the first draft of the manuscript. Her encouragement and enthusiasm have been unflagging. And behind all of these people stands Tillie Olsen, out of whose fiercely loving retention of all she has ever read by women writers first came the idea that The Feminist Press should publish a volume on Meridel Le Sueur.

Two pioneers in the Le Sueur revival deserve special thanks. John Crawford, whose West End Press publications of Le Sueur's works have done so much to bring her to a larger audience, has given unstintingly of his time, advice, and materials, and I hope that this book will justify his patient anticipation of it. Neala Young Schleuning most generously provided me with a copy of her unpublished dissertation on Le Sueur, a sensitive and comprehensive study of Le Sueur's life and work that has been invaluable.

It has been a pleasure to work with my editor, Elsa Dixler, who has read the manuscript with a sensitivity to both prose style and content from which I have richly benefited. Shirley Frank's painstaking work as copyeditor warrants special gratitude. Some texts presented difficult editing problems which she superbly solved.

The largest debt of all is, of course, to Meridel Le Sueur herself. Over the years in which this book has found its shape, she has been its nourisher, providing everything from food and shelter on research trips to Minnesota, to endless hours and days of her time for interviews. Above all she has given of her own indomitable spirit, to the book and its editor, as to all who meet her.

ELAINE HEDGES

CONTENTS

x   CONTENTS

Three Poems

LIST OF ILLUSTRATIONS

Introduction

ELAINE HEDGES

In 1940 a small book, *Salute to Spring*, containing twelve pieces of fiction and journalism by Meridel Le Sueur, appeared under the imprint of International Publishers. Its jacket carried blurbs by, among others, Nelson Algren, Sinclair Lewis, Zona Gale, and Carl Sandburg — testimony to the widespread recognition Le Sueur had achieved during the 1930s. During that decade, for example, sixteen of her published short stories were either reprinted or cited in Edward O'Brien's annual collections of best short stories; and one of her pieces of reportage, "I Was Marching," was reprinted three times, establishing itself as a classic of thirties literature.

Yet during the next twenty years Meridel Le Sueur dropped out of sight. What happened was of course what happened to many other radicals of the thirties in the aftermath of World War II. The repressive literary and political climate of the Cold War and McCarthyism forced Le Sueur underground, cut off many of her publishing outlets, and often made it impossible for her to find work of any kind. With the freer political climate of the 1960s and, toward the end of that decade, the emergence of the new women's movement, her work began to receive renewed attention. By now that work, and Le Sueur herself at the age of eighty-two, are enjoying a well-deserved revival. In 1970 a small collection of her work was reprinted under the title *Corn Village*. West End Press has published three collections of her reportage and stories, as well as her novel *The Girl*, written in the thirties but never before published; there have been interviews with and articles about her in Left and feminist journals; *Salute to Spring* has been reissued; a film, a dissertation, a one-woman performance, and several musical compositions have been produced by young women attracted to her work; and Le Sueur herself, having never ceased writing, is not only traveling, lecturing, and reading her poetry to large audiences, but is also publishing new work.

Meridel Le Sueur today is a woman whose ardor, energy, and sense of commitment are undiminished by age. Age, indeed, has released new energies, and "Ripening," the title for this edition of her work, is her metaphor both for her belief in the unbroken continuum of her work — its organic growth and unfolding — and for her sense of personal and literary fulfillment. Her writings include journalism, fiction (short stories and novels), poetry, history, autobiography, and biography. They comprise a record of over fifty years of faithful and passionate witness to many of the central economic, political, and social realities of twentieth-century American life — and especially to the lives of women.

Le Sueur was born at the very beginning of the century, in February, 1900, in Murray, Iowa; and the Midwest has remained her spiritual home. Her childhood and adolescence were spent in Texas, Oklahoma, and Kansas, in the care of several remarkable women, and in an environment that exposed her to a rich midwestern tradition of radical political thought and action. Le Sueur has written extensively about her grandmother, a third-generation Puritan, an Iowa pioneer, one of the first settlers, gun in hand, of the Oklahoma territory — and a militant temperance worker in the WCTU. Le Sueur's mother, Marian Wharton, was one of the "new women" of the early twentieth century: while raising three children she also, until well over the age of seventy-five, pursued an active career as a feminist and a socialist. In her youth, too, Le Sueur developed strong friendships with American Indian women (about one of whom, Zona, she writes eloquently in her autobiographical essay, "The Ancient People and the Newly Come") and with the Polish, Irish, and Scandinavian immigrant women who were settling the Midwest. Through these friendships she acquired a knowledge of women's lives and of attitudes and values that both enriched and challenged those of her own white, middle-class, Protestant culture.

In these years, too, through her mother and her stepfather, Le Sueur was exposed to that midwestern tradition of radical dissent that included the Populists, the Non-Partisan League, the International Workers of the World (IWW), the Socialist Party, and the Farmer-Labor Party. Arthur Le Sueur was a socialist lawyer whom Marian Wharton met and married while both were teaching at the People's College, a correspondence school for workers in Fort Scott, Kansas. Throughout their lives, Marian Wharton and Arthur Le Sueur were leading participants in the reform movements that were the midwestern farmers' and workers' response, from the late nineteenth century on, to the growth of railroad monopolies and grain cartels. The Le Sueur residences in Fort Scott and later in St. Paul, Minnesota, were meeting-places for Wobblies, anarchists, socialists, and union organizers. By her early teens Le Sueur had met Helen Keller, Eugene Debs, Alexander Berkman, and Ella (Mother) Bloor. And she had absorbed both the

IWW ideal of the worker-writer and a belief in the artist as activist and revolutionary.

By 1916 Le Sueur had quit high school, prompted by her dislike of the literary curriculum and by the ostracism she suffered as the daughter of socialists, and she had also spent a brief period in Chicago, where she studied dance and physical fitness at Bernarr McFadden's Physical Culture School. From Chicago she moved to New York, where, while living in an anarchist commune with Berkman and Emma Goldman, she studied at the American Academy of Dramatic Art and worked on the New York stage. Remembering her years in the New York theater, Le Sueur describes herself as having been "groomed like a mare"; she worked with David Belasco and appeared ("me from the Midwest prairie learning how to wear long skirts") in "Lady Windermere's Fan."[1]

Hollywood, where she moved next, was no better. Here she became part of what was known as the "meat market" of young women who worked as extras in the then-burgeoning silent film industry. She supported herself not only by working as a waitress but by taking jobs as a stunt woman. Usually she had to sign a statement releasing the studio from responsibility in case of her death, but the twenty-five dollars a day that she earned gave her free time to write. Once, she recalls, she stood in for Pearl White in a fencing scene in "The Perils of Pauline." Her eventual decision to leave Hollywood seems to have been prompted in part by being offered a contract on condition that she have surgery done on her "Semitic" nose.

Moving to San Francisco, Le Sueur worked there and in Sacramento in little theater, further eking out a living with jobs in restaurants and factories. And increasingly she wrote. For years she had contributed to labor and left-wing journals, including the *Worker* and *Masses*. Now she began publishing book reviews in the San Francisco *Call*; and toward the end of the decade her first short stories appeared.

The years from about 1917 to 1927 were bleak ones for Le Sueur: years of marginal jobs, uncertain income, and dislocation. And they were lived in a political climate that was equally bleak. World War I to Le Sueur was "a great and terrible drama," from which many of the young men she had known did not return; and the end of the war ushered in a period of political persecution and repression often overlooked in descriptions of the twenties as the "Jazz Age" or the "Age of the Flapper."

The postwar years saw Attorney General A. Mitchell Palmer's raids on private homes; the trials and deportations of aliens, including Le Sueur's friends Goldman and Berkman; the persecution of pacifists and socialists, including Le Sueur's mother and stepfather; and the collapse of the reform movements that had characterized the Progressive era. The tragic culmination of the period, for Le Sueur and many others, was the trial and, in 1927, the execution of the Italian immigrant anarchists Sacco and Vanzetti.

By 1927, Le Sueur recollects, "Everything had failed. Selling yourself, breaking your nose, failing at theater. . . . I had no job, no money." Yet in that year, while in jail for having participated in a protest against the Sacco and Vanzetti executions, Le Sueur made the decision to have a child. Some time earlier she had married Harry Rice, a labor organizer she had known in St. Paul. Born Yasha Rabanov in Russia, Rice was a Marxist and a conscientious objector who had spent the years of World War I in Leavenworth prison. Le Sueur's decision to have a child, however, seems to have been her own, not encouraged by her husband or her friends, who saw children — in the phrase H. L. Mencken made famous — as "cannon fodder" for another war. For Le Sueur, however, the decision marked a turning point; and since much of her writing, especially in recent decades, is inspired by the idea of the continuity of life through women, the reasons for her decision are worth noting. To have a child, she has said, was a choice for life in a world that (in the words of the story she would write about her pregnancy) was "dead and closed." It was her way of "giving a gift," even to a society that did not want it, and of giving a gift to herself as well. Looking back now, she remembers having in mind also a statement by Lenin that the primal relationship between mother and child is the only communality left in capitalist society.

Le Sueur's daughter, Rachel, was born in 1928. Less than two years later she gave birth to a second daughter, Deborah. By the time the stock market crashed in October 1929, she had moved to Minnesota, where her mother and stepfather were living, and she had begun a new period in her political and literary work.

The fiction that Le Sueur wrote and started to publish during the 1920s began to explore subject matter and to establish themes that she has pursued throughout her work. Central to these explorations in the early work is the figure of a "raw green girl," lonely, curious, seeking — Le Sueur herself as she began to transcribe and transform into literature her own feelings and experiences. In 1927, the same year in which she decided to have a child, she published in the *Dial* a story called "Persephone." She had begun the story in 1921 (the year of her own coming-of-age) at a time when, as she has recently explained, she felt rejected by her own mother and "lost" in the male-controlled world of Hollywood. "I wanted and expected to kill myself. . . . I was already dead," she recalls, and she did attempt suicide at the time.[2] Writing the story, with its controlling myth of Demeter and Persephone, sustained her. The story, set in rural Kansas, describes a young girl's innocent life with her mother, and the violent interruption of their relationship when the girl is abducted by a dark, Pluto-like figure, a man named March. Now mysteriously ill, the girl is being accompanied to a hospital by the story's narrator, who, distressed and anxious, ponders the meaning of the girl's life and her apparently fatal sickness.

Today Le Sueur says that her "identification with the myth of Persephone and Demeter saved [her] life," and certainly the story is a compelling example of the emotional and psychological power of the creative image.[3] It also marks Le Sueur's first use of what would become her central formulation of female experience. The separation from the mother, the plunge into the darkness of the underground, the woman (or the earth) as wounded, invaded, and raped — these are key images in her portrayals of women's lives. In time, Le Sueur added to them, as she explored the further implications of the Demeter-Persephone myth, the images of rebirth from the darkness and of a return to the mother and the world of women. In Le Sueur's later work, the young and wandering Persephone, "lost to the realm of her nativity," not only returns to the mother but is herself transformed into Demeter.

Sometimes, in the stories of the twenties, the Persephone figure is the central character, and the stories explore her inner life of thought and feeling. Sometimes she is the narrative voice, herself transcribing and trying to understand the lives and experiences of others. In these latter stories, it is particularly the lives of working-class women, and of the midwestern pioneers of Le Sueur's childhood, that are examined. In such stories as "Laundress" and "Our Fathers," Le Sueur began to show that deep concern for the lives of anonymous women and men that would inspire much of her work. The narrator of these stories is observant and sympathetic, if sometimes distanced or detached by her youth and inexperience, as she struggles to extract meaning from ordinary lives. In "Laundress," the narrator tries to comprehend the life of Mrs. Kretch, who has worked for her family. Mrs. Kretch's life of struggle, yet of efficiency and order, conveys to the narrator both a compelling dignity and some further, secret meaning that she cannot grasp. It is this as yet ungraspable meaning that the budding author wants to pursue. "Our Fathers" focuses on the lives of the narrator's own male ancestors: their restless movement across the country, their easy abandonment of roots and family, and the effects of this abandonment on the women — mothers, daughters, wives — left behind. "Laundress" appeared in Mencken's *American Mercury* in 1927, but "Our Fathers" was not published until 1937, and then only in a comparatively obscure journal. Le Sueur worked on "Our Fathers" through the twenties and thirties, and eventually the story grew into a novel, *I Hear Men Talking*, which she has recently returned to, revised, and completed. The novel describes the small-town, midwestern life of its narrator,

Penelope, and her rebellion against it as she moves through adolescence into young womanhood. Eventually she leaves her rural home for the city, and Le Sueur's recently published novel of the depression decade, *The Girl*, is in fact the continuation of Penelope's story in a new time and place.

Other stories that Le Sueur wrote in the twenties, although they were not published until later, show her beginning to explore the sexual dimension of women's lives. Such stories as "Wind," "Spring Story," "Harvest," and "The Horse" all have as central characters either adolescent girls or young, sometimes newly married, women. The dawning sexual awareness of the young girl in "Spring Story" induces both unease and an excited sense of new beginnings. The young wives in "Wind" and "Harvest" struggle with conflicting feelings of pride and disappointment in their new role, and of sexual desire and fear toward their husbands.

In treating women's sexuality, Le Sueur claims she could find few literary models. An important mentor for her in the twenties was the Wisconsin author, Zona Gale, who encouraged Le Sueur to write and helped get her work published. But Gale's own writings, like those of other women writers of her time, tend to avoid any direct treatment of sexuality. This was part of the price they paid in order to be accepted as writers, and it was to some extent also the result of their need to reject marriage, as they saw it in their mothers' lives, with its sexual obligations and reproductive responsibilities. A rupture seems to have occurred between Gale and Le Sueur when Le Sueur had her first child, an event Gale saw as interfering with her literary career.

The author to whom Le Sueur did turn was D. H. Lawrence. Although today Le Sueur agrees that Lawrence's influence was not always beneficial, in the twenties, she insists, "Lawrence saved my life. I'd never have gotten out of that Puritanism without Lawrence." "That Puritanism" was the inheritance, especially through her grandmother, of attitudes of shame, guilt, and disdain for the body, and of habits of sexual repression, against which she had early rebelled. Her memories of her grandmother, so full of a sense of self-reliance and courage, are also deeply shadowed by an almost appalled sense of her emotional and sexual self-denial. A home where bright colors were considered sinful, a grandmother dressed always in black who never looked at her own body naked and whose primary emotional outlet was singing Protestant hymns — these are key memories of childhood for Le Sueur. Growing up, she has said, was "a struggle to have sex at all," and her personal need to get away from the "terrible purity" of her family background became a primary motivation for her writing about women's sexual experience.

The Lawrentian element in Le Sueur's stories of the 1920s can be seen in the supercharged descriptions in "Harvest" of the farm wife's sexual feelings for her husband, Le Sueur's identification of the wife's pregnancy with the fertility of the fields, and her contrasting these natural proccesses with the husband's interest in "rational" and technological methods of cultivating the land. In "Wind" the eventual union of estranged husband and wife is accomplished through a Lawrentian epiphany of wind and rain; and "The Horse" echoes Lawrence's use of that animal to suggest male sexual virility and freedom, as the young woman in the story is attracted to the animal and rides it with increasing abandon. One finds also in Lawrence's work as in Le Sueur's the interest in the Persephone story and the idea of the dark underground. Lawrence's example may also have encouraged Le Sueur's own tendency to see sex as a central and transforming experience for women — and one that is achieved through the agency of the male. In Le Sueur's work women often acquire some essential but previously unavailable knowledge of themselves through their first heterosexual experience. On the other hand, these early stories also contain emphases Le Sueur would make her own: women's ambivalence within marriage, as in "Wind," and the loss of the mother as the young girl turns to heterosexual love, as in "Persephone."

By the end of the 1920s Le Sueur had begun to move beyond the Persephone character. "Annunciation," the story she wrote about her own first pregnancy, was, she has said, "the bud of a new flower within the time of the old," an advance beyond the isolation, narcissism, and loneliness that were so often the controlling emotions in the earlier stories. Although the story was not published until 1935, when it appeared in a small private edition, Le Sueur began "Annunciation" in 1927, in the form of notes to her unborn child. The story is set in the hard times that the poor experienced even before the stock market crash, and it describes a young wife living in a one-room flat with a husband who opposes her pregnancy. Alone most of the day while he looks for work, the woman becomes absorbed in thoughts of the new life quickening within her. She writes notes to the unborn child on scraps of paper; and in a prose supple enough to be both richly metaphorical and starkly literal, Le Sueur communicates a vision of the world transfigured by the woman's sense of "inward blossoming." The ordinary acts of her tenement neighbors take on new meaning: a boy leaning over a table reading a book, a woman hanging clothes on a line — these acts seem newly imbued with life and possibility. The pear tree that the pregnant woman observes from her porch during the long, solitary afternoons becomes Le Sueur's central symbol for life and its continuity even in the "darkest time." Rooted in the dark ground and spiraling upward through trunk, branch, twig, leaf, and bud to produce its fruit, the tree bestows its secular annunciation on the woman, offering her a vision of the world in which "everything seems to be moving along a curve of creation."

"Annunciation" has been called "a small American masterpiece," and it was well received in its time. It was hailed for its "gravely achieved affirmations of life" and for its poetic evocation of its author's "profound and passionate feeling of connection and union with all that lives and has ever lived."[4] By the time it was published, however, halfway through the decade of the thirties, Le Sueur had moved on to produce new work, in which she was expressing her "passionate feeling of connection and union" through explorations of the political, economic, and social realities of life in the depression.

As for many other writers, the thirties, and especially the early thirties, were years of intensely satisfying work for Le Sueur. In a time of unprecedented crisis, with the American economy in collapse, political activists could believe in radical social change as a real possibility. Josephine Herbst, a writer who also achieved a wide reputation in the thirties, once described what she called the "beauty" of the decade as its "communion among people, its generosity."[5] This sense of communion, of being part of a collective effort of shared revolutionary goals and expectations, both sustained and inspired Le Sueur. Although economically life remained precarious—for a time she lived with her two children in a single room; after working all day, she put her head under the cold water tap to stay awake and write—the quantity of work she produced suggests the stimulus she felt. A rough count (there is as yet no definitive bibliography) reveals over two dozen pieces of reportage; almost thirty short stories; a book, *Worker Writers*—a manual for writers derived from classes she taught under WPA auspices; the novel, *The Girl*; some poems and miscellaneous articles; pieces written for *Vogue* and *Harper's Bazaar* in order to make money; and the journals in which she wrote daily, as she has throughout her whole creative life.

The sense of having an audience for her work, and her participation in a wide variety of clubs, organizations, and groups working for social change, also gave her the satisfactions of involvement and activity, in sharp contrast to the isolation and despair she had felt during the 1920s. "Nourishing" is Le Sueur's word for the organizations of the Left in the thirties. For her these included the John Reed Clubs, established by the Communist Party to encourage new writers, through which she met Jack Conroy and Richard Wright; the *New Masses*, whose staff she joined for a time; *Midwest* Magazine, a regional publication she and Dale Kramer founded in 1936; the Workers Alliance, an organization of artists and workers for whose newspaper she wrote; and the Writers Project of the federal WPA. There were also meetings, formal and informal, with other professional writers — a group living in downtown St. Paul that included Le Sueur's friend Grace Flandreau and her husband. And there were the meetings in New York in 1935 and 1936 of the American Writers Congress, at the first of which she read a paper and was a member of the presiding committee.

Nourishing, too, were her associations with other women. After returning to Minnesota, Le Sueur lived for a time in the small village of Lakeland on the banks of the St. Croix River. With the money from her magazine writing she bought flour, with which other women made bread for all to share. It was a deeply rewarding experience in communal living for her. Later she lived with another group of women and their children in an abandoned warehouse in St. Paul. The women pooled their relief money and food and in the evenings wrote and told each other stories, with Le Sueur taking down the tales of those who could not write. The experience contributed to her reportage about women in the thirties, and to her novel *The Girl*, which describes a group of women who have bonded together to survive the depression.

One of Le Sueur's most transforming experiences in the thirties was her involvement in the Minneapolis truckers strike in 1934. In a year of widespread labor unrest, the Minneapolis strike halted almost all trucking in the city, and 35,000 other workers declared a sympathy walkout. Le Sueur worked with the women's auxiliary in the strike kitchen and hospital, pouring coffee, washing cups, dabbing alcohol on wounds, and finally joining in the massive protest march that followed the killing of two strikers, and the wounding of forty-eight others by the police. Josephine Herbst observed that one of the effects of the "communion" among people in the thirties was to enable writers, especially middle-class writers, to get out of "the constricted I"; and this was the effect of the Minneapolis strike on Le Sueur.[6] In her well-known article, "I Was Marching," she charts the stages of her participation in the collective strike effort, and presents a sense of fusing with a larger reality; as she merges with others, it is as if a new reality were coming into being. "For the first time in my life," she concludes in "I Was Marching," "I feel most alive and yet . . . not . . . separate."

A year later, Le Sueur described more precisely what she was by then calling the "communal sensibility." Her article, 'The Fetish of Being Outside," which appeared in *New Masses*, was a rebuttal to Horace Gregory's defense of the reluctance of some middle-class writers to join the Communist Party. Arguing for the writer's need "to stand for a belief," and indeed for a belief in something — a revolutionary future — that did not yet exist, Le Sueur urged writers to create out of the "chaotic dark." The writer must go "all the way, with full belief, into the darkness." "It is a birth and you have to be born whole out of it. In a complete new body."[7] This was not the first nor would it be the last time that Le Sueur invoked the metaphor of the dark underground to signify a germinal, fructifying chaos and rebirth. That underground which in "Persephone" had been threatening had become an energizing image of her own and society's potential for rebirth. Long after most writers associated with the Left in the thirties had abandoned their allegiance to "the working class" or "the proletariat," indeed through all the years since then, Le Sueur has remained loyal to her idea of the communal sensibility.

"I Was Marching" is an example of reportage, that special kind of journalism developed by the Left in the thirties. Described as "journalism with a perspective," and as "three-dimensional reporting" intended to make the reader see and feel the event, it eschews the presumed objectivity of traditional journalism.[8] Often it adopts elements of the short story, emphasizing character, carefully selected detail and image, and narrative line. Many of Le Sueur's pieces have been called both reportage and fiction. Le Sueur wrote a good deal of reportage during the thirties, and she continued to use the form in the forties and fifties as well. In the thirties she wrote not only about striking workers but about the devastating effects of dust storms and drought on farmers in the Midwest; about the silicosis contracted by miners on the Mesabi Range (which she investigated for the CIO in 1937-38); and about the political fortunes of the Farmer-Labor Party, which held office in Minnesota for much of the decade.

And she wrote reportage about women. Le Sueur's very first piece of reportage for *New Masses* in 1932, "Women on the Breadlines," was the beginning of a chronicle she would continue throughout the decade. Three million of the estimated thirteen million unemployed in 1932 were women.[9] The women about whom Le Sueur wrote were those she lived with; those she knew and met on the streets, in the relief agencies, and in the unemployment bureaus. They were women at the bottom of society — those who, she has said, leave no record, no obituary, no remembrance. She became their biographer. Such women, Le Sueur observed, were not usually seen on the breadlines; nor were there any flophouses for them. Some lived together, pooling their meager resources, hiding their one luxury, a radio, from the social worker. Others starved slowly in furnished rooms. They sold their furniture, their clothes, and then their bodies. A few, the young and pretty, sometimes found work as waitresses or clerks. But for others there was only the humiliation of applying for relief, of trying to prove "absolute destitution," like the desperate young schoolteacher in "Women Are Hungry," which appeared in the *American Mercury* in 1934.

Statistics make unemployment abstract, Le Sueur observes in one of her pieces of reportage. But her words and images create memorable pictures. Mrs. Rose, the old mother in "Women Are Hungry," with her dreary diet of bacon rinds and potato peelings, or the woman Le Sueur describes at the conclusion of "Women on the Breadlines"—her body, after a lifetime of working for others, "a great puckered scar"—are unforgettable examples of the destitution, the human loss and waste, of the depression. In a prose that is usually stark and clipped, relying on short declarative sentences and monosyllabic words, Le Sueur graphically conveys the psychology as well as the economic reality of these women.

In much of her work Le Sueur emphasized the suffering of women during the depression, because that suffering was "an immediate reality without romantic conceptions," and an advance, therefore, over the Lawrentian romanticism of some of her earlier work.[10] However, some of the editors of *New Masses* criticized Le Sueur's interest in suffering. One of them appended a note to "Women on the Breadlines" which cautioned this "new contributor" about her "defeatist attitude" and "nonrevolutionary spirit."[11] He urged her to write of the opportunities the Party's Unemployed Councils offered to poor women. Although Le Sueur, who accepted such criticisms as necessary in the development of any movement, later wrote reportage showing women actively involved in Unemployed Councils and the Workers Alliance—pieces that more obviously conformed to what the Party wanted—she continued to write about the suffering of women. For she saw suffering, not as negative and passive, but as a source of solidarity. She had written in her journal in 1930: "Whittle oneself down on the edge of suffering. We do not know ourselves except when we suffer. . . . In joy I know only myself, in sorrow I know others. . . . In happiness we are seperete [sic]. . . . In suffering we are fused." The journal entry concluded with the observation that "given a great enough strength, suffering would open the thick substance of the world heart."[12] Several years later, in an article about Mother Bloor, she described grief and sorrow as weapons in the class struggle, as materials out of which she hoped to make "a great song."[13]

Making a great song out of suffering might well describe Le Sueur's most sustained piece of prose about women in the depression, her novel *The Girl*. First drafted in 1939, *The Girl* is based on the oral and written accounts of the women with whom Le Sueur lived in the thirties, and represents, she claims, a composite of their words and her own. One publisher rejected the novel and requested that she return her $250 advance because the description of one of its main events, a bank robbery, was inaccurate. (Le Sueur claims that a local bank robber assured her of the authenticity of the details.) She seems to have been too discouraged or intimidated to seek another publisher, and the novel lay forgotten in the basement of her daughter's house in St. Paul until it was rediscovered and published in 1977 by West End Press as part of the current revival of interest in her work. *The Girl*, like Tillie Olsen's *Yonnondio*, is a retrieved treasure of women's literature of the 1930s — reborn, Le Sueur herself might say, out of the dark underground.

The girl of the title is an unnamed young woman who has left her rural home for St. Paul, where she has found work as a waitress in a speakeasy. The novel covers her involvement in a bank robbery planned by her lover, Butch, and his friends; the failure of the robbery and Butch's death; and the months the girl subsequently spends living with a group of women who struggle through the depression together. It concludes with the birth of her child, an event that becomes the occasion for the women to renew their commitment to life and to the future.

Despite the romanticism of the ending, *The Girl* is a work of literary power and political insight. Its depiction of many of the harsher realities of women's sexual lives — abortion, prostitution, sterilization, physical abuse by men — is especially notable for its time. As their needs demand, the men in the novel are sporadically tender toward "their women," but more often indifferent, even violent, using the women as scapegoats for their own frustrations — their inability to find jobs, their sense of hopelessness about the future. The women, in turn, submit to the indifference and the abuse, out of a fatalistic sense that this is the way things have always been and must be. Sex, the reassuring presence of another's body, is one of the few free sources of pleasure in the stark depression world of the novel. "His body had been good to me," the girl says. "It seemed like there was everything else bad and our bodies good and sweet to us." Innocent and naive, the girl uncomprehendingly accepts what attention she is given.

The women, meanwhile, who include a waitress-prostitute, a wife, Butch's senile mother, and a Communist Party organizer, live together after Butch's death, sustaining one another against hunger and madness, and against the violence of men. Through their own suffering they create a collective strength. Adrienne Rich has commented on what she has called the "double life" of women that novels like *The Girl* and Toni Morrison's *Sula* both describe, in different ways: a life with men in which sex is pleasurable but also destructive, and a separate life with women who provide each other with emotional and material support.[14] This sense of a double life also underlies the novels about women on which Le Sueur is currently working.

While writing about the sexual and economic conditions of the lives of working-class women, Le Sueur was also publishing fiction about those middle-class women she had begun to treat in stories like "Wind" in the twenties. Published in such journals as *Scribner's*, *Yale Review*, *Dial*, and *Kenyon Review*, these stories include a group — "Psyche," "The Trap," and "Fudge" — whose subject is the repressed sexuality of small-town, middle-class, and frequently middle-aged women.

They suggest an indebtedness to Sherwood Anderson, whose work Le Sueur admired and possibly also to Zona Gale, but their subject originates in Le Sueur's own middle-class upbringing, against which she continued to rebel. The stories describe the provincialism, the censorious morality, of small-town America, and its crippling emotional effects on women.

One of this group is especially striking in its stylistic sureness and thematic range. Also called "The Girl," it appeared in 1936 in *Yale Review*. The girl of the title is an unmarried schoolteacher who is driving through the Tehachapi Mountains on her way to a vacation in San Francisco. Drugged by the warmth of the sun and stirred by the physical presence of a young boy to whom she is giving a ride, she begins to feel in her body a diffused sensuality that eventually extends to include her perception of the surrounding landscape. Before her trip she has dutifully read about the Tehachapis, but now the mountains become "great animal flesh," instinct with a life of their own. Accepting her own sensations, she lives fully in and through her body for the first time. One is reminded of Edna Pontellier in *The Awakening*, where the relaxed vacation atmosphere of Grand Isle, the warmth of sun and sand, and the nearness of Robert LeBrun encourage Edna's emerging sensuality. Through a rich, imagistic prose Le Sueur evokes such sensuality, as well as a sense of the human body as related to all of nature in one living and breathing continuum.

The influence of Lawrence is still apparent in "The Girl," a story which also shows an unfortunate stereotyping that is to be found in much of Le Sueur's work. Like the schoolteacher here, Le Sueur's sexually repressed women are usually middle-class; and "intellectual" for Le Sueur is invariably a pejorative term. Working-class women, on the other hand, exhibit healthy sexual appetites. Despite such oversimplification, however, "The Girl" effectively conveys Le Sueur's sense of the importance of living within the body and, for women especially, of accepting their own sexual feelings without the guilt or denial that American middle-class culture has traditionally imposed on them.

The split in Le Sueur's treatment of working- and middle-class women undoubtedly resulted from her rejection of her own middle-class background; and it was a split that the political thinking of the thirties did not significantly address. In speaking of her radicalization in the thirties, Le Sueur once said that she "dropped feminism and identified with those below," that is, with the working class. What she meant was that she dropped — or found inadequate — the liberal, middle-class feminism of her mother and of those of her mother's generation for whom feminism had come to mean, narrowly, getting the vote. Although Marian Wharton had worked actively for birth control, to her daughter she remained a woman who lived in her mind, and who, in competing with men on their terms, denied the desires and claims of the body. It was with the farm, immigrant, and American Indian women of her youth, and with the Socialist Party and the IWW, that Le Sueur identified. As socialism became more and more a middle-class movement, however, after World War I, Le Sueur's affiliations became more radical. She had written for such journals as *Masses*, precursor to *New Masses*, since 1916; and she says she joined the Communist Party in 1924.

In the thirties her hopes, like those of so many others, centered in the Communist Party and in the potentialities of the working class. There was no viable feminist movement to articulate the unity and oppression of all women. To some extent, the Communist Party did recognize the special situation and needs of women, through a Women's Commission; special magazines; Party units devoted to the needs of certain groups of women, such as housewives; and support of strikes led by women workers. As Robert Shaffer has recently argued, women could find in the Party a structure that encouraged their participation in collective action, including activities that addressed their particular needs.[15]

On the other hand, the Party never recognized the special oppression of women: women's roles and needs were not significantly distinguished from those of male workers; and Mary Inman's feminist analysis, *In Women's Defense* — which, in any case, did not appear until 1939 — was not well received by the Party leadership. Inman argued that not just working-class women but all women were oppressed, and that housework was a major factor in capitalist oppression — an argument that conflicted with the Party position that wage labor was the key to oppression under capitalism.

Le Sueur herself was aware of the male orientation of the Party, and she criticized some aspects of it — the expectation that women organizers would adopt male life styles (Anna Louise Strong criticized her for having children and thus making herself less effective as a Party worker) and the dependency of the unpaid male leadership on their working wives ("the Party housekeepers," Le Sueur called them). In turn, she was sometimes criticized by the Party. Her style in some of her writings was considered "undisciplined." "They tried to beat the lyrical and emotional out of women," she has said.

But in the larger context the Party had much to offer Le Sueur. While it was antithetical to the spirit of some of her work, it was also helpful and supportive, and it provided a political theory and a program of action to which she could commit herself while at the same time retaining the freedom to be critical. As a midwesterner, Le Sueur was removed from the often bitter quarrels of the East Coast Party members that resulted from the shifts and turns in the Party line, and she remained, as she called herself, a "maverick." What mattered to Le Sueur was not ideology. She has described her impatience with those at the American Writers Congresses who delivered "great theoretic ideological speeches," attempting to make "a bureaucratic, intellectual, inhuman, non-human kind of thing of Marxism."[16] What mattered was "communal solidarity," and if this in the thirties was part reality and part hope, it was reality and hope that she shared with innumerable others.

Those others included many women writers. Although in the thirties women writers did not identify themselves as a special group, they were far from invisible, and Le Sueur knew many of them. Through meetings and conferences, as well as through their work, she knew Josephine Herbst, Grace Lumpkin, Agnes Smedley, Mary Heaton Vorse, and Muriel Rukeyser. And she had close friendships with Grace Flandreau, Margery Lattimer, and Sanora Babb. The thirties, Le Sueur has said, were "a good time to be a woman writer, or any kind of writer." The discussions and analyses of society and culture and of the writer's audience that took place at meetings like the Congresses, the sense of being among a group of writers who shared common goals and were part of a larger collective effort, provided a stimulus, a source of challenge and encouragement, which she would not again enjoy on such a scale until the 1970s, when the women's movement gave her a new sense of participating in a large, concerted effort for change and a new, responsive audience.

The publication in 1940 of *Salute to Spring*, a sampling of Le Sueur's thirties journalism and stories, marked a high point in her career and reputation. But *Salute to Spring* also marked an ending: the end of a decade of rewarding, shared work that was followed, beginning in the late 1940s, by bleak years of repression and neglect.

In the early and mid-forties Le Sueur continued to find ready publication for her work. From the mid-thirties on she had written about the developing unrest in Europe: the rise of Fascism in Germany, the Spanish Civil War, the outbreak of World War II. When the United States entered the war, she wrote both journalism and fiction defending the war effort and celebrating the young men who fought. "Breathe upon These Slain," which appeared in *Kenyon Review* in 1945, describes the last thoughts and lonely death of an American soldier on a Japanese island. Le Sueur transfers to the inarticulate, common soldier her belief in the solidarity of the working class: the soldier is sustained in the nightmare of his dying by recollections of the only companionship that he has known, that of his buddies.

During the war years, too, Le Sueur received some financial support for her writing. In 1943 she was awarded a Rockefeller Historical Research Fellowship, which enabled her to write *North Star Country*, an iconoclastic, impressionistic history of her Midwest region that was published in 1945 and chosen as a Book Find Club selection in 1946. *North Star Country* uses folklore and myth as well as more conventional historical materials to create what one reviewer called "a great weave of living legend."[17] It is a populist account of the settlement and growth of Minnesota, the Dakotas, and Wisconsin from earliest frontier times through World War II, and its poetic prose conveys both Le Sueur's sense of the continuing urgency of the people's struggle and her faith in its outcome.

It was with the arrival of the Cold War period in 1947 that Le Sueur moved into her "dark time," and her metaphor from the story of Persephone of "going underground" became once again painfully applicable to her own life. Like so many thirties radicals, Le Sueur suffered extensively from the persecutions and reprisals that were part of the Cold War period. In a time of loyalty oaths, the Smith Act prosecutions of Communists, and the investigations of Senator Joseph McCarthy and the House Committee on Un-American Activities, Le Sueur was blacklisted, cut off from publishing outlets, and hounded out of jobs. In 1954 the House Committee issued a subpoena, but process servers were unable to find her. By then, too, a rooming house that her mother had left her and that she used as a source of income was under constant surveillance by the FBI. Her boarders were harassed, and her telephone was tapped. Students in creative writing courses she was teaching were dissuaded from taking her classes, and she was fired from a series of waitressing jobs. In these years, too, the destruction of the Farmer-Labor Party in Minnesota, in which she had invested much energy and hope, the outbreak of the Korean War, and the trial and execution of the Rosenbergs added to her sense of "paralysis."

Nonetheless, she continued to write and to publish. Her reportage appeared in *Mainstream* and *Masses and Mainstream*, successors to *New Masses*. Acceptable to Alfred A. Knopf as the author of children's books, she published five of them between 1947 and 1954, centered on such figures as Davy Crockett, Johnny Appleseed, Abraham Lincoln, and Lincoln's mother, Nancy Hanks. Although the books were the subject of some red-baiting reviews and were banned by some libraries, they sold well enough to provide Le Sueur with a small but steady income for many years.

In 1955 a small press published *Crusaders*, Le Sueur's biography of Marian Wharton and Arthur Le Sueur. The book celebrates the lives and work of her parents and reaffirms her own faith in the Midwest populist tradition. The book's jacket called it an "antidote to fear," and together with her other writings in these years, it is a testament to her resilience during an era that "has to be measured," as a recent historian has said, "not only in individual careers destroyed but . . . in assumptions unchallenged, in questions unasked, in problems ignored for a decade."[18]

Le Sueur did not ignore the problems of the times. She reported on specific political and economic conditions, such as the investigations of the FBI and the efforts of the CIO to organize lead miners in Oklahoma. Her trip to Oklahoma to cover the CIO efforts also led to the writing of "Eroded Woman," another of her stark and compelling portraits of working-class women. And she began to travel extensively by bus, talking to people, asking them questions, and recording their stories, thus continuing the work as a social historian that she had begun in the thirties.

The result of the bus travel was a series of impressionistic accounts, most of them published in *Mainstream* and *Masses and Mainstream*, of American life in the late forties and fifties. They emphasize the persistent, restless movement of the people she met. Le Sueur's vision of America has always been of a people in motion. Restless movement, process, change, inform her interpretation of American history in "Our Fathers" and in *North Star Country*. And the idea of "movement" (actual physical movement creating ideological movement), was the key to her interpretation of the strike in "I Was Marching," where she described herself as participating in "the first real rhythmic movement I have ever seen," and as joining "with a million hands, movements, faces, and my own movement . . . making a new movement from these many gestures."

In the fifties, the movement was undirected. The people she met were dissatisfied, confused. In a piece called "American Bus," a passenger remarks, "In my home town you can't associate with anyone. We used to be liberal. Now everyone is afraid to think." One of Le Sueur's most effective pieces of reportage from the fifties is "The Dark of the Time," which describes a bus trip she took to visit the site where Nancy Hanks gave birth to Abraham Lincoln. Its rhythms are those of uneasy movement and discontent. As Le Sueur talks with and observes the other passengers on the bus, she conveys the bewilderment attendant on the Korean War, and the growing racial tensions as both blacks and whites begin to move out of the South in large numbers after World War II. And the visit to Lincoln's birthplace is itself a disappointment; the local people are ignorant of or indifferent to Nancy Hanks, and the site commemorates Lincoln, but not his mother.

But in the end Le Sueur's own faith sustains her. At the beginning of "The Dark of the Time" she describes herself as falling into "the dark flux of all on the move," and images of darkness and death, including the coffins of the dead soldiers being returned from Korea, pervade the

piece. But its conclusion reaffirms her unshakable belief in the possibility of new birth out of the darkness, and in her own role as a writer.
That role is to be "voice, messenger, awakener" for the people; to be a
writer, "partisan and alive," who will express "with warmth, abundance, excess, confidence," their hungers and their hopes.

Tillie Olsen has referred to any woman who manages to write as a
"survivor," and the term is almost an understatement when applied to
Meridel Le Sueur. As the 1950s drew to a close, she was herself nearing
sixty, still without any steady source of income. To support herself
both until, at sixty-five, she qualified for social security, and afterwards
to supplement it, she took jobs in garment sweatshops at $1.00 an hour,
was an attendant for women in the Minneapolis State Asylum, house-
sat in Santa Fe, drove a Cadillac for a handicapped woman who com-
muted between Santa Fe and Iowa, and even lived for several years in
Santa Fe in a condemned bus. After her mother's death in the mid-
fifties, Le Sueur began to spend time living and working among
American Indians, including groups in Northern Minnesota; in Taos,
Santa Fe, and Albuquerque; and in Mexico as well. Today she continues to spend part of each year in the Southwest, and part in St. Paul
with her daughter, Rachel.

The 1960s, meanwhile, saw the beginning of a new period in her
life and work. In a time of renewed political activism she found fresh
challenges and inspiration. Still traveling by bus, she observed and
took part in many of the protest and reform movements that emerged
in the sixties. She traveled to Berkeley at the time of the Free Speech
Movement at the University of California; to Mexico during the national railroad strike in the sixties; and to Washington, D.C., to join the
Poor People's March and demonstrations against the war in Vietnam.
And she continued to work with American Indians on issues of land
rights and land preservation.

With the development of the women's movement, beginning in the
late 1960s, she found a new audience for her work: "my own audience,"
she has said, "the women I was writing for."[19] And the existence of this
audience has helped stimulate in recent years a steady stream of new
writing — poems, novels, and essays. In addition, age for Le Sueur, with
its release from child-rearing and other social responsibilities, has been
a liberation. Citing the women in certain American Indian cultures, she
has said, "After a woman passes menopause she really comes into her
time. I feel that. I've never felt so well or had so many images before
me."[20]

Today, at over eighty, Le Sueur is celebrating what she calls her
"ripening." In her work, she has said, "I feel free for the first time in my
life. I think I am daring to write as crazily excessive abundant absolute-

ly in extremity . . . on the far edge of the circle."[21] She continues to travel extensively, speaking, and reading from her works to students and to women's groups throughout the country. Surrounded by her children, grandchildren, and great-grandchildren, and by a circle of friends and supporters, and linked through her work and her personal appearances to a younger generation of women, she has become the embodiment of her own idea of the "continuous woman": the woman linked to other generations of women both biologically, through the body, and historically and spiritually, through the reality of struggle and survival.[22]

Le Sueur's central concerns in her recent writings are women and the land—their centuries of parallel suffering and exploitation. Although she is no longer writing political reportage, her work is pervaded by the awareness that she is living in a time when recognition of the interdependence of human beings on each other and on nature has become imperative. Ecology has become an essential issue for Le Sueur—the need to save an earth already almost destroyed by war, speculative use, and chemical poisoning. And the lives of women, their suffering and their survival, are increasingly interpreted through metaphors and analogies to the land.

From "Persephone," "Harvest," and "Annunciation" in the 1920s and 1930s through "Eroded Woman" in the late 1940s, Le Sueur's interest in seeing women in relation to or in terms of nature was apparent. Today, writing in a style that is not only lyrical but, to use her own word, "abandoned," and that draws heavily on the suggestive power of myth and legend, she is expressing a view of women and the land that is at once sorrowful and celebratory, a view that acknowledges and extensively explores past suffering but ultimately embraces it within a vision of a transfigured future.

The myth that informs the writing is still that of Demeter and Persephone, the story through which Le Sueur first defined herself in the 1920s. But whereas then she was Persephone, now she is Demeter, the ancient mother, grieving, but protective, abundant, and fierce. This Demeter voice speaks in the poetry Le Sueur has been writing since the 1960s, in a series of novels on which she is currently engaged, and in a long essay she is composing on "The Origins of Corn."

A volume of Le Sueur's poetry, *Rites of Ancient Ripening*, was published in 1975. In a great many of the poems the voice heard is that of an American Indian woman, for the poetry shows Le Sueur's strong attraction in recent decades to the world view, legends, and imagery of certain American Indian societies, such as the Hopi. Whether the speaker is an old woman, the corn mother, or the earth itself, however, she is a manifestation of the Demeter figure, who, through her identification with the natural cycle of birth-death-rebirth, comprehends and transcends pain, division, and despair. What the voice chronicles in many of the poems is a tale of centuries of devastation: the pollution of the earth, American aggression against the land and people of Vietnam, the centuries of women's oppression, the history of accumulated wrongs visited upon American Indian societies. But counterpointing the despair is hope, derived from Le Sueur's conviction of the capacities and strengths of women, and from her faith in the cyclical process through which renewal may be achieved.

The poems celebrate the workings of this cyclical process primarily on the level of biology and nature. In the title poem (which also shows Le Sueur's indebtedness to Whitman) an old woman anticipates and welcomes her death, when the body will decay but also be transformed, in rejoining the earth, into nourishment for new life. The poems' imagery of fire, water, corn, bowls, earth, and sky, drawn from American Indian sources, intimately associates women's creative and specifically reproductive capacities with those of the land. *Rites* also contains some explicitly political poems, and in these, too, Le Sueur employs imagery of reproduction to convey her vision of a better future. "Doàn Kêt," for example, is a poem that Le Sueur sent to the North Vietnamese Women's Union during the Vietnam War, and it is literal, harsh, and gritty, in its descriptions of the bombing and napalming of the Vietnamese land and people and of the role of American corporations in providing weapons of destruction. But its conclusion subsumes political realities within a vision of women united through their suffering ("Doàn Kêt" means "solidarity" in Vietnamese), who have transformed that suffering "into bread and children/In a new abundance, a global summer."

In her recent fiction, Le Sueur examines the workings of this cyclical process in a more specifically historical context. She has projected and is writing a series of experimental novels, in which she returns to the midwestern prairie land and people of her origins. Only a brief excerpt from the first novel has so far been published. Essentially, the novels will explore memory and the past. On the occasion of her eightieth birthday Le Sueur said that in age "you become the monument, the grave, the memory of those who are dead," and the novels have a strongly elegiac quality. But as in the poems, elegy, or sorrow, is fused with celebration, as the past is discovered to reveal and provide resources for the future. In the thirties, over Communist Party protests that her treatment of women's suffering was defeatist, Le Sueur argued that out of suffering one can make "a great song." Her novel cycle is in some ways the culmination of this belief.

The first of the three novels, *Memorial*, describes three women who meet in a graveyard in a midwestern mining town, to which they have returned to seek the burial sites of a father, a mother, and a child.[23] As they narrate their stories to each other—first in the graveyard, then in a tavern, and finally in an abandoned mine pit into which they fall—they describe an American past of gutted land and gutted lives: impoverished families, fathers overworked in the mines, mothers worn out by child-bearing and child-rearing, daughters who flee to the city but succeed only in becoming prostitutes. But this past—in Le Sueur's words, the "underseas nightmares and realities of the submerged"—is, in the process of being recalled, given new meaning.[24] The descent into the underground, as always for Le Sueur, becomes an ascent. In her words, the women, through their descent and by reliving their suffering, "come together in a communal memory and illumination." Just as Mary Daly and Adrienne Rich are today using the word in their explorations of women's pasts, so for Le Sueur remembering becomes "re-membering": a healing process, reconstructive and transforming.[25]

Memorial dramatizes what some of the poems assert rhetorically: the union of women, accomplished through their recognition of their common suffering, struggle, and survival. Le Sueur has described the three women in Memorial as a whore, a mother, and an intellectual, and also as Persephone, Demeter, and Demeter's Holy Sow: a version of the Holy Trinity that, in incorporating woman as intellectual, overcomes that split between mind and body, between working- and middle-class women, that was evident in her writing in the thirties. For the distinguishing feature of Le Sueur's current use of the Demeter-Persephone story is her emphasis on the return of Persephone to the mother. "The non-return to the mother in Christianity is very hurting," she wrote upon the occasion of a recent reprinting of her early "Persephone" story, and it is women's rediscovery of the bonds that unite them that Le Sueur is describing in her current novel cycle.[26] Since, as her journals reveal, she was exploring some of the central images and ideas of Memorial at least as early as the mid-sixties, she thus anticipated the current feminist awareness of the need to rediscover the mother-daughter relationship that patriarchal literature has ignored or trivialized.

The succeeding novels in the cycle will continue to examine what Le Sueur frequently refers to as the "wound" of women; but here, too, suggestions of the healing or transforming process are not lacking, given the presence in both novels of a Demeter figure. The second novel will describe two women, an older and a younger, who, escaping from a Chicago mental institution, travel through the central Mississippi valley, where they recall and share their pasts. They are murdered, and their bodies are thrown into the hills; however, they are envisioned as nourishing the landscape. Le Sueur's description of the third novel is more elaborate and suggests that it may be the most experimental of the three. It is based on an actual encounter she had while traveling by bus from Albuquerque to Denver with a woman who revealed to her the carefully dressed body of a small, dead child that she carried in a vinyl bag. The woman in the novel is a field worker whose mother and grandmother, also field workers, have died of chemical poisoning; and the "perfection" in death of the child, on which the mother proudly comments, is poignant, ironic witness to their deaths. The novel is composed in three parallel columns: the woman's prose narrative will be bordered on one side by passages from Edgar Allan Poe describing an America of dead landscapes and immured bodies, and on the other by Le Sueur's own comments, compassionate and reconciling, on the woman's story.

All three novels will be written in the new style and will use new narrative procedures that Le Sueur has developed. *Memorial* interweaves past and present, prose and poetry, literal statement and suggestive image, to create not a sequential narrative but a matrix or web of relationships. And in the third novel the use of parallel columns will create a simultaneity of different time periods and layers of meaning. In this recent work Le Sueur is endeavoring both to create the sense of a space-time continuum — her analogy is often to the Hopi view of life as an unfolding spatial-temporal event on the order of the budding and growth of a plant — and to break down the distinction between the observer and the object observed, between the narrator and the story that is told.

This style has important political implications for her which she discusses frequently in her lectures. For Le Sueur, conventional narrative sequence, moving toward a conclusion as toward a target, is a male procedure. It is, she thinks, the aesthetic result of a linear perception of the world, which allows for and excuses conquest, appropriation, and pollution. To see the world as a circle, and movement within it as cyclical, on the other hand, is to recognize the necessary interdependence and interrelationship of all things. Le Sueur finds support for her ideas not only in the Demeter-Persephone myth and in Hopi culture, but in Einstein's theory of relativity and in the discovery of the spiral shape of the DNA molecule. In such a world of interrelated parts there would ideally be no conquest, since "You can't conquer anything unless it's outside you, and nothing lies outside the circle"; and there would be no pollution, since, as Le Sueur has vividly put it, "your shit returns to fall on you."[27]

This idea of relationship is crucial for Le Sueur today — and it is her way of expressing the need for what in the thirties she called the "communal sensibility." Today, more emphatically than in the thirties, the weave of relationship extends beyond class or sex to include all human beings, and nature as well.

Some of Le Sueur's most interesting formulations of this vision are to be found in her journals. Le Sueur's journals have always been a storehouse of ideas, as well as her way, through daily writing, of practicing and honing her craft. Today her journals number over 140 volumes, stored in the basement of her daughter Rachel's house in St. Paul. One entry, written in 1977, is a series of observations on a variety of disparate phenomena: glowworms, American Indian dances, corn fields, Japanese mobiles, radio signals from Belgrade, and women traveling down a river. The glowworms with their golden light, the movement and sound of the dances, the continuous vibration of the radio signals, the reflections from the glass pieces of the mobile, the fields in which the corn shakes, and the women who, as they travel, "enlarge each other's perceptions," all combine to create a world of process and movement, of energy which is shared and transformed — a world in which "everything moves to greater intensity, not less."

Le Sueur's central symbol for this energy that infuses and unites all things has become the corn. Corn engaged her imagination as early as 1931, when she published an essay, "Corn Village," describing midwestern American village life. Today she is composing a long work of prose and poetry on "The Origins of Corn." "Origins" treats the reality of corn as food, including its 2,500-year history of cultivation by American Indians and white settlers, and its exploitation as a crop for profit. But as Le Sueur describes the epic journey of the corn, both through history and though the processes of its natural growth, it becomes a symbol of the human journey through time, of human powers of love, solidarity, and survival, and eventually of all transforming and creative energy.

In this journey the essential, energizing act is the sexual encounter, the mating of pollen and cob, and Le Sueur describes that mating, often using religious imagery, in ways that invest it not merely with regenerative but with redemptive possibility. She speaks of the "congregation of cob," of the "holy wafer of conception," and of "resurrections." Where the novels concern the bonding of women and their rediscovery of each other and their pasts, "Origins" describes another state that Le Sueur sees as essential for human survival — a new relationship of the sexes. She calls this new relationship "a polarity of equals" or "a dialectic of equal opposites," and it assumes a world in which not only will women have ceased to be victims but men will have ceased to be "rapists" and "invaders," and the energies of both will be mutually, constructively joined. The intensity with which Le Sueur holds this conviction, not only in the necessity, but in the real possibility, of such a relationship and such a world, is evident in the heightened style and heavily freighted language of "Origins." The essay shows her at her most "abandoned," writing and thinking on "the far edge of the circle."

In discussing the visionary quality of much of her recent work, Le Sueur once said, only half-jokingly, "I come from a long line of preachers." (One of her grandfathers was a Campbellite minister.) She has become preacher and prophet, roles perhaps implicit in her description of the writer's function in "The Dark of the Time" as that of "voice, messenger, awakener" of the people. Today, in a period characterized by the deployment of enormous destructive power, she sees it as her responsibility to present constructive images of human and natural energies put to positive, life-enhancing use. And while such images of love, nourishment, growth, and interrelationship are visionary, she would argue that they are grounded in present reality — for example, in the recent emergence into voice of hitherto silenced groups, including women, blacks, Latinas, and American Indians.

There are nonetheless questions to be asked: about the nature of Le Sueur's images, the contexts in which they are presented, and the interpretation of women they convey. In the poems, the novels, and the essay on corn, women are defined primarily through their sexuality and their reproductive capacity. In the poems, woman is the corn cob, the bowl that is filled, the hidden cave, the nocturnal door; she is the earth, the harvested field, the ploughed flesh, the great smashed granary of seed. And in "Origins" she is associated with the "ardent" earth seeking the "loving" sun and finding fulfillment in the sexual act. The women in *Memorial* discuss themselves essentially in terms of having had, or not having had, children. The prostitute feels guilt because her womb is empty, and Yoni (the old woman introduced in the second section) interprets the meaning of her life mainly in terms of her sexual encounters and the children she has borne. In *Memorial* sex is the "something real" that the prostitute's mother had, despite her poverty; and Yoni sings the praises of the "great seed fathers."

This emphasis on women's reproductive capacity and identification with the earth runs the risk of reducing women to the biological role they have so long struggled to transcend. And it invests that biological role with mysterious power. As in her Lawrentian fiction of the twenties and thirties, Le Sueur still tends to present heterosexual relations as centrally transforming; a woman becomes initiated into some secret, incommunicable knowledge that distinguishes and defines her as Woman. Jan Clausen has argued that Le Sueur's emphasis on pregnancy and birth often functions "to suggest a kind of mystic regeneration which is natural, inevitable, rather than being, like a revolution, painstakingly prepared and uncertain of outcome."[28] Clausen has also observed that that regenerative possibility is frequently presented by way of a "fantasy" view of life lived in tune with natural rhythms.[29] Thus in her poetry Le Sueur relies on a world view and a

way of life that are no longer available even to the American Indians
from whom she derives it.

Le Sueur has acknowledged and spoken to some of these criticisms.
She does not, she insists, support the idea that women are confined to
their biological destiny. Having children, she said in 1973, is "not the
only or the ultimate [experience of women] but certainly a remarkable
one. I think the gestating part of the female consciousness is to give birth
to many things — a child is just one."[30] And more recently she has explained that she uses the child in her work for "creative connection and
symbol" of the need for human relationships and the need for continuity.

It is not always easy, however, to distinguish Le Sueur's
metaphorical meanings from her literal ones, and since the view of
women as mothers and as sexual partners for men is so central in her recent work, problems in reading it persist. Sometimes, her presentation
of women as nourishers sounds like a modern version of nineteenth-
century domestic feminism, the belief in women's special capacities for
nurturing and their instrumentality for improving the world. In this
connection, Le Sueur herself would claim that she is not describing a
biologically innate capacity but a culturally induced one, much as
sociologist Nancy Chodorow has recently argued in *The Reproduction
of Mothering* that women's historical mothering role has probably led
women to develop greater capacity for relationship than men. When Le
Sueur speaks of "the female concept of nourishing," she is referring to a
concept, not a trait, and one she wants to see extended to men and
located at the center of our culture, rather than being relegated, as it
traditionally has been, to marginal status, where it is sentimentalized
and demeaned.

It is also to be noted that women in Le Sueur's current work, even
in their role of nurturers, are far from being passive and self-sacrificial.
The women she describes are above all survivors, who have developed
strength through their suffering. One of Le Sueur's journal entries
reads: 'The great natural storms of these women, the wind, the stored
up whirlwind, the anger and oh, the wound. The great wound that they
were. I am also the wound . . . unbearable wound of sex, of lonely par-
turition and childbed. . . . I must write only this."[31] Such a wounded but
eminently strong woman is Yoni, in *Memorial*. Le Sueur's descriptions
of Yoni's "stealing the seed" from men and assisting at childbirths in the
midst of hurricanes show women as self-determining, if only within the
limited options available to them. Yoni has wrested joy and pleasure,
strength and defiance, from a life of brutality and hardship; and her
humor, irreverence, and sexual appetites are undiminished by age.
"Female knowing in America underground guerilla," Le Sueur once
wrote in some notes about the nineteenth-century feminist Margaret

Fuller — and Yoni is an example of what Le Sueur has called the guerilla woman.

It should also be noted that although Le Sueur's association of women with nature can be reductive, she is exploring through this association an issue of importance to other contemporary feminists. Her recognition of the historical connection between male analytical thinking and male manipulation and control of both women and nature anticipates an insight on which writers like Mary Daly in *Gyn/Ecology: The Metaethics of Radical Feminism* and Susan Griffin in *Woman and Nature* have based their work. Griffin, like Le Sueur, sees women as having developed, at least partly through their association with nature, both a special sensitivity to its processes and special ways of perceiving and knowing. All three writers see the imperative for a new relationship to nature, and all three have embarked on journeys of rediscovery and redefinition in which a new reading of the past is expressed in a new language and a new style.

Where Le Sueur crucially diverges from writers like Daly and Griffin is in the importance she accords the sexual relation between women and men, and in her optimistic anticipation of a world of rehabilitated men. Aside from the fact that men show little sign of becoming the "nourishers" and "shepherds" she desires, her way of describing the hoped-for new relationship of the sexes presents difficulties. In speaking of a "polarity of equals" or a "dialectic of equal opposites," she is using a vocabulary that retains and therefore risks reinforcing the very male-female dualism that historically has helped to establish and perpetuate women's subordination.

Nevertheless one reads Le Sueur's recent works with intense interest in her ideas and deep admiration for her indomitable energy and faith. What she said in *Crusaders* in 1955 of her mother, Marian Wharton — that she had "the courage to leap into new forms" — applies even more to Le Sueur herself.[32] In the 1930s she created a body of literature about women that, in sensitively recording their lives, showed respect for their unique experiences. She wrote of the culture of poor women, the psychology and sexuality of both working- and middle-class women, and the ways in which women experience adolescence, marriage, pregnancy, childbirth, the death of children, and widowhood. Both in the thirties and in later decades, and often well before they became topics of widespread social and literary concern, she wrote about American Indians, immigrant women, older women, the mother-daughter relationship, women uniting with other women, and ecology. Always she has written about the "common woman," the anonymous and inarticulate women whom poets like Adrienne Rich and Judy Grahn are today describing, who struggle to acquire some control over their lives, some dignity and meaning.

Le Sueurs commitment has always been to the common, the ordinary, the anonymous women and men who have traditionally lacked
a voice or expressive outlet. She has given them voice, brought them into conscious awareness. "Much of what is called culture is merely the
advertised, the expected, and the imposed," she once wrote, and her
writing has been her form of resistance to such expectations and imposi-
tions.³³ When she says today that "we [should] live to nourish life and
each other," she is her own best example.³⁴ Like the women in her journal entry who "enlarge each other's perceptions," she enlarges ours.

NOTES

¹Much of the material in this essay is based on correspondence and interviews with Meridel Le Sueur conducted in Minneapolis, Minnesota, and in New
York City between January 1977 and October 1980. Direct quotations from letters or from tape recordings of the interviews are attributed to Le Sueur in the
text but are not otherwise identified.
²Meridel Le Sueur, " . . . on the far edge of the circle . . . ," *Lady-Unique-
Inclination-of-the-Night* (Autumn 1977): 14.
³Ibid.
⁴Mara Smith, *Meridel Le Sueur: A Bio-Bibliography* (Mimeographed,
University of Minnesota, 1973), p. 13; Carl Sandburg, jacket comment, *Salute
to Spring* (New York: International Publishers, 1940); Cora MacAlbert,
"Review of *Salute to Spring*," *New Masses* (July 2, 1940): 27.
⁵Josephine Herbst, quoted in *Proletarian Writers of the Thirties*, ed. David
Madden (Carbondale, Ill.: Southern Illinois University Press, 1968), p. xxvii.
⁶Ibid.
⁷Meridel Le Sueur, "The Fetish of Being Outside," *New Masses* (February
26, 1935): 22, 23.
⁸Joseph North, "Reportage," in *American Writers Congress*, ed. Henry
Hart (New York: International Publishers, 1935), p. 121.
⁹Jeane Westin, *Making Do: How Women Survived the '30s* (Chicago:
Follett, 1976), p.164; Malcolm Cowley, *The Dream of the Golden Mountains*
(New York: Viking Press, 1980), p. 24.
¹⁰Meridel Le Sueur, "Journal Excerpts," *The Lamp in the Spine* 3 (Summer-
Fall 1974): 95.
¹¹"Editorial Note," *New Masses* (January 1932): 7.
¹²*The Lamp in the Spine*, p. 95.
¹³Meridel Le Sueur, "She Never Forgets," n.d., n.p. Many of Le Sueur's
writings are accessible only in xeroxed copies in her files, which are not always
fully annotated as to place and date of publication.
¹⁴Adrienne Rich, "Compulsory Heterosexuality and Lesbian Existence,"
Signs: Journal of Women in Culture and Society 5, no. 4 (Summer 1980):
654-56.
¹⁵Robert Shaffer, "Women and the Communist Party, USA, 1930-1940,"
Socialist Review 9, no. 3 (May-June 1979): 73-118.
¹⁶"Interview," *West End Magazine* 5, no. 1 (Summer 1978): 10.
¹⁷Smith, p. 17.
¹⁸Godfrey Hodgson, *America in Our Time* (New York: Doubleday, 1976).
¹⁹"Interview," *West End Magazine*, p. 13.

[20]Patricia Kirkpatrick, "Meridel Le Sueur: In the Cycle of Root and Bloom,": 12.

[21] "on the far edge of the circle," p. 14.

[22]The phrase, which Le Sueur uses in conversation, also appears in the title of an unpublished typescript on Margaret Fuller, "The Perpetual and Continuous Woman."

[23]Le Sueur has spoken of a cycle of five novels, including one about the women of Ireland. Most recently, however, she has referred to and described three novels.

[24]Quoted in Smith, p. 10.

[25]See Mary Daly, *Gyn/Ecology: The Metaethics of Radical Feminism* (Boston: Beacon Press, 1979), and Adrienne Rich, "Natural Resources," in *The Dream of a Common Language* (New York: W. W. Norton, 1978). It is interesting to note that in "Natural Resources" Rich uses the metaphor of a miner to describe women's past lives and their descent into their pasts.

[26]"on the far edge of the circle," p. 14.

[27]Neala Young [Schleuning], in "'America — Song We Sang Without Knowing' — Meridel Le Sueur's America" (Ph.D. diss., Univ. of Minnesota, 1978), extensively discusses Le Sueur's idea of the circle. See pp. 46-67 and passim.

[28]Jan Clausen, "The Girl," *Motheroot Journal* 3 (Spring 1980): 3.

[29]Jan Clausen, "Women on the Breadlines, Harvest, Song for My Time, Rites of Ancient Ripening," *Conditions: Three* 1, no. 3 (Spring 1978): 145.

[30]Kirkpatrick, p. 12.

[31]Quoted in Young [Schleuning], p. 14.

[32] *Crusaders* (New York: Blue Heron Press, 1955), p. 73.

[33]Quoted in Smith, p. 10.

[34]"Journal, May 31, 1977."

Origins

INTRODUCTION

"Literature," Meridel Le Sueur has said, must spring "from the deep and submerged humus of our life." In her case the rich soil was that of mid-America—of the Kansas, Oklahoma, and especially Minnesota lands where she lived as a child. A description of her "origins," therefore, should include some expression of her response to that region in which she is so deeply rooted. *North Star Country* is a history of Minnesota that she published in 1945; unconventional and ahead of its time in its use of folk materials as sources, it is the story of the workers and farmers, men and women, about whom she has since written so much. The book's opening chapter eloquently conveys Le Sueur's commitment to her region and ancestry. Her own forebears included both an Iroquois great-grandmother and some of the immigrants she describes in the chapter. These people, presented in the broad context of their political and economic struggles, are, to paraphrase her statement at the end of the chapter, "part of the deep" from which she emerged.

"The Ancient People and the Newly Come," an autobiographical essay published in 1976, is a backward glance, mellow and lyrical, into the formative years of her childhood and adolescence. It is also a memorial to that "maternal forest" of women who encircled her as a child—her mother, her grandmother, and her American Indian friend, Zona. In recreating their lives, Le Sueur is recalling not only an important part of her own past but some of that "half of history which is women," so often lost, forgotten or ignored. It has always been Le Sueur's purpose to record and retrieve that history. The domestic work and skills, the sufferings, and the perceptions and values of these white Protestant and American Indian women, at once different and complementary, were central threads in the fabric of early twentieth-century rural life and female culture out of which Le Sueur came. Enriching it also were the encounters and friendships she describes with Norwegian, Irish, Polish, and Finnish women, whose color, gaiety, and sensuality profoundly affected her.

To this deeply absorbed female culture Le Sueur added the heritage of political activism of her mother, Marian Wharton, and her step-father, Arthur Le Sueur. Through half a century and two World Wars, while American society became increasingly industrialized, and large-scale capitalism transformed the traditional rural way of life, the Le Sueurs worked unflaggingly for the rights of farmers and laborers. Inheriting and extending their ideas and beliefs, Meridel Le Sueur published a biography of her parents, *Crusaders*, in 1955, at a time when she herself was suffering from the political repressions of the Cold War period.

The excerpt from *Crusaders* fills out the story of Marian Wharton that is given in "The Ancient People," and it also provides another view of Le Sueur's grandmother, less genial than that in "The Ancient People" and equally important, therefore, for an understanding of her role in Le Sueur's life. The story of Marian Wharton does not end with the excerpt. Still active at the age of seventy-five in 1952, she ran for the United States Senate as candidate of the Minnesota Progressive Party in opposition to the Korean War. Le Sueur's relation to her mother, intense and often ambivalent, forms the basis for one of her most important early stories, "Persephone"; and the mother-daughter relationship itself has been of central importance throughout her life and work.

The NORTH STAR

*Should all things perish, fleeting as a shooting star, O God let
not the ties break that bind me to the North.*
— NORWEGIAN EMIGRANT EVENING PRAYER

*8 Goths and 22 Norwegians on exploration-journey from
Vinland over the West We had our camp by 2 skerries,
one days journey north from this stone we Were and
fished one day After we came home found 10 men red
with blood and dead Ave Maria Save us from Evil. . . .
Have 10 of our party by the sea to look after our ships 14
days journey from this inland Year 1362.*
— KENSINGTON RUNESTONE FOUND IN MINNESOTA

MEN AND THE EARTH

In the western reaches of the North Star Country a human skull was
found. The estimated time of burial was placed in the early Tintah stage
of Lake Agassiz, between eight and twelve thousand years ago. The
body of a young woman was found in an even deeper glacial drift, an
ax buried in her skull, murder ossified in the violent, remembering
earth. A pit of workmen with copper mallets in their hands and a
Norwegian ax were plowed up.

Interglacial plants found only in the Arctic have been unearthed,
also the teeth of chaetopods, small marine worms; the fossils of
elephants have been found at the edges of the glaciers, marks of their
roaming; gastroliths have been identified — the stones which dinosaurs
and other great birdlike reptiles carried in their crops as chickens and
turkeys now carry gravel.

These are witnesses that the tide of frost and northern lights, the
valley meeting of Arctic winds and tropical siroccos, has ebbed above
two-legged man for an unknown number of years, leaving the record of
his footprints — along with worm and dinosaur, the prairie bone,
flint — the mark of his coming and going, the smoothness of his palm
upon wood and copper. He has marked the land with the ruck of buffalo bones and made it a Golgotha of skulls. He has left songs,
drumbeats, the sounds of work in the air, stories, folklore, and the sad
wail of his tribal wanderings.

A lion does not write a book. The broken trail of the people must be followed by signs of myriad folk experiences in story, myth, legend, reflecting the struggle to survive; in the spore of old newspapers, folkway marking the rituals of birth, death, harvest, planting, in the embroidery on the pillow, the democracy quilt. These signs are not to be found easily or read lightly, measured like rock, estimated as metal. Folkways are malleable. They disappear as inland rivers do and reappear to flood a continent. They are submerged by time, shadowed by events, by sudden jets of power, changing into their opposite, a new harvest coming with a new tool.

Folklore is the hieroglyphics of all man's communication, both obvious and subterranean, as he struggles with growing society, changing tools, to create a place, a community, a nation. To read the meaning of the bones lying all one way in the buffalo wallow, the monuments erected by weather and by grief, requires a witch stick sensitive to deep channels. The weather erects monuments, but not at the place where a woman stopped in Wisconsin, after burying her first baby at sea, to give birth to the second in a shack before she and her husband went on over the frozen prairie into Dakota. The trail must be followed in the spore, in the blood stains and the marks of struggle: the desolation of tar-paper shanties, windows gaping still like the eyes of mad women who could not stand the solitude; the fleeing man seen in the unshut doors he did not close after him as he fled from Wisconsin to Minnesota, to the Dakotas, and then back again, losing a year's work, a wife, but never hope; the masks discerned, essential and instinctive in a new country full of danger and sudden weather changes, where a poker face saved your life, a tall tale hid a gun, a joke played for time, and tenderness was twin of cruelty.

Many signs mark the middle border country, a frontier nation not a hundred years old, with no connected primitive past, no deep historic shadow, no feudal fumbling of dark gestation. A swift action has taken place, recorded from the first day in diaries, newspapers, pamphlets, in a mass impulse for expression scarcely equaled, except perhaps in the Soviet Union. Expression grew like corn. Newspapers sprang up like whiskey stills. Democratic man wished not to die, but to be perpetuated, to speak in meeting, to write to the papers.

It was a new society, unique, set down green in the wilderness, adapting rapidly to climate, animals, minerals, mutually safeguarding new institutions, sharing prohibitions and extensions of freedom, rearing a new culture from the blend of diverse strands, sharing strengths, confidence, and myth, all in the bright humus of one idea: that the dignity of man is inalienable, and that by his own effort on this earth he can subjugate nature for the good of all.

Without the haven of the middle border country, the opening of the West, this belief might have died at the Cumberland Gap. Here it was given time, cradled and sustained in the Mississippi Valley and at the source of the great "Conception" River in the North Star Country.

The man and woman moving behind the westering sun wanted room to think fast and big, invent, speak, plant land and children with freedom's plow. They wanted new ways of being together. They hankered after something beside death and taxes. They wanted to see straight and live on earth. Like the growth of scientific thought, the twin of democracy, they wanted to examine the humus, look at decay, the minutiae of soil and society, honor the lowest labor and growth. Hard-headed, they wanted their pie in the "here and now," every man under his tree, no man a servant. Horse sense or common sense was "commin doin's"; they all had it together because without it they would not survive.

As de Tocqueville said in his time:

> These very Americans who have not discovered one of the general laws
> of mechanics have introduced into navigation an engine that changes
> the aspect of the world. The social condition and institutions of
> democracy prepare men to seek the immediate and useful, practical
> results of the sciences.

The task of this enterprising people was vast. They faced a boundless territory inhabited by hostile nations of red men, a country rich enough to haunt a man's dreams. Radisson had said when he first laid eyes on the verdant meadows:

> I liked noe country better, for whatever a man could desire was to
> be had in great plenty, viz.: fishes in abundance and all sorts of
> meat, corne enough. This I say that the Europeans fight for a rock in
> the sea against one another and contrariwise these Kingdoms are so
> delicious, plentiful in all things, the earth bringing forth fruit, the
> people can live long and lusty and wise in their ways. What con-
> quest would that be at little or no cost, what labyrinth of pleasure
> should millions of people have, instead that millions complain of
> misery and poverty

And the people flooded in at the opening of free lands, following the North Star, breaking the turf with four yoke of oxen, letting the daylight down into the deep wilderness — building, in the space of one generation, an Empire.

It was fast; it was big.

> Every morning Paul Bunyan grew two feet. When he laughed the
> folks in the villages ran into their houses and hid in the cellars think-
> ing it was a thunderstorm.
> He was quick as lightning, the only man in the north woods who
> could blow out a candle at night and hop into bed before it was
> dark.

He said he planted a kernel of corn and in five minutes the corn sprout-
ed up through the ground till it was fifty feet high, and Ole, the Big
Swede, climbed up out of sight.
Even the crumbs that fell on the floor were so large that the chip-
munks who ate them grew as big as wolves and chased the bears
right out of the country. Later the settlers shot them for tigers.
Paul had to invent the double-bitted ax, with a blade on each side,
so his men could work twice as fast. It was wide as a barn door and
had a great oak tree for a handle, and he chopped so fast, it got red
hot and had to be dipped into the handy lakes to cool off.
Paul and the Six Axmen logged off North Dakota in a single month,
and Babe, the Blue Ox, walked around on the stumps, pushing them
into the ground so that the Swedes could plow the next day.

Things were "opening up," they said then as now. Newspapers
were printed every week, on presses brought down on river boats, set
up in shanties and barns, with the latest news on science, political
theory, translating the Declaration of Independence and the Communist Manifesto. Simultaneously with building the sod shanties,
breaking the prairie, schools were started, Athenaeums and debating
and singing societies founded, poetry written and recited on winter
evenings. The latest theories of the rights of man were discussed along
with the making of a better breaking plow.

Inventions, new roads, tools, voyages, explorations, scientific
discoveries opened the horizon of man's brain. Excitement was high.
Fourier, Marx, Rousseau, Darwin were discussed in covered wagons,
along with electro-chemical equivalents. Knute, a woodsman, penned
the following after a lone winter in a cabin, seeing Indians through his
doorway as he wrote:

Having all my wood in and when I was thus alone I sent for a free
thinker paper in Norwegian, Dagslyset, and the writings of Ingersoll
and Spencer. And after long study I moved out of the orthodox faith
and into the faith of Ingersoll and after him I later named my first
son. It was a hard thing to do but a great relief to get rid of the hell
and damnation. I then slept sound and better nights.

Emigrants crowded the ports of Europe, Mennonites, German
revolutionists, the forty-eighters, French Communards who had swum
the Channel to the Jersey Isles. Gamblers, speculators, Yankee peddlers, three-card-Monty men, whiskey-sellers, quacks, dreamers,
hunters, planters, milled together on the river-boats.

As Emerson said at that time there were "madmen, men with
beards, Dunkers, Muggletonians, Come-Outers, Groaners, Agrarians,
Seventh-Day Adventists, Baptists, Quakers, Abolitionists, Unitarians,
and Philosophers." All these and more lashed their oxen west to take
part in Jacksonian democracy in a tide of farmers, mechanics, land-

hungry frontiersmen, with the marks of the knout on their backs, the prison pallor, famine color, breeding many kinds of tough, wild love of freedom.

So they came to the sun-down bailiwick writing a few notes, a letter that might go out when the thaws came. Some wrote back to New England in a tiny hand:

> Mama, you should come here. You can plow a mile straight and never turn a stone. Don't say I'm crazy.
>
> At night over the prairie we see a splendid mirage, a vast territory arising around us, a village in the air, with hay-cocks like castles, mirrored in the sky with no division between real and unreal.

Depending upon who you were and where you came from were your comments about the North Star Country. Margaret Fuller spending a summer in Wisconsin wrote of "its bold and impassioned sweetness, I do believe that Rome and Florence do not compare to this capital of natural art."

Englishmen like Basil Hall, Mrs. Trollope, Josiah Quince were willing to accept Boston society but the raucous frontier did not please them. The people, they said, were "convinced of their sagacity and acumen and proud of their shrewdness and independence . . . corrupt with political licentiousness which is producing turbulent citizens, abandoned Christians, inconstant husbands, unnatural fathers and treacherous friends."

While Harriet Martineau had the opposite impression, regarding the people as:

> . . . a great embryo poet, now moody, now wild, but bringing out results of absolute good sense, restless, wayward in action but with deep peace and a gentle heart; exulting that he has caught the true aspect of things past and the depth of futurity which lies before him, wherein to create something so magnificent as the world has scarcely begun to dream of. There is the strongest hope of a nation that is capable of being possessed of an idea.

What sextant can be used to shoot the sun of this people's migration; what spirit levels found to make their work live and hold? What delicate needle would indicate the flux of oppressed peoples into the free lands, opened as Utopia, a domain of rich earth bought by Jefferson from Napoleon, the North Star standing in the dark of that feudal night, inviting haven from the knout, the guillotine, the Bastille, shining as a beacon of the new, democratic man? What seismograph will chart such complex strains, beating the pattern, shifting like a reflection, full of antagonisms, despair and hope, mounting toward disaster, growth, and that great identity called a new nation?

Tradition was broken, relationships lost, the new man a green tendril full of loneliness, a bag of recollections: hair-braided portraits lost in Ohio, an old woman's fragmented memory, a child's horizon madness, a buck-and-wing, a mother with a harp, pictures in a rawhide trunk of people never seen again, the jokes of Abe Lincoln, songs of nostalgia — "We will meet by and by, in that beautiful land beyond the sky," "My old Kentucky home, good night," "They shall come rejoicing, bring in the sheaves."

A man having no more than a desire to become a Montreal merchant, opened the river, key to a continent.

Three men stealing out at night only to get ahead of an officer, founded a city.

The people of the North Star Country, because of their hatred of slavery, sent the first regiment in response to Lincoln's call and helped insure the solidarity of the United States.

Walking on giant paths, and being small and frightened, the north countryman created giant myths, sang to cover fear and nostalgia for old lands and bends of rivers he would never see again.

The mechanics, lumberjacks, the lakemen, rivermen, woodcutters, plowmen, the hunkies, hanyocks, whistle-punks; the women beating the chaff, the roof-raisers, the cradle-makers, the writers of constitutions, the singers in the evening along unknown rivers; the stone masons, the quarrymen, the high slingers of words, the printers and speakers in the courthouses, the lawmakers, the carpenters, joiners, journeymen — all kept on building. Every seven years they picked up the loans, mortgages, the grasshopper-ridden fields, the lost acres, the flat bank accounts, and went on, started over, turned a new leaf, worked harder, looked over new horizons.

The heritage they give us is the belief we have in them. It is the story of their survival, the sum of adjustments, the struggle, the folk accumulation called sense and the faith we have in that collective experience. It was real and fast, and we enclose it. Many unknown people lived and were destroyed by it. What looks to us grotesque or sentimental is the humor of the embryo, the bizarreness of the unformed, and the understanding of it is a prerequisite to our survival. It was real, and created our day. Perhaps it encloses us.

It is the deep from which we emerge.

Like a lion the people leave marks of their passing, reveal that moment of strength when the radicle plunged into the soil, in a fierce struggle on a strong day, and a nation held.

The ANCIENT PEOPLE and the NEWLY COME

Born out of the caul of winter in the north, in the swing and circle of the horizon, I am rocked in the ancient land. As a child I first read the scriptures written on the scroll of frozen moisture by wolf and rabbit, by the ancient people and the newly come. In the beginning of the century the Indian smoke still mingled with ours. The frontier of the whites was violent, already injured by vast seizures and massacres. The winter nightmares of fear poisoned the plains nights with psychic airs of theft and utopia. The stolen wheat in the cathedrallike granaries cried out for vengeance.

Most of all one was born into space, into the great resonance of space, a magnetic midwestern valley through which the winds clashed in lassoes of thunder and lightning at the apex of the sky, the very wrath of God.

The body repeats the landscape. They are the source of each other and create each other. We were marked by the seasonal body of earth, by the terrible migrations of people, by the swift turn of a century, verging on change never before experienced on this greening planet. I sensed the mound and swell above the mother breast, and from embryonic eye took sustenance and benediction, and went from mother enclosure to prairie spheres curving into eachother.

I was born in winter, the village snow darkened toward midnight, footsteps on boardwalks, the sound of horses pulling sleighs, and the ring of bells. The square wooden saltbox house held the tall shadows, thrown from kerosene lamps, of my grandmother and my aunt and uncle (missionaries home from India) inquiring at the door.

It was in the old old night of the North Country. The time of wood before metal. Contracted in cold, I lay in the prairie curves of my mother, in the planetary belly, and outside the vast horizon of the plains, swinging dark and thicketed, circle within circle. The round moon sinister reversed upside down in the sign of Neptune, and the twin fishes of Pisces swimming toward Aquarius in the dark.

But the house was New England square, four rooms upstairs and four rooms downstairs, exactly set upon a firm puritan foundation, surveyed on a level, set angles of the old geometry, and thrust up on the plains like an insult, a declamation of the conqueror, a fortress of our God, a shield against excess and sin.

I had been conceived in the riotous summer and fattened on light and stars that fell on my underground roots, and every herb, corn plant, cricket, beaver, red fox leaped in me in the old Indian dark. I saw everything was moving and entering. The rocking of mother and prairie breast curved around me within the square. The field crows flew in my flesh and cawed in my dream.

Crouching together on Indian land in the long winters, we grew in sight and understanding, heard the rumbling of glacial moraines, clung to the edge of holocaust forest fires, below-zero weather, grasshopper plagues, sin, wars, crop failures, drouth, and the mortgage. The severity of the seasons and the strangeness of a new land, with those whose land had been seized looking in our windows, created a tension of guilt and a tightening of sin. We were often snowed in, the villages invisible and inaccessible in cliffs of snow. People froze following the rope to their barns to feed the cattle. But the cyclic renewal and strength of the old prairie earth, held sacred by thousands of years of Indian ritual, the guerrilla soil of the Americas, taught and nourished us.

We flowed through and into the land, often evicted, drouthed out, pushed west. Some were beckoned to regions of gold, space like a mirage throwing up pictures of utopias, wealth, and villages of brotherhood. Thousands passed through the villages, leaving their dead, deposits of sorrow and calcium, leaching the soil, creating and marking with their faces new wheat and corn, producing idiots, mystics, prophets, and inventors. Or, as an old farmer said, we couldn't move; nailed to the barn door by the wind, we have to make a windmill, figure out how to plow without a horse, and invent barbed wire. A Dakota priest said to me, "It will be from here that the prophets come."

Nowhere in the world can spring burst out of the iron bough as in the Northwest. When the plains, rising to the Rockies, swell with heat, and the delicate glow and silence of the melting moisture fills the pure space with delicate winds and the promise of flowers. We all came, like the crocus, out of the winter dark, out of the captive village where along the river one winter the whole population of children died of diphtheria. In the new sun we counted the dead, and at the spring dance the living danced up a storm and drank and ate heartily for the pain of it. They danced their alien feet into the American earth and rolled in the haymow to beget against the wilderness new pioneers.

All opened in the spring. The prairies, like a great fan, opened. The people warmed, came together in quilting bees, Ladies' Aid meetings, house raisings. The plowing and the planting began as soon as the thaw let the farmers into the fields. Neighbors helped each other. As soon as the seed was in, the churches had picnics and baptizings. The ladies donned their calico dresses and spread a great board of food, while the children ran potato races and one-legged races and the men played horseshoes and baseball. Children were born at home with the neighbor woman. Sometimes the doctor got there. When I was twelve, I helped the midwife deliver a baby. I held onto the screaming mother, her lips bitten nearly off, while she delivered in pieces a dead, strangled corpse. Some people who made it through the winter died in the spring, and we all gathered as survivors to sing "The Old Rugged Cross," "Shall We Gather at the River?" and "God Be with You Till We Meet Again."

The Poles and the Irish had the best parties, lasting for two or three days sometimes. But even the Baptist revival meetings were full of singing (dancing prohibited), and hundreds were forgiven, talking in tongues. Once I saw them break the ice to baptize a screaming woman into the water of life for her salvation.

On Saturday nights everybody would shoot the works, except the prohibitionists and the "good" people, mostly Protestant teetotalers who would appear at church on Sunday morning. The frontier gamblers, rascals, and speculators filled the taverns—drink, women, and gambling consuming the wealth of the people and the land. There were gaming palaces for the rich, even horse racing in Stillwater. In St. Paul Nina Clifford, a powerful figure, had two whorehouses, one for gentlemen from "the Hill" and the other for lumberjacks coming in from the woods to spend their hard-earned bucks. It was said that three powers had divided St. Paul among them—Bishop Ireland took "the Hill," Jim Hill took the city for his trains, and Nina Clifford took all that was below "the Hill."

When the corn was "knee-high by the Fourth of July," and the rainfall was good and the sun just right, there was rejoicing in the great Fourth of July picnics that specialized in oratory. Without loudspeakers there were speeches that could be heard the length of the grove, delivered by orators who practiced their wind. When farm prices fell because of the speculation of the Grain Exchange in Minneapolis, the threatened farmers met on the prairie and in the park, the town plaza, and the courthouse to speak out against the power of monopoly. They came for miles, before and after the harvest, in farm wagons with the whole family. They passed out manifestos and spoke of organizing the people to protect themselves from the predators.

There is no place in the world with summer's end, fall harvest, and Indian summer as in Minnesota. They used to have husking bees. The wagons went down the corn rows, and the men with metal knives on their fingers cut the ears off the stalks and tossed them into the wagons. Then they husked the ears, dancing afterward, and if a man got a red ear he could kiss his girl. In August there were great fairs, and the farmers came in to show their crops and beasts, and the workers showed their new reapers and mowers.

There was the excitement of the fall, the terror of the winter coming on. In the winter we didn't have what we did not can, preserve, ferment, or bury in sand. We had to hurry to cut the wood and to get the tomatoes, beans, and piccalilli canned before frost in the garden. It was like preparing for a battle. My grandmother wrapped the apples in newspaper and put them cheek by jowl in the barrels. Cabbage was shredded and barreled for sauerkraut. Even the old hens were killed. I was always surprised to see my gentle grandmother put her foot on the neck of her favorite hen and behead her with a single stroke of a long-handled ax.

The days slowly getting shorter, the herbs hung drying as the woods turned golden. Everything changes on the prairies at the end of summer, all coming to ripeness, and the thunderheads charging in the magnetic moisture of the vast skies. The autumnal dances are the best medicine against the threat of winter, isolation again, dangers. The barns were turned into dance halls before the winter hay was cut. The women raised their long skirts and danced toward hell in schottisches, round dances, and square dances. The rafters rang with the music of the old fiddlers and the harmonica players.

When the golden leaves stacked Persian carpets on the ground and the cornfields were bare, we saw again the great hunched land naked, sometimes fall plowed or planted in winter wheat. Slowly the curve seemed to rise out of the glut of summer, and the earth document was visible script, readable in the human tenderness of risk and ruin.

The owl rides the meadow at his hunting hour. The fox clears out the pheasants and the partridges in the cornfield. Jupiter rests above Antares, and the fall moon hooks itself into the prairie sod. A dark wind flows down from Mandan as the Indians slowly move out of the summer campground to go back to the reservation. Aries, buck of the sky, leaps to the outer rim and mates with earth. Root and seed turn into flesh. We turn back to each other in the dark together, in the short days, in the dangerous cold, on the rim of a perpetual wilderness.

It is hard to believe that when I was twelve it was that many years into the century, fourteen years from the Spanish-American War, twenty-two years from the Ghost Dance and the Battle of Wounded Knee, and four years until World War I would change the agrarian world.

I hung, green girl in the prairie light, in the weathers of three fertile and giant prairie women who strode across my horizon in fierce attitudes of planting, reaping, childbearing, and tender care of the seed.

As a pear ripens in the chemical presence of other pears, I throve on their just and benevolent love, which assured a multiplication of flesh out of time's decay. I knew the first eden light among their flowers and prairie breasts, buttocks, and meadows, in their magnetic warmth and praise.

One was my grandmother from Illinois, whose mother was a full-blooded Iroquois who had married her teacher, an abolitionist preacher. She had come with him to the West and vowed she would die on the day of his death. She did. My grandmother herself was a puritan, fortressed within her long skirts and bathing under a shift. She divorced her husband, an unusual act in her society. He was drinking up the farms her father left her. Afterward she rode over the Midwest in a horse-drawn buggy, a shotgun beside her, for the Woman's Christian Temperance Union, crying in the wilderness for sobriety. We rode in hayracks in temperance parades, dressed in white and shouting slogans — 'Tremble, King Alcohol: We shall grow up, and lips that touch liquor shall never touch mine!"

Her daughter, my mother, went to college, with my grandmother cooking for fraternities to earn the money to send her through, and married a Lothario preacher at nineteen. She had four children; one died very young. She had read the works of Ellen Key and had heard Emma Goldman, and by the time her last child was born, she believed that a woman had the right of her own life and body. She took a course in comparative religion and broke away from the Christian church. Because the laws of Texas made women and children chattels with no property or civil rights, my mother kidnapped us in the night and fled north like a black slave woman, hoping to get over the border into the new state of Oklahoma, where the laws were more liberal. My father tried to extradite us as criminals or property but failed.

The third woman was a Mandan Indian we called Zona. She lived in the grove with the Indians who came in the summer to work in the fields, and she helped us out at canning time. Her husband had died of grief because the buffalo did not come back in the Ghost Dance and because, after the massacre at Wounded Knee, the government had prohibited her people from dancing and smoking the sacred pipe and had suppressed the shield societies. After that, she said, even the blueberries disappeared.

I grew in the midst of this maternal forest, a green sapling, in bad years putting my roots deep down for sustenance and survival. It was strange and wonderful what these women had in common. They knew the swift linear movement of a changing society that was hard on women. They had suffered from men, from an abrasive society, from the wandering and disappearance of the family. They lived a subjective and parallel life, in long loneliness of the children, in a manless night among enemies.

They were not waiting for land to open up, for gold mines to be discovered, or for railroads to span the north. They were not waiting for any kind of progress or conquest. They were waiting for the Apocalypse, for the coming of some messiah, or, like my grandmother, to join their people in heaven after a frugal and pure life. Their experience of this world centered around the male as beast, his drunkenness and chicanery, his oppressive violence.

They carried in them the faces of old seeds, ghosts of immigrants over land bridges, old prayers in prairie ash, nourishing rain, prophecies of embryos and corpses, distance opening to show the burning green madonnas in the cob, doomed radiance of skeletons, concentrated calcium, delayed cries at night, feeding pollen and fire. They carried herbs and seeds in sunbonnets, bags of meal, and lilac pouches.

We sat together after harvest, canning, milking and during cyclones in the cellar, and they seemed like continents, full of appearing children and dying heroines. The three of them had much to do with the primal events of the countryside — death, birth, illness, betterment of roads and schools.

I sneaked out with Zona often, crawling out the window over the summer kitchen and shinnying down the apple tree to go through the pale spring night to the Indian fires, where the Indian workers drummed until the village seemed to sink away and something fierce was thrust up on the old land. The earth became a circle around the central fire, and the skin stretched over the quiet and hollow skulls of the old and sacred traditional people of the Mandans. The horizon grew larger, the sling of the night stars moved above, and the horizon dilated in the repeating circle of the dancers.

I sat hidden in the meadow with Zona. She was tall and strong, like many of the Plains Indians. The structure of her face was Oriental, her woman's cheeks round as fruits, encased nutlike by her long black hair. She told me of how the grass once moved in the wind, winey in color — the ancient flesh of the mother before the terrible steel plow put its ravenous teeth in her. How antelope, deer, elk, and wild fowl lived richly upon the plains, and how in spring the plains seethed with the roaring of mating buffalo. How you could hear the clicking of their horns and the drumbeat of their feet in the fury of rut. How the warriors went out to slay the meat for the winter. And the summers of the wild berries and the plums and the making of pemmican, the jollity and wooing, the buffalo going south to the salt licks and the Mandans to their great mounded grass cathedrals where they spent the winter in telling stories and legends of the mountains and the shining sea to the west. She said they were the first people in the world. They had lived inside the mother earth and had come up on huge vines into the light.

The vine had broken and there were some of her people still under the earth. And she told how the traders threw smallpox-infected clothing into the Mandan village. Most of them died that winter. The whole northern plains stank with the unburied dead.

She showed me that the earth was truly round, sacred, she said, so that no one could own it. The land is not for taking, she said, and I am not for taking. You can't have anything good in the square or in five. All must be four or seven. You can't divide the land in the square, she said. She made the whole landscape shift and encircle me. She said the earth went far down and the whites could only buy and deed the top. The earth waited, its fingers clasped together like culms: she closed her brown fingers to show the interlocking. She said that men and women were rooted, interpenetrating, turning to the center. She did not believe in hell or heaven. She believed we were here now in this place. She said the earth would give back a terrible holocaust to the white people for being assaulted, plowed up, and polluted. She said everything returned, everything was now, in this time. She said past, present, and future were invented by the white man.

But it was the grass, she said: Grass was one of the richest foods on earth and the prairie grass had salts and protein more than any other food. Before the plow, the plains grass could have fed nations of cattle — all the cattle in the world — just as it had fed the buffalo. They did not overgraze when there were no fences because they walked away as they ate. She said that now the earthflesh was wrong side up and blowing away in the wind. The grass might never come back, the buffalo never return.

She said the government could not stop the Indians from prayer and the dances. They would take them underground with the unborn people. She swept her sacred feather around the horizon, to show the open fan of the wilderness and how it all returned: mortgaged land, broken treaties — all opened among the gleaming feathers like a warm-breasted bird turning into the turning light of moon and sun, with the grandmother earth turning and turning. What turns, she said, returns. When she said this, I could believe it.

I knew the turning earth and woman would defend me. I saw the powerful strong women, and I was a small green girl with no breasts and hardly a bowel for anger, but gleaming among them, unused, naked as the land, learning anger, and turning to cauterize and protect the earth, to engender out of their rape and suffering a new race to teach the warriors not to tread the earth and women down. At their own peril!

I saw them, the circle like the prairie holding the children within the power of the grandmothers, receiving the returning warriors from all thievery, defeats, and wounds. The fierce and guerrilla strength of the puritan and Indian women seemed similar, unweighed, even unknown, the totemic power of birth and place, earth and flesh.

Their fierce embraces seemed to crush and terrorize my brothers and me. There was something of anguish in them. They had the bodies of the fiercest exiled heroines in fiction and history, pursued, enslaved. They listened to each other and the horrors of their tales — how the Iroquois fled the assassins of my grandmother's village, how she came down the Ohio and brought a melodeon. My mother told of her flight from Texas, across the border into Oklahoma, where women were given the rights to their children. The Indian woman Zona told how her mother was killed in 1890 at the Battle of Wounded Knee, running with her suckling child till the soldiers gunned her down and left the child to freeze at the breast. How her father waited for the Ghost Dance buffalo to come out of the rock and they never came. The three women sat bolt upright in the afternoon with high and noble faces and told these stories so much alike in a strange way. I put it down in my heart that they were so fierce and angry and tempestuous, so strong, because they were bound for the protection of all and had a fierce and terrible and awful passion for vindication and the payment of ransom and the mysterious rescue of something.

My grandmother learned the native herbs and grasses and their uses from Zona. How the different parts could be used and how some parts of many plants were poison at some time in the growth cycle. The dried roots of chokecherry could be made into a gum to put into wounds to stop bleeding. The chokecherry bark could be eaten in the spring for dysentery. From the chokecherry wood spoons were carved. And the berries were crushed in pemmican, which was cut into strips and dried for winter or for a long journey.

My grandmother made a place for these plants in the root cellar and marked them clearly and neatly. The high four-o'clock that came up in the summer in the meadow was a drugstore, a friend. Nobody took too much, leaving some for seed so that it would appear again the next year, as it always did. Bear grass was used to weave watertight bowls. There were plants for digging sticks, brooms, and fishnets, plants for incense, incantations, clothing, soap, oils and paints, tanning, and branding. My grandmother especially loved to know about bulbs, roots, and tubers, for she always prepared for poor crops, famine, fires, disease, and death. Fifty plants were labeled for use in green salads, meal, flour, and syrup; five for beverages; three for contraceptives, remedies for snake bite, antiseptics, and astringents. She had twenty-six plants for the treatment of winter and summer diseases and for use as poultices, tonics, salivants, and thirst preventers. There were poisonous things, and they were used for poison. The pasqueflower, she said, would make a deadly liquor for enemies. The great sunflower was ground and made into a cake for long journeys. Some obnoxious distilled liquor was made from a putrefied toad. There was nothing like a worthless weed. Nothing was of no use. Everything was loved and cared for. I still cannot tear anything from the earth without hearing its cry.

It was a balm to feel from Zona the benevolence of the entire cosmos. Once she took me to Mandan, outside of Bismarck, across the river, to show me the most beautiful living space I have ever seen — the great mounded grass-covered excavations with no windows except at the top where the smoke escaped and the light poured down as in a cathedral. She showed me how they lived in that circle of the cosmos and the earth's orbiting around the round and burning fire of the grandmothers. She taught me that violence is linear and love spherical.

One afternoon as we all sat on the porch in the summer shade, shredding cabbage for sauerkraut, Zona told us about the Ghost Dance. When the government made it illegal for Indians to meet together for the practice of their religion, that was the end, she said; even the blueberries became scarce. My grandmother and mother nodded, fully understanding the strangeness of men and the dreams they get, invoking power on slim threads of reality. Zona spoke sadly of the Ghost Dance, saying that she hadn't believed in it fully and that she had hurt the power of the buffalo to come out of the rock by not believing enough. But her husband went on a long journey to talk with the prophet Wovoka and was convinced that the white man's Jesus was going to help the Indians, that if they all danced together the buffalo and all the dead would return and they would have the land again. She told how he came back and said that he had seen in Oklahoma a huge brass bed, a shrine on the sand hills, surrounded by prayer sticks and sacred objects, where it was said Jesus came and slept every night after helping the Indian people.

I am the one who held him back, she said, I couldn't believe this could happen. The dead appear, but they do not really return to eat the returning buffalo. She said the only thing you could believe was that the land might come back to them. All the grasses could return in one season if the overgrazing would stop. She remembered the real grass that moved and changed like a sea of silk. It took one color from the north, other colors from the south and the east and the west, but now it was short and leached of nitrogen and had only one color. The old rippling, running prairies were gone, she said. She could remember when the Indians had stood and called the buffalo to them, asking for the sacrifice of their flesh, asking them to give their bodies for food. There was great power and love in the earth then, she said.

Then came the last buffalo dream. The grandmothers brought their medicine in sacred bundles to bring the buffalo out of the rock. They brought the old-time power-songs back. She made her husband a ghost shirt through which it was said bullets would not penetrate. He went on a long journey to Texas to find a fresh male buffalo skin and skull for the sacred tepee. It was the last attempt to recover the Indian shield power. It was good power. Wovoka had seen the white savior who hung on the sun cross.

On four nights after the fast and the sweat bath, they sang, watching the rock out of which the buffalo and the dead were to come from the underworld. She said she didn't have the right thoughts. Once she wondered if she could get out of the way if they did come thundering out, and she almost laughed. She said she thought it was no use that way. The past did return, but not that way. But she watched all night. Some said they heard rumbling underground. They danced till they dropped. My husband, she said, stood sweating, his face dirty, his hide painted. My power, she said, was loving and good but not strong enough. My husband said his power was good and strong, she said, and I loved him for it, bringing the ancestors back and the buffalo, the good grass, and the fresh water.

And then in the night he stood with his hands out and cried, this is the way it is ending. No, no, she had cried, the circle never ends. But he did not hear her. He didn't live long after that. He just withered away, wouldn't eat, came to nothing. That was the end of the wild plums, she said, and the old life. We starved and wandered and went down into the culm. But we are locked together underneath, and living will go on. We have to keep things alive for the children.

My grandmother and mother nodded. They knew this. They had made long treks to farms they lost to the same enemies. We will have to do it, my grandmother said—keep the beginning of the circle, the old and the new will meet. And she sang her own ceremonial song then, "We shall come rejoicing, bringing in the sheaves."

There was always this mothering in the night, the great female meadows, sacred and sustaining. I look out now along the bluffs of the Mississippi, where Zona's prophecies of pollution have been fulfilled in ways worse than she could dream. Be aware, she had cried once. Be afraid. Be careful. Be fierce. She had seen the female power of the earth, immense and angry, that could strike back at its polluters and conquerors.

The great richness of growing up in a northwest village was in the variety and the excitement of all the ethnic cultures. I was free to go into all of them, even singing in Norwegian choirs and dancing with Finnish dance groups. The rituals were still celebrated. There was even a bagpipe group that marched on St. Patrick's Day, all in green, and in the park I listened to a lawyer, three sheets in the wind, recite the last speech of Robert Emmet. I liked to sample the rich foods, too, and secretly found in myself a riotous temperament different from my grandmother's.

I especially loved the dances. They were so colorful and varied, and some were so sensual and beautiful. They freed me from severe puritan sexual rigidity, from relating pleasure to guilt and sin. I remember my first dance. I don't know how my mother and my grandmother let me go, but it was not without warnings, threats, and a terrible armor against sin and excess. My first party dress was white, although I would have preferred red or even yellow. But only the Polish whores wore those colors, my grandmother said. So I wore a white dress and shoes that had a thin stripe of red around them and little heels. I had rolled my hair on newspaper to have curls, which seemed to me the height of voluptuousness.

Jon came to pick me up in a surrey with a fringe on top, though it was harnessed to a plow horse. The harvest was just over, and his huge forearms were browned from the sun and gleaming. He smelled of chaff, even though he was scrubbed to within an inch of his life and his wild straw hair was slicked down with bear grease. He seemed strange and huge as he helped me onto the high step. We drove slowly through the aspens, which were gold around us. I smelled of talcum powder and so did he. I had rubbed wet crepe paper on my cheeks and blackened my eyes with kitchen matches, passing my grandmother quickly so she couldn't see my whorish color.

The old horse turned, laughing, to see if we were there, we were so silent. In the grove wagons and carriages had stopped for spooning as it was early. I was glad we weren't going to do that. My grandmother had told me to drink nothing, just as Demeter told Persephone not to eat anything in Hades, though of course she did and was trapped by pomegranate seeds. She warned me that even grape punch could easily be tampered with. She meant spiked.

In the big empty hall everyone stood around kidding and waiting. The men seemed very tall and hung their heads. The girls seemed unbearably bright, each in her best bib and tucker, all laughing too loud and embracing each other to show how good it was to embrace.

But soon the bung was pulled from the beer barrel. Mugs were filled, and moonshine was nipped outside the door. But lips that touch liquor shall never touch mine. Besides, I was bold and spiced enough, going out with a boy, wearing almost high heels, and waiting to dance for the first time.

The fiddlers started warming up. An accordion joined them and we were off. I began to be tossed from one tall man to another. My feet hardly touched the ground, and the caller could have been speaking another language. I didn't need to know the dance, I just followed. I went from one great harvester to the other. They were laughing, some yelling and "feeling you up," as the girls said. Through the hours we were flying, sweating, pressed, tossed, stamping out the rhythms, whirling from embrace to embrace, touching – Hitch 'em up and hike 'em up a high tuckahaw, give me the dance of turkey in the straw. Sugar in the gourd, honey in the horn, I never was so happy since the day I was born.

As the night got deeper and the fiddlers hotter, we were flung into the men's arms, back and forth, a weave of human bodies. I couldn't tell one from the other. A girl took me outside with her. The girls lifted their skirts on one side of the field, and the boys stood with their backs to us on the other. I never heard such laughter or sensed such dangerous meaning in the night, in what took place in the woods, when the dancers returned with curious smiles and leaves in their hair. We seemed on the edge of some abysmal fire. But they seemed unafraid, plunging into the heat and the danger as if into a bonfire of roses.

I never was the same again.

My grandmother homesteaded a piece of land and built a house on it which was a simple pure expression of the Protestant needs of her severe religion, her graceless intensity of the good, thrifty, work-for-the-night-is-coming, dutiful labor. She came alone to the wilderness, hired stonemasons and carpenters, and demanded a design to match her dimensions and spirit. Did she make a drawing on a piece of paper, or did she spin it out of her memory, prudence, and frugality? It was a New England farmhouse with a summer kitchen, a birthing room on ground level, and a closed front parlor where one did not let the sun come. She probably did not consider that the house was squared off on an ancient land of mounds and pyramids and cones, on land that had not been plowed in a million years. Neither did she think the land had been monstrously taken from its native people. If she thought of it at all, she undoubtedly felt the Christian purposes of her Anglo-puritan world would bring only benefit and salvation to them.

The design and beauty of this house moved me then, and when I see its abandoned replica on the plains, I weep. It was a haven against the wild menace of the time, a structural intensity promising only barest warmth, a Doric hearth, and a rigid, austere, expectant growth.

On the day of the opening of homesteading she got a corner lot, a small parcel of land she could register, and she built her wooden democratic temple upon it. The lot ran to what became an alley when the village was formally platted. The outhouse was on this alley. She had two cellars dug the first thing. The root cellar was half under the house, and the cyclone cellar, prepared at all times for disaster with blankets, food, and water, was separate from it. Once during a forest fire the cyclone cellar saved us from the smoke. Her dream, which was common, was to have a piece of land, free of mortgage, with enough room for grapevines, gooseberries, strawberries, asparagus, and rhubarb (all of which would return every year), a garden, three peach trees, and an apple tree. We had one milk cow freshening once a year, and one pig bought from a spring litter. The pig would fatten on our leavings by fall, and we would butcher him, smoke the hams and bacon, and render the lard for the year's frying. Even in a bad year we were almost independent. We had to buy (or exchange work or produce for) only kerosene, wood, coffee, and flour, although we could make flour from acorns or our own corn or, like Zona, from the cattails that grew in the swamp. Zona also ate young cattail shoots in spring salad.

The basement was under only part of the house and was lined with river stone, which made a foot-high base for the house—the yellow sandstone, as I saw it years later, remained strong and faithful. The pine boards also were still aligned straight in their naive simplicity and symmetry, the center holding, the beams holding, the floor hardly warped or slanting. The house was earnestly made with a sturdy belief that it was built to last for a hundred years at the least and to give hearth and ceiling and walls for earnest, simple people who did not ask too much. It contained not one piece of wasted wood or embellishment; it was made to hold the weather out and to hold the faithful human for a century within its piney undecorated wood, straight-angled at the corners, the strong hide of wood stretched to its utmost to protect us. It displayed only two indulgences. One was a little bay window, not rich or ostentatious, projecting barely enough to permit a table or a desk in the alcove; from the window I could look down two streets. I had my desk there and wrote my first stories there. The other indulgence was the front door with its clusters of acorn carvings that had been painted black or had turned black.

The first front room was the parlor, which was used only for company. The blinds were always drawn in the parlor to keep the big red roses in the rug from fading, and on two easels were lithographs of my grandmother's father and mother. The room opening off the parlor was the sitting room, and from there the large kitchen extended under the peach trees. We mainly lived in the kitchen with its big wood-burning stove in front of which we took our Saturday night baths in the washtub. My brothers and I bathed in the same water because we had to carry it from the pump, which was outside, or from the rain barrel, which stood under the eaves. I envied those who had indoor cisterns in which the rain water could accumulate and be pumped directly into the sink.

Through a passageway half open to the weather was the summer kitchen and the little room called the birthing room. In the summer people who had the money to buy "Mr. Rockefeller's kerosene" cooked in their summer kitchen and did not have to heat up the house or waste wood. (My grandmother always said, "Mr. Rockefeller's kerosene has gone up two cents. If it goes up any more to add to his wealth, we'll have to use candles!") Another small room off the kitchen was the only bedroom. My brothers and I slept in the sitting room on couches.

Perhaps another small indulgence was the narrow wooden porch that went one-third of the way around the front of the house, upheld by small handmade wooden pillars. Later we had a sidewalk in front of the house.

This type of house, found all over the Midwest prairies, is a cultural wonder expressing the clean, rudimentary, sober symmetry of the pioneer's needs and speaking of the builders and their materials. Expressing the solid duty of worker and timber and time — earnest, rigid, no fooling, no laxness, spare as the puritan world. The extension of my grandmother's skeleton, of her needs: of her rebuke to the sensuality and wildness of the frontier, faithful to a vengeful god, severe but just; of her rebuke to the sensual stridency of violence and rowdiness. Single-handed in her long skirts and modesty — she never saw her own naked body bathing under that shift — she remarked in time and space of decency, uprightness, and duty. In her pure cabin she took the Ahabs back from their journeys. She cured the mad-drunk crew of beriberi and brought them back to the church altar and the brotherhood of Jesus.

Inside we had my aunt's mission furniture, a style that had been fashionable but then had given way to antiques, so that the poor relatives got the heavy chairs covered in imitation leather. In the spaces of that house I worshipped. I heard my first music in the evening as my grandmother sat at the little foot-pumped organ and sang the only songs she knew, in the homely voice the puritan women seemed to have, as if a joyful or immense tone might be excessive. At church the cords of her neck always swelled out painfully and the sound was painful, of sorrow and asking, and preparation to cross over the river Jordan into the heavenly land. Lead us home, take our hands and lead us out of the wilderness, let us rest in thee. Horrors were sung about rugged and lonely wilds: day after day I plot and moil, sorrow in my troubled glimmering breast, death shining in the dark mysteries beyond my dust, stars in gloomy graves glow and glitter, let me walk in the air of glory, this is where we were crucified, this tree, this agonizing light, and the flowers blanched by fear, poor I pine, what hidden place conceals thee? And she sang her only love song, "Jesus, Lover of My Soul, Let Me to Thy Bosom Fly."

Only though these songs did I know the depths of her sorrow, her terrible loneliness, her wish to die, her deep silence. Sometimes I heard her cry in the night, but I could not humiliate her by going to comfort her. In the day there would be no sign. In abrasive irony she would fulfill the duties inside the shell of her devotion, this fragile house flung up in tepee-curled light by the sound of hammers where a nail had not been known, this puritan citadel, fragile yet strong, a psychic mansion, a fragment of hope and despair. We crouched in an alien land under the weathers, tossing at night on this ancient sea, captained by women, minute against the great white whale.

These houses still gleam empty on the prairies, the same houses from the same puritan, democratic dream, lost and lost again as my grandmother's house was lost in the depression before World War I. They still live in the minds of those fled to the cities or to battlefields in strange villages. This small enduring white frame house is in nightmare and terrible dream proliferated, floating in the flood of time. Let yourself down, as if under water, into these lost walls, to hunt for treasure, to illuminate violence with meaning. Under sea-strange light these little houses glimmer in memory, powerful as radium.

In that little wooden nutmeg of a house my grandmother's mind was full of angels, the last supper, and Mary's ascension into heaven. We were together in the vengeful wilderness with a vengeful god. We read the psalms and the resurrection of Jesus and the women at the tomb that morning of his rising. She waited to go to heaven. She thought she would and so would all those she loved. This world was run by the devil.

The frontier was a hard place to hold up the Christian virtues single-handedly, in fichus of crochet, corsets, gloves, and hats and covered to the ankle by long skirts. She had a big iron rod up her spine and a small one in her curled ironic lip when she at last was released from hell at eighty-five.

After World War II I went out to the prairies to look for my grandmother's house. It was still there in the village that had changed to an industrial center. I followed the sun on my shoulder to find the street. The house still drew me with its light and shine. There was the wide street, the corner house. It had been painted white not long before by some faithful Protestant, and the little front porch was still supported by the undecorated pillars holding up the staunch and unslanting room. The bay window was still there. The back porch even had the same lattice, though the roses had died out. The faithful lilac bush was uncut, frowsy but still there, and the little irises still grew by the river stones that held up the house soberly and straight. The grape arbor had returned to wild grapes. One peach tree remained, spread out like an old matron, and I am sure in season bearing some kind of peaches. The people living in the house had had a hard time. The steps to the cellars were littered with whiskey bottles and coke bottles. A beheaded doll lay by the cyclone cellar. But repairs had been made, and a toilet had been added in one of the closets when the village had gotten water mains. The grass had held well, and I could even see some lilies of the valley near the back door.

When the front door was opened, I entered fearfully, the spaces of my girlhood still curving around me. Grandma's tall figure seemed to be about to appear in the doorway, her long arms under her apron. You see, she would be saying, I built a good house. Yes, I said, the floors even are not slanting: you built it solid.

The walls had been repapered time and again. It was wonderful and strange again to be inside the safe little square box. Not only the wood but the spirit of our flesh and all the harried flesh of a century now moved inside the snail shell, leaving the marks of movement intimate as marrow. I could see how the generations had made jelly from the grapes and had painted the good skeleton bright colors, the essential strength of my grandmother's being carrying her memory in this beautiful Doric shell.

Our fragility turns out to be strength. That sacred house seemed sunbonneted like my grandmother, spare and virginal. It had survived, as we have, the holocaust of our time, the human cyclone, and the hostilities of mid-America.

When we drove away, I didn't need to look back. That Pandora's box house had opened inside me, aswarm with apocalyptic light.

We lived from a frontier economy to the machine age in one generation. I saw the plundering of the wheat plains that impoverished thousands. The year I was born, despite antimonopoly laws passed by the Populist Party, there took the first gigantic amalgamation of wealth by the Hill and Morgan dynasties for the benefit of their children's children, they said, into eternity. I am glad I saw and suffered the desolation, distress, and sorrow of my people.

We lived through bonanza farming, absentee ownership, colonial oppression, wars, taxes, high interest, and mortgages. I participated in the organization of irate workers and farmers, Davids with slingshots against the Goliaths of power.

After a spell in Kansas we came back to the North Country during the time of the great strikes and depression, before the betrayal into World War I. At the People's College in Fort Scott, Kansas, my mother met Arthur Le Sueur, who with Helen Keller, Eugene Debs, and Charles Steinmetz had founded the greatest workers' school in the country. Thousands of farmers and hillbilly men, miners, and other workers took correspondence courses in workers' law and workers' English and workers' history.

My mother helped found one of the most amazing publications in our country, the *Little Blue Books*. In her course she used quotations from Marx, Jefferson, and Tom Paine, and the workers would ask her where they came from. It was impossible to get cheap editions of their works. She designed a book the size of the overall pocket and selling for a nickel. Millions of *Little Blue Books* were carried into the wheat fields, boxcars, and factories.

Arthur and Marian Le Sueur would not have said they were unique because they were soldiers in a large army of heroic people who with great courage stood against the kings of power in the vast new empire. They lived through many progressive movements, gave their lives to them, and never called anything defeat. Until he died at eighty-five, Arthur was still fighting for a change of venue against death. And Marian at seventy-five ran for senator, stumping the state to say a last word against war.

Arthur came from a militant family from the isle of Jersey. They had rowed across the channel after the failure of the French Revolution and were joined by the exiled Victor Hugo. They came to Minnesota for free land and settled in the rich Minnesota Valley across from Hastings in Ignatius Donnelly's town, Nininger, which was to be the Athens of the Mississippi. They broke the potato market in Chicago the first year and got their first lesson in monopoly and control of distribution. After Arthur's mother's death the three boys and their sister, Anne, all had to work to keep the free land during the depressions.

Arthur went to court the first time when his father horsewhipped the banker who came to foreclose the mortgage on the farm. He decided then to be a lawyer to defend the poor. His fare of oatmeal kept him short until he was sixteen, but he didn't get to school until he was too old to fit into the seats. By working in the harvest he got enough money to enroll in the law school at Ann Arbor, where he was called the bull of the woods. He bought an old McCormick reaper and hired it out in the summer to make enough money to finish law school. He opened an office in Minot, North Dakota, and furnished it with a kitchen table, two chairs, one law book, and a gun. He defended frontier justice and also picked up a little ready cash as lawyer for Jim Hill.

In his youth he had argued about God with the famous Bishop Whipple of St. Paul, who came to their farm. While he was plowing, only nine years old, he challenged God, asking him to make himself known or to be quiet. Asking him to strike him dead. There was no answer. He got his power when he left the fear and guilt and supplication and became a tribunal for the people. At night on the Mouse River he studied Marx and became a Socialist. He was elected the Socialist mayor of Minot and was arrested on his first day in office because he ordered the shackles taken off the ankles of the prisoners and the balls and chains thrown into the river. The city arrested him for destroying city property.

He loved the frontier way of life and missed it when it passed away. He was a stocky man with a fighter's stance, Indian color from prairie wind and sun, and a powerful plower's body. He had a curious stubborn quality of stolid incorruptibility, a solidity of responsibility, a devout social integrity. He believed in something called character, which was what you had of the root, something that could not be bought or sold or even dug out. What some men have as hunters for prey he had as public defender of his people. It was some kind of code of honor, of integrity and bravery. He had rigorous patterns for himself and the people. In a fight in court these strengths rose in him like a prizefighter's and he shone with all the powers of the cunning of the law used in defense of the oppressed. He stood on the soap box with the Industrial Workers of the World during the free speech fight and was arrested with them. He refused to be released and defended them all in court. When a banker was going to foreclose on a mortgaged herd of cattle, he brought the whole herd in to graze on the bank steps, saying, "Here is your herd!" Without a good fight he languished. He saw the enemy clear and never underestimated its power or his own.

He never drank, was chaste and shy, told a fantastic story to my children about Johnny Hoppergrass. He was full of frontier fantasy and Bunyan stories. He loved the poetry of Robert Burns and told funny stories in dialect.

His power was in the earth and the people. Above all, he liked to teach. He believed that the people had only to understand. He believed that he learned from the masses. He went to small towns throughout the Dakotas and Minnesota in his old car with his roll-down map. I went with him to many villages and passed out leaflets on Minnesota's iron range. Often we worked in secret because the Pinkerton spies and the company goons were watching every minute and people were shot outright for selling radical papers. We went in the afternoon, got permission to use the schoolhouse in the evening, and passed out leaflets saying, "Hear how the Grain Exchange robs you by a stroke of the pencil!" Then we would stop at some friend's house for supper, if we knew anyone, or would eat sandwiches in the village square. At seven o'clock we would ring the school bell, light the swinging kerosene lamp that hung from the ceiling, and hang Arthur's charts on the wall.

The charts showed how the Grain Exchange graded down prime wheat to third grade, robbing the farmer of millions. Arthur showed what was bad but also what was good and how it could be made better. He had charts of John Wesley Powell's study of 1878, showing how the 160-acre homestead was bad for the plains. Farmers needed more land and cooperative use of the land. They needed communal grazing lands and control of the public domain and water rights. The study showed why plowing was bad, why dust storms would result, why floods would come if all the forests were destroyed. The last page showed how only a few men were allowed to exploit the public domain through the railroads and the wheat monopoly — for example, the Pillsburys and the Washburns, who the farmers said had a congressional frank stamped on their buttocks at birth to assure them a seat in Congress.

The seldom discouraging word was being heard from orators in barns, at huge picnics where whole families and villages came in buckboards, the women setting out a rich feast and singing, "The Farmer Is the Man That Feeds Us All," "The Battle Hymn of the Republic," and sometimes "The People's Flag Is Deepest Red, It Waves above Our Martyred Dead." If you never heard the people singing together when you were a young person, shaking like an aspen in the thunder of history, then you can't imagine these political bacchanals in the cottonwood groves or in the open fields with guards staked out to spot the enemy at fifty or a hundred miles on a clear day.

The last chart bore Ignatius Donnelly's cry: To your tents, O Israel! Return the land to the American people, rescue the rich earth from predatory plutocrats, transfer the American people from pawns and automatons in the hand of monopoly to principals with a voice in their own lives and their country's life. The party of the common people, the child, is come, and it is a giant at birth. The blood is circulating in ten million hearts from which the people cry out for a better life. Its sledgehammer swings with the muscle of the toiling army. This is your party. The thrones of the despots are trembling. Get into the fight.

A great wind of talk was stirred up. Visions excited the men and women of the farms who lived a hundred miles from each other. They were of different ancestry and languages but were at last moving together with their planners, orators, and organizers. At last they were pointing out the charismatic leaders who were stealing their grain and the homestead itself. They asked themselves why, out of the rich humus and the protean grasses, they could not make a living, why machinery was so expensive, whether fences had ruined the land.

The bloody strike on the range broke out. I saw that workers could be killed if they asked for an eight-hour day. Bill Haywood was arrested on the range. The miners struck against low wages and long hours. Thousands of gunmen were imported, and scabs were recruited in the Minneapolis Gateway, the largest hiring street in the northwest. A company gunman killed Litvala, a peddler. And all the radical leaders for twenty miles around were arrested. The unarmed miners were charged with the murder. And the IWW leaders were arrested.

Arthur was one of the founders of the IWW at the 1905 convention. He went to the defense of the miners at Ludlow when the women and children were murdered by Rockefeller mining interests. He defended Wild Bill Haywood. He defended members of the IWW and objectors against the war.

Nowadays everyone seems to recognize and to be shocked at the insult and injury perpetrated against the IWW, the Socialists, and the conscientious objectors early in the century. It was different to know it then. Our family was not only isolated for our stand against the war, but we were shot at, our books were rifled and burned in our front yard on Dayton Avenue in St. Paul, rocks with obscene messages were thrown through our windows. Organizers for the Non-Partisan League were beaten and tarred and feathered. Tar is very hard to get off. I spent days with victims of beatings trying to get the tar off the skin without taking the skin as well. Minnesota had a vigilante committee, a state fascist organization with unlimited powers and headed by Governor Burnquist; it was called the Minnesota Commission of Public Safety.

Charles Lindbergh, Sr., was pursued from a parade in Red Wing, Minnesota, where the cars were covered with red paint. The participants in the parade drove to a farmer's field and the crowd followed them. The farmer's barn had been painted yellow. Lindbergh probably would have been tarred and feathered had not a train come across the meadow that happened to have at the throttle an antiwar engineer who stopped the train and hoisted the running Lindbergh into the cab and outran the pursuing vigilantes.

The Socialist Party was split in 1916 at the St. Louis convention on the question of the war. Arthur and Marian Le Sueur voted against the war. La Follette from Wisconsin stood alone in the Senate and voted against it. His picture in the statehouse in Madison was turned to the wall, and people spat upon him in the streets.

Frank Little, a member of the IWW who had worked on the iron range, had gone to join the fight of the miners in Butte. He had broken his leg but was taken out of his rooming house and was hanged on a Butte bridge. He was protesting the fate of 163 miners who had burned to death in an Anaconda mine explosion.

The years of the war were terrible years. Most of the young men I went to high school with never returned. As a family we were like underground exiles. We hardly dared to go to school. But the Non-Partisan League in North Dakota elected a socialist government in 1918. For one year they had the governorships and a majority in the legislature. They expropriated the grain elevators, the mines, and the newspapers. Arthur, with other lawyers and farmers, created the first legislation for workers and farmers. They included laws on social security, unemployment compensation, the legal takeover of monopoly, and the recall of elected officials. These laws were later made into national laws under the New Deal.

The amazing thing about the radicals of that day was their indomitable optimism. Arthur went though many periods when the struggles and organizations were betrayed, smashed down, destroyed, and sent underground into what appeared to be silence. The leaders and followers were blacklisted, threatened, and sometimes killed. Arthur was plowed under but never destroyed. He knew the people would rise again. He was nominated as a municipal judge when he was sixty, but he lost the election when moneys were put up to defeat him. He had only the poor. When he was over eighty and half blind, without many cases, he defended prisoners in Stillwater who he believed had been unjustly jailed.

In this landscape of linear violence I grew in many climates. I was fortunate in a moment of cataclysm to see the geological and sociological base of our roots. I saw we were not walking on air. I was in a place and a time when people were coming out of illusion. I saw that the earth and its people were moving and real and that we could love them.

I went to the best college. I lived in a unique place of immense geological upheavals and social tracery. Here as in the climate there were fierce oppositions, set down in the wilderness. The pendulum swings were visible and extreme. The immigrants, the native people, the exiles from revolutions were as militant and explosive as the soil or the landscape and the cyclonic weather. We moved in a forest carpeted with humus laid down during the million years since the river channels and the Great Lakes were formed. About five hundred million years before that the Mississippi Valley had been alternately inundated by seas and subjected to volcanic activity. We moved in a glacial drift, a terrain that burned, exploded, lay fallow, and burst upward into crops. The land lay above the iron, copper, nickel, and gold deposited four and a half billion years ago. The snow became radioactive in my time and the soil was poisoned by strontium 90. The lichen pointed in strange directions. Powerful men arose from these queer collisions. Return here from other space and you will see the deep roots and the turmoiled earth.

It is not unusual here that four or five generations have stayed where they were, being dissidents, radicals, mavericks, abolitionists, red republicans, and antimonopolists. These movements have deep and meandering roots like alfalfa.

I was nourished by this place and time and people. Through our house on Dayton Avenue there came the dissidents, the brave exploded root, the radicle. I think the IWWs had the greatest influence on me:

They believed that only from the working class could come the poets and the singers, the prophets, the heroes, and the martyrs. They rode the trains with their red membership cards and gathered wherever there was an attack upon their fellow workers. When they came to our house to recuperate, eat, and take a bath, they told hair-raising tales about riding the freights, the wheat fields, the docks of San Diego, the timber workers, the free speech fights in Seattle. They knew which were the best prisons to stay in all winter to learn, read, and eat till spring.

Charles Ashleigh, the son of an English lord, carried a cane and a volume of poetry and walked the wheat fields, teaching and reciting poetry. Joe Hill, tall and blond with amazing blue eyes, sang in the Gateway and at the meetings in the Smith and Rice parks in St. Paul, where classes were taught from a soapbox. The teachers were often interrupted by the police and given a night in jail.

They carried in their pockets poetry, the Little Red Song Book that also fitted the pocket, and leaflets of poetry and songs. They carried the *Appeal to Reason* and distributed a million copies of one edition of the paper. They would save the money they earned during the harvest and open a school on lower Hennepin Avenue or on the river flats and study the class struggle all winter. They prepared for prison by learning poetry and how to teach without books. They were transistors, conveyors of lightning.

Kate Richards O'Hare, a tall Irish woman, was arrested in North Dakota for opposing the war and came to our house before the trial. She had taken a children's march to Washington after their fathers were arrested in Oklahoma for what came to be known as the Green Corn Rebellion. They had hidden with their hunting rifles in the tall corn rather than go to the war, until the militia shot them out when the corn withered. She walked with these children across the country, fed by the farmers on the way. To the horror of President Wilson they stood before the White House in their hunger and rags and asked for amnesty for their fathers.

Our house was not large, an extension of my grandmother's puritan white house with an upstairs and a stairway upon which fifty people could sit. We heard the Colorado miners, a lean and terrible sight. Lincoln Steffens, his papers seized by Wilson, secretly came to tell the people of what had happened in Russia.

Bill Haywood, the one-eyed giant of the miners, hid out there. He talked to us and paced back and forth in the little wooden rooms. He was out on bail and he told us how you had to fight your weakness to be a fighter for the working class. He said he liked to drink and sometimes went on a spree, lurching in and out of saloons, brawling, taking on enemies, and reciting poetry. And then he would hole up and discipline himself for the working class, his class, and study Darwin and Morgan and London and Marx. Above all, he loved Shakespeare and would recite whole scenes. Sometimes, he said, he strengthened himself by fasts.

Haywood said his first school was with the miners. Each one would have a book and they would pass them around, and there was always a student, a scholar, among them who went around teaching. From such a scholar he first heard the slogan "an injury to one is a injury to all." He told how he had first been impressed by the Haymarket martyrs. He felt that a great light shone from them. He seemed to me to have grown out of the mines and the gloom and terror like some giant plant, fed by the lives of the miners. He would tell about their maiming toil and about the color of the lead miners, a deathly ashen gray, for they were dying of lead poisoning. He mourned them all and fought for them all. I had never before seen a man like that.

Clarence Darrow spoke eleven hours at Haywood's trial, and fifty thousand people marched in Boston alone. Roosevelt said Darrow was an undesirable citizen, so we all wore placards saying, "I am an undesirable citizen." Darrow said, "I speak for the poor, for the weak, for the weary, for that long line of men, who in darkness and despair, have borne the labors of the human race." The whole world waited and the jury found Haywood not guilty. He is buried in the Kremlin wall.

But Eugene Debs was a man the likes of which I had never seen before or since. He was a man who expressed love boldly. He loved and kissed the people. Kissing was not common on the puritan prairies, but he kissed comrades and children and women. He couldn't have been made anywhere else but in the Midwest. He knew poetry and the IWW preamble and all the people's expressions. It seemed to me theat his growth actually came from the people, his growth forced upon him by their needs, and he returned to them the image.

He was fed, matured, and consumed by the struggles of his time. He loved the American earth and its people. He would sit in our kitchen and recite the death speech of John Brown. He believed in oratory and poetry and love. He was a lanky, tall man, who moved, like so many farm boys, as if the shy body receded backward, hung on the bones; his delicate face and bald head and his whole being were full of a kind of tenderness. He also liked to drink in a bar with the workers and recite poetry, orations, and stories and to listen to theirs.

He was a marvelous speaker. In the time of no amplifiers his delicate message rang like a bell, as if his whole being became a resonance. He walked back and forth lifting his long arms and spoke like a lover and a teacher. Arthur had traveled with him on the "Red Special" in the 1908 presidential election. They spoke every hour from the train platform; the farmers stood in the fields to listen, and the workers came down to hear him at the station.

It was a tradition that the young girls, when he spoke, should present him with a bouquet of red roses. We wore white dresses and each carried a bouquet of red roses, the sign of the blood of the workers. We each could say something to him, and he leaned his tall frame down tenderly. I'll never forget the tears coming to my eyes, and I said to him a quote from his own speech, "All we want is the earth for the people." He took the flowers and leaned down and kissed each one of us. The audience was crying, too. It was a new kind of tenderness. I met an old man in Seattle once who after fifty years remembered the sunny day in the park and the exact words of Debs, and he cried, too, telling me about it.

I heard Debs tell with wonder how he confronted Jim Hill at the foot of Fourth Street in St. Paul, after he had held up Hill's trains in the Pullman strike of 1896 and how the big cyclops had said that not a man would go out on strike, that he knew every man who worked on his railroad (and he probably did). But they followed Debs and they won the strike, and Debs told how when the train pulled out of the St. Paul station, thousands of railroad workers stood silent and bare-headed beside the track. The greatest tribute ever paid him he said, was when they stood with their shovels and with happiness radiating from their faces, yet with tears in their eyes, their tribute more precious than all the bouquets in the world. These prairie agrarian prophets, these sagas of the people, still rise in the nitrogen of the roots, still live in the protein.

CRUSADERS

My people did not leave me land, or wealth, or great empires. I have on my desk a small inheritance, an instrument to estimate the prairie curve which my grandfather used, carrying out the plan of Thomas Jefferson, who saw a patterned, mathematical future in America, nothing hit or miss with a tree or a fence mark; but a survey clear as the Bill of Rights, set to the light of Polaris, of Aldebaran, of the Big Dipper, true to the moon and the sun and the needs of men, ignoring all that eroded, moved, changed like ridges and rivers. This was part of the democratic accuracy and justice.

The mapless, formless wilderness, alive in the subtle mind of Dakota, Pottowatamie, Fox or Chippewa, was henceforth marked clearly in orderly titles in the severe democratic court houses. Each township of six miles square was divided into thirty-six sections, each one mile divided into four equal quarters, each full section measuring six hundred and forty acres, including the road, with errors in curvature and measurement caused by the earth. Each quarter was the historic one hundred and sixty acres, the free homestead, the dream of every starving, hounded worker on the docks of Dunkirk. My grandfather carried this instrument through the dark nights waiting for the sight of the stars to set the meridian.

Now I have always cried to these forebears and cried to them for answers, for compasses, and seen their deeds, their actions, solid and muscular. They have always put a marker up at the place of disaster, guided your hand to the fissure of the mortgage and the quitclaim; pointed out the assassin, identified the murder, the usurer, the depraved. They have kept records of the Long Trail of Tears, the Battle of Wounded Knee and how many were killed by government bad beef; kept the bone splinter and the shoes of the dead child. Now, in a moment of crisis and cold, they point out where the warm ash of the old fires can give you warmth, where strength is cached. I can even catch their heraldic voices in the wind of struggle.

My family came from all the great migrations. They came on the stinking boats after the famine of '48; the black Irish, following the farms west. The migration is the common experience of us all, of both my red and white fathers and mothers. The Trail of Tears, still alive with migrations—the migration from seized tribal and ancient and deeded lands into raw dust and alien corn — is known to us all. Where I lived in Kansas it was said that ninety thousand went through there on the way to the Oregon Trail. They also trailed back. My grandmother sat in her buggy on the line of the Indian Territory of Oklahoma, when the stolen land was opened as a state. With her shotgun over her knees, she made the run and held the land till the claim was filed.

They wore the country on each foot. They salted it with their sweat, changed it with their labor, and had little more than six feet for their bodies. They kept alive the dignity of dissent and the right to impose upon it change; the cry for justice.

They were dissenters from England, Campbellites who could no longer stand the feudal property relations of the Church. They were circuit riders in Kentucky and educators at Oberlin, the first college in America to grant degrees to women. They manned underground stations before the Civil War.

They saw the steady impoverishment of land and people. Marian's family lost the rich farm lands her grandfather had helped to survey. Arthur's family broke the Chicago potato market, lost the rich land at Nininger, and homesteaded again in Dakota. His father went on to the mines hoping to strike it rich but died instead of tuberculosis.

As young people they saw their depressions, their wars, and the deepening of class war. In the 1890s great strikes involving thousands of workers hit back at the National Association of Manfacturers, which represented the new cartels. The Pinkertons, like the present F. B. I., organized violence and espionage against the workers, the destruction of civil liberties and the attack against the foreign-born.

It was the period of asking why for the petty bourgeois radical, the small business man and the farmer and intellectual, alike menaced by this rising power. It was the time of the panacea, of utopia, of the speaker at the small meeting, the church, the picnic, the opera house jammed for the anti-monopoly debate; of the tour over the farm country with the co-op chart, the Socialist books for sale, agrarian radical newspapers — the *Appeal to Reason,* and also the *Iconoclast,* edited by Arthur Le Sueur when he was Socialist mayor of Minot, North Dakota.

The village and farm agnostic was very verbal, for he had to break away from fear and the terror of Calvinism and its hellfire. It was the season of money panaceas and cranks. Anyone with a reform or solution for monopoly printed and distributed his idea or spoke from any prominence. It was a time of great creativeness of the people, of the development of wheat, of the blacksmiths' wrestling with the problems of the plow and the harrow and the great reaper. But alas, the people did not reap anything but disaster from this great bonanza. . . .

The strong democratic men felt the defeat of the law and education, of the beloved principles and practices of Jeffersonian democracy, of the Christian Socialists; they saw the defeat of the land, the wars and depression. The families broke up, as the fabric of the land, the lost villages shook, scattered, broke in a toll of dispersion, disappearance, death, drunkenness, amnesia, and silence. "Where he went I do not know. He disappeared in the gold rush . . . at sea . . . Lord knows where." A card in the horse hair trunk saying "I am fine hope you are the same. . . ."

The women were often left alone, the men gone to better fields. The pattern of the migrating, lost, silent, drunk father is a midwest pattern, and accompanying that picture is the upright, fanatical, prohibitionist mother, bread earner, strong woman, isolated and alone. My grandmother raised her own children, my mother hers, and I mine.

So upright in her beliefs, my grandmother carried on the upright puritan village life without ever knowing that the fight for the eight-hour day impinged upon her, that the growing labor movement and struggle for wages, or the wars of annexation, had something to do with the fact that she lost her land, was often poor, and saw the old Scotch and Irish pushed out of their land by the new immigrants whom she came to hate. Searching for a cause, she laid it all to drink and became the Secretary of the Oklahoma WCTU (Women's Christian Temperance Union) under the leadership of that courageous woman, Frances Willard, who later united with Susan B. Anthony and the intrepid women fighting for the vote.

With her peculiar single courage after going into Oklahoma at the opening of the territory and filing land, she packed her small bag every week, set out by buck board, into the miserable mining communities where she met in shacks and white steepled church the harried, devout, half-maddened women who saw the miserable pay checks go weekly at the corner saloon, and who attempted to stave off poverty and the disappearance of their husbands by smashing the saloons. They rode on floats in temperance parades with signs reading "Tremble King Alcohol we shall grow up" and "Lips that touch liquor shall never touch mine."

We became a kind of poor landed gentry without connection except with reforms that often met defeat. In my childhood, with the covert fear of the dispossessed, always with women, we set out on dark nights of migration, into the perils and the naked strife and the awful struggle of women, their faces set in rigid discipline so the children could not take terror from them; trekking to another farm, another city in the familiar unmarked trail from Indiana to Illinois into Iowa, into the Dakotas and Minnesota or down into Texas and back again. My grandmother, alone on her last trek, died on a train in the plains.

She always spoke of spunk and grit and barren intestinal courage. I have here a beautiful picture of the New England white house brought to my birthplace, Murray, Iowa. The shadow of a lost day chastely falls from the rigid angles of the straight house, and a tough agile old man stands laughing in the sun while the women rebuke him in their long skirts, which my grandmother wore to her death. The fichu and full bosom, the long sleeves and high at the throat for modesty, were the sign and signal of a last moment of "decency," as she always said. It was the decency of the rural agrarian primitive Christianity, of the flowering of the struggle for democracy.

She never knew that the great fathers Jefferson, Lincoln and Jackson had given way to Carnegie, Morgan and DuPont. She never knew it was so late; too late to turn the fiddle into the lyre, country reel into dancings, the songs of the Cumberland, the Kentucky Camp- bellites into lyrics and songs of the picket line; too late for the village and prairie dream of an Athens on the Mississippi. New Salem was deserted on the Sangamon (abundant) country; the wooden stool, the axe and the hoe had given way to the giant in the fields. She saw that the village life was gone but she did not see the factory in the field, turn- ing the farmer into the serf of Consolidated peas and corn!

Bitterly she had to oppose her daughters' militant struggle for the vote, or the new industrial developments. But she abandoned the talk of justice and beauty and the rights of all because she could not see how it would come about. She was pragmatic, puritan, realistic in her way. She knew in her bones that steadily, insidiously, and ruthlessly the enemy was winning; the sons of Tubal Cain had outfoxed the angels, and the great tumorous and drunk giants lay across the land. But she held to her passion and moral conviction to the last, and she believed in and held her own human dignity and that of her fellows above reproach.

It was not enough for her first girl child with the tall head and the great asking eyes, born in her lonely room in the New England house in the middle of Iowa.

It is hard to write about Marian Le Sueur, not because she was my mother, but because like myself she was a woman. In many ways her history is suppressed within the history of the man, the history of an oppressed people is hidden in the lies and the agreed-upon myth of its conquerors.

To those who remember her as an independent, aggressive, bold and brilliant woman it is difficult to understand that for each of these distinctions she had to fight most of society, public opinion and the laws of the land. Women especially would like to believe that her talents were God-given. But it was not so. Her anger, her strength, her determination, even her brilliance and her oratory were things she developed, often alone, and struggled and fought for, as much as

Frederick Douglass had to struggle to even read. In Texas her husband divorced her on the grounds of dangerous thoughts gleaned from reading books!

You have to think of her in the line of Elizabeth Cady Stanton, Susan B. Anthony, Amelia Bloomer, Carrie Nation, Frances Willard, Lucy Stone, Lucretia Mott, and the later suffragists of whom she was one. These courageous women set a pattern not understood yet, standing in their prim strength, in their sweetness and sobriety against cruel ridicule, moral censure, charges of insanity; for there is no cruelty like that of the oppressor who feels his loss of the bit on those it has been his gain to oppress. "Pine knots as we are," Susan Anthony said. They used the only means open to them — they became orators when it was considered immoral for a woman to speak in public; if she went to meetings she was only to listen and learn. But they could use their constitutional right of petition, and they could tramp up and down, getting signatures for the right to work, to get a divorce, to speak in public, to vote.

If the women in the Christian church did not sit separate from the men it was only an act of courtesy or perhaps a long lost act of rebellion on their part. St. Paul still sat in the front pew saying it is better to marry than to burn, and the heads of the women were covered. She had no legal right to her own property, or to her children; both were the property of the man. A man was responsible legally for the crimes of his wife as he was for his jackass or his cow.

It is touching to think of the young girl, the most brilliant mind in her family, yet a girl. Her father said why weren't you a boy? Her mother said you have too high a forehead for a woman, cover it up — as you covered your legs, your arms, your neck, and all the natural processes of becoming a woman.

The others in the family were jealous because she liked to study. Her brothers said you will never find a husband. The oldest brother, Frank, came back from the race tracks, the darling of his mother, and played practical jokes. At sixteen, after her father's death, she ran away from home to Chicago, bought a red wig and got a job. She did not go to her father's funeral, which my grandmother always said was attended by every "tramp" he had defended.

She went to Drake University, the school of the Christian church, and was a brilliant mathematician. She went back to Osceola on weekends. The young men who were training to be preachers drove down on Sundays in tandems with spanking horses. A year before her graduation, in her eighteenth year, she married one of them, and they went immediately to his first parish at Boise, Idaho.

The young and frightened wife at a meeting of the Ladies' Aid said that she didn't know if she had been poisoned by something, but she was nauseated. The ladies gave each other significant looks; two were delegated to take the young bride out to tell her privately never to mention again that she was sick because she was going to have a baby. I tell this to show the prudery, the medieval ignorance and darkness.

She came with her husband to the Chicago summer school. She took a course against his wishes on comparative religions, popular and very radical, and to her amazement she found there were other religions, older and as spiritual as the one she knew. She went to school the day before her baby was born.

Her baby died the next summer. I was born the following summer in Murray, Iowa. The rest of these years is the anonymous history of a mother following her husband except that she, with her vigorous and searching mind, studied and read, first William Ellery Channing, the liberals of the church, then Emerson, who remained a great influence, especially the essay on Self-Reliance which is worn out in many collections she still has. She had a son born in Oklahoma at her mother's house, and another son born in San Antonio, Texas.

Then she took one of the leaps of growth for which she was always ready. She welcomed change. She seemed, if she feared it, to always leap that fear and move in new directions. She came to the conclusion entirely outside the experience of her society, that it was a sin to stay with a man you no longer loved. But she had never earned her living. She could not possess any property that did not belong to her husband. She had no vote, no legal status, and divorce in her society was virtually unknown. She faced the poverty of the women she knew who, to raise money even for the church, had to have church suppers, for the only way they could filch money was to put it on the grocery bill, to make cakes and other things and sell them. She and her children were utterly dependent upon the man.

It must be remembered that at this time, outside the professions of nurse and teacher, there were few professions or jobs open to a woman. My mother opened a physical culture studio for women, and here she met Bernarr McFadden, who came to lecture to a large audience of women she organized to hear him. She dabbled in real estate and managed a large fig orchard, hiring Mexican workers. She told a liberal lawyer friend that the only way you could make money was to get something where you hire other people and make a profit off their labor. He said all by yourself you've discovered the capitalist system!

She got a bank account and the bank, without asking her, took her money to cover her husband's overdrawn account. She could not get a divorce and was threatened with the loss of her children.

We left everything sitting on the table, our belongings, our books, and left as if we were going on a vacation. But we fled over the "border," to Oklahoma, to my grandmother. Later, Marian's husband got the divorce on the grounds of desertion and her interest in "dangerous literature."

Lecturing by women was considered genteel, even though the platform had become a militant place for the voice of women. Susan Anthony had toured the mining towns and the villages. My mother felt a social responsibility toward women. She had read Ellen Key and found her problem was not her own, but a social problem, and she wanted to speak to women. She had taken the platform before. She was shy and conventional and intimidated by her long position as a housewife and her isolation from all but church life. Her husband's family said she was insane, that she was a wanton, a "free" woman, a bad woman. My grandmother gave up her hard-earned position as librarian in the little town of Perry to go back to family raising.

It was a daring and wonderful thing to take the road to talk about the rights of women, in the beginning to stand trembling with nervousness, to be the butt of jokes, to see the frightened, asking eyes of the women who packed the opera houses.

A Missouri paper carried this item in August, 1912:

> The Methodist Church reports a crowded house for Mrs. Wharton's physical culture lecture "The Glory of Superb Womanhood." In the evening she occupied the pulpit, speaking of Love and Bread. "Relating to the sexual science and the science of eugenics, ignorance has been called innocence. Prudery has reigned supreme," she said. "Women have been born and reared in ignorance, taught to feel shame toward the most sacred functions of life. Immoralities in and out of wedlock, the terrible white slave traffic, ruined lives, blighted homes, all can be traced to inequality of the sexes, and ignorance."

Later she barnstormed the little towns, to speak in tents with quartets, horn blowers and juggler acts; but always the farm and village women waited to speak to her and she saw their eyes, and the children at their skirts, and the weighted and torn bodies.

She became an orator, taking her courage from those eyes. Unequipped and untrained she studied, made massive notes, overcame her timidity, learned to let her voice go, to compose from the audience which became always the miracle of her speaking. She came to hate exploitation of women by men, at first hating the men, and fiercely struggling to get a place for herself in the world of men.

She started clinics for the miners' children in Oklahoma, but soon found that the wealthy middle-class women who supported them could go only so far, that they were bitted by their husbands and the economic interests of their husbands.

She began to find out that it was not all a matter of love, but of bread also.

She met the editor of the *Kansas City Star*, Billy Williams, who was a friend of Theodore Dreiser. She went down to the hall where the I.W.W., the Syndicalists, and the Socialists had school all winter between seasons. Here she went deeper to the roots of women's oppression and to the oppression of one class by another.

In Chicago she met Emma Goldman and Eleanor Fitzgerald; she studied anarchism. Later, she met Alexander Berkman, who was a great influence on her life and on my own.

But she became a socialist.

The Emergence of the Writer

INTRODUCTION

Many of Le Sueur's earliest stories show traces of the loneliness and isolation she experienced during the 1920s, as she tried to make her way in the theater and film worlds of New York and Hollywood. Looking back today at such early works as "Wind," "Spring Story," and especially "Persephone," she finds in them suggestions of the "lost girl" she then frequently felt herself to be. She also finds in these early pieces what she has called a "narcissistic" element, which she would later try to eliminate from her work, as in the more socially and politically informed writing she did in the thirties.

"Persephone," which describes the abduction from her mother of a young girl, and her subsequent mysterious illness, is Le Sueur's first use of the ancient myth of Demeter and Persephone, which has continued to figure prominently in her work. Haunting and unresolved, the story was her way of dealing with her own psychic turmoil at a time when she felt rejected by her own mother and immured within the male-dominated world of Hollywood. Many women writers today are rediscovering the myth of Demeter and Persephone and finding it compelling, revelatory of the experience of women in a patriarchy, where sexual initiation is likely to mean a severance of ties with one's mother. For Le Sueur its imaginative resonance also includes, in Demeter's search for her lost child, a celebration of that mother-daughter love which patriarchy suppresses, and an expression of women's traditional nurturing role. In the 1960s and 1970s, especially, she returned to the myth, exploring its implications anew in poems and in a series of experimental novels (see Section 5). By then, her own return to the world of women had long been accomplished, and the daughter was no longer, in the words of "Persephone," "lost to the realm of her nativity."

Although lacking the mythical overtones of "Persephone," "Spring Story" and "Wind" suggest archetypal situations in the lives of young girls and women. On the threshold of adulthood, the adolescent girl in "Spring Story" experiences the first stirrings of her sexuality as both exciting and disquieting. She feels both a sense of release into a new self (paralleled in the story by the blossoming cannas) and a sense of physical awkwardness and self-consciousness. Important in the story, too, is the girl's relationship to her mother, whom she both identifies with and rejects, and from whom she senses she is separating.

"Wind" takes a similar young girl through the early days of her marriage. Again the conflict is internal, as mixed feelings of sexual desire and fear, and of pride and disappointment in her new role, vie with each other. Although the ending is one that Le Sueur herself today calls romantic — a D. H. Lawrence-style ending in which the untamed forces of wind and rain somehow mysteriously effect a reconciliation of the lovers — the analysis of the young wife's conflicts, her dawning recognition that wifehood is in fact a "role," and the self-defeating strategies she contemplates for reconciling herself to that "role" (she will find meaning in a life of self-sacrifice, or deal with her disappointment in her husband by seeing him as a child to be cared for) all anticipate much contemporary feminist analysis of women's married lives.

"The Laundress" and "Our Fathers" show the young Le Sueur beginning to discover and define other subject matter that has continued to be important to her: the lives of working-class women, and those of the pioneers of her native Midwest. In both stories, characters are seen through the eyes of a young, inquisitive girl. In "Laundress," some meaning in the life of Mrs. Kretch, who washes and irons, cleans and mends, for the narrator's middle-class family, moves and interests her. It is a life of struggle but also of dignity, efficiency, and order: a life that may have carried a seed that will in future generations bear some special fruit. Raising her children alone, like Le Sueur's own mother and grandmother, Mrs. Kretch is an early example of the many "anonymous" working-class women whose lives Le Sueur would commemorate.

"Our Fathers" is a chapter from a novel, *I Hear Men Talking*, which Le Sueur began in the twenties, worked on in the thirties, and recently revised and finished. The chapter is a powerful, if not completely polished, treatment of a subject of major interest to Le Sueur — the restless migration and movement, and the resulting rootlessness, of an entire population during the decades of settling the West. Again there are some autobiographical parallels, particularly to Le Sueur's grandmother. The portrait of the grandmother here is harsher than that in "The Ancient People," and more akin to her depiction in *Crusaders*. In "Our Fathers" the women, and especially the grandmother, are sour and embittered. Although "The Ancient People" contains the statement that the pioneer woman's experience of men "centered around the male as beast, his drunkenness and chicanery, his oppressive violence," it is in "Our Fathers" that Le Sueur explores the effects of that oppression on women. It is only Pen, the daughter, who expresses sympathy and even some admiration for the roving men, as she tries to understand the hunger or vision that may have impelled them across the continent. Again one is in the presence of Le Sueur's determination to record and preserve the lives of people who have been lost and forgotten — this time even against the impulse of those whose flight into the future made memory "a menace" for them.

"Annunciation," the most artistically successful story in this section, was composed in the twenties although not published until 1935. Frequently reprinted, it has been called, quite rightly, a small American masterpiece. Based on Le Sueur's own first pregnancy, it is an evocation of the thoughts and feelings of a pregnant woman and especially of her sense of the relatedness and continuity of all life. "I've never heard anything about how a woman feels who is going to have a child," the woman in the story says, and Le Sueur's account is lyrical and compelling. For Le Sueur, as the spare decade of the twenties drew to a close, "Annunciation" was "the bud of a new flower within the time of the old." Its affirmations and celebrations of life signaled the beginning of that rebirth which "Persephone" had not achieved.

PERSEPHONE

We boarded the train at a Kansas town. Its black houses sat low amidst the fields which were hardening and darkening now the summer was over. The corn had been shocked, the seed lay in the granaries, the earth had closed, and now the sun hung naked in the sky. All was over — the festival, the flowering, the harvesting. Dark days had come and I was taking the daughter of Freda away to discover, if I could, the malady which made her suffer.

As the train moved from the station I watched Freda standing on the platform, her rounded face shadowed by the train as it passed between her and the low sun. The daughter leaned against the window for the last sight of her mother; as we left the town she sat with her small head bent as if half broken from her body.

We sped through the dying country, fleeing through the low land. Upon the fields as they lay upturned and dark, clear to the round swinging sky-line, there fell the eerie wan light of the dying season. The train as it traveled through this dim sea of light became uncanny and frail, touched, too, with the bright delicacy of decay. But upon the daughter of Freda the last light dwelt intimately as she lay half sleeping, like the fields, fatally within the cycle of the dying earth.

Fatigued after the preparations for the journey, she rested in utter weariness. Her black garments hung, about to exhaust her, while out from them, like sudden flowers, sprang her hands and face. Over her great eyes the lids were lowered and gave to her whole being a magical abstraction, as if she looked eternally within, or down through the earth. Only her mouth had tasted of violent fruit; it drooped in her face and turned red when she coughed, which she did frequently, dipping her head like a blind bird.

As I watched her an old pain brewed within me; a faint nostalgia which had come upon me all my life when looking upon her, or when in the presence of her mother, as if upon seeing these two women a kind of budding came about on all the secret unflowered tendrils of my being, to blossom and break in the spaces of a strange world, far from my eyes and hands.

Just when the round and naked sun hung on the horizon, three bulls, standing in the dim, nether light, turned and loped toward our train.

"The black bull," I said, "looked like your husband's."

She lifted the white lids from her eyes, but did not speak. When I repeated what I said, she turned away without answering and sat with her hands in her lap, her eyes lowered, in an attitude so fatal and hopeless that I knew it was of no use to take her on this train, through these fields, past these rivers and houses to our destination. Nothing lay in these things that could mitigate her illness. The malady was too deep.

As we sped through the fields, the fantastic conquering of distance threw a magic over us so that terrible and vast things became possible. With the dying of the sun the train traveled through a colossal cave, between the closed earth and the closed sky, and I half forgot our departure and our destination.

I have always expected some metamorphosis to take place in Freda and her daughter — a moment when the distant look would, by miracle, go from their eyes and they would reveal their nativity in some awful gesture. Nothing had ever happened beyond the natural ritual of our common farm life. But there came upon me now the old mystic credulity as I watched Freda's daughter sitting motionless, her white lids rounding over her eyes, her face glowing in the gloom.

Lying there she contained, like a white seed, the mystery of her origin. The marks of living were slight upon her, for from the first she seemed to carry most strongly the mark of a perpetual death. Paradoxically I thought that because death was her intimate, I could never come nearer her mystery than to her birth on the prairies, in the spring as the first white violets bloomed.

For the women of the Kansas town, shading their eyes, had seen Freda coming from the prairies, walking and carrying the child.

"Whose baby is that?" the women asked her when she had come to them.

And she answered, "Mine." And uncovered for them to see, bending down to them.

"When was it born?" these women, to whom birth was a great dread, asked.

She answered smiling, "In the night." And she went into a store and bought some goods with little flowers marked on it in which she wrapped the baby.

That year the days were bright and the earth bountiful. For each ear of corn heretofore, there were now two. The sun ripened all that had been sown. The soil was so hot we could not suffer our bare feet upon it. Freda's lands were the most fertile of all.

Her husband, Frantz, the strongest man in the country, was a ploughman. We saw him in the fields, dark and stocky, driving his big flanked horses, astride the black furrows that turned behind him. When he came to our fields we were frightened by his narrow eyes buried in the flesh, and by his hands matted with hair.

Together, Frantz and Freda ploughed the fields; there was a feeling abroad that never had Freda sown a seed that had not come to fruition. It was true that for her everything blossomed.

In the spring we met her in the fields or in the thickets, where the first flowers were springing alone. In the full, golden light she came towards us, full-bosomed, with baskets of wild berries hanging on her bright arms. When we ran to her, she gave us gifts, berries, nuts, and wild fruits unknown to us.

At harvest time she worked in the fields with the men. When we brought her water she straightened from the earth to loom above us, curving against the sky; a strong odor would come from her, like the odor of the earth when it is just turned; her yellow hair would glisten around her face and we thought it grew from her head exactly as the wheat grew from the earth. Once when she leaned over me, I grew faint with the fertile odor and at the same time drops of perspiration fell from her temples on my face.

When her mare was seen hitched outside the houses of the town, we knew that a great, natural, and dreadful thing was taking place within. The house became, after that, marked, possessing a strange significance of birth. We children, while the mare waited, sat on the curb watching for Freda, who, when she came, passed in a kind of confusion of her great body, the golden hair, and the strong, sweet odor. We would watch the hips of the horse, with Freda upon her, disappearing down the road, past the houses of the town, out into the open plains.

The child of Freda, delicate and pale from the first, was not much known or seen about. She came to town on the first spring days, with her mother, riding in the wagon atop the early vegetables. She carried with her always, falling from her hands, the first white violets. It did not astonish us that she was thus privy to the first stirrings of the season, since we glimpsed her through all the year in the prairies, by the streams, or hidden in the nooks of the fragrant hills. In the fall, returning from berry hunting, she brushed past us in the chill dusk. In the winter, as we went to the frozen creek, we glimpsed her peering from the naked bush. In the spring we saw her come by her mother, with the first violets. She never spoke to us, but covered her enormous eyes with her lids, standing quite still, before us but irrevocably hidden.

On Saturdays as Freda went about the town she hid behind her skirts, her eyes lowered in her slim, pale face. Some women would stop in the streets and say she was idiotic because of her little head. To me, however, she had a strange grace, with her swelling body, her little head and pale face, her eyes like minerals, and her hair light like her mother's, but fine and thin as if it had grown outside the light of the sun.

When Freda and her husband were ploughing the fields, the girl, who grew very tall, would run in the wake of the plough, singing. Frantz hated her, as everyone knew, and he hated her singing. When Freda with her horses went plunging through the black waves to the horizon, he would leave his plough and strike at the girl. She would veer away as if only the wind had struck her, still singing.

When I could run away from the town I used to lie in the damp thicket which bordered their field and watch them; the dark man straddling the furrows, following the rumps of his horses, holding the plough to the heavy soil; Freda with her skirts on the earth, the horses turning their great eyes to look back at her, the fields lying about her with their living secrets — I watched with satisfaction these two heavy figures, turning the vast earth, moving upon her stillnesses, and the slim girl, like an antelope, running in the fields beside them, singing high and shrill.

She coughed beside me, dipping her little head like a bird. Now no song was in her.

Outside rapidly past us moved the thickets, the fields, the villages. A woman stood in a doorway, half invisible in the dusk, hoisting a baby on her hip — a man came down the road with his team, the white breath of the horses flying from them in the dusk.

The visible world was sinking into another sea, into a faint dusk. The daughter of Freda lay like a fallen and despoiled angel, traveling through darkness, lost to the realm of her nativity, with neither memory nor anticipation. Still I watched her trying to spin around her the stuff of reality. Did there exist for her the seed of our common life or had she eaten only the fruit of perpetual strangeness and death? All that had happened to her, all the incidents of her life, I brought to bear upon her, but I had easier made a mark upon the wind. These things had made no mark upon her. The only mark was her mark upon life, upon all of us who saw her as a frail lost child in the fields of her mother, as a woman ravished by strangeness.

The young farm boys, still delicate with the wind and the fire which is the mark of light and air before the fields harden them, were the only ones who came close to Freda's daughter. They often told us in the evenings that they had met her in the thickets or coming across the fields, and had talked with her. But then they would say no more.

The older youths found it impossible to snare the footsteps of the delicate girl. Strange to say, on the other hand, the firm and serious farm youth were convinced of her wantonness, while old ladies rocking on their porches hinted dark things of her.

But one night a man came to town, from the west, driving his cattle, packed and bellowing through the deserted streets.

The next morning people said to each other, "Did you hear the cattle going by in the night?" We children thought it had been only a dream until, early in the morning, we saw on the lawn, the deep prints of cloven hoofs. When I went for the morning milk, just outside the town, I saw the cattle where they stood sleeping, knee deep in the grass and mist. As I was passing a man sat up, from where he too had been sleeping, and looked at me from the grasses. His beard stood out like bracken. From his low forehead the black hair sprang. When I saw him about to rise, I ran into the town shouting to my brothers that the cattle they had heard and thought were only the sound in a dream, had really gone down our streets, and had stopped on the outskirts of the town.

It came to be known that the man I had seen in the grasses went by the name of March. Saturday he came into the town riding a splendid horse. He went about the streets talking in a loud voice to the country people. He was to be seen, too, at the horse barns, or at public auctions. Saturday nights he herded what cattle he had purchased, sometimes only a fine bull, to the pasture he had bought next to Freda's land. He became famous through the countryside for his pedigreed bulls. The farmers came in season to lead them to their own pastures for breeding.

It happened in a very subtle way that the countryside came to think of Freda and her daughter and the man March, all three together, as somehow of the same blood. All the vital acts of farm life came to move around one or the other of them. Freda and her husband seemed intimate with the fields, and the half-mystical rites of planting and reaping. It was said in wonder that Freda even brought in the lambs as they were dropped in the fields in the spring as if she knew their time. She appeared to the women at the oven and her appearance augured good bread. It was out their road the farmers went for the breeding of their cows. The very lay of the land with its rich dark color was strange; so was the magic they had with the earth and with natural things. Freda's daughter held a more strange mystery. She seemed half evil at times. But after she saved the life of a boy, when his body had turned black, they sought her out for palliatives.

So that it came about that the country people as they dreamed over their work in the spring and autumn, were half unconsciously touched by the mystery of their tasks — a mystery between their own action and the secret of what they acted upon, by virtue of which alliance everything they did prospered and yielded in the field, the vine, the flesh. Probably because they were, in a manner of speaking, without a God, when in their dream, in a kind of blind ecstasy over the earth, within the heat, they attributed dimly to the figure of Freda, and with her the other two, an alliance and an intimacy with the virtue and the mystery, along with something sinister, of the natural things of which their lives were made.

After the corn had been husked and the dreary Kansas cold had set in, I was wandering in the thicket which ran along the stream in a little curve of the fields below Freda's. The pale sun, casting no shadow, shone on the naked sod and the land, low and flat, swelled a little to the sky. This side of Freda's, the bulls stood in the wind, quite still.

I had just left the path and gone further into the thickets for berries, when, out of the dying woods, with only a slight sound like a bird's, ran the daughter of Freda. March came after her. I could hear his feet strike the bare ground, and saw as he ran past me, his black beard and hair struck by the wind as he ran into the open. She had climbed the barbed fence and was running in the bull pasture, through the crisp grasses toward her mother's. But three bulls turned at the farthest fence and eyed her. When she turned back, frightened, March was running to her. Then she stood binding her skirts around her, her small head, like a dying bird's, thrown back. As she seemed about to cry out, he came upon her and bore her with him into the grasses. A young bull struck the ground with his forefeet and loped toward the sun. I ran back into the thicket.

The next days I was filled with terror because of what I had seen. I dared not go upon the road to the fields, or even out under the sky. The third day I came home and there in the dusk was Freda, leaning in our door.

"She is gone," I heard her say.

My mother spoke from the dark kitchen. "And is he gone, too, with all the cattle?"

"Yes," said Freda and stood suffering in the dusk. After a while she walked away down the dim road.

Frantz came in the night, knocking and pounding at our door to know where she had gone.

That winter she grew very old. The farmers, through the frosty moonlight, saw her wandering the barren plains. Children screamed when she approached the town. She seemed like an old woman whose time of fertility had gone. In the nights she came knocking at the doors of the village to ask for her daughter.

That year the spring never came. The flowers died beneath the ground and the fields burned in the sun.

Through the hot days of summer we saw her far off, unreal in the simmering heat. We found her by the old well in our orchard, sitting, sorrowing on the stones, her hair wild and white. We were young girls from school with bright ribbons in our hair. We had come to cool our faces over the black opening of the well and to cry down its sides to hear the sweet, far echo answer us. But when we saw her there we drew together, whispering and peering at her. She rose and came toward us, no longer bright and bold, but still terrible, looming above us. She went among us as we hid our faces in our aprons, stroking our hair and arms, calling each of us by the same name. It was a name I had never heard before and I could never, after that, remember it. She peered at each of us so close that we trembled when her breath came upon us. When she turned her sad eyes to the well again we ran from her in every direction, through the orchard, and for the rest of the afternoon watched her from behind the trees as she sat on the stones of the well, sorrowing.

One evening late in summer, as the land still lay beneath the drought, my brother came from the fields, and standing before us with the heat of the day on his face he said, "I saw Freda's daughter walking toward her mother's."

That night the country people thought it strange that the first rains fell, plunging ceaselessly into the earth.

The train stopped at a siding amidst the prairies in a sudden silence. The woman, aroused, sat up with her eyes wide open.

"How far are we?" she asked in a light voice.

I answered her very low, "From where?"

Before she could answer a fit of coughing shook her and the train started again.

The lights were lit. She was timid about going into the diner, but at last, with vague gestures, lifting her pale hands she put over her head an old velvet hat and rose and went down the aisle, forlorn and pale, with a kind of assaulted and pathetic dignity.

I came behind her, looking at the tall body as it moved with its peculiar grace. It was like this she had come back to Freda's, with this delicate, hopeless grace, as if she had touched strange fruits and eaten pale and deathless seeds.

After the summer, March had come back, driving his bulls through the street to the old pasture. He had knocked at Freda's door and Freda had given her daughter back to him. She had gone to live in his low hut. When we passed we saw her come out of the door to throw the dishwater over the bare ground. Her thick black skirts, given her now by the women of the town, would be pulling and dragging about her, her little head would swirl up from them, free as a serpent's. After she had thrown the water she would stand still, tall and hopeless, in that terrible abstraction, looking toward us with her blind, deep eyes.

In the diner she seated herself with timid, quick movements, then sat with her eyes lowered. Some arrangement of the heavy skirt annoyed her; she fingered it delicately beneath the table. She coughed, turning her head and frowning. In an effort to suppress it the tears started, and did not fall, but hung there magnifying her great eyes. Suddenly, unable to bear the light, she closed them. Again as the lids covered her eyes, by some bewitchment her face became beautiful and eternal. I felt again the imminent metamorphosis as if she were about to change before my eyes and as always in haste as if to prevent a phenomenon which I both hoped for and dreaded, I spoke.

"Did you see the fine bulls that ran toward our train?"

She lifted her eyes and looked at me, but did not answer.

"I believe the black one was the one your husband sold the up-state farmer." She was looking at me. "Did you see the bulls just before dark?"

"No," she said and the answer startled me.

Whether it was the natural desolateness of traveling between places, likely to give to the form of what reality we know a vast and fabulous temper, or the sorrow of the dying year, I do not know, but back in the car, I became desolate and afraid.

For the remaining hours I sat opposite, watching her sleeping. I brooded over her, half expectant as if about to startle from the mist that covered her, the winged bird which was the secret of her being. I watched her with pain as she moved me with her ancient mystery, as of something half remembered.

What strange realms had thrust her forth to be born of her mother in the night, to put upon her the burden of endless movement through fields, upon the earth, through many days under the burden of shadowless nights, marked with the mark of strangeness to be usurped by an unfamiliar man, to walk through unfamiliar places, and to carry unfamiliar burdens.

Watching her glow before me with her terrible veiled identity, a strangeness of everything came upon me and a terror. I felt suddenly that after this journey, in which after all nothing had happened, I should never be the same; that by looking upon her I was partaking of some poisonous drug, like the poison of early spring flowers and the poison of late berries.

I dared not move in my terror, afraid she might stir, but she sat still, preoccupied, with her eyes hidden, dreaming of what she had never forgotten. Cautiously I came near to her mystery. She among us all had known that living was a kind of dying. When in these realms, she had refused to partake of our fruits and so become enamored, but had closed herself in the dream which is real and from which we die when we are born.

Soon, now, we would come upon the city glittering on the plain, above the bluffs of the river. A terror of all that lived came upon me; a terror of Freda's daughter who lay as if dead, glowing already in the mineral worlds of her strange lord. Because of the terror I said to myself, this woman is only the wife of a Kansas stockman—but who is the stockman? We saw him driving his bulls through the night, but who is he? Who is her mother? We saw her in the ripe fields, and turning the soil to fertility — but who is she?

All in that town came to me, all I had known passed before me, and I said, who are they? And I did not know.

SPRING STORY

She opened her eyes and knew it was Easter morning. The white-lawn curtains blew out and in the half-open window as if signaling to someone outside. The air blew in upon her, cold, but with a strange fertile promise in it. She had been lying a long time, listening to the wind and the morning sounds outside. Her mother had called up the stairs many times. She was calling again.

"Eunice, aren't you going to get up at all? You must go with the boys to nine o'clock mass."

Eunice did not answer, but lay still, listening to the wind, pretending sleep. That freshening air seemed to blow right through the house. Her youngest brother had been shouting and running in and out all the morning, leaving the doors open. It was funny how suddenly, from the very sound of the voices, one knew that it was no longer winter. As she lay half dreaming she heard the laughter and the shouts of children on the street outside and behind the house. The voices seemed bright and shaken out. A milk-cart went by and the jingling of the horses' hoofs and the sound of the wheels had a new sound too, a loose, gay sound. In winter everything seemed muffled, sounds were frozen, but now outside they began to flow again, awaken and rouse and blow in her window with the strong sweet wind.

She sprang out of bed, the gusts of wind on her body, ran to the dresser and turned it about, moving the mirror downward at an angle. Now she could see herself lying in bed with her thin gold hair on the pillow, and her frail face smiling. She lay looking at herself, half entranced, while her mother called at the foot of the stairs, the voice sounding nearer than it did from the kitchen but still far away to the dreaming girl. "Eunice, I'm not going to keep those cakes warm another minute. It's eight o'clock!" The mother's voice, though near, sounded from another world. But in a few moments the girl got up, watching herself move in the mirror, as if in this way doubling her pleasure in her manner of being. She wandered about the room, touching her things that lay about; she leaned close to the mirror and lifted the fine hair from her forehead, gazing for a long time at her face. Sitting on the bed she began to slowly pull her stockings on, stopping to look at her feet, then to see her own face again, far away and lovely, in the slanting mirror.

Lying, walking, sitting in this room, she felt herself ripening and coloring. It was as if she felt upon herself, as upon the world outside, the blowing of a nourishing wind from some unseen space. She hung on a strange tree and day by day felt herself ripening and rounding in her flesh. This morning the wind blowing in the window seemed freighted, not only with the promise of the physical spring of the world, but with other promises for herself, blowing in upon her the dream of her future, the scent of unripe meanings which would one day mature.

Looking at her hands and feet they seemed to be shining with the vision of the things to be touched and the ways to be trod. "I will not close the window," she said to herself without voice, her lips moving, although she could not have told if she had spoken or not. "No, I will not close the window. Something will come in, something is sure to come in if I have the courage to leave it open. I am sure not to miss life then."

The cold air blew in silently. The white curtains waved, blowing out and then in, sudden gusts blowing with the wind upon her. Straight out the window she could see the great elm rising from the back yard. The top limbs looked as if they had begun to break open. They looked as if an excitement were upon the branches; a faint aura of reddish brown seemed to surround the tree. You really could not see the buds at all, but could only sense this excitement and the red irritation of the spiked branches. She could only see the top antlers rearing against the pale-blue sky. At that instant the sun came out in a faint shower of golden light that seemed to shatter down in a crystal rain upon the still-frozen earth. She ran to the window and put her bare arms in the light. They looked white with the little reddish hairs alight in the sun. Perhaps she too was going to burst into leaf and bloom. She laughed to think so and leaned out the window, the wind striking her, the curtains blowing about her in a confusion.

From below in the alley came up the sharp gay banter of young boys, excited like sparrows with the air and light. She could see them scrambling over the old fences, digging the last of the black snow up from the corners to throw at each other.

Then her uncle came up out of the cellar as if from the earth itself. He had a shovel and a rake.

"You've forgotten your coat," she shouted down at him, feeling she had to shout against the strong wind and the shattering light. "You've forgotten your coat," she sang out, feeling happy to cry out into the air like that. Startled, he looked up into the tree as if a blackbird had shouted at him. Eunice laughed, shaking her loose hair. "Here I am in the window, Uncle Joe."

He turned his face upward to her, so he looked like a gnome, half his size. "What if I have? What if I have?" he mumbled, half smiling. She saw that he was pleased with her.

"What are you going to do? Working on Sunday?" she shouted down, laughing.

"I'm going to uncover these canna bulbs so they'll get a sniff of this air and some warmth in them." He went with his shovel and rake to the corner of the house and began raking where the canna-bed had been the summer before. The girl, looking down on him, had for an instant, a sharp picture of the dark leaves of the cannas standing there, amidst them in the rising fold of scarlet leaping in a twist of flame. The last year she had felt them as a rich, a troubling thing, as she had run past them in the dusk. Then the flames had withered and the rich stuff of the leaves had dried. Now, after a certain time, there they would be again, standing still and secret at the corner of the house for her to pass, a rich dark presence from another world. This year they would mark for her a different time. This she knew. No longer would she run past them in young play. These red flames would burn in a different time for her, stand up, marking a time that would be stranger and disquieting.

The uncle raking back and forth was a sharp figure in the morning and held for her some enchantment of meaning. For he was uncovering a plant that would grow up in a new time for her. She watched him raking back and forth, his stooped back, his whole figure swinging to the rhythm of the raking. His body seemed to have grown to a curve, with a pull to its lines that had come from the many seeds he had uncovered in his time, the hoeing and the raking. This uncle had just come from a farm in Iowa the past year after Aunt Emma had died and his heart had got so bad the family thought it unsafe to leave him alone, so isolated. Now they passed him around from house to house among the uncles and aunts, and he did odd jobs like this. Eunice looked at him thinking his life was over; behind him and before him was only death. Still he came out to give the first life to the cannas.

He kept raking back and forth as she leaned out the window watching. He had on a blue shirt and a small black cap. His figure was unlike the figures of the other men of her family. It was short and stocky, despite its age, with a vigor unknown to her before, with black hair on his square wrists and on his neck where he opened his shirt a bit. He had a strong odor of tobacco about him, almost overpowering, which she associated somehow with his strength, with his long past on the farm with horses and wheat and with the silent Aunt Emma, who was like some powerful wild grass herself. He moved in a way unknown to her. Not like her father and her uncles who lived in the city. He moved as if the meaning of his life were in his body and not in anything else, as if the pleasure too were there. So it was a satisfaction to her to be near him or to watch him working as she was watching him now as she leaned out of the upper window.

He raked back and forth, stooped and picked up the débris of winter, which was black and slimy, lifted it and put it in an old tub he had standing beside him. He uncovered the earth, which then looked as delicate as skin when the bandage has been removed, and there were the white blades of grass and the naked sprouts of the canna bulbs.

He turned his face toward her with pleasure. "Here they are. You can't fool them even under this rubbish. You can bet your boots they know when it's spring."

"How do they?" she called. He looked up at her again and his blue eyes looked blind. He did not answer her question. She felt awkward, as she often did around him when she had been foolish. He stooped again and picked up more of the slimy débris, dropping it into the tub. Above him the black elm was budding.

The wind blew off his black cap, exposing his close-cropped round head. He ran after the cap and put it tightly on his head, and came back to the canna-bed, leaning again over the dark earth, his short, strong body bent over it. The young girl leaned over too, looking down at the black earth he was uncovering. Still the wind blew fresh with something in the odor of it. The stocky man below went back and forth with the decay of winter, bending, lifting the dead stuff, raking again, uncovering the mist of green rising out of the earth.

"What time is it, uncle?" Eunice finally asked. He straightened and took a large gold watch out of the small pocket of his trousers. "It's quarter after eight. You've missed them pancakes with honey your mother give us for breakfast. I ate a lot of them."

"Say!" Jim, the brother next to her in age, came out of the kitchen door. He had just put on his shirt and was buttoning it. His face shone, newly washed. "You better hurry, Eunice. I been up since seven." He was pale in the bright light. "Jim," the mother called, "come out of that cold. And right after your bath, too." Jim went inside, banging the kitchen door.

Eunice turned back to her room, now dark to her dazzled eyes. She slammed the window down. The room seemed close and stifling, and she hurried, glad to be gone from it.

The way to the cathedral where the children were going led through a park whose winding paths went among the tall, upstanding trees. "Like black candles, they look," Eunice said to herself, walking between her brothers. Through the black maze of trees one could see the people hurrying, men and women with their children, groups of boys loitering, feeding the many squirrels that frisked greedily from the branches in spring hunger. Snow lay in the crotches of the trees yet and lay too at the bases. In places they had to step over little rivulets that ran over the walks. Men were taking up the board runway that had run from the warming-house down to the lake for skaters. Soon the ducks and swans would be upon the water. Pigeons came strutting down the walk with them, singing in their arched throats. From high among the budding branches came the sharp conversation of sparrows. Her brothers as they passed the croquet grounds were talking of spring sports, baseball, tennis. Eunice walked amidst her own thoughts and heard them as she now heard all the talk of her family, as something that went on at a distance.

This year she wouldn't play ball or run in the park at dusk with the gang like a wild girl. This year she would put on a good dress after supper and walk delicately along the paths, with the boys in awe and amazement at the sudden beauty of her ways. She felt a new mode of life, a new way of being. "Jim, I don't see why you wear that crazy hat." His sallow face under the upturned collegiate hat annoyed her. "Well, you know what you can do," he said, for he felt the hat exactly right, going well with his own immediate idea of himself. The answer seemed so rude, she thought she would cry, but she began looking at Johnny, who went beside them erratically, kicking an old tobacco can. He would not stop it and only grinned at her.

They rose over a hillock and saw the towers of the church with pointed caps like two witches. Up a flight of stairs from every street, the people were hurrying into the black spaces of the three dark doors. The bell was ringing from the bell-towers that rose amidst the sunlight. The fresh strong wind kept the trees blowing in a wild movement and seemed to have something to do with the gaiety and excitement of the many people hurrying to church. The three children walked faster, fearful lest they be late and have to attract attention. They half ran up the steps, slowed down at the doors, and entered with the hurrying people, hastily crossing themselves at the inner doors with the holy water from the font. They paused before the darkness of the interior, which came up on them softly after the wind and the light outdoors. Far down at the altar two little boys, moving in strict unison were lighting the candles for the mass. The three children walked together down the central aisle, feeling they were being watched, and after a hasty bob by way of a genuflection, they slid one by one into a wooden pew and onto their knees.

Amidst her prayers, which she knew by heart and said without thinking, Eunice looked at the altars decorated with lilies and ferns. There was a smell of burning wax and of the incense from the last mass which still floated above them in the vaulting ribs and buttresses.

The priest came, his black garments rocking about him. He was a slim old man, with a face looking as if it had been carved out of old wood like the statues of Saint Joseph and Gabriel on the side altars. He began the mass in a low humming voice. The little boys came, with the incense, the gong, moving in awkward youngness, their slim necks protruding from the white yokes, their big young feet swinging beneath their black robes. It gave Eunice a stab of pain watching them. They made her feel so much a girl.

The meaning of the mass she made up mysteriously herself. It made her sit in the trance of her own destiny, feeling through the ritual some hint of meaning that was never wholly graspable. The organ sounds came from behind them and fell and rose through the spaces; the choir of young boys sang in a high pitch. Their voices were strangely moving to the young girl. Hearing them, she had again a sharp knowingness that she would be a woman; something in the single, plaintive young male voices made her feel in her every fiber her own femininity. She could imagine their open mouths, their blank young faces, their earnest necks stretched upward, while out of their young throats came this high, plaintive singing, so effortless, so pure.

In the midst of her own dreaming she saw the thin white body ahead, hanging from the cross. Behind the flickering red candles in the dim recess stood that woman, His mother, amidst her draperies, that benign head drooping, looking down. Seeing the figure, she knew herself to be a woman too. Tears came to her eyes. The wooden altar in the apse of the dim church, the quaint figures looking outward with their pigmied human pathos, with so gentle a human grace, seen through her tears, filled her with a strange, a tumultuous compassion. There seemed to be sorrow in the world; the saints on the altars stood like any human men gentle from sorrow; the woman standing above the body of the prone man dead in anguish; the ways of the cross with the small tortured figures; and the priest proceeding about the mass, his tall, thin body, a line of tenuous sorrow, with a gentle droop lifting with effort upon itself the gray, lovely head.

The bells were ringing. Incense rose with the rising gray pillars, and above all, as if from a tree-top, fell that high-song of the boy choir, the single sustained pure note coming from the delicately upstanding throats of young boys. The many male voices all sounding together so sharp and clear made the girl feel confused and heavy. Looking at the back of the seat in front of her, she felt again that heavy knowledge of being a woman. The nearest she could get to the pain of such knowing was the vision of her mother, frail and sad and somehow defeated. To be a man was to be single and pure and unbroken. To be a woman was to be broken by an obscure defeat and mysteriously mellowed.

The ritual of the mass went on far down before her, as if the participating figures were so minute she might hold them in the palm of her hand, or as if the whole movement were going on within her.

And in all these symbols she felt vaguely a meaning of herself and what she would become and of a knowledge dimly awaiting her. Some faint knowingness of herself moved in her as the mass was enacted before her with its revealing of an inner altar, with all its intricate and provocative gestures of revealment. She too might turn at any moment and with as single a gesture as the priest made opening the great book before him — revealing the sacrament, taking from its inner place the chalice — with so simple a movement she too might open a space in whose depths lay the seed of her being. In this tension of suspense she watched the giving of the sacrament.

To her surprise it was all soon over, the moment had passed. She saw her brothers sitting beside her. The congregation wavered from the hard form into which the mass had seemed to mould them; it now broke, and moved. The two boys marched in again to the altar and snuffed out the candles. People were hurrying down the aisles to their Sunday dinners. Jim and Johnny wanted to be gone. The girl felt unhappy, baffled, but she rose and went with the scattering crowd out into the wind.

Outside the light seemed pale and wan upon the chill air. They hurried along buttoning their collars. Johnny found his tobacco-can, which he had hidden under some snow, and began kicking it home.

When they saw their own red brick house, Eunice dreaded the Sunday meal. Their dog came running out of the yard to meet them. Jim pushed the animal away and went on ahead alone. Eunice stooped to pat the beast but his affection apalled her. He wagged all over, his red tongue hanging out in an agony of gratitude for her attention. She could not stand it, having him all over her like that. "Go 'way," she said. "Go 'way, Spud." Johnny went around the corner of the house still kicking his tobacco-can, and the dog followed, turning his little doggish eyes back upon her in reproof and sadness.

Going in the front door, she felt almost a fear that someone would stop her before she got to her room. There was her father calling out from the front room, where she knew he would be sitting without any collar on, reading the Sunday papers. "Hello, want the funny paper?" he called. She stopped tragically on the stairs. "Ye gods," she murmured, closing her eyes dramatically, "The funny paper!" Out loud she shouted crossly, "No, I don't," and ran up the stairs making a clatter.

In her room she flung herself on the unmade bed and lay like an animal in ambush listening to the sounds downstairs. Johnny was now batting the can around the back yard. She could hear him. There was the incessant rattle of the many Sunday papers, and the voice of her father sometimes reading the scandal or the news out loud so her mother going from the kitchen to the dining-room might hear snatches of it at least. As she feared, she heard her mother ask where she was; then the tired, slow tread ascending the stairs. She flung herself against the wall, her back to the door she knew her mother would open in a moment.

When she heard the familiar woman behind her she could see with her eyes closed the face and figure of this woman, and she was glad she had come into the room. If she might turn and ask the older woman some question. But she did not know what the question would be, and she had a feeling her mother would not be able to answer it even if she found herself able to ask. "She must have looked like me when she was young," Eunice often thought. "What has happened?" Lying on the bed, the bewildered mother standing in the room behind her, the girl saw every feature of the woman — her delicate body worn thin, her slender neck, her face once whittled to its delicacy by many hopes, now gone into a tension of bewilderment and fatigue. Something was marked there clearly. This marking signaled a warning to the young girl, signaled some blight that had fallen on a dream her mother once had had. The imminence of a like blight haunted her.

The smell of pork roast came up the stairs through the door the mother had left open behind her. "Eunice, are you ill? What is it? Aren't you coming down to dinner? You haven't felt well all morning, have you?" she was asking, hovering over her in her delicate bewilderment.

"I'm all right. Please go away." She felt her mother pause, leaning over. "Oh, mother," she said to herself, wishing the mother of her own accord would say something to her. She felt the thin hand on her head: "You don't seem to have a fever." Eunice flung herself to a sitting position: "Of course I haven't. I suppose I've got to go down to dinner." She felt hunger with the strong warm odor of the pork coming up the stairs. Fixing her untidy hair at the mirror, she saw her mother reflected there too as she stood in the small space of the room, the worn hands under her apron, her flushed, worried face peering at her daughter in the little mirror into which they both were looking.

But nothing was said. Eunice followed her down the stairs, watching the familiar body, with its slight, dejected droop, go ahead.

"Well," said her father at the dinner table as he put a slice of roast on each plate, and they all knew by the tone of his voice that one of his jokes was coming. "So you don't read the funny paper any more, Eunice? She must be growing up, mother." He related — grinning palely, for he knew really how much he was hurting her — how he had been willing to share the funnies with her and she had shouted out to him, "like a fine lady," that she did not want them. Eunice looked down at her plate, feeling her cheeks flush.

Her mother changed the subject, speaking to Johnny: "Your cheeks are red as a beet, child; you must have been playing hard." Eunice saw the round face opposite her, his full apple cheeks chapped and reddened, his hair shaggy just as the wind had blown it. Uncle Joe, sitting alongside, looked at the boy affectionately, as if there was something between them.

"Let's go to the park, Johnny, and the keeper will take us over to the island and show us the duck eggs he is hatching," he said to the boy shyly, conscious of the others. "That'll be fun," the boy said, hacking his meat. Before she thought, Eunice was asking: "Can I go too, Uncle Joe?" "You stay home, Eunice," Johnny said, for he no longer liked her as well as he did. She had changed. "All right," the girl said quickly, ashamed and afraid lest her father tease her again, "I've got a date anyway."

But she had no "date." After the dishes were done she prepared to leave the house. She passed the door into the living-room and saw her father sitting by the window smoking. Her mother was sitting in her rocker looking almost as if she did not live there at all, but was a stranger who had come on a very long journey and was tired.

"Good-by, mother," Eunice paused in the door, "I'm going for a little walk." She hated to see her mother sitting there all afternoon like a stranger in the house. The mother looked up with her quick, startled eyes at the sound of her daughter's voice.

"All right, dear," she said, lowering the book she held. "Are you going with the bunch?"

"No, I don't know where they are. I just thought I'd go alone," Eunice said, feeling again that queer desire to cry.

"Oh," her mother said, raising her book.

Eunice stood still in the doorway looking into the littered room where sat her father and mother. Conscious of her there, the mother laid her book down on the floor and got up. Eunice started toward the outside door, saying hopelessly: "Well, good-by." And the woman followed her with that baffled air of indecision she so often had about her. At the door the two stood close together for a moment. "My, it's a fine day," the mother said, not looking at the day at all but smelling the fragrance of the close presence of her daughter.

"Yes, it is," Eunice said, not attending to the day, her eyes gone blind to the outside light as she stood so near her mother.

The girl turned suddenly and put her arms around the older woman, who stood awkwardly in the young embrace, not knowing what to think. Eunice let her go and ran down the walk to the street.

"You better wear your heavier coat, Eunice. There's a right chill wind blowing."

"No," called the girl, turning as she half ran and seeing the slight woman in the door of the shabby house, so that, walking along, she began to cry.

On the street she was afraid she might meet someone, so she stopped crying. The park was still deserted. She felt romantic and melancholy walking along under the tall, vaulting trees, but she met no one, so she soon lost interest in the feeling. She thought she would go to

Fourth Street, where there were shops, and where the gang often "hung out." She would buy a chocolate bar, she thought, making sure she had a nickel in her pocket.

Coming onto the street she began to walk in an agony of self-consciousness, wondering whom she would meet. She saw ahead of her, at the corner of the cigar-store, a group of boys. She saw them become conscious of her as she was still in the next block. They turned, still talking and laughing, but with half an eye upon her approaching. She didn't know how she should carry herself, how she should walk approaching them. She felt herself superior and yet vulnerable. It was a confusing way to feel. As she came near, the boys stopped talking and stood watching her cross the street. She felt in an agony lest she slip on the melting snow, or perhaps her skirt was hanging in some way below her coat. Some of the boys in the group she knew at school.

"Hello, Red," she said in a mincing voice and they all took off their hats. At last she got by and into the drug store. Inside she bought her candy.

One of the boys followed her. He leaned against the soda-fountain and talked to the clerk, wise-cracking for her to hear. She went over and began looking at a magazine. She felt the boy looking at her and she wished she had not come, yet she felt too that she was glad to be there.

She had not enough money to buy a magazine, so she was afraid to stand there looking at it too long. She feared that if she went toward the door the boy might open it for her. But she could stay no longer, so opening her candy bar she went to the door, feeling the boys turn to watch her walking. The boy did not offer to open the door. She went out and passed the window, seeing the two boys laughing inside, their grinning faces so young and so disordered.

Should she speak again to Red? She had decided against it when she found herself looking straight into his eyes and saying again in that queer high voice that disgusted her, "Hello, Red," and seeing all the boys raise their hats at once, so comically. She felt then like running as fast as she could. She felt almost as if she were running swiftly and was afraid she was, but she knew she was walking quite slowly really, peeling the tinsel from the chocolate.

After she had turned the corner out of sight of the group, she felt depressed and would have liked to go back again. She went on toward the park feeling lonely, wishing some of them might follow her, imagining what might be said to a young man.

She sat down on a bench, watching uneasily the streets which led into the park, thinking perhaps one of them would come. Strolling couples came around the curve of the lake, stopped and took each other's pictures, taking off their winter coats boldly. She thought them common, holding each other's hands, kissing so secretly behind the bare lilac-bush where she could see them quite plainly.

Uneasy was her afternoon. She thought she would go back for another candy bar but had not the nerve.

The young boys frolicked around the lake like monkeys, seeming quite mad in the spring wind, climbing trees, digging in the mud, shouting at each other, fighting, screaming, calling half around the lake, running to the cold water to get their feet wet, shoes and all. Last year she had climbed that elm slanting out over the lake. She remembered the thrill of sitting there between the sky and water, her lean young self, like these boys, shouting and singing.

The cold was getting into her limbs. The sun hung low behind the trees, a pale, shaggy, round ball. The heat was all gone and only the wind blew. She wondered where she could go, sitting miserably on the cold bench while the dusk gathered in the dark trees and the last couples and the last children went away. Far around the lake, on their way home, she could hear two young boys calling to each other.

Above her in the dusk arched the darkening trees. Occasionally a man passed along the walk behind her and she went tense listening to his steps. Once a dark figure stopped uncertainly and she heard him say something to her. She sat rigid, looking blindly out over the lake until he had gone on. She became afraid after that and got up and from habit went toward her home.

She saw the lights in the windows of her house. Someone turned the light off in the front room, so she knew they must all be in the dining-room. They would have cold-pork sandwiches.

Instead of turning into the house, she went on past it. She imagined that she did not live there. She went straight on in the uncertain dusk ahead.

Turning the corner out of sight of the house she trembled in excitement. It was as if she had disappeared from her familiar world. She might go on, making the right turnings, and come to the house where she would live, and to the companions she did not yet know.

But she walked around the block and came upon the old house again. The light was still on in the dining-room. She crept around the house. Standing on tiptoe she looked in at the window where they were eating.

The light seemed to lie like a glare in the room and the family seemed horrible in it. Her mother sat at one end, her father at the other. Facing her sat Jim, his pale face looking ill in the light. She could see the back of Johnny's head and the broad back of Uncle Joe. Their lips moved as if they were speaking but she could not hear. The storm-windows had not yet been taken off.

She looked a long time. Tired of standing strained upward, she slumped down and seemed to fall out of the light into an abyss of darkness.

Creeping around the dark corner of the house, she smelled the newly upturned soil of the canna-bed. The morning when her uncle had uncovered them to the sun seemed a long time in the past. She felt herself leaning out the upper window watching him, having that moment of brightness and wind.

Down on her hands and knees by the canna-bed she could see the white curved sprouts like scimitars just thrust from the earth. She put her finger on one of them and felt them hard and cold but with a moisture and this strong urgency, this upward thrust of power. They thrust upward, hard and single in the darkness, awaiting their day of flowering.

She parted the hard, naked stubs of the limbs of the lilac-tree and crawled behind it close to the house, sinking down on the ground. The body of the house was warm and she could hear going on inside the vague noises and movements of the people within, her father, her mother, her brothers. She listened and listened.

A stillness came up out of the blackness around her. People passed in front of the house along the walk. She could hear the quick steps of invisible children, the firm tread of many young men in the darkness.

She felt her eyes unbearably wide open and she listened and listened. The wind blew about her in the darkness as from another world.

After what seemed a long time the back door opened and her mother came out and stood on the steps. Reaching out, she could have touched the woman's skirt.

"Eunice," her mother called softly peering beneath her hand into the deep shadow that lay under the elm. The woman stood there a moment listening too. Then she went back into the house.

WIND

Since she had been married she could not get over the feeling that the night was a voyage, a journey through a strange land. Waking beside him she felt they had been traveling down a mysterious river, with banks gliding by and at last, in the morning, they were waking in a foreign land hearing unfamiliar sounds, voices speaking a language unknown to them, and peeking out, they saw a strange land, and the stamping, bustling, moving of the waking city was a great excitement.

Sometimes too, Ken became a strange fellow traveler and she looked at him with horror, putting on his shoes or shaving, and she threw the covers over her head wishing she would never have to get up. Who was he? Whom had she come away with? Mama, mama, she called to herself. Someone was standing just inside the bathroom door shaving and she did not know who he was. Mama, someone has come in, that's why we should always lock the front door. When he wasn't looking she would fly into the kitchenette and put on the coffee.

She was uneasy, but not he! He understood everything. He understood perfectly that she was his wife. He was never frightened seeing her in the morning and when he left he kissed her neatly as if he sealed her forever as his wife, in a little nutshell.

It terrified her. Why wouldn't he see HER? But the minute he had disappeared down the steps and she had run into the hall waving at his disappearing face and heard him go three flights of stairs and had run to the window and looked down and saw him minute below and had waved and waved until he was out of sight — that moment she became very happy.

She knew then instantly that she was Ken's wife. She had to stop making the dust fly and write it down on a piece of paper, "Mrs. Ken Swanson." Then she flew about the small room that was bedroom, parlor, dining-room in one, tidying everything. The hours simply sped and she quite forgot her childhood, her girlhood in a perfect bliss of happiness. She forgot all their quarrels then. She never once thought of them. She often spoke to an imaginary person, "Oh, Ken and I never quarrel," — and it did seem incredible that they ever ever should. She perfectly believed with the imaginary person that they did not.

Ken left at exactly fifteen minutes to eight every morning and four minutes later to the dot, something else happened that she could not miss.

It was early spring so she could throw open the window and lean out and wave to Ken far, far below as if she were a bird leaning out of a precarious nest and he could see her far up, her hair blowing and her girlish face against the sky with the clouds flying swiftly above her. He would want to wave her back, fearful she would fall but he was afraid of being silly and the street was full of people going to work. She saw him lift his hand for the last time as he turned the corner and she leaned out for a moment sniffing the air and seeing the clouds race inland swiftly. There was a tangy smell of the sea too and a smell of spring coming from the earth. The street below was full of children and girls and young men coming from sleep tumbling out into the world again and they seemed loath to leave their own nests. She was glad she was so snug, that she did not have to leave this warm mysterious voyage of her own being and another's. The houses just opposite were shut up. One could not see into them. She knew absolutely no one in this town where Ken had brought her.

She ran to the kitchenette and stood on tip-toe looking out the tiny window. It was through this window that she saw the only people that were familiar to her. She saw the back of an apartment house with dozens of criss-cross stairs marking it and fire escapes and she could see right into the houses, see people moving, standing a long time like herself looking out, then going back, back into the dimness behind them, visible to her only a moment, like some strange undersea animals coming up in the dim water for an instant, flashing over in the light, then receding again into another element.

Giving off each back room there was a tiny balcony that looked as if it might drop off any moment and behind these were broad windows through which she could see. A window with an orange curtain was opposite her and she felt she knew the stout woman who sat there nearly all day and who must have been an invalid. She sat reading or sewing and sometimes she lifted her head and looked out right at Fran, straight into her eyes so she felt she must dodge back but she found then that the woman saw nothing, so she stood still with the woman's face lifted, looking right at her, and she felt in an invisible coat. It was eerie. She had to giggle to herself a bit nervously.

Above that there were two rooms. In one a negro slept late in the morning. He just got up usually when she set her salad out on the kitchenette table for her lunch. She could see the bed dimly. Sometimes she wondered if he were really sleeping there. Perhaps he was a gambler and stayed out nights and lived a life of chance and excitement. She could go only so far imagining such lives and then there seemed to grow up a kind of wall and she could see no further over it, no matter how she stretched on her toes there was always the wall shutting her in.

But what she was waiting for was about to happen. In the next room there was another man who always got up exactly four minutes after Ken had gone. An alarm must go off in that other room and the unknown man get out of bed at exactly the same time every morning. She could almost see him, a pale shaft in the darkness of the receding room. She always felt very excited watching the unknown man. It was an excitement she imagined she should have felt when she married Ken and she had not felt. Or to be more truthful, she had felt it before she married him, or when he was gone, but never when he was near. It was very curious.

She stood on tip-toe in her little red bedroom slippers that her mother had given her for a wedding present and that were quite new of course. And this unknown, dim man was Ken and all the men she might have married. He would be moving about receding, coming nearer so her breath stopped but he never came to the window, never. Then he would put on his coat coming to the window so she could ALMOST see him, just as when she was a girl, in the spring out in the hay she had closed her eyes and at first little gold splotches had chased each other and then dimly almost, not quite, she could see the man she would marry coming toward her — but then she would always have to open her eyes, something would happen, she would forget. . . .

He would lean toward an invisible mirror and stand a moment looking at his face; then he would go back into the room, receding, and he was gone. She would stand bewildered, a great gap inside her from his going. Yet who was he? What could it mean? Sometimes in despair she went back to bed and slept the whole day.

But most often she let her heels go back down into her wedding slippers and there she would be shut into her little kitchenette where she could reach out her arms and actually touch the walls on all sides, there she would be shut in, shut in. . . .

When the dishes were done she got her basket and started out for the market. She took off her red slippers and put on her black pumps. She still wore her new black wedding pumps and her good suit; she felt so new, as if everyone must know that she had bought them in that awful excitement that was almost an illness, before she was married. It never ceased to be a wonder to her that she had bought the shiny pumps before she was Mrs. Ken Swanson and she was now putting them on after being married three months. There was something mysterious about it.

She let herself out into the dark hall, locked the door, tip-toed to the banisters and peered over. It gave her a fright to be going through the unknown house, past doors where unknown people lived, through the corridors where unknown smells roamed so hostilely. Her heart beat like a trip hammer. As luck would have it she hardly ever met anyone. She crept down, every creak sounding like an explosion but at last with a little run she was out on the high steps with the clouds racing dizzily above her head. She ran down onto the street and went sedately with her basket on her arm. What a day! The air was full of life, the white frothy clouds simply flew over the sky like giant tropical birds. The shops were full of shirts, suits, neckties, dresses, baby clothes. How gay it was. A little white dog ran down the street chasing nothing, simply beside himself with joy barking so he shivered from stem to stern. She had to laugh when he fell over his white paws turning right over in the street with joy.

She felt she was flying. She could NOT keep from running a few steps. Really she thought she would take off right into the air. And when she saw all the stores with food in the windows she was entranced. What would she buy? Here was food for their own precious life and future. Oh it was too lovely. There were pickles, black bread, meats prepared in onion and garlic, little fishes, whole hams, chickens, new shining eggs at every price. Women sat in front of the stores that were full of laughing talking joking customers. She went into the warm-smelling bakery and carefully, oh carefully, chose a fat loaf of rye bread Ken liked because "there is absolutely no value to white." He was positive of that. There seemed to be not the slightest doubt about it. Then she went out the door with the warm balmy bread odor around her somehow like warm woman's hands, like her mother. Out out into the delicate morning again with the street's sound surging around her.

The children were looking down the street and the old women were peering. There was the sound of horns blowing and bells and drums. Marvelous. She craned her neck standing on tip-toe in her little black pumps, her hands clasped, her lips parted in wonder. What was it? What in the world, then it came, a parade! Oh, joy! Coming around the corner, a bright wagon with balloons and huge bright signs — BLUE RIBBON ICE CREAM — and a picture of a giant cone with its pouf of cream; cars followed and the horns were blowing and bells ringing and a huge clownish voice poured out of a radio. And the bright light simply poured down over them all.

Fran stood by two Italian children, enchanted, and the white clouds raced above changing and changing the light so nothing looked the same ever. One blink of the eyes and everything was plunged into a different gilding light as if it were all moving silently, flowing with such musical swiftness it took one's breath. And she closed her eyes feeling the swift moving light over her and something white silent blissful moved in her; she felt this swift passage within shadowless and fleet that was the movement of her whole mysterious life from beginning to end. . . . What was it? Bliss. . . .

The parade went by and Fran ran into a delicatessen and quite to her own astonishment she was saying, "I want a bottle of pure pure milk for my baby." The Jewish woman smiled. "How old?" she said as she dropped the white milk bottle into a brown bag. "Oh. . . very young. . . ." Fran smiled so idiotically lovely with her hat just a little awry, her wispy hair escaping. She took the milk and simply ran out. What if the woman should want, should demand to see the baby. She thought everyone on the street was looking at her curiously. They all seemed to have babies and were looking at her with sad disapproval, but just the same it was so pleasant that she went on pretending she was buying all the vegetables with an eye out for Ken Junior.

She stopped beside a barber pole with her carrots hanging out of the basket. A sudden awful fear shot through her — what if there should be. . . nonsense. She soon forgot about it watching a girl with a stunning fox fur. But she stopped dead still again right at the curb as she was crossing the street — what had Ken said — Oh he said he didn't believe in women voting. How terrible, how simply awful. How could she have married a man who didn't believe in women voting? She had never voted herself but she certainly believed in it. Why hadn't she asked him before? And then he didn't take a bath every day. That DID upset her. He said it was nonsense taking a bath every day. How hideous. How could she ever bear it? By the time she had dodged a truck, crossed the street, she quite forgot about it.

Suppose Ken should get run over by a truck. Oh, for an instant she saw it all vividly, vividly. They would bring him up and lay him on their bed. . . she saw it all distinctly. For half a block she was quite positive he was lost to her forever.

She dawdled up the street looking at all the people, at the women coming out on the stoops shaking rugs, seeing her for an instant. She wanted to raise her hand to them, "I'm married too," but they shook the mop or the rug and went into the unknown houses again slamming the doors.

When she got back the place seemed very alien. She stood in the room and she thought she could not bear for Ken to come home that night. If only that night he wouldn't come back there. She lay down on the couch and went straight to sleep. The world went on noisily outside. The window was open just a fraction and the wind came in wandering about the room. Once it lifted her hair very gently and laid it back across her cheek. The clock ticked. She slept sprawled like a child her arms up in a strange abandon, in a rather awful innocent abandonment as if anything might happen to her. She seemed like a victim, one simply could not have helped but think of a victim. She lay with her arms thrown up and out over her head, and her neck and breast were thrown back. The thin childish brows were drawn up in a kind of anguish. Was it bewilderment or anguish? And the wind kept lifting her skirt, her hair, as if some invisible thing was breathing on her gently, very gently.

She opened her eyes thinking someone had touched her and sat up wondering where she was. She thought at first she was in the sunroom at home, then she saw the tiny place, the kitchenette through the door whose sides she could touch. She looked at the little clock and saw with a start that it was four-thirty. She had been asleep for hours. Her basket of groceries with the carrots hanging out sat right in the middle of the floor. What a housewife she was! She got up and tried to bustle in as her mother would have, getting supper. Ken would be there at five-sixteen exactly. Oh, she wanted to be a girl again, if this would ever ever let up, but every day for years and years he would be coming at five-sixteen. A hideous languor came over her. She stood on her toes to look across the alley, supper must be in every room. As she was depending on cans pretty much anyway she managed to get things started.

Then people began coming home; the front door far below kept opening and closing and then she would listen standing still, in fear almost anguish. What did he look like? What was he? Then at last there were the steps coming up past the second landing, up the stairs. She stood in fright knowing that in one minute, one second, he would open the door. Then it happened. The door opened and she turned in fright watching and there he stood and he had flowers in a green shiny paper curling up.

"Here honey," he said, handing them to her, sort of "shoving" them at her, "shoving" she said gingerly taking the flowers. She didn't want to look but she had to see him his compact closed little back, his stubborn blond head. . . . He was taking off his coat and she saw that he took it off, folded it up in exactly the same way every single night. She thought she would scream.

"Gee, it feels good," he said, "the spring — doesn't it honey?"

"I wish you wouldn't call me honey," she said from the kitchen leaning over the string beans.

He laughed, "Gee it's funny, I always forget."

She took the flowers out of the wet funneled paper. They were lilies-of-the-valley. Why would he bring her lilies-of-the-valley? She left them lying beside the carrots. She dished the beans and it was all she could do to face him, go in and put them on the library table over which she had spread the bluebird cloth.

"How's my little sweetheart?" Ken said awkwardly fumbling, trying to encircle her waist. She always felt he was laughing in some way when he touched her because she was so new. He seemed to know all about touching.

"Don't," she said in a panic, backing away, the dish of beans between them and some of the hot liquid spilled on her and she began to cry.

"Oh honey that's too bad," he said taking the beans and setting them on the table. He was solicitous but she couldn't stop crying and he kept making out as if it were the spilt beans she was crying over. "That's all right," she kept saying. "That's all right. It's not that I'm crying about. It's not that."

He got impatient, taking on like that over a little burn. "Never mind," he said. "Look, we'll put the flowers on the table." He went out and got the flowers and put them on the table and set them right in the middle where they sat ringing out joy from their minute bells.

She sat down opposite him in front of the lilies-of-the-valley and tried to eat and he kept looking at her as if he were spying on her.

"Oh why do you look at me like that?" she said.

"Like what?" He looked at her startled. What was the matter with her? He thought he had been patient.

"You look at me funny." She was trying not to cry.

"Good Lord," he said laying down his fork. "I've had about enough." Instantly his face got smaller and smaller as if it were going to disappear altogether, simply diminished like a hard knot and his lips set. He looked as if he positively hated her.

"I don't know," she said, "I don't know who you are. . . ."

"You don't," he said bitterly. "Well you better eat," he said and to her horror he began eating as if he were starving. What a boor he was. She was offended to the soul.

"Why do you eat like that, like a . . . a . . . a beast?" she said in a little gasp.

"So . . . now I'm a beast," he said. "I'm a beast. That's pretty good a wife calling her husband a beast. . . . "

Oh my husband, something in her cried. "I didn't call you a beast."

"You mean to sit there and say you didn't? Can't even argue with a woman."

She bit her lips. Oh, God keep her from quarreling. She would be forgiving. Her breasts and arms ached with the beauty of her own forgiveness, washing over him because he was her husband. . . . In a storm she would warm his hands under her armpits. Oh why wasn't there a dreadful cataclysm and she would save him. She said in a small voice, "How did things go today?" She could hardly say it, it ground like dust in her mouth.

But he was amiable and began telling her about the office. How simple everything was to him and he never never wanted to know about her life. She did not eat. She would probably get very thin from sorrow and grief. Oh if only he would notice that she did not eat. She thought of the man across the way and of his imagined tenderness. Then suddenly in the midst of his telling her about having lunch with John Hays she couldn't help saying, "At home now mama is just putting everything on the table. They are just sitting down to dinner. . . . "

"Well, for Christ's sake," he said suddenly, "Why don't you go home then?" He stood up and sat down again. She was pleased to see how moved he was.

"You don't love me."

"I do love you, Fran," he said hanging his head. "I don't make you happy. We thought we would be so happy."

And to think of all the things they had said to each other about happiness made her choke. "You don't want to know about me. You only want to sleep with me."

He didn't say a word. His neck bulged out above his collar and she was frightened and went on in a low scared voice, "At home Gracie and Lizzy liked to hear me talk. Oh, you would be a writer they said, you talk so well, you tell such good things, and now. . . now. . . ."

"You're always thinking about everyone at home. . . . You're not here, you're still at home. You're not married to me, you're still with your mother."

"Oh no, no . . ." she said ashamed. Why couldn't she tell him of the day, how she had felt?

"You're with your girl friends," he said, "Gracie . . . Gracie," he mimicked, "That's all I hear."

She was furious, "Don't you say anything about Gracie, don't you dare. . . . " She got up and flew to the couch, flinging herself down on her face. He went on eating his dinner and she was furious, furious. She got up blindly, put on her coat and hat and blindly went flinging out the door. "Where are you going?" he said but she ran expecting him to run after her but he came to the banisters calling her name just once. . . . She ran down the stairs, down the dark halls and flew out the door. Oh where could she go to die? She went around the streets looking behind her for him. Why didn't he come and get her? A strange man followed her. Where could she go? She ran back to the house and up the stairs and into the door and to her relief there he sat reading the paper. She wanted to fling herself in his arms.

"I forgot my purse," she said instead.

"It's on the dresser," he said.

She saw he had cleared away the table.

"Shall we go to a picture show?" he said trying to be casual.

But then she remembered how he had not followed her. "No," she said. Oh, would he let her go out again alone on those dreadful streets where men followed her. "I guess I'll stay here," she said miserably straying away from the door.

She took off her coat and hat and instead of flinging them down she hung them up very unctuously, but she could hardly bear to turn back into the room. What would she do? She could not go to bed right in the room like that with him watching her. If only she could go into her own bedroom and lock the door but there was no place to go away from him. She stood in the room thinking he would notice her. Now he's going to read the paper and neglect me, she thought. I have to wash the dishes. How lonely I am. She felt very lovely suddenly. I shall never complain, she thought and it was very sweet imagining herself dying a dear old lady after years of sacrifice during which she had never complained.

After washing the dishes she came back and was startled to see he had gone to bed. There he lay in the bright room in bed. She was horrified. A terrible desire to shake them both, for something tremendous to happen came over her. She sat down miserably in the only rocker, "Oh I think I'm going to have a baby, Ken," she said and the words frightened her nearly out of her skin.

There was a moment's silence, then he said from the mound on the bed, "Oh, I think you're imagining it Fran, anyhow it's too early to know now."

But since she had said so, she was sure of it. She sat dejectedly on the chair. She even felt as if she was going to be sick. "I don't know. I feel awful," she said, and it was true enough really.

"You poor kid," he said and "kid" was a word she could not stand at the moment. "Come here," he said.

She sat perfectly still. "Won't you come here," he said.

"No," she said faintly leaning over herself in terror.

"Oh, all right," he said flouncing over, "Stay there then."

She sat very quietly. The clock ticked and the wind crept in through the still open window. It crept low on the floor like an invisible cat flicking at the fringes of things, leaping in play at her feet as they crouched under her. The room was very still and presently she forgot all the quarreling. And a pleasant sensation came over her again, of their being up so high in their nest alone. "Ken," she said softly but there was no answer. She knew how he fell asleep like a child instantly, just when she was most awake. The curtain stood out and the wind was in the room like a presence and that same bliss she had felt in the afternoon put a little smile on her lips as if she were smiling with her whole body. She got up and tip-toed to the bed and looked down where he was sleeping and his face no longer looked knotted and angry but it was all smoothed out and there he lay the man she had wanted to marry. Her heart was filled with tenderness.

She crept over and put the window up, clear up so the wind blew straight in upon her, then she took off her clothes and stood naked for a moment in that fertile spring wind. The clouds were still flying overhead like a huge migration of giant birds and again her life seemed to be flying high within her so silently, swiftly. She dropped her lacy nightgown over her and crept through the room that was chilling rapidly from the wind.

Very carefully so as not to wake him she crept in and lay far over perfectly straight her toes stretching down. She still suffered but it was a thick lovely suffering in her, a kind of tangible thing she could touch. I shall suffer all my life, she said and smiled blissfully.

Cautiously she raised on her elbow and looked down at him, his face toward her. She saw the flushed skin, the tender neck going down into the white of his body. His head was flung back now and he was off guard in a lovely innocence, and she was free to love him as she liked. He was like a child . . . child . . . child . . . where was it?

Then she wanted to shake him rouse up the man who had courted her, startle out the tender lover but she was afraid of the look of his eyes when they should open, the little possessive look again.

If she were dead, then, then he would lean over her tenderly. She would be a bride again. She folded her hands over her breast. He would waken, call her, touch her little hands. My little hands . . . she said.

Without knowing it she went to sleep and the wind rattled the evening paper he had left on the floor.

She wakened with a start knowing something was happening. The wind blew a gale straight through the room. She propped up on her elbows. Outside the window the darkness was illumined with a soft flower-like burst of lightning, as if magnolias were bursting on the outside air, and there came a far delicate rumbling just shaking the air around them, rumbling through her body deliciously and the wind blew right in making the curtain stand straight out like a ghost in the room and the smell of that wind — it smelled of loam and sprouting seeds. She breathed it right into her body like a madness.

Then there was a sharp crack and a stroke of lightning that seemed to cut her flesh and she screamed, "Ken . . . Ken . . . " Then again the great cracking of thunder and suddenly as if at a signal the rain began to come down striking straight down from the sky to the earth and into the earth directly. There it was on the roof, all around them striking straight down. It was wonderful and frightening. "Ken. Ken," she called; her eyes dilated as the lightning pierced the room, as if it was a light cocoon hanging on a bough, and pierced her body too, cauterizing the grossness.

She heard feet running past, doors slamming and the black rain like javelins fell in a torrent outside the window and flowed even into the window and the whole room seemed to be shaking with the wind blowing it out. There was a terrible excitement in the air. "Ken. Ken," she called and he waked instantly as he did and his eyes dilated too with wonder as he saw the exciting windy darkness in the room and the rain was like an unknown army below the window.

"Fran," he said in wonder and that fright a spring storm is bound to give you, "Fran," and she went straight into his breast, and the fresh wind kept summoning them, blowing and blowing in the room straight over them in its fertile chill.

And most delicately he felt for her, calling her; so she answered for the first time, stirring to him, struck by the freshening wind. It blew and blew in the window straight over them.

The LAUNDRESS

I

I remember my first sight of her as I stood behind my mother in the doorway. We had advertised for a laundress. It was early morning, and the sun shone white and pleasant.

A little woman confronted us, but strongly built, with black eyes, sharp nose and firm lips.

Not at any time did she seem to us like a servant.

She came, after that, to our house twice a week. Upon one day she did the laundry; upon the other she mended, cleaned and attended to odd jobs.

She always came on her days somewhat early, before we children were off to school, usually while we were still at breakfast. She would come in silently and be standing at the door looking at us, and always, upon her appearance, we were surprised, astonished somehow, that she should be there. It was the same way with her departure; the same inexplicable sense of phenomena accompanied it. She would greet us pleasantly, and immediately she seemed to surround the chaotic atmosphere of morning strife with something of order, of efficient and quiet uniformity, so that one had the feeling that life was small and curiously ordered.

In the many years we knew her, her habit of dress almost amounted to a uniform — a black jacket, which she took off and placed on the back of a chair, and a black hat which she put beside the jacket on the seat. I can say no more than that they were black and seemed to belong to her; they were as irrevocably a part of her as a nun's costume is part of her, though, of course, in an entirely different manner.

One other thing was part of the secret air about her: always upon the removal of the black hat, her hands edged themselves beneath the raven wings of her hair, lifting it bodily from her low white forehead. Her hair always made me think of the beautiful German fashion of expressing the hair as plural. I always thought the gesture, even in the early morning, a tired one — not of the body particularly, though.

We could prepare nothing for her breakfast.

"No. No. I will eat what is here. Very good, very good for me."

Her speech was broken and halting, full of ejaculations. When her feeling rose she never spoke, but uttered these lovely singing sounds. I thought she must have come from some foreign land. My mother said it was Germany.

She would roll her sleeves above the elbows and sit down at table with my mother. They had a kind of militant feminism in common, and both were very unusual and beautiful women, I thought, as I watched and listened to them. Both had left husbands for their personal freedom, and both had gone out alone with children when that was no small thing to do. Kretch had been her husband's name; and I suppose because she was predominantly the mother of those children, she had automatically kept the name. There were four children, two boys and two girls.

"But it is something to have no man for boys," she would say in her full-throated voice. "I can manage my girls, but boys — it is different. I am a woman. A man they need, I feel." She would make a little clucking sound and go on eating.

Kretch, a German land-owner, had married her for his farm. She worked like a drudge, but when he bullied the children she brought them to town, and, to his surprise, earned their living until they were large enough, one by one, to add to the family budget.

"My oldest son Franz — ." She ate methodically, dark and stalwart in the morning light, which fell on the littered table, and on my mother, who leaned her face in her hands listening. "I think a man should have a trade. So. He works in machine shop; the noise has made him a little deaf. You know boys; he is restless, he doesn't like too much work. Oh, I can tell you, he goes wild so often. It is a man he needs. My other boy is sweet. But boys need so much a man. Ach, you know too!"

It was fine to see her work, so thoroughly, with a hardy pride in working well with her hands.

Through the pantry one could see her standing, stolid and efficient in the middle of the room, ironing.

I would go and sit on the step in front of her to be near the shining skin of her arms. She was always pleasant and quick with sympathy.

"You never sing, Mrs. Kretch."

"Sing, no, no. I never sing." And she would go on ironing with her strong naked arms.

She would put on her black jacket, her black hat. Her face would be sharp and strong in the evening and she would smell of soap and heat.

Then, more than ever, she seemed to have come from a foreign land, and a lonely secret would be upon her. Her face had a passionate pure look, as the faces of ascetics have, or of any persons consecrated to the sustaining of an act. The same feeling which accompanied her entrance, of astonishment and surprise, would surround her exit as she would turn at the door in her black garments, her dark eyes sad, looking out, the two wings of her hair in tired and secret flight beneath her hat, and her hands lying against her sides.

"Good-by," she would say, and there was mysterious portent in the word.

We would run to the window, loath to have her leave, and see her sturdy figure, like an ordained shadow, go down the walk, into the street between the rows of middle-class houses, and disappear suddenly in the dusk.

In the interim between her work and her return to the two-story wooden house where she kept her children, strange things must have taken flight within her.

II

One evening her voice, hardy and foreign, spoke over the telephone. She was in dire straits over her oldest girl, who was, despite her wishes, about to leave with a medicine man. My mother, in great sympathy, went to her immediately.

The house was one of those unpainted houses that rise perpendicularly with blind windows on the flat surfaces. The door opened nearly into the street, after three wooden steps. The room we entered was papered newly, with light faintly-flowered paper. The odor of soap and iron heat filled it faintly. Mrs. Kretch admitted us. She gave the entire house — with its corridors, its straight walls, its wooden stairs beyond the room where we sat, the littered room behind the young girl who stood in the doorway to our right — a transitory air, as if it were a scene that she would leave. Nuns give the world the same aspect when they pass through the streets.

"My girl Lilly — ." She pointed to her, and with customary directness, after we were seated, leaned forward, "Tell them all, Lilly, they are our friends."

Lilly was a faint replica of her mother, lighter, more delicate. She sat straight and unembarrassed and talked in a pure, simple, though high, voice. She had the same high directness. They both looked proud and hardy, sitting in their room with the gas-flickering.

A boy came in, tall and sullen. Mrs. Kretch turned. "My boy who is learning a trade." She looked up at him impersonally as he stood enormous beside her. The foreign look came into her eyes as she watched his tall, stubborn back disappear into the next room.

My mother persuaded the girl to take up stenography — a trade for a girl, Mrs. Kretch felt, too, in her clear, stubborn way.

All the time we were there, a young girl kept going back and forth setting the table for the evening meal; she was very blonde, and tall with a slender neck, and she raised her eyes timidly, watching us. There were little pictures on the wall, of ladies done in water color, which I suspected she had done. Yes, Mrs. Kretch said, she had done them. She called the girl softly.

"Hilda . . . Hilda, leave off setting the table and come." I started. Again I had the feeling that this woman who smelled of soap, this vital sibyl, had uttered phenomenal secret words. The girl came in and stood looking at her mother. They looked at each other, held in each other secretly. I felt very near to solving the enigma of the woman and the girl. My heart beat. I felt excited for some unknown reason. Yet, it eluded me, and I came no nearer to the secret. I could not understand.

Later the girl studied design, and though she became nothing phenomenal, she did pretty things, and sometimes her colors and lines startled one unexpectedly, with something hidden and exciting, exactly and in the same manner as the appearance of Mrs. Kretch. Perhaps that was the secret thing in them—perhaps several more generations will produce something. One cannot with certainty trace those things, but surely great expression has somewhere a beginning, a vague and terrible budding.

I left the city and was gone for several years, though during that time my mother, in writing to me, often spoke of Mrs. Kretch. Besides having her always for her work whenever she kept house, my mother was very fond of her, with that peculiar devotion which often springs up between a very simple and vital woman and a complex and intellectual one.

When I returned, other things occupying me, I did not turn my attention to the woman. I didn't think of her one way or the other. My mother had told me that the children were self-supporting, and successful, and that the younger boy had turned out to be a student. But I paid scarcely any attention to it, until one day she said: "Do you know Mrs. Kretch is dead?"

Her dying produced in me again that astonishment, that shock as of something mysterious and unusual. I stood quite still, a feeling of incredible sadness filled me — or was it sadness? It was scarcely more than a great tidal feeling. What the woman had done when she stood at the door of our breakfast-room many years before she repeated now, only colossally. The entire world seemed to shift suddenly, and change, to become a thing new-touched and secretly, with meaningful ritual. . . . The same whole and complete feeling her living aspect produced was repeated a hundredfold in the act of her death.

III

By some power, almost as if we were led by the hand, my mother and I were drawn to the funeral. The oldest daughter had telephoned to us. Her mother had died suddenly, she said. Of course. We used to see her go suddenly into the dusk after uttering that phenomenal word, Goodby. The daughter gave us an address of a little undertaking establishment. We got off the car, in the middle of the day, when the traffic of the city was at its height. We passed the perpendicular house. It was entirely vacant now, the windows terribly blind, the door closed as if it would never open again.

A hearse stood at the curb, and a small line of cars. We turned into the white wooden house. We were late, we could hear a voice. Nothing mattered, none of these little things. The door was opened by a little sandy man, who took us through the hot room to seats near the front. A man was standing on a carpet in the backroom, a Bible in his hands, talking in a lisping, sentimental voice. Nothing mattered.

The room was close and sweet. Flowers lay in one corner, banked on the gray coffin. Nothing mattered but the woman's head, lying in a cloud of satin. I was astonished. It was white and colored with a beautiful unnaturalness—the black hair on the narrow forehead; the fine nostrils, sharp with the breathing of death; the vital cheeks, vacant of their blood, and the chest shrouded in lavender. The rest of the body was covered by the coffin. But chief in beauty was the forehead; wide and organic, such as some women have, it lay beneath the flight of the strong hair as if she had flown hence through it, touched it in the last passage.

The man kept talking, changing his position from one foot to the other, smiling a vacuous, sickening smile.

Her four children sat before her, the two boys looking down abashed, the girls, their hats shrouded in black, hands folded tightly in their laps, looking straight at her, like strangers, quite tearless. Her mark was on all their faces, and she lay like a pod when the seed has flown.

But even her body seemed to have lost the memory of its children. She was as virgin as a girl, but with a subtle difference: it was a religious virginity, a mask-like secret consecration that possessed her, as if she were witness to most secret temple fires. A vast abstraction lay upon her.

She had been stout, but now she was slender, as she must have been when young, only strong as a vestal, for she had somehow entered into a vast virginity.

I thought, looking at that consecrated, ecstatic face, that death must be the most beautiful thing in the world and the most strange.

Some women back of us sobbed.

The man in the frock coat stopped. There was no music. No outward grace anymore than there had been in her life. With the ceasing of his voice the beautiful doomed body in the coffin, trembling in the fragile moment of disintegration, seemed to possess the room. All eyes turned toward it. There was complete silence.

No one moved to pass the coffin. A heavy step came up behind us, plodded past. A man with a thick back stood before the coffin—on one foot, so that his huge body slanted. His little head was cropped closely, and he pulled his hat in his hands. Kretch. He stood looking down at her. She was young in death, as young as on her bridal day and more beautiful, for her beauty was more spare, more proud, more certain. In her final bridal, he respected her and was afraid. He turned, and plodded heavily back and out the door.

The four children rose and walked together to her. Her eyes looked half open, like those of a woman dreaming half voluptuously. Only her lips bore the mark of a terrible touch, and lay on her gray chin. Her virile brows half met in the center. Her black hair, like the wings of released birds, took flight from her face. The voluptuous, heavy padding of the coffin came around her. Ah, that ascetic! In death she lay on the couch of a courtesan.

The sandy-haired man walked in briskly and took the flowers from the coffin.

For a moment I seemed near the secret, heartbreakingly near it. He took the white ruffles of her last couch in his hands and put them about her. Her children watched him impassively. In a moment the light would be taken from her, shut away. What was the mystery? She had fulfilled some rite in her life, of which she had been conscious — she had done her work, she carried upon her the secret of her order. What?

A man who is born is like a man falling into a sea. When he dies he leaves his body, washed up from that sea, an instant before decay, livid upon a foreign shore, illumined by a terrible light, chilled by the gusts of eternity — he looks back upon it before he enters the caves, and for an instant it glows in that illumination of death; he leaves the white sands of the sea, the body sinks into the ground it lies upon, the light fades within it, and there is nothing more visible.

The lid was lowered over her face.

OUR FATHERS

I

They had only one room above the barber shop and of course they could not let her father lie there for the two days before the funeral, but the undertaking parlor was only a few doors away, next to the beer joint, and she could go there with Mona and her grandmother to see him any time of day. There were lots of others there too, men and women she had never seen before who said they were from the unemployment council. It never seemed very real to Pen tiptoeing softly over the thick carpet past the huge urns to see her father lying, rouged and colored, upon a bed of silk. It made her want to laugh as though they had a joke together and his skinny face seemed to twist, and the thin black mustachios twirled up on the waxen cheeks and she thought they ought to have let him have his hat on that he always wore pulled down over his eyes. He seemed exposed with his narrow forehead showing whiter than his face. And then to lie in that silken bed. She had to run out to keep from screaming because she could see his thin mouth in talk as it had been the night before the demonstration when he had been shot.

"We've got a right to be living, see?"

"Sure, you said it."

"It was us made this country, it was us, the bones of my people lie along Hill's railroad and there was a man dead for every tie laid and that's a fact. . . . "

"That's a fact all right. . .that sure is true."

"My fathers dug in the earth, threw up bridges, that's what they done, tilled the god-damned soil, that's what, froze on the prairies. We've been buckers and loggers and made nothing while those that held the land became wheat, lumber, coal kings and us lean to the guts."

"Yes sir, that's right, Tim. . . ."

"Stand together. Be together. I got brothers to my fathers who joined up with John Brown, stormed Harpers Ferry. Lie now face up in Kansas dirt but they done something, showed us something. . . ."

Penelope heard voices talking in the day and sleepwalking voices murmuring in the night, but not one of them said where they were, or what they would be doing in that long and tangled journey and a darkness would come over her asking of that space they traveled. Who are we? Where have we come from? What movement of lost seed in a had a meaning.

Until they came to the moment of her father's death, which became a moment they had been running toward. They were living up above this barber shop and the barber came up knocking at the door, and Mona threw her kimono on and opened it a crack and the barber said, "There's somebody calling you on the phone." And Penelope looked up from the book, knowing what it was since Mona knew no one in Kansas City who would be calling her. And Mona started toward that man she held in hate, waiting for this. "Come on, Pen," Mona said and her grandmother stood back with anguished eyes knowing too it had come.

They got a taxi to follow that man — father — wherever he led, in hatred but compelled. They went into the stone hospital and found him lying very white without hat or cigar, squinting one eye at them.

And Mona began to weep, not knowing what he had been doing all those years, "I knew you wouldn't come to no good, always talkin'," she moaned, because she never had any of the things she might have had, an automobile, a silk dress for Sunday. He looked at her patting her arm as if he had long since forgotten her. He looked at Pen though, he took her hands, "Don't forget," he said but the time was short with him now and he looked as if he had much more to be saying but had to go. "Those god-damned bastards," he said and his body flew up as if a pulley jerked him from the chest, then fell down as if released, as if the skin began to fall clean to the bone now, his cheeks sinking down where he was too lean from bad food and not enough of it until before their eyes between one word and another his breathing stopped.

II

Back in the room above the barber shop Mona sobbed, "Poor Tim. . .Poor Tim. . .," but not for him but for some obscure loss more terrible, because they had not been "successful." The grandmother kept spilling the milk and trying to cut a hunk of dried bread off which a mouse had already eaten. "Eat. . . Eat. . .," she kept on saying, licking her lips, her bad eye running water as if weeping alone, unknown to her. "Men . . . men . . .," she said bitterly and her broken pelvis hung half to her knees from childbearing, from working in textile mills, from berry-picking and tobacco-hoeing.

She held the glass of milk to Pen. The light struck off her great flanks. The thick flesh moving slowly upon itself, the gimlet eyes looking out. What was buried there? What girl? What bright youth? Face peering around, caught in the torso like a burr.

"Mother, who was he?"

"Who?"

"My father? Where did he come from?"

"He was born in Indiana. I wisht he had a dress suit."

"A dress suit," the grandmother snorted, "Oh my god."

Mona laughed. They both laughed. Penelope looked up startled, saw the two huge women's throats and bodies thrust back, wild laughter and wild grief festering in them, lost women. Penelope sat small and thin, her knuckles caught between the knobs of her knees, thinking. The many dead in each, the many dead lying in mounds over the middle states. Who lies dead in you? Where are cousins, uncles? Where are faces to see, hands to touch? Where?

III

"Why, you have cousins in Butte, in Des Moines. Let me see, doesn't that fifth son of Uncle Ev live in Kentucky now?"

"God knows, Mama, God knows."

"Yes, sir, it do beat all how they scatter, it do beat all. Yes, sir, we ought to write tell them he is dead — but they never knew him much and that's a fact. . .but we ought to write. . . ."

The grandmother went to an old candy box and took out the six old pictures. Penelope had seen them, thumbed them, but now she looked closely to see some trace of that dead man, father, soon to be in the earth.

There was no mark on them except on the back the name of the photographer. . . J. A. Edmiston, Bushnell, Illinois. . . M. C. Stanley, Ann Arbor, Michigan, where they had stopped on a sunny day, felt her need perhaps, the need of Penelope not yet born, gone in, sat down, had their heads vised, sat for a moment to make a mark of their passing which she now held in her hand. Who are you? What did you have to say? What did you know? And they made no answer, lost and dead, they would never tell, even if they knew.

They spoke only for that one moment, looking out like dreamers, like sleepwalkers, they had known a moment of ease in hard riding lives, when, the swift winded movement stopped, they had sat in a moment of ease and dream.

Penelope looked at them to know which way to let the seed of her own life blow, to find some mark abruptly ended that she could catch from her father, take on with her giving direction across prairies.

There was Grandmother Gregory. Her own grandmother leaned over, her dirty spatulate thumb on the tiny picture, "She was a woman I heard quoted all my life. Grandfather married her straight from Ireland, so Irish when they sent her out for corn she began digging in the ground for it. . . ." Penelope saw a woman whose old body was like a pod where the seed has flown, frail in age, delicate again and insubstantial as a girl — as if instead of being matured and made abundant by bearing five sons and four daughters she had been ravaged by a ghost, worn away by a dream at once fatal and tender, inwardly ravished by a melancholy that became like love, sublimated in longings that could never be fulfilled in this world. Her eyes looked far away in fanatical consecration to an ideal world, as if everything her hand touched in the real world failed and withered, while fruits grew heavy and honey flowed in the streets of the promised land. She had borne sons and daughters who became lawyers, doctors, witches, breaking the land, felling trees, surveying new land, going mad at religious bacchanals in Ohio, but all going a swift tense pace, so fast as not to be remembered, going out in a bright flash without trail.

Penelope had come to think of Grandmother Gregory's children as running weeds on the prairie, that travel a hundred miles in the wind to plant their seeds in another place. John married a girl in Kentucky and was a doctor. Emma was a harlot who married a butcher. Bernice was like her father and was a missionary. Two of the boys went to sea and sent home things from foreign lands.

"And this is one of her girls and my mother," Penelope's grandmother said, and they both looked down into the face of a stern and angry woman with a mouth tasting of bitter drouth, and a tempest in her which never gave way to any peace. Penelope looked up from the picture and saw that both Mona and her grandmother and this woman in the picture were made that way by the hatred of their men, but she could not ask why feeling that brew would be in herself and then she would know and never be cured of it.

From that childbed of a virgin had come hunters, trappers, killers, bitter women, along with stillborn babes and boys who tramped the prairies, pushing further west, to tramp, ride, plant a seed, pushing the margins back and back and secretly preparing for a great destiny, which never came to them.

The next picture was of her first son, Herbert. Penelope knew what a wild one he had been, and his picture spoke no lie for him now, showing a fierce man, reared back with a glowing belief that shone in his torso and in his eyes cutting down with a fine knowing, as if he had something to ask, going wild and drunken over a dark continent, lusting for the blood of righteousness. Black hair curled over his round skull and the thick brush of beard was thrust from his fair and awe-full face.

Penelope knew how he had been with John Brown at Harpers Ferry. The women spoke of it bitterly saying he had twenty scars already from Kansas warfare but the women thought it was only a disgrace for their world.

There he was, the only one who seemed more than a phantom with a grievance, as if he touched something and was willing to be seen, bearing witness to this far lost girl for the blood of his belief. The others, beside him, seemed never to have died even as if they might have their ghostly presence somewhere still, perfect, enclosed like some wild animal in a new country, the mystery intact, seeking a grievance to explain themselves. He seemed about to lift his hand from where it hung unseen in the picture, to speak to her and to her dead father, the unknown word, to form that meaning over the prairies, the cities, villages, making a meaning of fire stand up over them. She saw the way the wind of the prairies had shaped that skull and that grimace and imagined or hoped to see a likeness in her father now with his spare face and grotesque look of lostness and fatigue.

She had looked at this picture in this same wonder, at all that was left of such a man, looking and asking of his face in Oskaloosa, in Orleans, in the tobacco country, in the cotton, hog, corn countries. . . .

IV

There was not one word of what they had felt, not one record, even on these remote and earth-dreaming faces.

The next the grandmother turned over was a tintype of a gentle amused man, his cheeks tinted pink by the photographer, with a wide head, a stiff beard, a coat too big for him so he rested easy in it, bending a little forward, leaning to that future. He was sitting on a horsehair couch leaning on his arm.

"That's McGavery, my old man," the grandmother said. "He was in Iowa when I married him. I was teaching school then. . . ."

Oh, how did you know him? What was there? What did you say to him? What was there between you?

"He had a grand funeral if I do say it." She was quiet a moment and they could hear Mona sobbing. "Yes, that's Samuel. That's him." She leaned over and the truth was that she could hardly see the picture at all. It blurred and moved away and then came too close, she only knew it at all from the position of the body like a design. "That's Samuel," she said again looking over her glasses. "I left him after twenty years and never saw him again until the funeral."

Penelope looked over at Mona lying on the bed, sobbing.

There was no remembering, as if the will was set against it, as if such memory would be a menace. Mona and herself and her grandmother would go down like the rest, grim mouths speaking no word, with the cry that would be praise or calumny unheard. They would bear it like a martyr, as a matter of forbearance of some mischance of which they would say nothing, shut in like stars and darkness, without record of their service or their love, through anxiety and fear.

Penelope could hear the sound of wagon wheels over frozen ruts, of men shouting and women screaming, but words she could not hear, the moments of these men and women were now fled without record, each gone moment heavy to their breaths, weighting the eyelids, making the lifted hand momentous. She senses that rising and falling breast harvest of men and women who had thrown her forward, leaving no word.

Leaving only the shadow of many departures, of many journeys, many arrivals, and all without chronicle. Is there no letter saying we have arrived or we are going on the next journey? Was such a letter lost, destroyed? You cannot go over half a continent on horseback carrying letters, and if such letters said only, "We have arrived, all is well, hope you are the same" — less reason to carry them at all.

Was there no word spoken, no gesture made, no stone, no grave?

"Is anyone buried here we know?" Penelope would ask going through a town, stopping at a tourist camp.

Her grandmother answering, "You do beat all."

Is there then no grave? Men going across like wind over the wheat, their footsteps as ghostly as that. GRANDMOTHER? WHERE WAS IT? WHAT SPOKE TO YOU? WHERE HAVE YOU COME FROM?

Her grandmother saying, they were thus and so; they lived here, they moved there because a mine had opened, because new territory was opening at the shot of a gun; because it was good cattle country, because gold was discovered, or there was adventure, women, safety, risk — and here they died of safety or risk or dream or poison.

BUT WHAT DID THEY SAY? WHAT DID THEY KNOW?

Gold was tied up in Lucinda's skirt worth twenty thousand and it was a cold day when they took off for the funeral of Uncle Rolf and the family fighting over the household furniture before he was cold.

"Who is she?" Penelope asked, for in her hand was a picture of a grim woman rising out of her full skirts and sleeves and curving bodice, a baby who was to die curved in her arm, looking at nothing, its bald head between embryo and death. The woman did not look at the child, let it fall loosely in her lap as if it could not have been the Christ child, or any child worth much, giving it over to death more than to life, and looking out, her mouth grimly set, blighted already by the spirit's longing.

"Who is she?"

"I don't know who she is at all."

A chill went over Penelope, "Hasn't she any name? Didn't anybody know her?"

"If she had a name I don't know it," her grandmother said.

"How do you have the picture then?"

"I don't know how, some woman of the men folks probably — some wench."

They both leaned over looking at the picture while they could hear Mona sobbing from the bed.

Her grandmother snickered over the next picture, "That's me," she snorted, "Just afore I married Samuel. My you wouldn't believe it. A handsome one, I was." And there she was buried now in an accretion through which you might cut and still find that lovely girl within the mighty folds of flesh. In the picture the curls were drawn back, falling to the slender shoulders and the buxom breast; the full lips were smiling, waiting for that future that would never come, the eyes eager that were now crafty, the face thrusting forward to touch cheeks, the hands ready to greet other hands, "Yes, that was just afore I married Samuel, just afore. . . ."

Penelope looked up into the small crafty eyes, "Samuel that no account. If I'd known what I do now about men it would a been different. Men. . . men. . .," she sneered.

Then she told again how she got the better of Samuel when he came crawling back that night before he died, wanting her to take him back, and how she let him lie down behind the broom hedge, without even stopping the supper and the children peeking around the curtains trying to see him there. As if she was only glad to remember in order to deride him.

The grandmother seemed like a woman triumphant, flushed with victory because she had them all buried, and they giving her no meaning to trouble her. She was proud of this, and wore it like a banner of death and silence more terrible than the dead father at the undertaker's, so that a fear came into Penelope of her own future, lest it fall into such an abyss and touch nothing. The fear was in her for those she did not know and for those she knew, walking like sleepers that one word of rebellion could awaken.

V

In another candy box the grandmother had put away pieces of quilting, a snapshot of an old wooden house where she had been born, it was covered with grapevine and for a moment a woman had looked up from the doorway straight out of the picture. There were a few letters and postcards from her own sons whom she never saw anymore and heard only rumors whether they were alive or dead, had gone to this country or that, having from them now only old postcards of old journeys saying, "Dear mother, how are you, your loving son J. P. McGavern." There were postcards from the Grand Canyon, from San Francisco, from the opening of the Panama Canal, with cheery quips on the backs, saying "Well, here we are." The last picture she put back was of a rakish-looking boy with his head over the hump of a papier mâché camel at Coney Island as if to prove that nothing really happened at all.

"It beats all," the grandmother was saying, "It beats all how they've scattered. Why they're not two of them in the same place. My children are all lost somewheres as if they'd never come."

"There's us," Penelope said hugging herself with her thin arms.

"Us!" her grandmother snorted her great flesh shaking. "For the Lord's sake, two women and a half." And she chuckled noiselessly and it didn't sound much different than Mona's low sobbing from the bed.

Mona never looked at these pictures but slept and moved in a dark wild squalor, saying nothing.

Who would speak for them, then, now her father would lie prone in the Kansas soil like the man who had been killed at Harpers Ferry? Penelope stood up watching the pictures being folded away, her mouth open, the breath coming sweetly into her living body, looking up, wanting to be, hearing her grandmother running on about what had been.

"The men were no accounts running here and there, always off to the ends of the earth, I'll swear. That no account Samuel, I guess my kids take after him, every hide and hair of 'em. I never saw him after I left him except lying dead like Tim is now." Mona burst out sobbing louder and Penelope saw the way her body lifted up on itself like a worm that has been cut into. "My youngest came in one evening and said, 'Father's down behind the hedge.' Come back as big as you please. I recollect it was just supper time. Did I go? Well, not so's you could notice it and him leaving me every time I had a chap and going off to the gold fields, the corn fields, the wheat fields, God knows where. I never saw or heard of him again until he was dead at Joliet and then I done the decent thing by him."

She put the lids on the candy boxes and bore them away with her into the next room leaving Penelope sitting in the room with that huge mound of mother, whose windy sides had stretched over her, wild, dark, and angry, and her convulsed body looked as if it ran hugely from violence to violence. She heard the great steps of her grandmother in the next room and knew she was buried in the long accretion of her desires and had been thrown forward deep into the flesh by a cursing, striding race, thrust from powerful women and men who were in fear and terror of a flight they had to take, across unknown prairies having no myth and no speech, upon which they were forced into endless action without word, fighting, brawling, conceiving without song.

And FATHER, too, a vain man, but glancing off, leaving no mark as father or as man, who would now lie beneath Kansas earth with all the lean desperadoes and she could hear his speech now a murmur without words and would see the lean bodies of other men like his, leaning over a fence, talking on a corner, all making a sharp pain in her knowing their defeat and their poor fright, hearing words now from cotton picking time to fruit picking and wheat harvesting, through Pawnee and Georgia and Tennessee, lean men, standing alone and bitter, fleeing from their women, lifting a hand to stress a point, voices droning from

Omaha to Chicago, across Iowa, Illinois, Indiana, and the Dakotas. . . .
Our fathers. . . .

She sat quite still and her grandmother began to rock and sing
from the next room —

> Jeeesus lover of my soul
> Let me to thy bosom fly. . .

Like an old wolf baying. The only love songs she had ever had.

> Now wash me and I shall be whiter than snow,
> whiter than snow, yes. . .
> whiter than snow. . .
> Now wash me and I shall be whiter than snow.

This her only urgency. "I'll go where you want me to go, dear Lord,"
and never going an inch along with Samuel.

"My life and love I give to Thee. . .," she quavered changing from
song to song, knowing only one verse or perhaps only one line of each.
And she never gave her life to a living one though they hungered and
Samuel so derided, her will mowing him down, like a spouse of the
Lord being betrayed by earth's little men.

Mona turned over and let her arms fling upwards. Penelope sat
leaning over her knees to stop the pain in her thin stomach. Her grandmother kept rocking. The street cars scraped through the heat below,
clanging sharply as if ploughing right through the room. Soon it would
be time to go to the funeral parlor. The long howl of her grandmother
followed and fell through the body of Penelope as she hungered.

> I need Thee,
> O I need Thee,
> Every hour I need Thee. . .

An anguish came to the girl listening and she bent over thinking
she was about to die.

YOUR HUSBAND IS DOWN DEHIND THE HEDGE. LET HIM LIE. HE IS DURNK
BEHIND THE BROOM BUSHES AND THE SUN IS GOING DOWN. WON'T YOU GO?
DON'T LET THE POTATOES BURN, MARK. DON'T LET THE BEANS BOIL DRY, LUCE.
. . . WHERE? WHERE? THERE? RIGHT BEHIND THAT FLOWERING BROOM TO THE
RIGHT OF THE PEAR TREE. HE'S WAITING. TRIM YOUR WICKS. FILL YOUR LAMPS
WITH OIL. THE BRIDEGROOM COMETH. . . . THAT COULDN'T BE HIM BEHIND
THE HEDGE NOW COULD IT? THAT BUM? THAT WASTREL? THAT LIVING MAN?
THAT NO ACCOUNT SAMUEL. THAT COULDN'T BE HIM. . . .

Mona sat up magnificent and wild, rocking and crying. "Poor Tim.
Poor Tim. . .," weeping not for the living man but only for the dead.

"Land sakes," said her grandmother, "How time goes. It's time we
got ready to go to the parlors. Get your good dress on, Pen. What will
people say? Mona, pull yourself together."

Pen looked at the two women with hate because they did not see what was going to happen, what her father saw and John Brown. . . . She began to cry and beat her fists together. . . . I won't go. . . . I won't go. . . . Her mouth tore open. Mona and her grandmother began to strike her. She saw their wild torn faces and she could not hear but saw the screams tearing like bright threads from their tortured mouths, from their distressed faces rising above her. . . . They began to beat her to relieve themselves. . . .

"My father. . .," she screamed crouching down, "Our fathers. . .," she screamed, "Our fathers. . . ."

ANNUNCIATION

FOR RACHEL

Ever since I have known I was going to have a child I have kept writing things down on these little scraps of paper. There is something I want to say, something I want to make clear for myself and others. One lives all one's life in a sort of way, one is alive and that is about all that there is to say about it. Then something happens.

There is the pear tree I can see in the afternoons as I sit on this porch writing these notes. It stands for something. It has had something to do with what has happened to me. I sit here all afternoon in the autumn sun and then I begin to write something on this yellow paper; something seems to be going on like a buzzing, a flying and circling within me, and then I want to write it down in some way. I have never felt this way before, except when I was a girl and was first in love and wanted then to set things down on paper so that they would not be lost. It is something perhaps like a farmer who hears the swarming of a host of bees and goes out to catch them so that he will have honey. If he does not go out right away, they will go, and he will hear the buzzing growing more distant in the afternoon.

My sweater pocket is full of scraps of paper on which I have written. I sit here many afternoons while Karl is out looking for work, writing on pieces of paper, unfolding, reading what I have already written.

We have been here two weeks at Mrs. Mason's boarding house. The leaves are falling and there is a golden haze over everything. This is the fourth month for me and it is fall. A rich powerful haze comes down from the mountains over the city. In the afternoon I go out for a walk. There is a park just two blocks from here. Old men and tramps lie on the grass all day. It is hard to get work. Many people besides Karl are out of work. People are hungry just as I am hungry. People are ready to flower and they cannot. In the evenings we go there with a sack of old fruit we can get at the stand across the way quite cheap, bunches of grapes and old pears. At noon there is a hush in the air and at evening there are stirrings of wind coming from the sky, blowing in the fallen leaves, or perhaps there is a light rain, falling quickly on the walk. Early in the mornings the sun comes up hot in the sky and shines all day through the mist. It is strange, I notice all these things, the sun, the rain falling, the blowing of the wind. It is as if they had a meaning for me as the pear tree has come to have.

In front of Mrs. Mason's house there is a large magnolia tree with its blossoms yellow, hanging over the steps almost within reach. Its giant leaves are motionless and shining in the heat, occasionally as I am going down the steps toward the park one falls heavily on the walk.

This house is an old wooden one, that once was quite a mansion I imagine. There are glass chandeliers in the hall and fancy tile in the bathrooms. It was owned by the rich once and now the dispossessed live in it with the rats. We have a room three flights up. You go into the dark hallway and up the stairs. Broken settees and couches sit in the halls. About one o'clock the girls come down stairs to get their mail and sit on the front porch. The blinds go up in the old wooden house across the street. It is always quite hot at noon.

Next to our room lies a sick woman in what is really a kind of closet with no windows. As you pass you see her face on the pillow and a nauseating odor of sickness comes out the door. I haven't asked her what is the matter with her but everyone knows she is waiting for death. Somehow it is not easy to speak to her. No one comes to see her. She has been a housemaid all her life tending other people's children; now no one comes to see her. She gets up sometimes and drinks a little from the bottle of milk that is always sitting by her bed covered with flies.

Mrs. Mason, the landlady, is letting us stay although we have only paid a week's rent and have been here over a week without paying. But it is a bad season and we may be able to pay later. It is better perhaps for her than having an empty room. But I hate to go out and have to pass her door and I am always fearful of meeting her on the stairs. I go down as quietly as I can but it isn't easy, for the stairs creak frightfully.

The room we have on the top floor is a back room, opening out onto an old porch which seems to be actually tied to the wall of the house with bits of wire and rope. The floor of it slants downward to a rickety railing. There is a box perched on the railing that has geraniums in it. They are large, tough California geraniums. I guess nothing can kill them. I water them since I have been here and a terribly red flower has come. It is on this porch I am sitting. Just over the banisters stand the top branches of a pear tree.

Many afternoons I sit here. It has become a kind of alive place to me. The room is dark behind me, with only the huge walnut tree scraping against the one window over the kitchenette. If I go to the railing and look down I can see far below the back yard which has been made into a garden with two fruit trees and I can see where a path has gone in the summer between a small bed of flowers, now only dead stalks. The ground is bare under the walnut tree where little sun penetrates. There is a dog kennel by the round trunk but there doesn't ever seem to be a dog. An old wicker chair sits outdoors in rain or shine. A woman in an old wrapper comes out and sits there almost every afternoon. I don't know who she is, for I don't know anybody in this house, having to sneak downstairs as I do.

Karl says I am foolish to be afraid of the landlady. He comes home drunk and makes a lot of noise. He says she's lucky in these times to have anybody in her house, but I notice in the mornings he goes down the stairs quietly and often goes out the back way.

I'm alone all day so I sit on this rickety porch. Straight out from the rail so that I can almost touch it is the radiating frail top of the pear tree that has opened a door for me. If the pears were still hanging on it each would be alone and separate with a kind of bloom upon it. Such a bloom is upon me at this moment. Is it possible that everyone, Mrs. Mason who runs this boarding house, the woman next door, the girls downstairs, all in this dead wooden house have hung at one time, each separate in a mist and bloom upon some invisible tree? I wonder if it is so.

I am in luck to have this high porch to sit on and this tree swaying before me through the long afternoons and the long nights. Before we came here, after the show broke up in S.F. we were in an old hotel, a foul-smelling place with a dirty chambermaid and an old cat in the halls, and night and day we could hear the radio going in the office. We had a room with a window looking across a narrow way into another room where a lean man stood in the mornings looking across, shaving his evil face. By leaning out and looking up I could see straight up the sides of the tall building and above the smoky sky.

Most of the time I was sick from the bad food we ate. Karl and I walked the streets looking for work. Sometimes I was too sick to go. Karl would come in and there would be no money at all. He would go out again to perhaps borrow something. I know many times he begged although we never spoke of it, but I could tell by the way he looked when he came back with a begged quarter. He went in with a man selling Mexican beans but he didn't make much. I lay on the bed bad days feeling sick and hungry, sick too with the stale odor of the foul walls. I would lie there a long time listening to the clang of the city outside. I would feel thick with this child. For some reason I remember that I would sing to myself and often became happy as if mesmerized there in the foul room. It must have been because of this child. Karl would come back perhaps with a little money and we would go out to a dairy lunch and there have food I could not relish. The first alleyway I must give it up with the people all looking at me.

Karl would be angry. He would walk on down the street so people wouldn't think he was with me. Once we walked until evening down by the docks. "Why don't you take something?" he kept saying. "Then you wouldn't throw up your food like that. Get rid of it. That's what everybody does nowadays. This isn't the time to have a child. Everything is rotten. We must change it." He kept on saying, "Get rid of it. Take something why don't you?" And he got angry when I didn't say anything but just walked along beside him. He shouted so loud at me that some stevedores loading a boat for L.A. laughed at us and began kidding us, thinking perhaps we were lovers having a quarrel.

Some time later, I don't know how long it was, for I hadn't any time except the nine months I was counting off, but one evening Karl sold enough Mexican jumping beans at a carnival to pay our fare, so we got on a river boat and went up the river to a delta town. There might be a better chance of a job. On this boat you can sit up all night if you have no money to buy a berth. We walked all evening along the deck and then when it got cold we went into the saloon because we had pawned our coats. Already at that time I had got the habit of carrying slips of paper around with me and writing on them, as I am doing now. I had a feeling then that something was happening to me of some kind of loveliness I would want to preserve in some way. Perhaps that was it. At any rate I was writing things down. Perhaps it had something to do with Karl wanting me all the time to take something. "Everybody does it," he kept telling me. "It's nothing, then it's all over." I stopped talking to him much. Everything I said only made him angry. So writing was a kind of conversation I carried on with myself and with the child.

Well, on the river boat that night after we had gone into the saloon to get out of the cold, Karl went to sleep right away in a chair. But I couldn't sleep. I sat watching him. The only sound was the churning of the paddle wheel and the lap of the water. I had on then this sweater and the notes I wrote are still in the breast pocket. I would look up from writing and see Karl sleeping like a young boy.

"Tonight, the world into which you are coming"—then I was speaking to the invisible child—"is very strange and beautiful. That is, the natural world is beautiful. I don't know what you will think of man, but the dark glisten of vegetation and the blowing of the fertile land wind and the delicate strong step of the sea wind, these things are familiar to me and will be familiar to you. I hope you will be like these things. I hope you will glisten with the glisten of ancient life, the same beauty that is in a leaf or a wild rabbit, wild sweet beauty of limb and eye. I am going on a boat between dark shores, and the river and the sky are so quiet that I can hear the scurryings of tiny animals on the shores and their little breathings seem to be all around. I think of them, wild, carrying their young now, crouched in the dark underbrush with the fruit-scented land wind in their delicate nostrils, and they are looking out at the moon and the fast clouds. Silent, alive, they sit in the dark shadow of the greedy world. There is something wild about us too, something tender and wild about my having you as a child, about your crouching so secretly here. There is something very tender and wild about it. We, too, are at the mercy of many hunters. On this boat I act like the other human beings, for I do not show that I have you, but really I know we are as helpless, as wild, as at bay as some tender wild animals who might be on the ship.

"I put my hand where you lie so silently. I hope you will come glistening with life power, with it shining upon you as upon the feathers of birds. I hope you will be a warrior and fierce for change, so all can live."

Karl woke at dawn and was angry with me for sitting there looking at him. Just to look at me makes him angry now. He took me out and made me walk along the deck although it was hardly light yet. I gave him the "willies" he said, looking at him like that. We walked round and round the decks and he kept talking to me in a low voice, trying to persuade me. It was hard for me to listen. My teeth were chattering with cold, but anyway I found it hard to listen to anyone talking, especially Karl. I remember I kept thinking to myself that a child should be made by machinery now, then there would be no fuss. I kept thinking of all the places I had been with this new child, traveling with the show from Tia Juana to S.F. In trains, over mountains, through deserts, in hotels and rooming houses, and myself in a trance of wonder. There wasn't a person I could have told it to, that I was going to have a child. I didn't want to be pitied. Night after night we played in the tent and the faces were all dust to me, but traveling, through the window the many vistas of the earth meant something — the bony skeleton of the mountains, like the skeleton of the world jutting through its flowery flesh. My child too would be made of bone. There were the fields of summer, the orchards fruiting, the berry fields and the pickers stooping, the oranges and the grapes. Then the city again in September and the many streets I walk looking for work, stopping secretly in doorways to feel beneath my coat.

It is better in this small town with the windy fall days and the sudden rain falling out of a sunny sky. I can't look for work any more. Karl gets a little work washing dishes at a wienie place. I sit here on the porch as if in a deep sleep waiting for this unknown child. I keep hearing this far flight of strange birds going on in the mysterious air about me. This time has come without warning. How can it be explained? Everything is dead and closed, the world a stone, and then suddenly everything comes alive as it has for me, like an anemone on a rock, opening itself, disclosing itself, and the very stones themselves break open like bread. It has all got something to do with the pear tree too. It has come about some way as I have sat here with this child so many afternoons, with the pear tree murmuring in the air.

The pears are all gone from the tree but I imagine them hanging there, ripe curves within the many scimitar leaves, and within them many pears of the coming season. I feel like a pear. I hang secret within the curling leaves, just as the pear would be hanging on its tree. It seems possible to me that perhaps all people at some time feel this, round and full. You can tell by looking at most people that the world remains a stone to them and a closed door. I'm afraid it will become like that to me again. Perhaps after this child is born, then everything will harden and become small and mean again as it was before. Perhaps I would even have a hard time remembering this time at all and it wouldn't seem wonderful. That is why I would like to write it down.

How can it be explained? Suddenly many movements are going on within me, many things are happening, there is an almost unbearable sense of sprouting, of bursting encasements, of moving kernels, expanding flesh. Perhaps it is such an activity that makes a field come alive with millions of sprouting shoots of corn or wheat. Perhaps it is something like that that makes a new world.

I have been sitting here and it seems as if the wooden houses around me had become husks that suddenly as I watched began to swarm with livening seed. The house across becomes a fermenting seed alive with its own movements. Everything seems to be moving along a curve of creation. The alley below and all the houses are to me like an orchard abloom, shaking and trembling, moving outward with shouting. The people coming and going seem to hang on the tree of life, each blossoming from himself. I am standing here looking at the blind windows of the house next door and suddenly the walls fall away, the doors open, and within I see a young girl making a bed from which she had just risen having dreamed of a young man who became her lover. . . she stands before her looking-glass in love with herself.

I see in another room a young man sleeping, his bare arm thrown over his head. I see a woman lying on a bed after her husband has left her. There is a child looking at me. An old woman sits rocking. A boy leans over a table reading a book. A woman who has been nursing a child comes out and hangs clothes on the line, her dress in front wet with milk. A young woman comes to an open door looking up and down the street waiting for her young husband. I get up early to see this young woman come to the door in a pink wrapper and wave to her husband. They have only been married a short time, she stands waving until he is out of sight and even then she stands smiling to herself, her hand upraised.

Why should I be excited? Why should I feel this excitement, seeing a woman waving to her young husband, or a woman who has been nursing a child, or a young man sleeping? Yet I am excited. The many houses have become like an orchard blooming soundlessly. The many

people have become like fruits to me, the young girl in the room alone
before her mirror, the young man sleeping, the mother, all are shaking
with their inward blossoming, shaken by the windy blooming, moving
along a future curve.

I do not want it all to go away from me. Now many doors are
opening and shutting, light is falling upon darkness, closed places are
opening, still things are now moving. But there will come a time when
the doors will close again, the shouting will be gone, the sprouting and
the movement and the wondrous opening out of everything will be
gone. I will be only myself. I will come to look like the women in this
house. I try to write it down on little slips of paper, trying to preserve
this time for myself so that afterwards when everything is the same
again I can remember what all must have.

This is the spring there should be in the world, so I say to myself,
"Lie in the sun with the child in your flesh shining like a jewel. Dream
and sing, pagan, wise in your vitals. Stand still like a fat budding tree,
like a stalk of corn athrob and aglisten in the heat. Lie like a mare panting with the dancing feet of colts against her sides. Sleep at night as the
spring earth. Walk heavily as a wheat stalk at its full time bending
toward the earth waiting for the reaper. Let your life swell downward
so you become like a vase, a vessel. Let the unknown child knock and
knock against you and rise like a dolphin within."

I look at myself in the mirror. My legs and head hardly make a difference, just a stem my legs. My hips are full and tight in back as if
bracing themselves. I look like a pale and shining pomegranate, hard
and tight, and my skin shines like crystal with the veins showing
beneath blue and distended. Children are playing outside and girls are
walking with young men along the walk. All that seems over for me. I
am a pomegranate hanging from an invisible tree with the juice and
movement of seed within my hard skin. I dress slowly. I hate the smell
of clothes. I want to leave them off and just hang in the sun ripening. . .
ripening.

It is hard to write it down so that it will mean anything. I've never
heard anything about how a women feels who is going to have a child,
or about how a pear tree feels bearing its fruit. I would like to read these
things many years from now, when I am barren and no longer trembling like this, when I get like the women in this house, or like the
woman in the closed room, I can hear her breathing through the afternoon.

When Karl has no money he does not come back at night. I go out
on the street walking to forget how hungry I am. This is an old town
and along the streets are many old strong trees. Night leaves hang from
them ready to fall, dark and swollen with their coming death. Trees,
dark, separate, heavy with their down-hanging leaves, cool surfaces

hanging on the dark. I put my hand among the leaf sheaves. They strike with a cool surface, their glossy surfaces surprising me in the dark. I feel like a tree swirling upwards too, muscular sap alive, with rich surfaces hanging from me, flaring outward rocket-like and falling to my roots, a rich strong power in me to break through into a new life. And dark in me as I walk the streets of this decayed town are the buds of my child. I walk alone under the dark flaring trees. There are many houses with the lights shining out but you and I walk on the skirts of the lawns amidst the down-pouring darkness. Houses are not for us. For us many kinds of hunger, for us a deep rebellion.

Trees come from a far seed walking the wind, my child too from a far seed blowing from last year's rich and revolutionary dead. My child budding secretly from far-walking seed, budding secretly and dangerously in the night.

The woman has come out and sits in the rocker, reading, her fat legs crossed. She scratches herself, cleans her nails, picks her teeth. Across the alley lying flat on the ground is a garage. People are driving in and out. But up here it is very quiet and the movement of the pear tree is the only movement and I seem to hear its delicate sound of living as it moves upon itself silently, and outward and upward.

The leaves twirl and twirl all over the tree, the delicately curving tinkling leaves. They twirl and twirl on the tree and the tree moves far inward upon its stem, moves in an invisible wind, gently swaying. Far below straight down the vertical stem like a stream, black and strong into the ground, runs the trunk; and invisible, spiraling downward and outward in powerful radiation, lie the roots. I can see it spiraling upward from below, its stem straight, and from it, spiraling the branches season by season, and from the spiraling branches moving out in quick motion, the forked stems, and from the stems twirling fragilely the tinier stems holding outward until they fall, the half-curled pear leaves.

Far below lies the yard, lying flat and black beneath the body of the upshooting tree, for the pear tree from above looks as if it had been shot instantaneously from the ground, shot upward like a rocket to break in showers of leaves and fruits twirling and falling. Its movement looks quick, sudden and rocketing. My child when grown can be looked at in this way as if it suddenly existed. . . but I know the slow time of making. The pear tree knows.

Far inside the vertical stem there must be a movement, a river of sap rising from below and radiating outward in many directions clear to the tips of the leaves. The leaves are the lips of the tree speaking in the wind or they move like many tongues. The fruit of the tree you can see has been a round speech, speaking in full tongue on the tree, hanging in ripe body, the fat curves hung within the small curves of the leaves. I imagine them there. The tree has shot up like a rocket, then stops in midair and its leaves flow out gently and its fruit curves roundly and gently in a long slow curve. All is gentle on the pear tree after its strong upward shooting movement.

I sit here all the afternoon as if in its branches, amidst the gentle and curving body of the tree. I have looked at it until it has become more familiar to me than Karl. It seems a strange thing that a tree might come to mean more to one than one's husband. It seems a shameful thing even. I am ashamed to think of it but it is so. I have sat here in the pale sun and the tree has spoken to me with its many tongued leaves, speaking through the afternoon of how to round a fruit. And I listen through the slow hours. I listen to the whispering of the pear tree, speaking to me, speaking to me. How can I describe what is said by a pear tree? Karl did not speak to me so. No one spoke to me in any good speech.

There is a woman coming up the stairs, slowly. I can hear her breathing. I can hear her behind me at the screen door.

She came out and spoke to me. I know why she was looking at me so closely. "I hear you're going to have a child," she said. "It's too bad." She is the same color as the dead leaves in the park. Was she once alive too?

I am writing on a piece of wrapping paper now. It is about ten o'clock. Karl didn't come home and I had no supper. I walked through the streets with their heavy, heavy trees bending over the walks and the lights shining from the houses and over the river the mist rising.

Before I came into this room I went out and saw the pear tree standing motionless, its leaves curled in the dark, its radiating body falling darkly, like a stream far below into the earth.

The Thirties

INTRODUCTION

The thirties were stimulating years for Le Sueur, a time of heightened productivity. Immersed in the radical political activities of the Left, she produced a large amount of both fiction and journalism. She continued to write about the lives of women, and she wrote about a variety of other subjects as well: the unemployment, labor unrest, and strikes of the period; the drought that devastated parts of the Midwest; mining conditions; and both state and national political campaigns. The pieces of reportage about depression women included here, "Women on the Breadlines" and "Women are Hungry," appeared, respectively, in *New Masses* in 1932 and the *American Mercury* in 1934. They contain that combination of deep sympathy and absorbed attention to detail that characterizes Le Sueur's best writing about women in the thirties. Often portraits of individual women are unforgettable. Le Sueur captures their poverty, the relentless monotony and dreariness of their lives, their suffering, and their survival. Such reportage, along with her novel *The Girl*, provides an important record of the lives of women in the 1930s.

"O Prairie Girl Be Lonely" has been called a "flawless embedded narrative" within the novel *The Girl*, which Le Sueur wrote in the thirties but which has only recently been published in full for the first time. ("O Prairie Girl" itself was published separately as a short story in 1945.) The girl of the title, a nameless farm girl driven by the depression to seek work in St. Paul, takes part in a bank robbery with her lover, Butch. The excerpt describes the robbery and the escape, which ends with Butch's death. Butch's long, delirious speech reveals the waste of his life, which has been an unequal scramble for jobs and money within the capitalist system. His has been a more desperate, twentieth-century version of the restless seeking of the pioneer wanderers Le Sueur described in "Our Fathers." The original version of "O Prairie Girl Be Lonely" appears below; Le Sueur revised it for the publication of *The Girl* in 1978.

"Women Know a Lot of Things" was published in March 1937, on the occasion of International Women's Day. More an editorial than a piece of reportage, it suggests who, in the thirties, political and economic events at home and abroad — ranging from the strikes in the United States to the Spanish Civil War to the growing unrest in China — were leading Le Sueur to think of women and their common experi-

ences across both class and national boundaries. In those common experiences of wives, mothers, and workers, Le Sueur finds and defines
sources of women's strength and political power.

"I Was Marching" is probably Le Sueur's best-known piece of
reportage, describing a crucial experience in her life — her participation
in the Minneapolis truckers strike of 1934. Her report describes the
radicalizing effect of the strike on her, her sense of participating in a
new reality that was being forged out of the collective effort of large
masses of people. It conveys her sense, profoundly felt, of getting
beyond the separate self and merging with what she has since called a
"communal sensibility."

Of continuing concern to Le Sueur in the thirties was the plight of
the farmers of her native Midwest. She wrote several pieces of reportage about the dust storms and droughts that swept from Texas to the
Dakotas in 1934 and lasted for more than two years. By 1936, as many
as 90 percent of all farm families in some counties of North Dakota
were on relief. Le Sueur traveled through the stricken areas to witness
and record the human misery. Again, carefully observed detail is informed with sympathy, and report transforms itself into story, complete with suspense and plot, as we watch farmers heroically but futilely
try to deal with the starvation of cattle and the withering crops and
then in despair abandon their land. Images — of children walking with
wet cloths over their faces, of farm wagons loaded with furniture moving through denuded fields, of cattle like "bleached hulks" — convey the
terrible cost in human suffering of the drought.

In contrast, "The Girl" and "Gone Home" come not out of the
economic conditions of the depression but out of Le Sueur's interest in
writing about male-female sexual relations and about female sexuality.
"The Girl" is one of her most successful treatments of the presence and
power of the erotic. Through its rich poetic prose the story creates an
almost hypnotic mood of sensual release. A desire to return to women a
sense of the validity of their bodies is the feminist impulse that lies
behind this and other of Le Sueur's treatments of female sexuality.

But always Le Sueur is aware of the damage that has been
perpetrated by denying the body, and by such exploitation of women
as Butch's in *The Girl* and the men's in "Our Fathers." "Gone Home" is a
further, powerful exploration of some of the ways in which, in
American society, relations between the sexes have been profoundly
destructive. Nearing death and feeling a sense of urgency to do or say
something special before dying, Jonathan Hanks tries to show
tenderness to a frightened and lonely widow. But what Le Sueur calls in
the story the "conditioned enmity between men and women" perverts
tenderness into hostility and leads to a terrifying dénouement.

WOMEN on the BREADLINES

I am sitting in the city free employment bureau. It's the women's section. We have been sitting here now for four hours. We sit here every day, waiting for a job. There are no jobs. Most of us have had no breakfast. Some have had scant rations for over a year. Hunger makes a human being lapse into a state of lethargy, especially city hunger. Is there any place else in the world where a human being is supposed to go hungry amidst plenty without an outcry, without protest, where only the boldest steal or kill for bread, and the timid crawl the streets, hunger like the beak of a terrible bird at the vitals?

We sit looking at the floor. No one dares think of the coming winter. There are only a few more days of summer. Everyone is anxious to get work to lay up something for that long siege of bitter cold. But there is no work. Sitting in the room we all know it. That is why we don't talk much. We look at the floor dreading to see that knowledge in each other's eyes. There is a kind of humiliation in it. We look away from each other. We look at the floor. It's too terrible to see this animal terror in each other's eyes.

So we sit hour after hour, day after day, waiting for a job to come in. There are many women for a single job. A thin sharp woman sits inside a wire cage looking at a book. For four hours we have watched her looking at that book. She has a hard little eye. In the small bare room there are half a dozen women sitting on the benches waiting. Many come and go. Our faces are all familiar to each other, for we wait here every day.

This is a domestic employment bureau. Most of the women who come here are middle-aged, some have families, some have raised their families and are now alone, some have men who are out of work. Hard times and the man leaves to hunt for work. He doesn't find it. He drifts on. The woman probably doesn't hear from him for a long time. She expects it. She isn't surprised. She struggles alone to feed the many mouths. Sometimes she gets help from the charities. If she's clever she can get herself a good living from the charities, if she's naturally a lick spittle, naturally a little docile and cunning. If she's proud then she starves silently, leaving her children to find work, coming home after a day's searching to wrestle with her house, her children.

Some such story is written on the faces of all these women. There are young girls too, fresh from the country. Some are made brazen too

soon by the city. There is a great exodus of girls from the farms into the
city now. Thousands of farms have been vacated completely in Minnesota. The girls are trying to get work. The prettier ones can get jobs
in the stores when there are any, or waiting on table, but these jobs are
only for the attractive and the adroit. The others, the real peasants,
have a more difficult time.

Bernice sits next to me. She is a Polish woman of thirty-five. She
has been working in people's kitchens for fifteen years or more. She is
large, her great body in mounds, her face brightly scrubbed. She has a
peasant mind and finds it hard even yet to understand the maze of the
city where trickery is worth more than brawn. Her blue eyes are not
clever but slow and trusting. She suffers from loneliness and lack of
talk. When you speak to her, her face lifts and brightens as if you had
spoken through a great darkness, and she talks magically of little things
as if the weather were magic, or tells some crazy tale of her adventures
on the city streets, embellishing them in bright colors until they hang
heavy and thick like embroidery. She loves the city anyhow. It's exciting to her, like a bazaar. She loves to go shopping and get a bargain,
hunting out the places where stale bread and cakes can be had for a few
cents. She likes walking the streets looking for men to take her to a picture show. Sometimes she goes to five picture shows in one day, or she
sits through one the entire day until she knows all the dialog by heart.

She came to the city a young girl from a Wisconsin farm. The first
thing that happened to her, a charlatan dentist took out all her good
shining teeth and the fifty dollars she had saved working in a canning
factory. After that she met men in the park who told her how to look
out for herself, corrupting her peasant mind, teaching her to mistrust
everyone. Sometimes now she forgets to mistrust everyone and gets
taken in. They taught her to get what she could for nothing, to count
her change, to go back if she found herself cheated, to demand her
rights.

She lives alone in little rooms. She bought seven dollars' worth of
second-hand furniture eight years ago. She rents a room for perhaps
three dollars a month in an attic, sometimes in a cold house. Once the
house where she stayed was condemned and everyone else moved out
and she lived there all winter alone on the top floor. She spent only
twenty-five dollars all winter.

She wants to get married but she sees what happens to her married
friends, left with children to support, worn out before their time. So she
stays single. She is virtuous. She is slightly deaf from hanging out
clothes in winter. She had done people's washing and cooking for fifteen years and in that time saved thirty dollars. Now she hasn't worked
steady for a year and she has spent the thirty dollars. She had dreamed

of having a little house or a houseboat perhaps with a spot of ground for a few chickens. This dream she will never realize.

She has lost all her furniture now along with the dream. A married friend whose husband is gone gives her a bed for which she pays by doing a great deal of work for the woman. She comes here every day now sitting bewildered, her pudgy hands folded in her lap. She is hungry. Her great flesh has begun to hang in folds. She has been living on crackers. Sometimes a box of crackers lasts a week. She has a friend who's a baker and he sometimes steals the stale loaves and brings them to her.

A girl we have seen every day all summer went crazy yesterday at the YW. She went into hysterics, stamping her feet and screaming.

She hadn't had work for eight months. "You've got to give me something," she kept saying. The woman in charge flew into a rage that probably came from days and days of suffering on her part, because she is unable to give jobs, having none. She flew into a rage at the girl and there they were facing each other in a rage both helpless, helpless. This woman told me once that she could hardly bear the suffering she saw, hardly hear it, that she couldn't eat sometimes and had nightmares at night.

So they stood there, the two women, in a rage, the girl weeping and the woman shouting at her. In the eight months of unemployment she had gotten ragged, and the woman was shouting that she would not send her out like that. "Why don't you shine your shoes?" she kept scolding the girl, and the girl kept sobbing and sobbing because she was starving.

"We can't recommend you like that," the harassed YWCA woman said, knowing she was starving, unable to do anything. And the girls and the women sat docilely, their eyes on the ground, ashamed to look at each other, ashamed of something.

Sitting here waiting for a job, the women have been talking in low voices about the girl Ellen. They talk in low voices with not too much pity for her, unable to see through the mist of their own torment. "What happened to Ellen?" one of them asks. She knows the answer already. We all know it.

A young girl who went around with Ellen tells about seeing her last evening back of a cafe downtown, outside the kitchen door, kicking, showing her legs so that the cook came out and gave her some food and some men gathered in the alley and threw small coin on the ground for a look at her legs. And the girl says enviously that Ellen had a swell breakfast and treated her to one too, that cost two dollars.

A scrub woman whose hips are bent forward from stooping with hands gnarled like watersoaked branches clicks her tongue in disgust.

No one saves their money, she says, a little money and these foolish young things buy a hat, a dollar for breakfast, a bright scarf. And they do. If you've ever been without money, or food, something very strange happens when you get a bit of money, a kind of madness. You don't care. You can't remember that you had no money before, that the money will be gone. You can remember nothing but that there is the money for which you have been suffering. Now here it is. A lust takes hold of you. You see food in the windows. In imagination you eat hugely; you taste a thousand meals. You look in windows. Colors are brighter; you buy something to dress up in. An excitement takes hold of you. You know it is suicide but you can't help it. You must have food, dainty, splendid food, and a bright hat so once again you feel blithe, rid of that ratty gnawing shame.

"I guess she'll go on the street now," a thin woman says faintly, and no one takes the trouble to comment further. Like every commodity now the body is difficult to sell and the girls say you're lucky if you get fifty cents.

It's very difficult and humiliating to sell one's body.

Perhaps it would make it clear if one were to imagine having to go out on the street to sell, say, one's overcoat. Suppose you have to sell your coat so you can have breakfast and a place to sleep, say, for fifty cents. You decide to sell your only coat. You take it off and put it on your arm. The street, that has before been just a street, now becomes a mart, something entirely different. You must approach someone now and admit you are destitute and are now selling your clothes, your most intimate possessions. Everyone will watch you talking to the stranger showing him your overcoat, what a good coat it is. People will stop and watch curiously. You will be quite naked on the street. It is even harder to try to sell one's self, more humiliating. It is even humiliating to try to sell one's labor. When there is no buyer.

The thin woman opens the wire cage. There's a job for a nursemaid, she says. The old gnarled women, like old horses, know that no one will have them walk the streets with the young so they don't move. Ellen's friend gets up and goes to the window. She is unbelievably jaunty. I know she hasn't had work since last January. But she has a flare of life in her that glows like a tiny red flame and some tenacious thing, perhaps only youth, keeps it burning bright. Her legs are thin but the runs in her old stockings are neatly mended clear down her flat shank. Two bright spots of rouge conceal her pallor. A narrow belt is drawn tightly around her thin waist, her long shoulders stoop and the blades show. She runs wild as a colt hunting pleasure, hunting sustenance.

It's one of the great mysteries of the city where women go when they are out of work and hungry. There are not many women in the bread line. There are no flop houses for women as there are for men, where a bed can be had for a quarter or less. You don't see women lying on the floor at the mission in the free flops. They obviously don't sleep in the jungle or under newspapers in the park. There is no law I suppose against their being in these places but the fact is they rarely are.

Yet there must be as many women out of jobs in cities and suffering extreme poverty as there are men. What happens to them? Where do they go? Try to get into the YW without any money or looking down at heel. Charities take care of very few and only those that are called "deserving." The lone girl is under suspicion by the virgin women who dispense charity.

I've lived in cities for many months broke, without help, too timid to get in bread lines. I've known many women to live like this until they simply faint on the street from privations, without saying a word to anyone. A woman will shut herself up in a room until it is taken away from her, and eat a cracker a day and be as quiet as a mouse so there are no social statistics concerning her.

I don't know why it is, but a woman will do this unless she has dependents, will go for weeks verging on starvation, crawling in some hole, going through the streets ashamed, sitting in libraries, parks, going for days without speaking to a living soul like some exiled beast, keeping the runs mended in her stockings, shut up in terror in her own misery, until she becomes too super-sensitive and timid to even ask for a job.

Bernice says even strange men she has met in the park have sometimes, that is in better days, given her a loan to pay her room rent. She has always paid them back.

In the afternoon the young girls, to forget the hunger and the deathly torture and fear of being jobless, try to pick up a man to take them to a ten-cent show. They never go to more expensive ones, but they can always find a man willing to spend a dime to have the company of a girl for the afternoon.

Sometimes a girl facing the night without shelter will approach a man for lodging. A woman always asks a man for help. Rarely another woman. I have known girls to sleep in men's rooms for the night on a pallet without molestation and be given breakfast in the morning.

It's no wonder these young girls refuse to marry, refuse to rear children. They are like certain savage tribes, who, when they have been conquered, refuse to breed.

Not one of them but looks forward to starvation for the coming winter. We are in a jungle and know it. We are beaten, entrapped. There is no way out. Even if there were a job, even if that thin acrid woman came and gave everyone in the room a job for a few days, a few hours, at thirty cents an hour, this would all be repeated tomorrow, the next day and the next.

Not one of these women but knows that despite years of labor there is only starvation, humiliation in front of them.

Mrs. Gray, sitting across from me, is a living spokesman for the futility of labor. She is a warning. Her hands are scarred with labor. Her body is a great puckered scar. She has given birth to six children, buried three, supported them all alive and dead, bearing them, burying them, feeding them. Bred in hunger they have been spare, susceptible to disease. For seven years she tried to save her boy's arm from amputation, diseased from tuberculosis of the bone. It is almost too suffocating to think of that long close horror of years of child-bearing, child-feeding, rearing, with the bare suffering of providing a meal and shelter.

Now she is fifty. Her children, economically insecure, are drifters. She never hears of them. She doesn't know if they are alive. She doesn't know if she is alive. Such subtleties of suffering are not for her. For her the brutality of hunger and cold. Not until these are done away with can those subtle feelings that make a human being be indulged.

She is lucky to have five dollars ahead of her. That is her security. She has a tumor that she will die of. She is thin as a worn dime with her tumor sticking out of her side. She is brittle and bitter. Her face is not the face of a human being. She has borne more than it is possible for a human being to bear. She is reduced to the least possible denominator of human feelings.

It is terrible to see her little bloodshot eyes like a beaten hound's, fearful in terror.

We cannot meet her eyes. When she looks at any of us we look away. She is like a woman drowning and we turn away. We must ignore those eyes that are surely the eyes of a person drowning, doomed. She doesn't cry out. She goes down decently. And we all look away.

The young ones know though. I don't want to marry. I don't want any children. So they all say. No children. No marriage. They arm themselves alone, keep up alone. The man is helpless now. He cannot provide. If he propagates he cannot take care of his young. The means are not in his hands. So they live alone. Get what fun they can. The life risk is too horrible now. Defeat is too clearly written on it.

So we sit in this room like cattle, waiting for a nonexistent job, willing to work to the farthest atom of energy, unable to work, unable to get food and lodging, unable to bear children — here we must sit in this shame looking at the floor, worse than beasts at a slaughter.

It is appalling to think that these women sitting so listless in the room may work as hard as it is possible for a human being to work, may labor night and day, like Mrs. Gray wash streetcars from midnight to dawn and offices in the early evening, scrub for fourteen and fifteen hours a day, sleep only five hours or so, do this their whole lives, and never earn one day of security, having always before them the pit of the future. The endless labor, the bending back, the water-soaked hands, earning never more than a week's wages, never having in their hands more life than that.

It's not the suffering of birth, death, love that the young reject, but the suffering of endless labor without dream, eating the spare bread in bitterness, being a slave without the security of a slave.

WOMEN ARE HUNGRY

Let others sing of the hungry pain of Life,
Let others sing of the hungry pain of love,
I will sing of the hungry pain of hunger.

When you look at the unemployed women and girls you think instantly that there must be some kind of war. The men are gone away from the family; the family is distintegrating; the women try to hold it together, because women have most to do with the vivid life of procreation, food, and shelter. Deprived of their participation in that, they are beggars.

For this reason also they feel want and show it first: poverty is more personal to them than to men. The women looking for jobs or bumming on the road, or that you see waiting for a hand-out from the charities, are already mental cases as well as physical ones. A man can always get drunk, or talk to other men, no matter how broken he is in body and spirit; but a woman, ten to one, will starve alone in a hall bedroom until she is thrown out, and then she will sleep alone in some alley until she is picked up.

When the social fabric begins to give way it gives way from the bottom first. You can look at the bottom and see what is happening and what will continue to happen. The working-class family is going fast. The lower-middle-class family is also going, though not so fast. It is like a landslide. It is like a great chasm opening beneath the feet and swallowing the bottom classes first. The worker who lives from hand to mouth goes first, and then his family goes. The family rots, decays and goes to pieces with the woman standing last, trying to hold it together, and then going too. The man loses his job, cannot find another, then leaves. The older children try to get money, fail, and leave or are taken to the community farms. The mother stays with the little children helped by charity, until they too are sucked under by the diminishing dole and the growing terror.

Where are the women? There is the old woman who has raised her children, and they have all left her now, under the lash of hunger. There is the unattached woman, and the professional one, and the domestic servant. The latter went down two years ago. The professional woman began going down only recently. There are the young school girls — more than a million of them — who were graduated into unemployment two or three years ago. Many of them, particularly those coming from the industrial centers, who never went beyond grammar school, are now hoboes riding on the freights. Their ages run from eight to eighteen. They are the lost children.

You don't see women in bread lines. Statistics make unemployment abstract and not too uncomfortable. The human being is different. To be hungry is different than to count the hungry. There is a whole generation of young girls now who don't remember any boom days and don't believe in any Eldorado, or success, or prosperity. Their thin bones bear witness to a different thing. The women have learned something. Something is seeping into them that is going to make a difference for several generations. Something is happening to them.

II

Old and Young Mothers

We went up three flights of stairs and down a crooked corridor flanked by shut doors. There was not a sound. It was early afternoon. In that house there were about twenty families, and often four lived in one or two rooms, but now everything was pretty quiet. Everybody was taking a nap; the children had not yet come in from school. In the whole building only about five are employed regularly, and about two now and then in the Munsingwear just down the street; the rest are on charity. Six of these families are without men, just holding together like bees, in this huge desolate hive.

Anna, who lives on the top floor, is a cook and supports four people, her mother, sister, and two sons, on her $45 a month. Her man left three years ago to find a job in another city, and at first wrote now and then, and then didn't write at all, and now is lost. Anna comes home every Thursday to see her family, and the rest of the time she does not see them. This is Thursday, and she is home reading out of a Swedish Bible to her mother, who broke her leg last spring.

We listened at the door and then we knocked. The reading stopped. Anna opened the door. Leaning over a round table sat her old mother, her sister, her two blonde sons, and Mrs. Rose. Mrs. Rose is an elderly woman who has raised six tubercular children whose whereabouts she has not known for four years, since they were out of jobs. One was in a foundry in Pittsburgh, another on a wheat ranch in Montana. The other four were on the bum for a while and sometimes wrote her, but now they do not write. Mrs. Rose tries to support herself getting jobs as a housekeeper but has a hard time. Either she doesn't get paid at all or the man tries to sleep with her. She has hair that was hennaed a long time ago. She is lean and bitter and has a great deal of hate in her. She has nothing to do now, so she comes to talk to Anna and her mother in the afternoon and stays to eat there.

Many men have been killed making America. Many were killed laying the railroad, making docks, coal mines, felling the lumber, blasting the land. There were a lot of widows in the last century left to support their children with their physical labor. Everyone remembers many such women even in one small town. They were the women who took in washing, who scrubbed office buildings at nights, or made the party dresses for the merchants' wives and daughters. Everyone remembers many such women and there are many who live in nobody's memory at all.

Anna's mother is such a woman. She had seven children, and her man was killed on the docks in Duluth while she was raising her children on the sand bar. After that she supported them herself, scrubbing office buildings every night until five-thirty. She sent them all through high-school, because in America education would lift them out of the physical labor of her class. Two of her sons were killed riding back and forth from coast to coast on the freight cars. Only one has a little property, a farm, but it is mortgaged and he is likely to lose it at any time now.

They all live in two attic rooms. You can see over the roofs of the town.

They begin to talk, as everyone does, of how to live. It is all nip and tuck. They are used to it, but you never get quite used to being trapped. At any time you may look up with amazement and see that you are trapped. "I've worked all my life," Anna's mother says, "with these arms and hands and sent seven children through high-school and now I can't get enough to eat."

The women all look at one another. The youngest boy, about four, is playing on the floor. The other boy is reading. They all look at the little boy, who looks like his father who was swallowed up, just as if some big crack had opened and swallowed him, or as if a war had devoured him whole. Mrs. Rose has lost all her children like that now. They all seem to be looking at something. Anna gets up to make supper of a sort.

"A person can't get paid nowadays for what a person does," Mrs. Rose says, and she begins telling about the last place she was working in, and the man was a widower with four children, and she worked like a dog for three months without any pay, and bacon rinds cooked with potato peelings most of the time because the garden had burnt up in the sun; and then she couldn't get a cent, not a red cent, and so now she is without work at all, and the cancer growing inside her, and nothing to show for her life and she might as well die.

Anna's mother sits with her broad arms over her stomach. She is full of words about it and pounding the Bible and saying she will write a letter to the President. "It's all in the Bible," she shouts, the tears going down her wrinkled face. "You cannot live by bread alone." She looks at the little boy again. "Anna, we left some milk for him. There will be a glass left. What are you going to feed him?" she cries. "He has got to have milk. You can't make bones with just bread. Everybody knows he has got to have milk."

The women all look at the child. Anna stops by the stove looking at the child. You can't feed a child cream tomorrow to make up for his not having milk today. They know that. Anna goes over and picks him up. It's really to feel his ribs and his legs.

It's hot in the room, all the heat goes up to the attic, and it's turned a bit warm out so they have left the door open, and women keep going by slowly in the hall to the lavatory. They have been going by heavily in the dark hall with swollen faces.

"There are four pregnant women in this attic," Anna's mother says bitterly. "If they knew . . . if they knew . . . they would cut their children out with a butcher knife. . . ."

"Mother!" Anna says. "Sh! they will hear. . . ."

"Better to hear it now than later, and only one has a man working now and then only for the city, and there hasn't been any snow yet this winter to speak of and besides the city is going broke and can't hire so many men."

"What do they do then?"

"Well, when you are going to have a baby you have got to have it. You go ahead and have it, whether a war is going on or not you go right ahead. They got so many women now having babies at the city hospital they only keep them eight days now. The better ones they turn out sooner. They got to have room. It's got so a woman can't have a baby. It's got so a woman is crazy to have a baby."

The other women look at her in fright. The child keeps on playing. Another pregnant woman goes slowly looming in the dark. Anna looks wildly at her two blonde boys. She gives her mother a cup of hot water with milk in it and sugar. The old lady cries pounding the Bible. "It says it all here. Under your own tree . . . it says. Every laborer is worthy of his hire. Every man should be under his own tree and should be paid at sundown. . . ."

Nobody knows what the poor suffer just for bread and burial. Nobody knows about it. Nobody has told about it. Nobody can know about how it feels unless you have been in it, the work there is, just for bread and burial.

The women look at one another. The child plays on the floor, never showing his bright face, his yellow hair shining. The snow keeps falling very softly outside the window.

We all seem to be sitting within some condition that we cannot get out of. Everyone is bright and ready for living and then cannot live.

Pretty soon it gets darker and people begin to come in, doors slam below and the smell of food comes up, and it smells terribly good when you know how hard it is to get, how it takes a whole life and all the energy of a man or a woman to get it for the born and the unborn and the dying, and how it takes some kind of splendid courage to still have children to keep alive when it is the way it is.

The winter evening settles slowly and the snow falls sadly.

The two bitter women tell about their lives in a loud voice and we listen, and something keeps going on and on, something that is killing us all and that nobody seems to stop.

You keep feeling how rich everything is except the thing of making a living. You feel how rich these women are in their necessity to have rich experience and then how they are crippled in their bright living, having too hard a world in which to get bread for the living and burial for the dead.

"I might have been a great singer," Anna's mother suddenly says softly. "Everyone said I might have been a great singer when I sang at Christmas in Sweden and everyone in Stockholm stopped on their way to listen. . . ."

"Is this all the milk?" Anna says pouring out half a glass.

"All the milk," the old woman screams. "My God, everybody knows you can't make bones out of water, doesn't everybody know that you can't make bones out of water? I took that woman next door a little milk. You can't make bones in her without something to eat, can you? Doesn't everybody in the world know that, you can't make bones, a woman can't make bones without the stuff to make it in her?. . ."

"Mama, mama, sit down," Anna cries. "Sit down, mama. Drink your pink tea, mama."

The woman next door, far gone in pregnancy, comes in. "Look, Anna, it is snowing. There will be some shoveling to do."

All the women turn to look at the feathery flakes drifting down. It will have to snow like this a long time before it makes any shoveling.

Milk went up two cents today. Milk is dearer.

III

Farm Girl

Bernice lives in an old block building that was condemned by the city long ago, but is now full to the brim with people because you can get a room for two and three dollars a month. Everyone in the building is on charity. Bernice has been on charity for two years now. She no longer looks for a job. She looked steadily for a job until about six months ago and then she stopped looking. She has been all her life working in other people's kitchens. She is pretty deaf now from hanging out wet clothes in the cold. She doesn't care about that kind of work any more even if she could get it. For the first time in her life since the depression she has had leisure to enjoy herself and find out about things, and have a bit of pleasure. She runs around the streets now with other girls, sometimes with a man, having a good time, talking, laughing, going to picture shows, dancing sometimes when she can pick up a guy.

Bernice is quite moral, because she is afraid of the hazard of being unmoral. She is afraid of what men do, she knows how men are, that you can't trust them a moment and they get you into trouble. Her friend Grace makes that plain. Grace is always in trouble with men, always trying to get out of trouble. Bernice wants to get along and keep out of trouble. Her life has narrowed itself down, like a wary animal's, keeping herself out of trouble and having the best time she can.

The police are pretty hard on a lone girl. When the police see you wandering they always think you are bad if you are a girl. Bernice and her kind are simply hungry. But the police wouldn't think you were wandering out of many kinds of hunger.

No, if you are a girl you are either good or bad and that is all there is to it.

Next to Bernice lives her girl friend Mabel, who has to keep pretty clever, too, to keep the charities from running her into Faribault. They want to have her sterilized and put into the home for girls at Faribault. Mabel is from a farm in Minnesota; she likes men pretty well and isn't clever keeping herself out of trouble. Last year she had a baby, so of course all the charities are down on her, and if any of the workers or the police see her talking to a fellow they are right after her. She is pretty and likes fellows so it is kind of hard on her. A girl has to live, she only has one life.

Mabel has worked in the five-and-ten since she was fourteen and lied about her age. When she had her baby they gave her an intelligence test when she was scared stiff anyway, and it was about forests and she has never seen more than one tree at a time in her life, just growing between the sidewalk and the curb.

Of course, she failed pretty thoroughly, because she was shaking like a leaf all the time because of fright about having a baby. If they had asked her how a girl wolf gets by in a city, where to get the best handouts, how to catch a guy that will take you to a show maybe, and a feed after, and how to get away without giving him anything, she would have passed one hundred percent. They asked her about the wrong kind of jungle.

Mabel hasn't worked for three years. She doesn't look for work any more either, and they all refuse to work in women's kitchens in this new arrangement of working for room and board that lets rich women save a lot on their help so they can go to Miami during the winter. They are all on to that. This old block is honeycombed with lone girls like this, wolf girls who get along. There are girls in the building who have been machine operators, trimmers, pressers, button sewers. They all get five dollars' worth of groceries a month from the charities. Sometimes they get an order of Pillsbury's best flour and practice making fancy cakes that are advertised in the ladies' journals, and then they eat cake for a week and have nothing the next three weeks, but it is worth it.

This is incomprehensible to the charity virgins. They can't understand either why the girls leave those stinking holes where they live and go to a picture show whenever they can. They try to go to as many shows as they can. The rooms are heated only by stoves. The charities give them a little wood or coal. The rooms are always cold and infested by the odors of all the foul humanity that has lived in them since 1850, and, besides, cockroaches, bed bugs and lice and enough rats to keep all the cats they can get very fat.

The girls live a great deal on hand-outs from restaurants. Sometimes they beg clear to the other side of town until they get some dish that touches their fancy. Before Mabel's baby was born she had a hankering for spice cakes, and they used to walk from restaurant to restaurant turning down chicken dinners and asking for spice cakes.

Sometimes a man gets sweet on them for a while and if he has a job gives them money now and then. They always manage somehow or other to have a good hat and a bright scarf. They rummage around at the Salvation Army store and fix themselves up for about a quarter. It is pretty marvelous how vivid life stays in a woman, how she always washes out her socks, and looks pretty clean and has some powder for her nose, no matter how pinched she is and how miserable. Women sometimes have a kind of indestructible lust for living in them that is pretty hard to douse.

But they are now seeing something pretty clearly. Keep alone as much as you can, look out for yourself. Keep away from men and marriage, because there isn't anything in it for a girl but a horde of children to be left with. Lie low, get along, beg, borrow or steal, go a lone wolf's way.

It is a philosophy of war and famine. They stay strong and alive and terrible with it. They are like wolves in a jungle, not even traveling in a pack. They sit for hours in wash-rooms, looking, waiting.

Their families are gone. They are alone now. Let the State take care of them. The State is their only family now and they look to it. They have transferred even the quarrels with their families to the charities and the State. They complain lovingly and bitterly about the food they get, the coal, the care at the clinics. They adore going to the clinics; they enjoy the sensation of importance that they have, as if for a moment the State cared passionately for their health.

The boys may still think they are going to be successful, that they are going to step into the big guys' shoes, but there is something funny about the girls. They are thrown up, lost from all the folkways for women, derelict from the family, from every human hunger except the one for bread.

They talk and they say only one thing, "I ain't going to have nothing to do with any of it. I ain't going to have nothing to do with guys. I'll have a time. I want what I want. I'll drink when I like it and have a time but no guys for me. I ain't going to work for nothing either. I ain't going to slave for nothing. I ain't going to do nothing."

So there it is, a strike. They understand something that is going to make a difference for a generation or two. They are on strike. They aren't going to have anything to do with it. They don't like the terms, so they aren't having any of it, and it will make a difference to all our living for a long time.

IV

Teacher

To get any relief work, if you are a teacher, and haven't had any work for a couple of years and have spent all your savings and let your insurance go and pawned everything you own, you have to go to the Board that is handling the relief work for teachers and *prove* to them that you are destitute. You not only have to be destitute but you have to prove it. They are both hard but the last is harder.

Nancy Sanderson's father had been a skilled glass blower. He had made pretty good money in his time before they invented a machine to take the place of the man. They lived pretty well and they always thought they were going to find some splendid new opportunity and go into business for themselves and be smart merchants and have the best house in town and servants. He educated all his six children because he knew that education was a thing that could get you on in America and anyone who had it could get what he wanted. So his four girls were school teachers and his two sons he educated to be engineers, and now they are all out of jobs. Old Sanderson fortunately is dead, but his daughters and his sons are not dead, except one daughter who is now dead because she chose it.

To prove you are destitute you have to go to the State House after having sent your application in before so it would be there ahead of you and everybody would know thoroughly about your being destitute, and then you have to put on your best things and go up there and see if they will give you one of those night classes for the unemployed, to teach. They are going to have classes for the unemployed, for adults, to keep up their ambition in this trying time; besides, it will employ a few teachers who, if they work steadily, will make as much as fifty dollars a month. Anyway, each State has appropriated so much money for this relief work. Some say it is a plan that comes from the educators who are afraid that they are not going to be supported so bountifully in the future, and are trying to make themselves important in the crisis. Some people wonder who is going to pay for it all anyway, whether the teachers will spend enough to put it back where it is taken out. Well, there is a lot of speculation, but probably there is a great deal too in the mind of a girl like Nancy Sanderson going up toward the State House on a frosty morning in a light spring suit to prove she is destitute.

She is alone, and it is hard for a lone woman to get much attention from the charities. She spent the last of her money last spring, all but about fifty dollars, and she does not know how she has been living. She has some friends who do not dream how destitute she has been. They ask her for dinner now and then but she eats so much, as you do when you are hungry, that it generally makes her sick afterwards. Well, there are ways of doing when you are destitute, and you get by some way and you don't know how you do it. A person can see you stand there and you look all right, but of course you have on quite a bit of rouge, but still you don't look starving or anything out of the usual and at the same time you may feel your knees dropping down and the greatest terror in the pit of your stomach. Lack of food is the best thing to give you terror. And, of course, Nancy's family always expected to get ahead, to better themselves. Never for a moment did they expect this.

So you feel very terrible going up to the capitol office building. You've gone up there a lot of times to get a position but that is different. Then you had your Ph.D. and your fur coat and the knowledge that you were going to get on in the world, and you didn't have to watch to see that your elbows did not come through and that your last pair of silk stockings did not spring into a run. The great building with the chariot of horses high above looks terrifying and you feel guilty, as if you had failed somehow and it must be your own fault.

You walk around a long time before you go in and then you go in and up the elevator without thinking and down the long hallway where women who have jobs are working, and you know who they are, like yourself nice girls who work very hard and save for a fur coat and to put some linen by in case of a wedding. And they are always looking to better themselves, too, in some mystical and obscure way that seldom comes about. A pang goes through you for what has happened to women.

There is a bench outside the door where people wait. The bench is full of rather thin but rouged women, waiting. You stand against the wall. Someone is in the office talking to the man who is in charge and there is a stenographer who goes to the huge file and hands him the application he wants.

You stand there. Perhaps there will be too many applications before yours. When you get in a big machine like this office building, then you don't think. You are in the machine. It can do what it likes. How many human lives are filed in a building like that! The woman in the office says desperately, "Twelve hundred new applications for work relief today. . ."

"Good Lord," the man says. He goes on talking in a loud desperate voice to the applicant who is a man and stands doggedly, twisting his cap and trying to answer. You can tell from the voices of both men that they are both caught in something, strained to the breaking point. The man who is asking the questions is part of a machine, too. He has to answer to someone higher up. "Well, you see," he shouts too loud, "you've got to answer these questions. You've got to answer them. You see, we'll give some of this work to someone who has a car, or a bank account, or owns a house, and then we'll be in dutch. . . ." The other man tries to answer in a low voice so no one will hear. He has had dreams, too. He has thought to have some power of his own, like any other man. . . Then another and another, all squirming, answering in low voices and going away and the man talking more shrilly.

Nancy Sanderson sat down, biting her teeth together, holding her wet hands tight in her lap. She looked all right. To look at her you would have thought she was all right. But hunger tears through you like a locomotive. You can hear your own heart like a trip hammer. You can hear your own blood in your ears like a cataract and you can't hear anything else. You are separated by your tremendous hunger from the ordinary world as if by a tragedy. You can't see what is happening. You can't hear what is being said.

The man was going over her application, trying to make it more definite. He was trying to be patient.

"You see, to get this, you have to prove absolute destitution."

"Yes," she said, wetting her tongue. When you don't eat the saliva begins to dry up in your mouth.

"Do you understand that?"

"Yes, I understand," she said again.

"Well, look here, you say you had fifty dollars left from your savings in the spring. Have you still got that?"

Where was that gone, fifty dollars? Why, fifty dollars doesn't last long.

"No, then what have you been living on? You must have been living on something. How have you been living?"

"I don't know," she cried in agony, and she felt all the starved blood rise and push against her throat like a million crying voices, but she did not cry out and she knew she must not cry because everyone would be embarrassed and they were all embarrassed already, as if they could not help something that was happening and they all felt ashamed and embarrassed.

"What have you been living on since?" the man suddenly shouted.

Everyone looked up, faces looking up from all around.

"I don't know," she barely said, and knowing all of them there squirming like worms when you uncover them.

"You've got to prove it, don't you understand that, you've got to prove it. . . ." The man seemed to be wild and shouting. "You've got to prove it."

She stood up amidst the eyes and saw the long corridor stretching out. She got up and started to walk as if she stepped among fetid and rotting bones and empty eye sockets. A silence followed her, and the people spoke to her in the common silence of hunger.

The manager got up and took a few steps after her, his pencil held out. "Wait," he said. "Perhaps something can be arranged. . . ." It sounded like a speech in a dream.

She went on down the white corridor so clean and white and warm, down into the rich lobby, out into the rich country with the fall light like gold upon the faces of the hungry people, and the horses of state gleaming and roaring into the sky, and she walked down past the nigger shanties and the Jewish tenements and people saw her walking and she looked all right so they paid no attention until she was dead.

When she came to the high bridge she let herself ease off into the air that was so sweet, as if you might skip winter.

They found her and took her to the morgue and of course they knew it was suicide.

V

Moon Bums

The winter moon was hanging down over the stacks of the city. We were to meet down by the fish hatchery where the freights slowed down at the switches to be shunted with the empties. The two girl bums, Fran and Ethel, were taking off for the South. This country is no place to spend the winter, so they were hopping off. I went down past the jungle, down into the thicket, across the tracks to the cliff side where they are hollowed out below into small caves. I saw a tiny fire low down in the cliff and somebody hallooed, "Hey!"

I stooped down and crawled in. They were leaning over a small fire of smoking twigs. They both had on overalls and a lot of sweaters but they were blue from the cold and Ethel's scar on her cheek looked bad.

She had come in from Seattle with that cut festering. She had let go of the grab irons and tried to alight running, but her knees had buckled and her face ploughed through the gravel along the tracks. It left a pretty bad cut. It was hard getting some hospital to fix it. You have to be pretty sick if you are a bum before they'll take you in. They shunt you on some place else for repairs. These kids aren't allowed more than twenty-four hours in each place if anybody knows it.

I met up with them just after they landed here from Seattle. I heard a lot of tales from them. They had been traveling and mooching around the country for a year and a half. They were old hands. They knew their onions. They might have been anywhere from sixteen to eighteen. They look like a thousand girls, they have a thousand names. Workers' kids, they have graduated from poverty, sweat shops, machines, diets of pigs' feet, stale hamburger and old bread.

Fran worked in a shirt factory since she was twelve at $1.97 for a fifty-five-hour week. Ethel is younger, and she went to eight grades in school and then worked as a learner in Connecticut where they have young girls work for a dime a week learning, and then most of them are fired when they learn and others are hired. Her family strung safety pins on a wire at night for awhile and then set out in an old car to make the canneries, but they soon separated; the father and mother stayed in a town in Carolina with the three younger children, and the older ones set out on their own. When Ethel made the town last summer the family were gone and nobody had heard of them for six months, so that's out now. She's on her own now for sure.

The South-bound refrigerator empties aren't due for half an hour. We all squat down and hold out our hands. It is bitter cold. I can see the new moon hanging just outside the cave.

"Boy, well we're off again," Fran says. Fran is a thin eerie-looking girl. Kind of a Botticelli-looking girl, with the stone cave behind her and her delicate face on the thin drooping body. But she's wiry, and she told me their life was better than the life in a factory, that they were healthier really.

"Yeah, we're off," Ethel says. She can't talk very well because of the long gash on her cheek. It will make a scar.

"Where are you bound?"

"Boy, I don't know where, I don't know where this car goes. I only know it's headed South and that's enough for me." She swore like a sailor about the cold.

We sat listening to the trains coming up the grade and the wind tearing around the rock like a sea. We looked at one another. We probably never would see one another again. It was like it is in a war.

They had told me a lot of tales, wonderful and terrible. Last winter they had lived in dry goods boxes outside of Chicago with two fellows who were carpenters and made the shacks, and the girls did the cooking and the fellows did the foraging. They didn't live with the men because they didn't want to. The men were awfully homely, so they didn't want to. They just took care of the house and the men did the mooching, because a man isn't picked up in the city like a girl is. A girl is always considered a moral culprit when she begs in the city, and she is sterilized or sent away to a farm or a home which she hates.

You have to look out for this. In the summer this causes a curious return to an old matriarchy. The girls gang up and live in the jungles and the boys do the mooching and the foraging, and the girls keep the jungles clean and cook the mulligan and make the boys wash, and sometimes they sleep together. They warm each other. But there is principally one kind of hunger, the hunger for bread. There isn't much prostitution because there is no money. The girls want to keep away from pregnancy and disease.

"It ain't honey and pie," Fran told me. "You get slapped and kicked around plenty and it's root, hog, or die. A girl don't have it any worse than a boy, not as bad maybe, because there is some terrible homos on the road, but it's bad. You got to roost anywhere and be ready to high tail it any old time."

Now they were high tailing it again. The long, long hoot of the train coming up the grade came right into the low cave. "There she is," Ethel said, her eyes dilating, and she reached nervously for her bundle. "I get kind of nervous when I hear that. I never get used to it. My stomach gives right away."

"With that feed in you," Fran said. "We got all the leavings at the fort. Tasted all right but you never can tell about garbage. We ate garbage in Spokane and our stomachs have been yelling."

We listened to the long long hoot. "She takes her time coming up the grade," Fran said.

How did she know? Had she been in Minneapolis before?

"Sure I been here," she said looking at me. "I don't know when. I been so many places, but I remember these caves and the long grade with the bullengine hooting like that for about ten minutes. We might as well stay inside out of that wind."

I felt queer. I wanted to make them stay. But the statistics kept going through my head . . . one million vagrant children. . . . The long wail of the engine came nearer. The two girls got up. Fran stepped on the fire. The young moon hung brighter.

Ethel had told me, "No more jobs for me. There's nothing to it, working your guts out. My family did it and look at them, no better than if they'd been on the bum."

Fran said, "No marrying for me and our kind. A fellow can't get a job now the way I see it. No kids for me when I see what happens to them. I should stand around like my mother and see my kids thin as rails and going up in a puff of smoke every winter, all that blood and work going up. There's nothing in it. . . ."

The ground began to shake as if it were about to crack open and swallow us. We ran out into the cold wind. The ground shook more. The blackness before us seemed to gather and mount. Number 29 was coming up the hard grade along the Mississippi. Fran and Ethel stood with their bundles. They looked like twigs as the light from the engine swathed over them. They looked like nothing.

"Fran . . . Ethel . . .," I screamed. The black engine came in a blast and forced us back against the cliff for a moment, then passed, and we all ran forward together as if released. Fran and Ethel were shouting something at me. I could see their mouths and their ghastly grins, trying to smile at me. Ethel went ahead waving her bundle, the gash showing livid down her cheek. I shouted at them but they could not have heard. They were shouting back at me, but I could only feel the ground shake and the ghostly force of the wind. I ran after them as if some ghastly suction were taking me in too.

The train stopped banging back upon itself . . . the engine let out a great hiss. The two girls scuttled like mice through the couplings between the cars and I ran down looking through every space, but I couldn't see them any more. I read the lettering . . . Golden California . . . Seedless . . . Chicago . . . Omaha.

I didn't see them any more. I shall never see them any more.

I WAS MARCHING

MINNEAPOLIS, 1934

I have never been in a strike before. It is like looking at something that is happening for the first time and there are no thoughts and no words yet accrued to it. If you come from the middle class, words are likely to mean more than an event. You are likely to think about a thing, and the happening will be the size of a pin point and the words around the happening very large, distorting it queerly. It's a case of "Remembrance of Things Past." When you are in the event, you are likely to have a distinctly individualistic attitude, to be only partly there, and to care more for the happening afterwards than when it is happening. That is why it is hard for a person like myself and others to be in a strike.

Besides, in American life, you hear things happening in a far and muffled way. One thing is said and another happens. Our merchant society has been built upon a huge hypocrisy, a cut-throat competition which sets one man against another and at the same time an ideology mouthing such words as "Humanity," "Truth," the "Golden Rule," and such. Now in a crisis the word falls away and the skeleton of that action shows in terrific movement.

For two days I heard of the strike. I went by their headquarters, I walked by on the opposite side of the street and saw the dark old building that had been a garage and lean, dark young faces leaning from the upstairs windows. I had to go down there often. I looked in. I saw the huge black interior and live coals of living men moving rest-lessly and orderly, their eyes gleaming from their sweaty faces.

I saw cars leaving filled with grimy men, pickets going to the line, engines roaring out. I stayed close to the door, watching. I didn't go in. I was afraid they would put me out. After all, I could remain a spec-tator. A man wearing a polo hat kept going around with a large camera taking pictures.

I am putting down exactly how I felt, because I believe others of my class feel the same as I did. I believe it stands for an important psychic change that must take place in all. I saw many artists, writers, professionals, even business men and women standing across the street, too, and I saw in their faces the same longings, the same fears.

The truth is I was afraid. Not of the physical danger at all, but an awful fright of mixing, of losing myself, of being unknown and lost. I felt inferior. I felt no one would know me there, that all I had been trained to excel in would go unnoticed. I can't describe what I felt, but perhaps it will come near it to say that I felt I excelled in competing with others and I knew instantly that these people were NOT competing at all, that they were acting in a strange, powerful trance of movement *together*. And I was filled with longing to act with them and with fear that I could not. I felt I was born out of every kind of life, thrown up alone, looking at other lonely people, a condition I had been in the habit of defending with various attitudes of cynicism, preciosity, defiance, and hatred.

Looking at that dark and lively building, massed with men, I knew my feelings to be those belonging to disruption, chaos, and disintegration and I felt their direct and awful movement, mute and powerful, drawing them into a close and glowing cohesion like a powerful conflagration in the midst of the city. And it filled me with fear and awe and at the same time hope. I knew this action to be prophetic and indicative of future actions and I wanted to be part of it.

Our life seems to be marked with a curious and muffled violence over America, but this action has always been in the dark, men and women dying obscurely, poor and poverty-marked lives, but now from city to city runs this violence, into the open, and colossal happenings stand bare before our eyes, the street churning suddenly upon the pivot of mad violence, whole men suddenly spouting blood and running like living sieves, another holding a dangling arm shot squarely off, a tall youngster, running, tripping over his intestines, and one block away, in the burning sun, gay women shopping and a window dresser trying to decide whether to put green or red voile on a manikin.

In these terrible happenings you cannot be neutral now. No one can be neutral in the face of bullets.

The next day, with sweat breaking out on my body, I walked past the three guards at the door. They said, "Let the women in. We need women." And I knew it was no joke.

At first I could not see into the dark building. I felt many men coming and going, cars driving through. I had an awful impulse to go into the office which I passed, and offer to do some special work. I saw a sign which said "Get your button." I saw they all had buttons with the date and the number of the union local. I didn't get a button. I wanted to be anonymous.

There seemed to be a current, running down the wooden stairs, toward the front of the building, into the street, that was massed with people, and back again. I followed the current up the old stairs packed closely with hot men and women. As I was going up I could look down and see the lower floor, the cars drawing up to await picket call, the hospital roped off on one side.

Upstairs men sat bolt upright in chairs asleep, their bodies flung in

attitudes of peculiar violence of fatigue. A woman nursed her baby.
Two young girls slept together on a cot, dressed in overalls. The voice
of the loudspeaker filled the room. The immense heat pressed down
from the flat ceiling. I stood up against the wall for an hour. No one
paid any attention to me. The commissary was in back and the women
came out sometimes and sat down, fanning themselves with their
aprons and listening to the news over the loudspeaker. A huge man
seemed hung on a tiny folding chair. Occasionally someone tiptoed
over and brushed the flies off his face. His great head fell over and the
sweat poured regularly from his forehead like a spring. I wondered why
they took such care of him. They all looked at him tenderly as he slept.
I learned later he was a leader on the picket line and had the scalps of
more cops to his name than any other.

Three windows flanked the front. I walked over to the windows. A
red-headed woman with a button saying "Unemployed Council" was
looking out. I looked out with her. A thick crowd stood in the heat
below listening to the strike bulletin. We could look right into the windows of the smart club across the street. We could see people peering
out of the windows half hidden.

I kept feeling they would put me out. No one paid any attention.
The woman said without looking at me, nodding to the palatial house,
"It sure is good to see the enemy plain like that." "Yes," I said. I saw that
the club was surrounded by a steel picket fence higher than a man.
"They know what they put that there fence there for," she said. "Yes," I
said. "Well," she said, "I've got to get back to the kitchen. Is it ever hot!"
The thermometer said ninety-nine. The sweat ran off us, burning our
skins. "The boys'll be coming in," she said, "for their noon feed." She
had a scarred face. "Boy, will it be a mad house!" "Do you need any
help?" I said eagerly. "Boy," she said, "some of us have been pouring
coffee since two o'clock this morning, steady without no let-up." She
started to go. She didn't pay any special attention to me as an individual. She didn't seem to be thinking of me, she didn't seem to see
me. I watched her go. I felt rebuffed, hurt. Then I saw instantly she
didn't see me because she saw only what she was doing. I ran after her.

I found the kitchen organized like a factory. Nobody asks my
name. I am given a large butcher's apron. I realize I have never before
worked anonymously. At first I feel strange and then I feel good. The
forewoman sets me to washing tin cups. There are not enough cups. We
have to wash fast and rinse them and set them up quickly for buttermilk
and coffee as the line thickens and the men wait. A little shortish man
who is a professional dishwasher is supervising. I feel I won't be able to
wash tin cups, but when no one pays any attention except to see that
there are enough cups I feel better.

The line grows heavy. The men are coming in from the picket line.

Each woman has one thing to do. There is no confusion. I soon learn I
am not supposed to help pour the buttermilk. I am not supposed to
serve sandwiches. I am supposed to wash tin cups. I suddenly look
around and realize all these women are from factories. I know they
have learned this organization and specialization in the factory. I look
at the round shoulders of the woman cutting bread next to me and I feel
I know her. The cups are brought back, washed and put on the counter
again. The sweat pours down our faces, but you forget about it.

Then I am changed and put to pouring coffee. At first I look at the
men's faces and then I don't look any more. It seems I am pouring coffee
for the same tense dirty sweating face, the same body, the same blue
shirt and overalls. Hours go by, the heat is terrific. I am not tired. I am
not hot. I am pouring coffee. I am swung into the most intense and
natural organization I have ever felt. I know everything that is going
on. These things become of great matter to me.

Eyes looking, hands raising a thousand cups, throats burning, eyes
bloodshot from lack of sleep, the body dilated to catch every sound
over the whole city. Buttermilk? Coffee?

"Is your man here?" the woman cutting sandwiches asks me.

"No," I say, then I lie for some reason, peering around as if looking
eagerly for someone, "I don't see him now."

But I was pouring coffee for living men.

For a long time, about one o'clock, it seemed like something was
about to happen. Women seemed to be pouring into headquarters to be
near their men. You could hear only lies over the radio. And lies in the
papers. Nobody knew precisely what was happening, but everyone
thought something would happen in a few hours. You could feel the
men being poured out of the hall onto the picket line. Every few
minutes cars left and more drew up and were filled. The voice of the
loudspeaker was accelerated, calling for men, calling for picket cars.

I could hear the men talking about the arbitration board, the truce
that was supposed to be maintained while the board sat with the Governor. They listened to every word over the loudspeaker. A terrible
communal excitement ran through the hall like a fire through a forest. I
could hardly breathe. I seemed to have no body at all except the body
of this excitement. I felt that what had happened before had not been a
real movement, these false words and actions had taken place on the
periphery. The real action was about to show, the real intention.

We kept on pouring thousands of cups of coffee, feeding thousands
of men.

The chef with a woman tattooed on his arm was just dishing the
last of the stew. It was about two o'clock. The commissary was about
empty. We went into the front hall. It was drained of men. The chairs
were empty. The voice of the announcer was excited. "The men are

massed at the market," he said. "Something is going to happen." I sat down beside a woman who was holding her hands tightly together, leaning forward listening, her eyes bright and dilated. I had never seen her before. She took my hands. She pulled me toward her. She was crying. "It's awful," she said. "Something awful is going to happen. They've taken both my children away from me and now something is going to happen to all those men." I held her hands. She had a green ribbon around her hair.

The action seemed reversed. The cars were coming back. The announcer cried, "This is murder." Cars were coming in. I don't know how we got to the stairs. Everyone seemed to be converging at a menaced point. I saw below the crowd stirring, uncoiling. I saw them taking men out of cars and putting them on the hospital cots, on the floor. At first I felt frightened, the close black area of the barn, the blood, the heavy moment, the sense of myself lost, gone. But I couldn't have turned away now. A woman clung to my hand. I was pressed against the body of another. If you are to understand anything you must understand it in the muscular event, in actions we have not been trained for. Something broke all my surfaces in something that was beyond horror and I was dabbing alcohol on the gaping wounds that buckshot makes, hanging open like crying mouths. Buckshot wounds splay in the body and then swell like a blow. Ness, who died, had thirty-eight slugs in his body, in the chest and in the back.

The picket cars kept coming in. Some men have walked back from the market, holding their own blood in. They move in a great explosion, and the newness of the movement makes it seem like something under ether, moving terrifically toward a culmination.

From all over the city workers are coming. They gather outside in two great half-circles, cut in two to let the ambulances in. A traffic cop is still directing traffic at the corner and the crowd cannot stand to see him. "We'll give you just two seconds to beat it," they tell him. He goes away quickly. A striker takes over the street.

Men, women, and children are massing outside, a living circle close packed for protection. From the tall office building business men are looking down on the black swarm thickening, coagulating into what action they cannot tell.

We have living blood on our skirts.

That night at eight o'clock a mass-meeting was called of all labor. It was to be in a parking lot two blocks from headquarters. All the women gather at the front of the building with collection cans, ready to march to the meeting. I have not been home. It never occurs to me to leave. The twilight is eerie and the men are saying that the chief of police is going to attack the meeting and raid headquarters. The smell of blood hangs in the hot, still air. Rumors strike at the taut nerves. The dusk looks ghastly with what might be in the next half hour.

"If you have any children," a woman said to me, "you better not go." I looked at the desperate women's faces, the broken feet, the torn and hanging pelvis, the worn and lovely bodies of women who persist under such desperate labors. I shivered, though it was 96° and the sun had been down a good hour.

The parking lot was already full of people when we got there and men swarmed the adjoining roofs. An elegant café stood across the street with water sprinkling from its roof and splendidly dressed men and women stood on the steps as if looking at a show.

The platform was the bullet-riddled truck of the afternoon's fray. We had been told to stand close to this platform, so we did, making the center of a wide massed circle that stretched as far as we could see. We seemed buried like minerals in a mass, packed body to body. I felt again that peculiar heavy silence in which there is the real form of the happening. My eyes burn. I can hardly see. I seem to be standing like an animal in ambush. I have the brightest, most physical feeling with every sense sharpened peculiarly. The movements, the masses that I see and feel I have never known before. I only partly know what I am seeing, feeling, but I feel it is the real body and gesture of a future vitality. I see that there is a bright clot of women drawn close to a bullet-riddled truck. I am one of them, yet I don't feel myself at all. It is curious, I feel most alive and yet for the first time in my life I do not feel myself as separate. I realize then that all my previous feelings have been based on feeling myself separate and distinct from others and now I sense sharply faces, bodies, closeness, and my own fear is not my own alone, nor my hope.

The strikers keep moving up cars. We keep moving back together to let cars pass and form between us and a brick building that flanks the parking lot. They are connecting the loudspeaker, testing it. Yes, they are moving up lots of cars, through the crowd and lining them closely side by side. There must be ten thousand people now, heat rising from them. They are standing silent, watching the platform, watching the cars being brought up. The silence seems terrific like a great form moving of itself. This is real movement issuing from the close reality of mass feeling. This is the first real rhythmic movement I have ever seen. My heart hammers terrifically. My hands are swollen and hot. No one is producing this movement. It is a movement upon which all are moving softly, rhythmically, terribly.

No matter how many times I looked at what was happening I hardly knew what I saw. I looked and I saw time and time again that there were men standing close to us, around us, and then suddenly I knew that there was a living chain of men standing shoulder to shoulder, forming a circle around the group of women. They stood shoulder to shoulder slightly moving like a thick vine from the pressure behind, but standing tightly woven like a living wall, moving gently.

I saw that the cars were now lined one close fitted to the other with strikers sitting on the roofs and closely packed on the running boards. They could see far over the crowd. "What are they doing that for?" I said. No one answered. The wide dilated eyes of the women were like my own. No one seemed to be answering questions now. They simply spoke, cried out, moved together now.

The last car drove in slowly, the crowd letting them through without command or instruction. "A little closer," someone said. "Be sure they are close." Men sprang up to direct whatever action was needed and then subsided again and no one had noticed who it was. They stepped forward to direct a needed action and then fell anonymously back again.

We all watched carefully the placing of the cars. Sometimes we looked at each other. I didn't understand that look. I felt uneasy. It was as if something escaped me. And then suddenly, on my very body, I knew what they were doing, as if it had been communicated to me from a thousand eyes, a thousand silent throats, as if it had been shouted in the loudest voice.

THEY WERE BUILDING A BARRICADE.

Two men died from that day's shooting. Men lined up to give one of them a blood transfusion, but he died. Black Friday men called the murderous day. Night and day workers held their children up to see the body of Ness who died. Tuesday, the day of the funeral, one thousand more militia were massed downtown.

It was still over ninety in the shade. I went to the funeral parlors and thousands of men and women were massed there waiting in the terrific sun. One block of women and children were standing two hours waiting. I went over and stood near them. I didn't know whether I could march. I didn't like marching in parades. Besides, I felt they might not want me.

I stood aside not knowing if I could march. I couldn't see how they would ever organize it anyway. No one seemed to be doing much.

At three-forty some command went down the ranks. I said foolishly at the last minute, "I don't belong to the auxiliary — could I march?" Three women drew me in. "We want all to march," they said gently. "Come with us."

The giant mass uncoiled like a serpent and straightened out ahead and to my amazement on a lift of road I could see six blocks of massed men, four abreast, with bare heads, moving straight on and as they moved, uncoiled the mass behind and pulled it after them. I felt myself walking, accelerating my speed with the others as the line stretched, pulled taut, then held its rhythm.

Not a cop was in sight. The cortege moved through the stop-and-go signs, it seemed to lift of its own dramatic rhythm, coming from the intention of every person there. We were moving spontaneously in a movement, natural, hardy, and miraculous.

We passed through six blocks of tenements, through a sea of grim faces, and there was not a sound. There was the curious shuffle of thousands of feet, without drum or bugle, in ominous silence, a march not heavy as the military, but very light, exactly with the heart beat.

I was marching with a million hands, movements, faces, and my own movement was repeating again and again, making a new movement from these many gestures, the walking, falling back, the open mouth crying, the nostrils stretched apart, the raised hand, the blow falling, and the outstretched hand drawing me in.

I felt my legs straighten. I felt my feet join in that strange shuffle of thousands of bodies moving with direction, of thousands of feet, and my own breath with the gigantic breath. As if an electric charge had passed through me, my hair stood on end. I was marching.

Cows and Horses Are Hungry

When you drive through the Middle West droughty country you try not to look at the thrusting out ribs of the horses and cows, but you get so you can't see anything else but ribs, like hundreds of thousands of little beached hulks. It looks like the bones are rising right up out of the skin. Pretty soon, quite gradually, you begin to know that the farmer, under his rags, shows his ribs, too, and the farmer's wife is as lean as his cows, and his children look tiny and hungry.

Drive through Elbow Lake, Otter Tail County, Elk River and Kandiyohi County, Big Stone County, Yellow Medicine County and Mille Lacs, and you'll see the same thing. These are only the counties that are officially designated as in the droughty area by the federal government. This is only in Minnesota. In the Dakotas they say cattle are leaning up against the fences. There is a shortage of water as well as of pasturage.

If you are officially in the droughty areas you will come in on the government purchasing of starving cattle. On May 31, the day after the last hot wind and temperature at 112° in some areas, the papers announced the working plan of the machinery set up by the federal government to aid farmers in the drought-stricken areas of the Northwest. The animals will be bought and those that are not too far gone will be fattened and given to the F. E. R. A. for the relief departments. If you're on the breadlines you'll be getting some starved meat for your own starved bones. They could feed you some choice farmer's ribs, too. But you can't buy up farmers and their wives and shoot them. Not directly.

The government has been pushing straw into these communities all winter to keep the cattle from starving for lack of grain until the pasturage came in. Well, now there is no pasture. The grass is brown and burnt as if it might be mid-August instead of May and June. The farmer is milked at one end and given relief at another. Well, the farmer says, they wanted a scarcity, and by God, now they have it. They shot off the pigs and cows, they tried to keep what was left alive because they couldn't feed them, now they're trying to keep them from dying off and rotting on the ground and making too big a stench.

The farmer can't sell his cattle to the stockyards. They're too far gone, too thin. The cattle thus turned over to the government will be left temporarily on the farms, fed by the administration and then moved to the packing houses or redistributed to other farmers or turned directly over to relief channels.

The administration of this plan seems similar to the other plans, with a regional director for seven Northwest states: Minnesota, North and South Dakota, Montana, Wisconsin, Iowa, and Nebraska; with state directors from the farm-schools working through county agents. The county director will have an advisory committee made up of the members of the corn-hog allotment committee that functioned in the county. This organization will appoint township committees that will visit the farms, check the stock, classify, appraise the value and fix the purchase price, secure necessary farmer and creditor signatures to sales contracts, and arrange for final check to see that the animals have been disposed of as agreed. They will also approve vouchers for payment. The same old rubbish. Committees and committees and committees. But the farmer will keep on starving. He has been rooked by nature and now he will be rooked by the federal government.

II

The farmer has been depressed a long time. For the last three years he has been going over into the abyss of pauperism by the thousands. This spring after a terrible winter there was no rain. The village where I live has not exchanged money for two years. They have bartered and exchanged their produce. Last year some had nothing to exchange. We cut down trees in the front yard for fuel and tried to live off the miserable crop of potatoes of last year.

Since April there has been hope of rain and even up until the day after Decoration Day, until that bitter afternoon when the hot winds came and made any hope after that impossible. During April the farmers said that the winter wheat would be all right if it would rain even next week. The peas went in. They raise a lot of peas for the canneries both in Wisconsin and in Minnesota. The peas came up a little ways and then fell down as if they had been mowed down. We waited to put in the corn day after day.

Then came a terrifying wind from the Dakotas, blew tens of thousands of dollars' worth of onion seed away and half of North Dakota blew into Ohio with the spring sowing. That wind was a terror and blew dust and seed so high you couldn't drive through it in midday.

A kind of terror grew in the folk. It was too much, added up with the low prices they got, the drought, heat, and high wind. A peculiar thing happened. Very much like what happened in the flu terror after the war. No one went outdoors. They all shut themselves up as if some terrific crisis, some horrible massacre, were about to occur. The last day of the wind, the radio announced every half hour that there was no menace in the dust, it would hurt no one actually. The wind died down, but it didn't rain. Well, they said, it *will* rain. It has to rain sometime. The winter wheat and rye began to whiten. A thin stand. You could sit in your house and look about and see the fields whiten and the wheat seemed to go back into the ground. You could see it stand still and then creep back into the ground.

But the farmers kept on ploughing in case it would rain. First you had to plough with two horses and then with four. You couldn't rip the earth open and when you did, a fume of dust went up like smoke, and a wind from hell whipped the seed out. Some planted their corn, though, in corn-planting time, some waited for rain. They waited until the day after Decoration Day.

Every day the pastures became worse. The grass became as dry as straw in May and the cattle lost their flesh quickly. They weren't too well padded because of scarce food all winter. You had to look for a green spot every morning. Children were kept out of school to herd the cattle around near streams and creeks. Some farmers cut down trees so the cattle could eat the leaves even if they were poor picking. The leaves on the trees are poor, falling off already in some places due to the searing, driving wind and the lack of moisture at their roots. The man up the road has turned his cows into his winter wheat which is thin as a young man's first beard anyway.

On Decoration Day the wind started again, blowing hot as a blast from hell and the young corn withered as if under machine gun fire, the trees in two hours looked as if they had been beaten. The day after Decoration Day it was so hot you couldn't sit around looking at the panting cattle and counting their ribs and listening to that low cry that is an awful asking. We got in the car and drove slowly through the sizzling countryside.

Not a soul was in sight. It was like a funeral. The houses were closed up tight, the blinds drawn, the windows and doors closed. There seemed to be a menace in the air made visible. It was frightening. You could hear the fields crack and dry, and the only movement in the down-driving heat was the dead writhing of the dry blighted leaves on the twigs. The young corn about four spears up was falling down like a fountain being slowly turned off.

There was something terrifying about this visible sign of disaster. It went into your nostrils so you couldn't breathe: the smell of hunger. It made you count your own ribs with terror. You don't starve in America. Everything looks good. There is something around the corner. Everyone has a chance. That's all over now. The whole country cracks and rumbles and cries out in its terrible leanness, stripped with exploitation and terror — and as sign and symbol, bones — bones showing naked and spiritless, showing decay and crisis and a terrific warning, bare and lean in Mid-America.

We kept driving very slowly, about as slowly as you go to a funeral, with no one behind us, meeting no one on the road. The corpse was the very earth. We kept looking at the body of the earth, at the bare and mortgaged and unpainted houses like hollow pupas when the life has gone. They looked stripped as if after a raid. As if a terrible army had just gone through. It used to be hard to look at the fat rich-seeming farms and realize that they were mortgaged to the hilt and losing ground every year, but not now. Now it stands a visible sign. You can see the marks of the ravagers. The mark of that fearful exploitation stands on the landscape visible, known, to be reckoned with.

The cows were the only thin flesh visible. They stood in the poor shade of the stripped and dying trees, breathing heavily, their great ribs showing like the ribs of decaying boats beached and deserted. But you knew that from behind all those drawn blinds hundred of eyes were watching that afternoon, that no man, woman, or child could sit down and read a book or lie down to any dreams. Through all these windows eyes were watching — watching the wheat go, the rye go, the corn, peas, potatoes go. Everywhere in those barricaded houses were eyes drawn back to the burning windows looking out at next winter's food slowly burning in the fields. You look out and see the very food of your next winter's sustenance visibly, physically dying beneath your eyes, projecting into you your future hungers.

The whole countryside that afternoon became terrifying, not only with its present famine but with the foreshadowing of its coming hunger. No vegetables now, and worst of all, no milk. The countryside became monstrous with this double doom. Every house is alike in suffering as in a flood, every cow, every field mounting into hundreds, into thousands, from state to state. You try not to look at the ribs, but pretty soon you are looking only at ribs.

Then an awful thing happened. The sun went down behind the ridge, dropped low, and men and women began to pour out of the houses, the children lean and fleet as rats, the tired lean farm women looking to see what had happened. The men ran into their fields, ran back for water and they began to water their lands with buckets and cups, running, pouring the puny drops of water on the baked earth as if every minute might count now. The children ran behind the cows urging them to eat the harsh dry grass. It looked like an evacuated countryside, with the people running out after the enemy had passed. Not a word was spoken. In intense silence they hurried down the rows with buckets and cups, watering the wilted corn plants, a gargantuan and terrible and hopeless labor. Some came out with horses and ploughs and began stirring up the deadly dust. If the field was a slope, barrels were filled, and a primitive irrigation started. Even the children ran with cups of water, all dogged, silent, mad, without a word. A certain madness in it all, like things that are done after unimaginable violence.

We stop and talk to a farmer. His eyes are bloodshot. I can hardly see from the heat and the terrible emotion. . . . How do you think my cows look? he asks. I think they are a little fatter today. I try not to look at his cows at all. Pretty thin, though, he says, pretty thin. I can see the fine jersey pelt beginning to sag and the bones rise out like sticks out of the sea at low tide.

We both know that a farmer across the river shot twenty-two of his cattle yesterday, and then shot himself. I look at him and I can see his clavicle and I know that his ribs are rising out of his skin, too. It is visible now, starvation and famine. So they are going to buy the starving cattle and shoot them and feed the rest to the bread lines. A man isn't worth anything – but a cow. . . .

We drive on. When I shut my eyes the flesh burns the balls, and all I can see is ribs – the bones showing through.

The banks protest the federal government's price for starving cattle. From six to twenty dollars, with your pedigreed bull thrown in. No difference. Hunger levels all flesh. When the skeleton shows through, all meat is worthless. The banks don't like this. Most of the cattle are mortgaged and they won't get much. The banks are protesting. All this sounds different in the language of the banks. . . .

They say in their bulletin. . . . We report further deterioration of crops since the May 1 report. In addition, weather conditions in a large part of the Ninth District, which embraces the states of Minnesota, North and South Dakota, Montana, and part of Wisconsin, are bad. . . . And abandonment of 16 percent in Montana and 60 percent in South Dakota of winter wheat acreage. . . . Reports from grain, trade and railroads serving the grain-raising areas show condition poor of both winter wheat and rye.

In addition, weather conditions in the Ninth District have been more than usually favorable for the hatching of grasshopper eggs and tend to increase the seriousness of this menace.

In human terms, of life and not credit and interest, this means – winter wheat and rye gone, pasturage gone, cattle gone; wholesale prices low, retail prices soaring; the government piles in feed, straw, and now buys up the lean cattle, but they milk the farmer faster than they resuscitate him.

Starvation stands up in the blazing sun naked at last; and bare and lean ribs for all the coming winter.

WOMEN KNOW
a LOT of THINGS
...That they don't read in the papers, and they're acting on what they know

Minneapolis

Women know a lot of things they don't read in the newspapers. It's pretty funny sometimes, how women know a lot of things and nobody can figure out how they know them. I know a Polish woman who works in the stockyards here, and she has been working there for a good many years. She came from Poland when she was a child, came across the vast spaces of America, with blinders on, you might say, and yet she knows more than anybody I know, because she knows what suffering is and she knows that everyone is like herself, throughout the whole world. So she can understand everything that happens, and moving between the shack where she lives on the Mississippi bluffs and the canning department of Armours, she feels the hunger and the suffering of Chinese women and feels as if she is in Flint with the Woman's Brigade.

I was having a cup of coffee with her the day the Woman's Brigade knocked out the windows so the air could get into the factory to the gassed sit-downers and she told about how they were all singing a song we knew:

> "We shall not be moved
> Just like a tree standing by the river
> We shall not be moved."

And how they were all leaning out of the windows singing this song, hundreds of them probably, with machine guns mounted on the buildings opposite and she got up and walked around the little stove that warmed her shack. She couldn't sit still.

"Imagine that," she said, "Can you believe it, them all singing that song, with the guns pointing right at them and the women, scooting in there and smashing those windows. O, say, I woulda like to have been there." And she wasn't in that shack at all, the boundaries of that shack weren't anything.

That's the way it is with women. They don't read about the news.

They very often make it. They pick it up at its source, in the human body, in the making of the body, and the feeding and nurturing of it day in and day out. They know how much a body weighs and how much blood and toil goes into the making of even a poor body. Did you ever go into a public clinic to weigh your child? And you feel of him anxiously when you put his clothes on in the morning. You pick him up trying to gauge the weight of his bones and the tiny flesh and you wait for the public nurses to put him on the scales, and you look, you watch her face like an aviator watches the sky, watches an instrument register a number that will mean life and death.

In that body under your hands every day there resides the economy of that world; it tells you of ruthless exploitation, of a mad, vicious class that now cares for nothing in the world but to maintain its stupid life with violence and destruction; it tells you the price of oranges and cod liver oil, of spring lamb, of butter, eggs and milk. You know everything that is happening on the stock exchange. You know what happened to last year's wheat in the drouth, the terrible misuse and destruction of land and crops and human life plowed under. You don't have to read the stock reports in Mr. Hearst's paper. You have the news at its terrible source.

Or what kind of news is it when you see the long, drawn face of your husband coming home from the belt line and the speed up and feel his ribs coming to the surface day after day like the hulk of a ship when the tide is going down?

Or, what price freedom and the American Way so coyly pictured on the billboards, when you go up the dark and secret and dirty stairs to a doctor's office and get a cheap abortion because you can't afford another baby and wait for the fever that takes so many American women, and thank heaven if you come through alive, barely crawling around for months?

A woman knows when she has to go to work and compete with other men, and lower the price of all labor, and when her children go to work, tiny, in the vast lettuce and beet fields of the Imperial Valley and Texas. She knows when she has to be both father and mother, her husband like a fine uncared-for precision machine, worn down in his prime, or eaten by acids in Textile, or turned to stone by Silicosis.

In the deeps of our own country, the deep south, Arkansas and Tennessee and Alabama women are beginning to read the news right. In the center earth of China women who for centuries have been slaves, are lifting their faces from the earth and reading a sign in the skies.

In South America, in the deepest and most inaccessible mountains, a woman walking behind a donkey, or working in the sugar cane, is preparing to vote, if she was asked, the way of her international sisters.

It's the same there, wondering if there is enough meal in the sack, if watered thin, for a meal. Anxiously looking at the lank husband's body, the dark quick hungering eyes of children, measuring with eagle eye their appetites, knowing to a grain how much would send them from the table without a roving eye.

Hunger and want and terror are a Braille that hands used to labor, used to tools, and close to sources, can read in any language.

International Woman's Day is the recognition of that mutual knowledge leading to the struggle of women throughout the world.

When we look at Germany and Italy we know that the coming of fascism exploits men and women alike, and takes from woman the painful civic and political gains she has bought with a century of struggle.

This year promises to be a crucial one for women, and one that will unite them in even closer bonds with the international struggle against war and fascism, those twin beasts that threaten our frail security. The cause of women will be the cause of all toiling humanity.

Men and women alike are beginning to know this. No longer does the good union man keep his woman at home to mind the kids. The Woman's Brigade at Flint was an important weapon in the strike. The Woman's Auxiliary came out of the kitchen and fought side by side with the men. This is only a beginning.

Immediate in the struggle in America is the Woman's Charter. This document will draw up a Legislative plan, uniting all women against reaction which strikes at democratic rights and at the labor movement while pushing women back into the dark ages. The basic principles of this Charter are: that women should have full political and civil rights; full opportunity for education; full opportunity for employment according to their individual abilities, and without discrimination because of sex; and security of livelihood, including the safeguarding of motherhood.

This coming year will see the tide of war and fascism rising high, but it will also see the strong and invincible wall of working men and women, locked in stong formation in a party of farmers and workers everywhere, in a Farmer Labor Party, saying with the international workers, in Spain, Russia, China, FASCISM SHALL NOT PASS.

Maria Simarro, one of the young women of the Spain Youth Delegation now touring America, told me that in Spain when they gave the women the vote, everyone was very nervous. Here were thousands of illiterate peasant women, held for many years in medieval ignorance and darkness, kept in subjugation to the church, to endless toil and childbearing. What would they vote for? How could they understand international problems, the great program of the United Peoples Front of Spain and the world? It was a problem that worried everyone. They held the election in their hands. The Liberal Spanish government was afraid. These newly enfranchised women could turn the tide of the election. They needn't have worried.

The so-called ignorant peasant women of Spain were not ignorant. They voted with their hands, their feet, the knowledge bred and seeped in sun drenched labor, in every bone and muscle, in grief in the night, and terror, of hours of walking behind the plow, their sweat dropping into the furrows, birthing children on straw with only the blessing of the priest to ease the pain.

They voted from this knowledge, solid, with one voice, one body, for the Peoples' Front of Spain, voted for that democracy they later showed themselves ready to defend against the Church and the Landlords.

This is the kind of knowledge the women of 1937 must have. They are no longer negative mourners, weepers at the weeping wall, shrouded in the black of grief and defeat. The old English folk song says, "Men must work, and women must weep. . . ." No longer. The International women of 1937 will protect democracy with their lives, demanding food that can now be so abundantly provided out of the earth's rich land and factory, demanding security for loved ones — standing militant in the wheat fields, at factory gate and bench, raising her cry of — Land . . . Bread . . . and Peace.

O Prairie Girl,
Be Lonely

...there is a song deep as the falltime redhaws, long as the layer of black
loam we go to, the shine of the morning star over the corn belt, the
wave line of dawn up a wheat valley.

—CARL SANDBURG

Look, honey, Butch says, it's now more than ever.

Oh, we're not going to do it now? I said.

If we don't do it now, when would we do it? No matter what we do
we got to have it now. If you get rid of it we got to have it and if you
have it we got to have it.

Yes, I said, that's the way it is.

All right, he said, then we got to go through. Are you game?

Yes, I said, lifting up my face. How can we be together, that's the
point. It's no good if we can't be together at all, it's no good, any of it.

We got to be together, honey, he said.

I feel strong when he says that, and everything in me seems to rise
and bloom and cry for growth. Sometimes he looks at me and seems to
raise me up and put his hands within me like in an orchard, and then he
seems like a devil to me and I know there is no way to be having what
we need and want and then everything in my whole being sinks down
like into a sea and I can feel my hair standing up and everything looks
unreal like in an old movie and cracked apart as if cement was nothing.

Are you game? he says.

Yes, I say, if there's no other way, but not until we know it.

Don't you know it? Lord, when do you learn? You got to be cracked
up complete?

Don't get mad, Butch. Please.

All right, he says, I show you how to do it and you won't do it,
you ain't got the guts, you're crummy.

No, I said, please don't talk so loud, everybody's looking.

All right let them look, so what? Why don't you get some sense, then you wouldn't have a child. Live and let live, that's my motto. It's no thanks to bring a child into the world now. You have to feed them or they'll die if you don't, won't they? Sure you have to feed them for years and years. They'll get sick and all that kind of stuff because you can't take care of them. They'll have all kinds of stuff, and then they'll get bombed like in other countries and I don't care what happens to grown people, get what I mean, they can take it, but kids is different. What happens to kids is a hundred percent different, get what I mean?

Yes, I said.

You should get smart so you won't be having a child. You got yourself into this. Now you got all the big odors sniffing around. Since you live with that whore.

I won't listen to your foul language, I said. Everybody in the joint was looking at us. The sun was shining outdoors.

You can listen to all that crap of everyone else and enjoy it, he said.

Who, what, who do you mean, what are you talking about?

You know what I'm talking about.

Lord, O God.

Anybody can tell you anything and you make off you enjoy it, he said.

Who? Who told me anything?

Oh, everybody, anybody.

Mention one person.

Well, Ganz. . . .

You told me to be nice to him.

All right don't expect anything of me. I haven't got anything. I told you that from the start, didn't I? Didn't I? I didn't make off anything I wasn't. I didn't hamstring you along, did I? Did I?

No.

There you see. Don't slap your brats on me.

I don't care, I cried, leave me alone! I don't see why we can't have a life. We don't want much.

No, not much.

Oh, we'll cry our strong cry, something will come.

Sure, howl to the moon. . . .

Well, I will, I said, standing up in the booth, I will.

Sit down, he said, don't get excited. Nobody cares a rap in hell what happens to you, might as well get that first as last. Get rid of it. I could do it myself with a pair of scissors, there's nothing to it. Listen, you are just like Clara, why are you looking at that little dago, giving him the come-on?

I began to sweat with cold. I wasn't looking at anyone but Butch.

Cut it out, I cried. I could smell food cooking. I want something to eat. I began to cry. I'm hungry.

I haven't anything to feed you. I told you that.

I began to cry.

All right, Butch said, touching me suddenly, putting his hand over mine on the table. All right don't make a noise, you might wake him up. He's Irish and he likes his sleep.

I smiled at him. I felt like bells were ringing in all my flesh. I felt lovely and quick, laughing. It's not a fault being hungry and it's not a fault men hate the hungers in women now that they can't be filling, it's not a fault asking for child, food, love.

I wanted to warm him.

Ganz opened the door, the December sun shining on him too. He came over and sat down and said, A round on me, to the bartender. And then he said, How are you? to me and I said, All right, and Butch was watching me like a hawk. He said, Butch, we got to go see about the car. Butch said, It's got to have the license plates changed on it.

Shut up, you crumb, Ganz says, and smiles at me.

Ganz and Butch drank up and they both got up and Butch made out he dropped his scarf and touched my leg and smiled at me. Wait here for me, he said, no matter how long. And then he and Ganz went out the door.

I looked at the clock; it was five-thirty when they left.

You can't sit in a room alone now quiet. I got desires now, wild, like the dark sweet fruit of the night that breaks on your tongue. How can you sit down now in a room and mend your stockings and polish your nails and maybe think about your mother, with your flesh like the wild breaking of spring, like a tree after a storm, weighted to the ground and rain water in your throat and your hair springing wild out of your skull and the strong root terrible in the earth with bitter strength?

It's a quarter to seven. You look at the clock. In a short time he can be gone and back again. Somebody comes in and asks for Hoinck and Belle says in her full voice, Hoinck went out. He mixed a Tom and Jerry, then put on his hat and checkered scarf and went out. My husband went out. Man, husband, what is he? Why should grief sit on your body like a carrion for knowing one?

And Butch, wild with longing and anger, weeping in his sleep. He picked up a bottle last night and filled his own glass, and left mine empty and then threw the bottle at me. Then he threw the rye-bread rinds from his sandwich.

Ack has been drunk all night and now he is up to no good, coming in with a suitcase full of bootleg.

I am sitting here alone. He has to hate me. The way it is he has to. It is funny how you can stand more than you thought, and feel yourself inside get stronger, and taste the salt of your own wounds, and the weight of the things that have happened to you.

At seven Butch came back and when he came in the door I could see he didn't like anything. I knew I would say the wrong thing. I knew whatever happened it would be wrong. We had a beer and I said I don't know whether to do it or not. I had a dream I thought I would have the child, and I would go south in the sun to have it and I dreamed I was looking through a little hole like in those candy eggs we used to have where you saw lambs grazing and a little house and children playing in the sugar. I said, It's Friday, and I ought to decide if I'm going to do it.

Butch said, I don't give a damn if it is Friday.

I said, Well, I could go south and have it, then I wouldn't be any trouble to you.

Oh, so you're going south, he said, so you are going away with my own kid. I'm not supposed to have even that, am I? Or maybe it ain't mine, so I am going to have a baby by somebody else.

No, Butch, honest it's yours.

Why don't you tell me?

You wouldn't want to give me anything.

The hell with you, Butch said, another beer — my father did that with me, made me come home and pray and mumbo-jumbo. To hell with women.

I feel an awful hunger in me. I feel like an idiot with my mouth open and my eyes hanging out. Clara came over.

They were going to do a square dance, she said.

They want to do a square dance, I said to Butch. The big apple.

There isn't enough people, Clara said. Come on, I'll get you a man.

Don't you want to dance the square dance? I said to Butch.

No, he said. He looked so cold and when he looked at me his eyes were cold.

Come on, Clara said.

Oh, no, I couldn't, I said. We sat there.

Butch said, We've got to do it with Ganz. Ten dollars more and I can get a lease from the Standard Oil — I can have a station of my own, I can have a station, then we will be sitting pretty.

He kept on drinking. What is to become of us? Why do we fall apart? He sat there so silent. We seem so good. . . what happens to us? We are being eaten by some rot. Why do we give in to it? He didn't answer. It's like it isn't in us. . . like we didn't do it. He just sat there. I don't like to feel it. I don't know what there is to do. I don't want a success like Butch. I want to be. . . I love to be. . . .

A ballplayer came over. Listen, he said to Butch, when were you with the Wisconsin Blue Socks?

I sat there. People's heads kept going by the window. You could just see their heads and they looked like a strong wind was pushing them, yet it was very still outside. It looked as if it might snow. The sky was low down and looked full.

After the ballplayer left Butch said, You've got to do it, that's all. You've got to have it.

I sat looking down at the wood of the table. It had little lines in it. Then I saw that he was sitting quite still, and he was crying.

Don't, Butch, I said.

Honey, he said, you know I'd like to have a kid, you know that now, don't you?

Sure, Butch, I said.

I looked out the window across the street. It said Garbo Coke. . . 20 percent more heat, lasts longer—no ash. It was upstairs you got it. Some girls went there at noon and had it and then went back to work. The doors have no doorknobs on them, you can only open them with a key, no one can open the door from the outside. Clara told me that. Clara says it smells awful and he doesn't wash his hands.

I suppose you like to stay with Clara because of the men, Butch said.

Oh, yes, the men. Oh, I entertain men all the time. I'm crazy about men.

We sat there. Another beer, Butch told Clara.

The little pad the beer sat on said, In my old cupboard who wants bones cried Mother Hubbard I like Schmidt's. The radio was announcing that the White Sox made a home run. We won't ever take a home run ring the bell beat the race come in first. . . there's nothing to it, science is wonderful. Listen, honey, don't cry. . . . It's nothing. I'll do it. I'll do it.

You'll do it, he cried, you don't care for it, you don't want to have it.

Don't cry, I said. I knew he would get mad next.

Listen, I'll be back in a jiffy and I'll be O.K. Everything will be O.K. You sit right here and I'll be back in an hour. The way science has it now it's wonderful. Don't worry.

I walked out the door, and across the street.

I could hear men's voices. It seemed dark where I was but there was a light a long way off. I lay quiet like an animal when hunters are near.

The clerks get there early, Ganz was saying. Eight o'clock. We wait outside. The girl here drives the stolen hack. Ack has another waiting out beyond the bridge to transfer the dough. Butch stands by the corner at five after eight. We have to wait for the vault to open. If we go in before the vault is open then we're done for.

How much do you think it will crack? Hone said.

I could smell them sitting there under the light, bending over the map of the bank in South St. Paul that Hoinck had made. I had seen it before. It was a good map. You could see the pillars and the door and a black space in the back where the vault was and the places were marked where each clerk stood by the cash drawer. I knew it by heart.

Hone was leaning over me sharp as a knife.

He pushed me into a chair between them. I looked at the drawing spread on the table. I could feel their awful bodies on each side of me, the soft putrid body of Ganz and the sharp-knifed body of Hone. I felt sad.

I felt bad and like I would never feel any different.

How much you think it'll crack? Hone repeated.

If the vault is open—plenty.

How much?

Don't worry, Hone, you'll get yours all right, you bloodsucking bastard.

Oh, I'll get mine, Hone said. To me he said, If people only knew how square I am. They're always misjudging me. I'm always trying to do the right thing and where does it get me?

Oh, bull! Ganz said.

When the vault is open, Ganz said, Butch moves in. I cover the cashier from the side. . . . Butch has got to be good. You think that mewling baby of yours can do it?

I didn't answer.

And you, he said to me, see if you'll be any good at this. You sit in the car. There's a copper on the corner with red hair. You watch him. He'll be directing morning traffic at that hour and he'll be standing on that corner, and that's where he should stay. If he moves you give the signal.

I tried to remember it. I knew I ought to remember it good. Our lives might depend on it now. What we had left.

What's the signal? I said.

Ganz said, and he put his heavy hand on my shoulder—I tried not to move—you lean out the window on the opposite side and toot the horn like you was tootin' for someone in the building opposite. One long, two short. That's for you to remember.

I'll remember, I said and looked at him. I'll remember forever. Even dogs don't do it that way.

And watch in back for the bulls. They come up from behind now in plain clothes. Watch in the mirror but don't look uneasy. Look quiet and sleepy. Look natural and dumb like always.

Yes, I said. I guess I am dumb.

Keep your foot on the clutch all the time . . . ready for a getaway. Everything depends upon speed with us in there. We got to do it quick and easy, see? Everything depends on it like Hitler does it. Know how

Hitler does it? Surprise, that's his racket, that's the thing Hitler's got, surprises . . . the poor rubes don't know what's up and don't believe anything's going to happen and before they know it he's over the hurdles with the dough in his jeans pretty as a picture.

Yeah, Hone says, that baby's smart.

Plenty, Ganz says. I'd like to hone in on his racket. What we need in this country is somebody like Hitler, that's what we need. Hitler knows we don't need so many people, kill off half of 'em, leave only the best people, who know what it's all about. We don't need all these wops and Jews. God, I hate Jews . . . I would like to snipe off a few Jews myself.

Jews ain't so bad, Hone whined.

That's the way it is, Ganz said. I don't want anybody to argue with me, see? Hey, are you a Jew? he asked Hone.

Hone said, Hell, no, Ganz, you know I'm not.

Well, you better not be. I hate Jews. I don't like 'em, see?

O.K. Hone looked scared. Take it easy. No kiddin', Ganz, how much will she go for?

You mean the girl or the bank? Ganz laughed. She's not so bad. Nice and young. The way I like 'em.

I mean the bank—her too. Hone grinned.

If we spike the vault and she's open, she ought to come through with thirty grand.

Whew! Hone said.

As long as no one gets out of there it's all right. Butch has got to watch that. Think he can watch that? That baby of yours?

Yes, I said. He can do it all right.

God, love is wonderful. Ain't love grand, Hone?

Hone got up and began to skip around the room like he was holding his skirts. Ganz laughed. Speed's the thing a fast clout.

Speed's the thing, Hone said.

One man getting past your sweet potato will queer it. You better tell him to be good. I'll turn around and plug him where he stands if he lets a man get through that door and get out again with a loud mouth.

I looked at Ganz. I never hated anyone before—I knew that now.

What about my friend here? he said.

You're both rats, I said.

All right, Ganz said. Never mind, Hone, get you another, the woods are full. But keep your mouth buttoned up, he said to me.

You keep yours, I said.

And I ran out and down all the stairs, past the clerk at the desk, and into the street and I looked back and saw all the windows behind me brightly lighted and the smooth furniture inside and the nice beds. I always wanted to see what they did in there. Now I knew. I ran into the

park and I touched the trees and I leaned down and picked up some dirt
and ate it. It tasted bitter. . . .

And I kept walking and looking at men and now I knew
something. This is what happened. Now I knew it. I was going to know
more. Nobody knew anything that didn't do it. Down below you know
everything and there are some things you can never tell, never speak of,
but they move inside you like yeast.

Belle said, Tomorrow night this time they might all be dead.

Stop it, Belle, I said. Hoinck was playing poker with three other men.

Cut it out, Hoinck said, and have a drink. Hit me.

I wanted him to quit for years, I'm going to kill myself if he doesn't,
Belle cried.

Have a drink, I said.

A fine way to talk the night before a big job, Hoinck said. We got
to go to work tomorrow for sure.

Go to work, Belle said in scorn. She began to cry. It isn't worth it,
all the money in the world, it isn't worth it.

It'll be all right, Hoinck said. Play, he said to Ack, go on play.

I'll be all right, Belle said. A thieves' phrase.

What do you want? Hoinck said. I take it.

What do I want! Belle shouted. Godlordchrist and the Virgin
Mary, what do I want!

Cut that out, Hoinck said, what do you think this is? Because you
have a fit I'm supposed to call everything off.

I'd better be dead.

Stop saying that. What in the name of God. I'm giving you all I can.

What did you ever give me, living in ratholes from one minute to
the next? Stop stealing.

Everybody steals, Hoinck said. My play.

Nuts! There must be some other way.

Well, you know it as well as I do. Hit me. Go on hit me. We tried
that.

We're better dead and all our kind.

The men slapped down the cards.

Hoinck yelled: Here's a rod, blow your brains out, or else shut up,
and have a drink.

I'll never shut up, Belle screamed. Look, she said to me, I got him
extradition papers, got a quick straw bond for him, didn't I? I got him
out of jail. I got bail for him. I hitchhiked from Baltimore, Maryland, to
Dallas, Texas, to get him out of the can once. I took the rap for him.
What else could I do? I might as well blow my brains out.

All right, Hoinck said, do it. If the women would only shut up.

Sure, say nothing. See everything blown to hell and sit quiet knit-
ting. Belle cried. Sure, don't say a thing.

Have a drink.

I'll have a drink. Sure.

Butch came in and walked by me without speaking. He sat down and watched the game and Belle noticed it too, and she said, What's the matter? Tomorrow we may all be dead and he can't speak to you.

He said, Shut up, Belle, mind your own business. Butch said to me, So you want a father and husband? Well you won't be getting them. Nobody's going to get them.

I stood by the stove.

You want me to bring you something, give you something. Everybody could hear him. You Goddamned chiseler, you lying whore. I wouldn't bring you anything.

The men playing cards looked at me.

Did you have a good lay? he said. Did you have to sell me down the river?

Shut up, Hoinck said. We want to be good for tomorrow.

Yeah, you all know it, Butch said, you all know it. I phoned here and you all knew she was lying up there with that skunk. That lying red-headed bitch.

Belle was laughing, I could hear her laughing. . . . He was drunk. He would have a hangover.

Butch, I said, come with me, come on out. I took hold of him and he came with me easy. I was surprised, he just followed me and we went outside in the hall. We stood against the wall and he put his body close to me. We stood there and I thought he had forgotten. It was good to smell him.

Why in hell did you do it? he said.

I felt cold. Do what? I said.

Instead of answering he struck me full in the face with the flat of his hand. I leaned against the wall. I couldn't see. Then I saw his face awful in front of me as he came toward me and I put out my hand and pushed against his chest and when I touched him I loved him then. Somebody was coming up the stairs. Don't, Butch, I whispered, someone will see. I could see his hand lifted, this time in a fist, and it struck me in the mouth. The man who had been coming up the stairs passed us and I tried to look like nothing had happened. But I couldn't help the blood coming out the side of my mouth.

It's funny to be hit. Nobody ever hit me before but Papa. He didn't hit like that. I took hold of Butch's arm and we went downstairs leaning on each other. It wasn't snowing.

Butch said, It isn't snowing, a good thing too. I hope it don't snow tomorrow.

I hope so too, I said. I could see my mouth. It was swelling. The inside of my lower lip was bleeding where my teeth had cut.

Butch said, What's the matter? Your mouth is bleeding. He said, I'll hit you again, don't ever let me catch you again. Jesuschrist, why did you have to do it?

You told me to do it, I said. You told me to be nice to him.

Sure, go on, blame it on me. That's my fault too. Everything's my fault. That's what my mother used to think. Sure I can take it, go ahead. I'll lead with my chin.

No! No! I cried and we walked along the dark, rotten streets. I didn't know where my legs were and fountains seemed to be rising and breaking behind my eyes. No, no, I cried, it's not your fault. I only thought I'd help with the money.

How much, he said, go on tell me how much?

I hadn't had a single drink but I felt drunk. I could hardly see.

Look, Butch, I said, let's go to a hotel.

Listen, he said, I suppose you think I can't pay for a hotel. I suppose you think only that bloodsucker Ganz can pay for a hotel. Well, I want you to know that I got dough, see? I can pay. I pay my way. I always done that. I don't depend on no one on God's green earth, get me? Since I was eight years old I paid my way in this lousy world. You're not going to take *this* baby to any hotel. You're not going to pay for me. I can pay for my own room, and for my own girl, see?

Sure, I said, Butch, I know you can. I know that. I've never paid for you. I've never never paid for you.

All right, he said, don't act like it's any different.

Before we went in the hotel on St. Peter, Butch stopped by the pawnshop and took a drink.

Don't drink, Butch, I said, pulling him. Remember in the morning. You got to have your wits.

I suppose you don't think I can drink either. I suppose you think I can't hold it. All right, belittle me, see? Go ahead, I'm used to it. I'll show this cockeyed world.

Sure you will, Butch, sure you will. Oh, I know you will. You're wonderful. You're a good mechanic, you're the best. I know that.

Do you, sweet? Do you?

Sure, sure, I cried. Oh, I love you. I know it is going to be all right.

Do you love me? Honest?

Honest, Butch. Oh, hurry, come on. Sure I love you. Better than anything.

All right, Butch said, that's enough for me. I know when I'm lucky. That's all I need to change my luck. That's absolutely all. I don't need a rabbit's foot. I don't need to take a black girl. I don't need an eleven. I don't need nothing. Tomorrow is going to be silk. Look, he said, you help me get a picture of this. I stand by the pillars, see, until Ganz gets in the side door, then I go in, step over the swinging gate and cover the clerks from the right.

I'll help you, Butch, I cried, pulling him. We'll get it all down.

We went into the lobby and I stood back a little and he signed the register and then he looked in his pants pockets, and then his vest and then all his coat pockets, and he took out a bunch of letters and keys from his back pocket and then he started over and went through them again.

I said, Gee, honey, I forgot you gave me your purse to hold while you were changing the tire. I said, We had a blowout just outside the city, can you imagine, we came clean from Washington, D.C., without a blowout and then just before we get to the city we have one. I put a dollar on the counter and the clerk gave me the key and Butch leaned against me going upstairs and he said what number we got this time? The number on the door was 23.

Twenty-three skiddoo, Butch said. Three and two is five. Five is a lucky number for me. Is it for you?

Yes, I said.

We went in and I didn't turn on the light. I laid Butch on the bed and he went to sleep like a baby. I sat on the edge of the bed. it was an inside room with a shaft. There was no outside window. The window led on the shaft and I could hear men talking in the room above. At first it sounded like wasps and then I heard one of them say, . . . We got to be careful. And another said, . . . But doughnuts is sure.

I didn't want to go to sleep because I dreamed about it every night. I could see it all plain. I've read about robberies but I didn't think anything of it. I have seen it in the papers, banks robbed and pictures of a young man or maybe a girl. I never thought anything of it. I can see myself sitting on the bed dim in the mirror. Tomorrow everyone will know it if we are caught. I am afraid to get up and look close to see if tomorrow already shows in the way I am made. This must show, make the bones go different, and the flesh different.

I am to drive the car. We are to meet Ack at the corner of Third and then we are to part. He is to go across the bridge for the transfer. I am to drive down Fourth and stop in front of the bank just six feet from the hydrant and from there I can see the cop directing traffic on the next corner. I am to watch him and watch behind me in the mirror and keep my foot on the clutch.

I wake up at night and dream that I've forgotten the shift. But that would be impossible. Then I dream I am paralyzed and have become rooted in the walk like when we were kids and put our footprints in the fresh cement. Sometimes it is raining in the dream and sometimes the sun is shining. And I see people broken on the streets by explosion.

It is awful to bear these things at night and horror in your dreams of things unknown to you, not thought of by you at all. I didn't think of these things. It wasn't my own evil. I never dreamed of them nor looked to doing any of them. Was I evil? Was I a monster in my youth? Did my mother think of this? Who thought of these crimes and hatched them out to scatter our flesh?

I can see dead on the walk by the corner of that building. I never saw the corner of a building like that before. How far is six feet? How far is it from the door to the car six feet from the hydrant? . . . I must ask Butch to step that many feet for me. I never was good on distance. Distance is very important in this, time and distance. They blow up to big sizes in my dreams. One foot more, one foot back, is the difference of a bullet. One minute more, one second less. I can see all this mixed up in time like a movie when you run it fast and then slow or run it backward.

The voices above said, . . . We got to have racks we got to have a lot of racks to make it pay. Then the voices lowered.

I lay down beside Butch and he put his arm over me. In his sleep he did it. Some voices outside the door must have wakened me. I was dreaming that it came, that moment when Butch was at the front door and Ganz came out the side door with three satchels of money and there were four coppers coming around the corner at the same time. I shot at them and one officer pumped an automatic in Butch. In the light I saw Butch whirl, fire at the officer and then fall in a heap. I lifted a rifle and fired at the fourth officer again and he raised a shotgun and blasted away half my head.

I woke up crying and woke Butch. I said, That's funny, I never fired a gun in my life.

He said, I hope it's clean tomorrow. I feel better. How about something to eat?

I said, You get it. I didn't want to see those streets again.

There was a commotion in the hall. A woman kept saying, Go on get going go on what's the matter. I won't take a thing! she cried, I don't want a thing. Then the man would mumble something like he was moved and ashamed, and then you could hear them kiss and then she shouted, Go on get going get out get going get along, and he didn't want to go. Voices in old hotels at night sound funny, and finally he went back in with her and we could hear them laughing. . . .

Butch turned on the light and killed a bedbug walking up the wall. He wanted to go out and get some beer. It was after twelve. I said, No, you better not drink any more beer. We have to be out there at seven-thirty sharp.

Jesus, maybe we won't wake up, maybe we ought to stay up.

No, we got to get some rest.

He said, Have you got a dime? I'll get you a hamburger. I wait at the front, light a cigarette, lean against the pillars like I was just waiting. I can see through when Ganz gets the clerks covered and then I go in and cover them from the other side.

I said, You put the money out of the drawer on the counter and sweep it into a satchel. Then you take the satchel to Ganz and watch the front door.

Yes, he said, that's right. It can't miss. We ought to make a cleanup.

Yes, I said. We ought to.

Why don't you be easy? he said.

I don't feel easy, I said. I feel awful.

You take everything too personal, he said. Look at me, I can stand anything.

Yes, I said, I'm looking at you. He was still pretty drunk and I knew nothing could keep him from getting drunker, nothing in heaven or hell.

He went out for the hamburger and didn't come back for a long time. They started a party next door. They must make these walls out of paper. I lay in bed listening. I thought if I wouldn't move I wouldn't remember. It was two o'clock. I thought I better get some sleep. I tried to figure things out. I couldn't figure it.

I could hear them through the wall moving like huge rats, like talking rats very funny. I thought they would look like great rats with long snouts and blood hanging from their teeth. The shooting craps and the loud bad talk went on and the low roar and murmur of men's voices with the cries of the women riding them like birds on a wave.

The clock struck two-thirty and I could feel all this come into me like a misery seeping into you.

I certainly wouldn't forget, if the copper moved, to look across the street, up at the empty windows, and one long and two short. Yes, I would remember that. One long and two short. You might say that on your deathbed. Last words, one long and two short.

Didn't anyone ever go to bed here? Were they all waiting for seven-thirty, for the holdup? The men upstairs kept figuring out how much to start a doughnut racket.

I went downstairs and it was snowing but the black street showed through. I had a cup of coffee and two hot dogs. I only had fifty cents left of the five bucks. I left twenty on the table.

I had only been upstairs ten minutes when Butch knocked and came in with a hot dog still warm in a paper. He was very drunk. He said he had been talking to a fellow who made two thousand a month before the depression. Think of that, he said, two grand a month selling shoes. Jesus!

You better get some sleep, I said, it's near three.

Do you think I can step over that swinging gate O.K.? he said. I'll have to step over it because it will be locked, ten to one.

Sure, I said. How far is six feet from the hydrant?

Don't you know six feet? he said. Look, and he stepped it off from the window to the dresser. Not much smaller than the room. I looked at the space. Space could blow up, it could stretch like rubber.

I tried to eat the hot dog because he brought it.

Butch took off his pants and sat on the bed in his shirt, his strong legs hanging down. He was very drunk. His eyes were glazed.

I put on my coat and ran downstairs and brought up a milk bottle full of coffee. Now I only had fifteen cents left. The coffee cost ten with five deposit for the milk bottle. But that was enough until morning.

Here, I said, drink. I began pounding his arms. You got to eat, I said. You got to sober up.

So, Butch says to the air, I am your father.

Father, I almost screamed. Who was he talking to? A step came down the hall, somebody tiptoeing. He was talking in a low steady voice. The glare of the single bulb fell on his black head.

I held the coffee to his mouth.

I am your father, he says. Go back to the grave, Father, lie still. So, he says, my son, it was better for you not to be alive, it was better for you dead. You wouldn't be a white feather, you would have made the big team. Pitcher for big time, you hear me, that's for certain. My lousy old man wouldn't have known you and you could pitch on Sunday.

Drink, I cried. Drink.

He pushed it away. I was scared. He kept on talking. He wasn't talking to me.

I will talk to you when you are dead, he said, when they lower you in the ground, when everything is dead.

We will have it, I cried, if it goes good tomorrow. Drink. We will have it. You got to sober up.

Too late, he said, it's against us.

No, no, I said. We're lucky.

Luck, he said, that bitch.

He swore to himself, like a wasp ready to plunge into you.

Drink, I shouted, drink. Somebody knocked on the wall. I was shaking like a gourd.

What's the matter? he said. This place smells like a perspiring corpse. Who's been in here? Has that nest robber been in here? I'll kill him.

Drink, I said. You got to be sober tomorrow. You got to be.

He looked at me. If the cop from the corner comes back we are going to be scattered, he said.

Don't think about it. Stop thinking about it.

All right, you stop too.

What time is it?

Almost four.

This time tomorrow we'll be through with it.

It will be all right. Everything will be all right.

Yes.

It won't though. It will be stinking. Lousy.

Don't say that.

Might as well look yourself in the eye.

It will be all right. We'll make it.

We'll be dead.

No, no.

We'll be dead and forgotten.

Oh, we will live forever, I cried.

Sure, nuts, forever. You sweet nut. Come here.

Don't, Butch, you shouldn't. You got to sleep.

Come on now, honey, turn over, turn to me.

Not now.

The man and woman in the other room were laughing in bed. You can hear them strong, through the buggy walls, like grapes hanging in summer, like heavy wheat blowing in Wisconsin.

Now! Now! Butch cried. Before it is too late.

It's funny how anything begins to happen how clear it gets. When it begins to happen you don't worry about it. When you are doing it you don't think about it.

At six-thirty I got Butch out and filled him with black coffee and walked him along the river. The street looked quiet and clear. It was a clear cold morning and it wasn't snowing. I walked him along the river and then he looked better and we went to the tavern and Belle was cooking coffee holding a wrapper over her breast and looking around from the stove. Her ruined face was frightened in a way I never saw it. What a life, she says, get up all hours of the night. Can't sleep a wink. Here's some coffee.

We can't stop, I said.

Oh, yes you can, she says. It's only quarter after seven.

I gave Butch some more coffee and put a little brandy in it.

Ganz came in the kitchen and said, We can't stop here, it will look bad.

You look bad anyhow, Belle said, you look terrible.

All right, no remarks, give me some coffee. What's the matter with him? he said, pointing at Butch.

He's all right, I said.

Hoinck came in, his hair sticking up. He had a bag in his hand.

You can't use that, Ganz said.

What's the matter with it?

Jesus Christ, man, you can't walk in a bank with a satchel like that. What a man!

Shut up, will you? Belle said.

Belle, Hoinck said, get that bag upstairs, will you?

Drink a cup of coffee, baby.

Ganz went into the bar, which was still dark.

Don't do it, honey, Belle said.

We'll quit after this, Belle. Don't rag me now, this is a hard one.

At seven-thirty we went out on the street. The car was in front, the one I had driven to have the license changed. I could see in the back, all the guns, rifles and shotguns on the floor.

The men all wore revolvers besides. I could see them under their coats. It made them all look funny.

I got in. Ganz sat beside me and I could feel Butch leaning forward from the back.

Drive easy, girl, Ganz said, like I told you, in the middle of the street so nobody can see in and we don't have to put the curtains down. If we got nabbed now with all this arsenal we'd have to shoot it out.

I hope it's a nice job, Hoinck said, I hope it's clean.

Drive easy, girl. Don't break any rules. Today we're dynamite.

Leave her alone, Butch said.

Who's talking?

I am, Butch said.

I screwed down the window. There was sweat on my head.

Speed between crossings, go slow at the crossing, Ganz said. Stop at all stop signs.

I could see both sides of the street at once like I had extra ways of seeing. A man moving down the street toward us walking to work struck me like a blow and I watched him. Everything looked so single, so clear.

A nice morning, Hoinck said.

It looked like in a show, everything so clear, and the buildings looked like they were painted on. I saw three men talking on the corner. They raised their heads and looked at us. I can see one has a mustache like my father and a thin face. They go on talking. I look back and I can see the back of one's pants come down to a little peak behind like my father's pants always were.

We came across the bridge to meet Ack where we were supposed to meet him with the car that they were to change to and Ack wasn't there.

There was a tire store on the corner. Somebody was inside sweeping the floor.

Where is he? Ganz said. What the hell is this, a kindergarten? We drove around the block and back. He wasn't there.

Don't look, Ganz said. Don't gawk.

I drove around again slow, and back, and the man was still sweeping the floor and he looked up this time.

Don't let him see you, Ganz said, cough in your handkerchief.

I felt like laughing. I didn't have a handkerchief.

We drove around again and this time the man came to the window and looked out at us, his broom in his hand.

I never saw everything before so clear and flat, as if it was the end of it, as if you could never get behind or around or even remember it. Like there was no place to go into, to hide. It was crazy. I kept saying to myself, There's still time, we can stop now. Ganz leaned forward, looking up and down the street. I could feel Butch at my back. I could see him there. I could see him plain.

I could see the street, tiny and sharp in the mirror behind me.

The police squad car was coming behind us. I saw it. I said, The squad car is coming behind us.

Ganz said, For Christ's sake!

I said, Sit still, look natural. It's nothing. They are going back to headquarters, around the block.

Ganz was white as a sheet. You're not so brave, I said to him. You're a rat.

The squad car drove alongside and past us and the two tired cops didn't even look at us.

It's a quarter of eight, Ganz said. What does he think this is?

He'll be here, Hoinck said.

Get off this street, Ganz said. Get the hell out of here, we'll drive a few blocks and come back. Get out of here, get off this street, get away, Ganz said.

All right, Butch said, you can speak decent to her.

To who? Ganz said. Don't be too sure about that.

What do you mean? Butch said.

Be still, I said. There's Ack. I could see him a block ahead.

Tail in half a block behind, Ganz said.

He saw us, I said. All we need to do is just pass him so he knows we're set.

O.K. We drove back to the tire store and Ack leaned out a little and raised his hand. I raised my hand.

Stop, Ganz said. I pulled alongside. It wasn't necessary. Where you been? Ganz said in a whisper. Where you been?

Never mind, Hoinck said, let's go.

Tell you later, Ack said.

All right, Hoinck said, let's take a gander at it, get it over with. It's not too late. We'll get something. . . .

Make it snappy, Ganz said.

The streets were beginning to have more cars. I drove fast. I drove very well. I turned down Fourth and drove slowly around the corner. I saw the cop a block ahead directing traffic like we knew he would be. When I saw the hydrant I jumped as if it was looking at me. I remembered the wall of the bedroom. I stopped five feet away.

I turned and looked at Butch and he smiled at me. I felt better.

The lights were on in the bank and we could see in clear. The doors weren't open yet. The sun struck across the pillars just like the morning we cased it. I left the engine running. Butch got out easy and just then I could see the steel vault opening.

There it goes! both Hoinck and Ganz said. Ganz opened the door, took out his brief case and walked around the car and back around the corner.

Hoinck got out and slowly followed him. Butch was leaning up against the pillar, taking a cigarette out of the pack. He looked natural. Everything looked terribly natural. I saw the woman secretary clean off the desk of the president. She had a white lace collar on, very neat. The clerks came out with locked trays which they took to the cages and opened, sorting the bills into the open drawers.

I felt almost happy, as if I knew all this would happen and now it was happening just like it should. I could feel my heart beating high up in me. A woman walked by Butch and he looked at her. I watched him look at her.

He put his hand up to his face so she couldn't see him clear. I remembered his saying, Cover your face, honey, or I'll see you in the papers.

I saw Ganz inside.

Butch, I said softly to myself, just moving my lips, and as if he heard me he threw his cigarette into the gutter and turned his face and went through the pillars into the bank. I could see the long hard nervous cat life in him. It was lonely now on all sides.

Now I couldn't tell what time it was, whether an hour passed or a minute. I felt lightheaded. A man walked by and looked at me and I thought his eyes got larger.

It was very queer. Not many people seemed to be on the street. The cop kept turning full face to me and then sideways as the traffic went by him. I kept my foot on the clutch. I could see my foot far down as if it had gone to sleep. I couldn't feel it, as if it had been cut off and was lying down there.

GET SET TO GO. Words kept going in my mind. GET THE HOT HEAP READY. TAKE OFF IN A MINUTE, SPEED SPEED THAT'S IT LIKE HITLER.

I looked at the street behind, tiny in the mirror. I could see the buildings slanting a little, and darkening.

I said to myself for Butch, Step over the counter, counter ends at avenue window, small gate there, step over it, you're tall, darling, step over it. Clerks and money drawers will be in line with you, cover them. Motion them back, give them their orders, keep them away from the alarms. Don't forget anything, Butch, and if they hit it and start the big buzzer, remember that's a lot of battle for us for sure, that's for sure. Be careful. Clean the drawer now as you come to each cage, throw the dough onto the counter and push it into the bag. That's right.

Hoinck has vaulted the other end at the second pay window. . . .

I didn't look in. The big windows flashed now like glasses in the sun.

A dog started across the street and stopped. He's afraid too, I thought, and he went back to the curb and stood by the hydrant and then lifted a leg.

I turned my head and looked at the door. I could see Butch standing by the door. Now Butch had emptied the drawers, given the satchel to Ganz, now he was watching the door. Don't let anybody in, Butch. Watch it!

A stout man with a brief case was let out on the corner. A pretty girl was driving the car. She said, Good-by, Father. . . . He pulled down his vest and pushed up his mustache with his fat finger, walked toward me without looking, and turned in between the pillars. Butch saw him too and when he got in the door, I saw his head disappear like he had been dropped.

Everything was quiet. I could see the bank so clear like it was made of ice with the sun moving a little over the pillars, such lovely pillars.

Another man got out of a car that stopped alongside. A chauffeur was driving. He got out, slammed the door, threw away a cigar and went toward the streak of light between the pillars.

I watched now like it was something in a story, something I was reading. He went inside and then almost instantly he ran out fast and squealing in a high voice like a stuck pig. Everything on the street changed. Someone was running. I raced the engine. I felt lightheaded. I could see the air.

Then it broke like glass all around me and I heard the guns go off and the repeater Ganz carried, and two single sharp cracks, and the cop on the corner whirled like a doll, and then it was still again with people running.

Butch came backward out the bank door. I kept my eyes on him. He came out with his back to me, and he was holding his side. He was bent over and then he straightened, turned toward me and ran four steps, then he turned again facing the door of the bank, through which people were running. I kept my eyes on the back of his head as he moved toward me. I raced the engine and when he was near I took hold of the door handle and opened the door. I held it open until I saw his head and the backs of his ears, close to me.

People seemed to be running past him into the bank. No one seemed to be paying any attention to him. I held the door until he backed into it, then he opened it and got in. I could see the street in front of me and in back of me in the mirror and everyone was running toward the bank.

I raced the engine and when he closed the door I threw in the shift, grating it a little because my foot had gone to sleep.

Butch said, They're both dead.

I didn't know who. I didn't ask him. I hoped it was Ganz anyway. No one seemed to notice us. I drove down to the end of the street, turned down the river hill. I drove fast and over the bridge without thinking because that was the way I was supposed to go. I drove very fast and I could see very well. Everything looked very clear, like on a morning after a storm. I was over the bridge on the way to meet Ack before I thought of it and then when I realized it I turned off the road and kept going until we came to the country. Then I looked at Butch. He was very white and he was holding his side. I slowed up. Let me look. I pulled back his coat and his side looked like a tree that had been struck by lightning. He was almost split in two, the skin stripped down like bark.

I knew now nobody was following us. I couldn't figure it. I didn't even try to figure it. I just drove on as fast as I could but not too fast. I took off my coat. Put that on your side, I said, and try to stop the blood.

Where are we going now? he said. It don't much matter now, does it? Go on blame me. I got you into this, go on blame me, I can take it.

Don't say anything, I said, it makes it worse.

We were driving through flat lands. I hoped we were going south. I tried to keep to the little roads so we wouldn't be seen but I knew nobody was following us.

Well, you were right, go on tell me you were right. This is a fine end to come to.

We aren't coming to any end, I said.

He didn't say anything and it scared me.

We kept on driving and after a while he said, We haven't got a bit of the haul. Nobody following us and we haven't a thing. After all that and not a thing. That bastard Ganz made it all up so he would carry the money. I could of just as well had a satchel but he would carry the money. It could have been every man with a satchel and his chances.

He seemed excited. I couldn't keep him from talking. I felt better now than I felt before the holdup. I felt light as if I had dropped about a hundred pounds. He kept on talking and I was scared. I thought he was getting delirious now.

There was a short fellow at the bar, he said, in a black makinaw. He had a pointed nose and he was always having a fine time. He died of rot gut but he had a good time while it lasted. And he said, what kind of cup is this? The chalice of McCarthy—he was a card—that was Mc-Carthy's saloon, and he said, this is the chalice of McCarthy. I am going to wear a green tie, he said, if I have to bust a gut. I won't buy beer for any sons of guns that are drunk. If you are sober you need a beer—oh, he was a card all right—but if you are drunk you don't need a beer. He was the greatest gambler in town, used to gamble with Joe Hill and he knew what it was all about and he knew the cards were stacked. He told me then—Butch, he said, the cards are marked—when I was just a punk, he told me that, but I was smart—I was pretty smart all right.

There was no use to tell him to be quiet now. I had to find someplace to take him. I thought, Should I take him to a doctor? I was afraid to take him. It seemed like we were against everybody now.

Now we haven't got a thing, Butch said. After all that, and all that money in my hands, I can still feel it, what we could have done with even a little bit of that sweet money.

You're alive, I said.

He looked at me.

I was thinking, he said, standing by them pillars before we went in, when that girl went by, there was a few seconds there, I could have walked out then, we could have lived our lives like you wanted. I could have walked out of there then.

Don't talk, I said. I kept on driving through the country, going around the towns and villages. I just kept on going and I got out and took the extra gasoline can out and filled the tank and took off my petticoat and dipped it in a river and washed his side, and put the skirt in along the wound.

I kept driving and nobody was coming after us now for sure, and we must have been about a hundred and fifty miles by afternoon and the land was very flat and I thought maybe we were in Iowa, and it seemed so flat I looked at the sun and turned east because I had a crazy idea we would drive into the dark quicker and maybe get into Missouri or some wooded country. It was frightening to see it so flat with no place to go but into the ground.

I kept driving and nobody was coming after us. Farmers' wives came out and stood at the door. We drove past like lovers. Butch looked all right from the chest up and he leaned a little against me. The women stood in the doors of their houses, and children looked out the windows. All wives are beautiful.

I did everything just like we planned it, Butch said. I couldn't catch hold of that fat bastard, he slipped out of my hands like a greased pig. He let out an awful squeal.

I heard him, I said. Don't talk. I'm going to stop now and get some gas before it is dark. Sit up, I said, pull that coat around.

You don't think it was my fault, do you? Butch said. I mean

the whole mess.

No, I said, it wasn't your fault. You couldn't help it, any of it. Be still now.

I drove into a service station. Five gallons, I said. Could we fill our can too? We are going camping.

Sure, he said, going south?

Yes, I said. Maybe it's warm in Arkansas. I hoped we were going toward Arkansas.

It didn't surprise him. Yes, he said, good hunting down there too.

He took our can from the back seat. It was a service station built like a cottage. There were paper geraniums at the window.

This is a swell place you got here, Butch said.

The young man looked at us and went inside.

How much money you got, Butch?

I got a fiver Ganz gave me for gas, he said.

Good, I said, that's one thing Ganz did that was O.K.

The young man came out and Butch said again that it was a fine place he had. He looked at us. Oh, yes, he said, wiping the windshield. Butch and I leaned together so he wouldn't see.

I put everything me and my wife had into this place, he said, and now the oil company is going to take it away from me.

How can they do that? Butch said. Didn't you get a lease on it?

Oh, sure, he said, that's a racket. They make you feel like you got your place, like you're going to be the boss, a big shot. They take all your dough and they got it fixed so you can't make good. You could work twenty-eight hours out of twenty-four, you could starve your wife and kids and throw them in with it. They got you milked from both ends. It's a racket. They hold the cards. You can't win. And when you give up, when they've sucked you dry, they get another sucker.

Holy mackerel, Butch said.

It was getting night. He gave us the change and when we drove on down the road Butch began to swear. I never heard him swear like that.

Butch, I said, don't.

Oh, the Goddamned dirty bastards. They got you coming and going. They got you.

Be quiet, I said. Be quiet.

I had to stop somewhere. It was getting dark.

Once it began to snow a little and I was disappointed. I thought we were going south. I hoped we were going south.

I knew if we drove long enough we would come to a river and rivers always have dark places near them, caves and trees.

Butch got very delirious. I couldn't see him but all the time I was looking for some place to drive into I could hear him talking.

Yes, Butch said, honey, it's got to show pretty soon. Where are we going? It's got to show soon. What are we looking forward to? You got to believe in the future. I knew a man, he wasn't my father, but he said, Son, I can't tell you anything but you will find out something. You'll learn something. He wasn't my father but he told me that. I wouldn't pay him no mind. I was a cocky buck.

We were coming to some trees and rolling hills. It was nice to drive into them and not see any road behind. I drove as good as I could and not jar him.

No, he wasn't my father, Butch said. Do I owe my father any grief? Answer me that, he said. You don't owe your father anything. Here we are kicked around all our lives, what do you owe your father, spawning you in it? He began to sing. It sounded terrible. I cried a little so he wouldn't know it. He began to sing like he was drunk, to the tune of *The Star-Spangled Banner*: My father's gone to sea of thee I sing. . . . This is a dirty day, he said, a hell of a day. . . .

My mother, he said. She was the darnedest bawler out and had all those kids, Lord, there were kids everywhere like a brood of chicks. And where are mine? Where's my son? He'd make the big team, wouldn't he? He wouldn't be a white feather. Got to take the old carcass somewhere. I sleep anywhere, don't worry about that, I can sleep anywhere. I'm pretty sleepy. Hell, nobody'll bother you. One summer I slept in the morgue every night. Now that's a good place. Joe at the morgue don't like to stay alone with all the stiffs and it's cold in summer, it's about the coolest place in summer, crawl up on a nice cool slab.

Joe was goodshakes, once, going for a fare-you-well. It burnt him up. That's the trouble, you burn up. You don't bail out soon enough. I never saw anybody get out soon enough to save his hide. Joe was runner up. He used to track around Como and Rice in winter. I'd be coming down driving the truck, all bent out of shape with my kidneys killing me, and there'd be Joe warming up running like a dog. You can't hurt him now. Why should I be quiet? Can't I even speak? He's been knocked over so often his brains are addled. Jock Malone started a gym, that was a long time ago. Once Joe came back to town with a Packard. Boy, oh, boy, that was something. And then he didn't have a Packard, just like that, and I met him staggering down Fourth with a breath—Got a nickel? he hollers, and him in the big money not six months before. You see, that's the way it goes, in again, out again Finnegan. Got a nickel? he hollers. Damn if I know, I says, shake me and if you hear anything we'll split. Found a quarter and we split. My girl wants to go to a show, he says, and I went with him and I slept until a guy came along with a broom. That was another blank, that's all. I've got a lot of blanks. I draw a lot of blanks. You gotta have. My mind doesn't register now. Have I been knocked over?

No, I said, you're all right, Butch.

I saw a bridge ahead and I thought, There will be a road on the other side going down, to the river.

I know the porter at the Union Station, Butch said, he would help us. I know where you can get nigger gin. He would get us some. Five cents a pint, lay you in lavender for a week. And Mabel Martino the check girl is half-baked, short and plump, keeps herself fried. It would help, wouldn't it?

No, I said, we're all right.

Oh, we're fit as a fiddle, he shouted, and began to sing. The bellboy was drunk, he said, and started to lean where the old court-house was and it was gone, the bells are gone now. I better hit the hay, honey. Come down close. This old carcass better get someplace, take this old carcass home, wherever that is. . . .

We'll be home, I said, and I drove across the bridge and turned to the left where the road went straight down in the brush by the river. It was a dirt road and I drove very slow and eased the car down the frozen ruts. I stopped and turned off the lights.

Butch said, Don't do that, don't make it dark, and I turned them on again.

Once, he said, we were coming into Oshkosh between games and there I saw two ballplayers at the bar. One was a guy named Pinkey. It was mahogany beams, pretty swanky. Pinkey said, Hello, boy, I'm in the big money, I'm staying at the Fondulac over here. There was O'Leary and he was in the big money too and we had some drinks. We had gin rickies. Pinkey had pockets full of money, his old man just kicked off beside.

Say, he said, this must be the road to my mother's. My mother's goofy now. I used to go see the old girl. It seemed to cheer her up so to see her best effort, this son of Erin. Does it cheer you up?

Yes, it does. I began to go on slow. Sometimes there are old shacks along a river.

Gee, he said, when I remember it when I was young. I thought this old world couldn't live without me. Honest. I thought men couldn't live without me. I worked up until I was head of the route. I had to be in the alley back of the News at four o'clock in the morning. I thought I was doing a swell job. I didn't think they could get the paper out without me. Honest. I thought I was a public servant. I was a goof. Now a woman's got to give me food, hand-feed me. . . .

Charlie had three fingers from N.Y. came from Miami by freight. We flipped. Charlie and I had to sleep together, Red started telling about his kids. He was a steel worker too saved money and lived in a house and paid so much a month a steel-rivet man worked with a boy friend didn't have to push the bell button often to warn the men below they always worked together Sam fell off the fifty-fourth floor of the Empire State. Shouted I'm going down. I tried to grab his leg. All I could do then was ring bells. I had a pretty big funeral. All the gang. I felt terrible. I worked with different fellows . . . worked in factories. In October I met Charlie again he was a sight didn't care about anything but Baby Ruth candy bars. . . .

Remember my brother?

Yes, I said.

Bill was used to it. When he was a punk he climbed the company poles to fix wires in every kind of a gale so the hairs on his belly would freeze from the sweat of his armpits. I remember I met Bill. When I heard he was born I pulled up my didy and went out to give him howdy and welcome to this mortal coil and he was growing about one foot out of the linoleum in the kitchen and I was a little bigger than him. We had another boon companion named Sad Eye Morton and he was a bad boy. We were not good boys but he was a bad boy. Where are you going?

I'll be back, I said. I got out easy and tried to prop him up. I thought I would walk down the road and look in the thicket. I walked down in the light. I could hear the river on my left. I saw a path and I turned off. It led to a shack close by the banks. I ran back and I could hear Butch still talking. I got in.

Butch said, He was the greatest tipper over of outhouses and feeler under women's skirts and now he is a bank teller, very respectable, it just goes to show. Maybe he was that fat little squealing pig that got out of my hands.

I said, We are almost there.

Where? He said.

I drove into a clearing where a car had been before.

I feel like my old man's feet that time, Butch said.

How? I said.

Well, I was wandering around and the old man was sick and I happened to see his dogs sticking out of the bottom of the bed so I felt them and they were stone-cold. The old man's feet were like stones. I told my old lady that and she let out a yell. It turned out he was dead.

I said, You'll have to help me. We are going to get out now.

I'll help you, he said, I'll do anything you say.

All right, I said. I opened the other door. You'll have to put your good arm around me.

Why, that's easy, he said, that's a pleasure. Why, that's cooperation.

I left the lights on and they pierced the bare winter trees that looked like the beard of a man.

When I got him on the cot in the shack his whole side was a big mouth opening and shutting, with his shirt and coat caked in it. I ran down and took off my undershirt and broke the thin ice and dipped it in the water and ran back putting it under my armpits to warm it. I hated to put it on so cold. I put the cloth in and I didn't know how that mouth could ever be closed.

I went to get some wood because it was cold. I ran in the brush like mad. Some of it wouldn't go in without the stove door staying open but that was nice. I could watch Butch by the light of it.

He didn't say anything now. He slept and I watched to see that he was breathing. It was his being so quiet made me know.

Once, he said, You better drive on, honey, and leave me here.

I found an old stew pot and boiled some water. It seemed like it had been night for a long time. I thought I should have taken him to a doctor before. I must have been insane. Why didn't I do it? I thought, As soon as it is light I will do it.

We did everything O.K., Butch said, except that bastard slipped out of my hands like a greased pig. If it hadn't been for him.

Something else would have happened, I said.

It was funny, Butch said, there was a fat lady clerk and I told her to get down on the floor and when I was getting out of there to the door I almost stepped on her face and she looked at me. I didn't plan it, Butch said.

What? I said. Now he was going to tell it.

Take it on the natural out, Ganz told us. That's what I did. I came out of there natural and nobody followed us, I did that O.K., didn't I?

Yes, I said.

Well, just before that little pig came in Ganz said O.K., boys, take it on the natural, get out now, natural, walk easy, get that dough in the car. Hoinck had one satchel from the vault and Ganz had the one I gave him. The way I doped it sometime in my sleep was that Ganz was figuring with Hone to get all the dough one way or another.

Yes, I figured that too, I guess.

Ganz saw the pig slip out of my hands all right and he turned and I saw Hoinck fall as he was making for the door and it was Ganz shot Hoinck straight through the heart from the back. It was Ganz. Hoinck fell by the door. I saw him. He was so big and he just fell like he was cracked from behind. Ganz took the money on the run from his hand so he had both satchels and I took aim and shot him in the back.

I didn't say anything. I took his hand.

I saw him and I shot him. I never liked to look at him from behind.

All right, I said, neither did I.

And he kind of twisted around spinning to the floor and he saw me and raised his automatic and shot the whole wad. Ganz could shoot straight but I guess I got him bad.

All right, I said, try and sleep.

Sleep, he said, I been sleeping all my life. My God, do we belong to the human race or don't we?

Some people don't think so, I said.

To hell with them, I feel so tired.

Sleep, I said.

I had found a bottle of whisky in the car. I put some in the hot water and made him drink it and I drank some. I began to rub his body. The bleeding had stopped but he was spitting blood like he was bleeding inside. I rubbed him all over slow, his feet, his thighs, his neck and shoulders. I thought of everything he ever told me.

His body had been good to me. It seemed like there was everything else bad and our bodies good and sweet to us. He said, Get in beside me, I'm so cold. I got in with him and put our coats over us and he held on to me and if I would move he would draw me back. It was a narrow cot and I felt the fever mount in him. Sometimes he talked serious and I talked to him.

I haven't been good to you.

You've been good to me, I said, the best.

I hate it the way my brother looked when he was dead. I went out and I saw him face down in the gutter, and when I turned him over he looked at me.

There was Rafferty traveled and got his expenses paid, two thousand a month think of that met big men too. It brings the best out in you Rafferty used to say, ten years in hotels the best hotels give a tip of one dollar as easy as sneezing. I saw his report it was two thousand for one month what we couldn't do with that in one year even if we had it. The boy's doing well. I hope he makes a million.

Butch, I said, you know it wasn't anything with Ganz.

I know, Butch said, don't think about it. We're trapped, honey. Don't say anything.

This would happen anyway, he says, the sooner the better, eventually why not now? We couldn't do anything we didn't do. We put everything into it like they say. We shot the works. It was all in the cards.

Don't think of anything now, I said, and began rubbing his back.

Haven't done you much, he said.

Oh, you're good, I said. Haven't I done what you said, gone with you, followed you?

Yes, he said, you're sweet.

What was I doing all my life? Butch said. *What was I doing, what in high heaven and low hell was I up to? St. Peter Street, Wabasha, St. Paul 3rd and 4th and 5th. Remember Hogan's used to be up two flights and in the back and Rifle Joe's and Dodo? What in God's name? Three-story stone building that's Belle's, I recognize that an old stone building can be sweet saloon tailorshop restaurant fruit stand hotel upstairs,*

*rubber word off a red globe in the entrance the alley was a blind
remember that. Smell of sour whisky, rotten fruits, horses, catgut and
beer. I worked in a hat factory on that second floor when I was a punk
you didn't know me then I hadn't slept with you then I was looking for
you the girls used to hang out their towels in the hotel and we bet on
how many towels that was the first thing I bet on and the machines
made a steady one two stop one two you got so you liked it you could
jig it we used to do it.*

We both fell asleep. He woke me shouting: *What have they done
to this, what have they done to this now? Where are the oats, the
wheat? I was sure they were planted. Look, Mrs. Hinckley, the wealth
of the country, the iron ore wheat with my body I thee wed, with my
worldly goods I thee endow. . . . What are they doing to you now,
honey? They own the town. They own the earth and the sweet marrow
of your body. Watch out they'll shoot at you from all the windows and
blow up the town.*

*All my life there what in hell was I doing? Who said anything?
What happened? Going around those streets year in and year out boy
and man, those narrow dark godriddendevil haunted whorish drunken
grand streets upstairs and downstairs O Christ my God my heavens
good morning good evening with nothing Christ was it who made it
what got us we come to this bad end.*

Be quiet, I said.

We didn't mean any of this, we didn't think of any of this, he
screamed.

I couldn't make him quiet now. He talked about other things, some
he had told me and some of it he hadn't. He thought of all the people he
knew ending up with me and then he died.

It was Saturday night then. I tried not to go through towns. I tried
to keep going south. Butch sat beside me on the seat like he was asleep.
He was cold when you touched him and the blood had stopped. I was
glad of that. A scab closed his mouth.

I was going south but the cold was like the little teeth of Belle's cat
going into your skin, sharp. I had to wear Butch's coat. I was frightened
once, I thought I heard a shot, but then I saw it was a laundry truck
parked by the road and the driver was up in the hill, shooting. I didn't
want to hear it.

I went slow, and all night on Saturday I passed parties and taverns
and could see the girls sitting in the cars with their fellows. Toward
morning the roads got empty except for drunken boys, driving from
hell to breakfast, just like I was doing, and I saw a bar hill rise toward
the sky and I drove into a field of shocked corn. It seemed nice, the
round prairie hill. Like a mound.

It must have taken a long time for me to get him over my shoulder like a jackknife. It got a little lighter and some cows came and looked at me. The grasses at the top of the mound were tall and made a soft shhhhh where I laid him on his side, because I couldn't bend him now, and a black beard had started on his face.

I got the blanket and I covered him and I left him there.

The GIRL

She was going the inland route because she had been twice on the coast route. She asked three times at the automobile club how far it was through the Tehachapi Mountains, and she had the route marked on the map in red pencil. The car was running like a T, the garage man told her. All her dresses were back from the cleaner's, and there remained only the lace collar to sew on her black crepe so that they would be all ready when she got to San Francisco.

She had read up on the history of the mountains and listed all the Indian tribes and marked the route of the Friars from the Sacramento Valley. She was glad now that Clara Robbins, the math teacher, was not going with her. She liked to be alone, to have everything just the way she wanted it, exactly.

There was nothing she wanted changed. It was a remarkable pleasure to have everything just right, to get into her neat fine-looking little roadster, start out in the fine morning, with her map tucked into the seat, every road marked. She was lucky too, how lucky she was. She had her place secure at Central High, teaching history. On September 18, she knew she would be coming back to the same room, to teach the same course in history. It was a great pleasure. Driving along, she could see her lean face in the windshield. She couldn't help but think that she had no double chin, and her pride rode in her, a lean thing. She saw herself erect, a little caustic and severe, and the neat turn-over collar of her little blue suit. Her real lone self. This was what she wanted. Nothing messy. She had got herself up in the world. This was the first summer she had not taken a summer course, and she felt a little guilty; but she had had a good summer just being lazy, and now she was going to San Francisco to see her sister and would come back two days before school opened. She had thought in the spring that her skin was getting that papyrus look so many teachers had, and she had a little tired droop to her shoulders and was a little bit too thin. It was fine to be thin but not too thin. Now she looked better, brown, and she had got the habit of a little eye shadow, a little dry rouge, and just a touch of lipstick. It was really becoming.

Yes, everything was ideal.

But before long she was sorry she had come through the Tehachapi Mountains. Why hadn't someone told her they were like that? They did her in. Frightening. Mile after mile in the intense September heat,

through fierce mountains of sand, and bare gleaming rock faces jutting
sheer from the road. Her eyes burned, her throat was parched, and
there was mile after mile of lonely road without a service station and
not a soul passing. She wished, after all, that Miss Robbins had come
with her. It would have been nice to be able to say, "What an interesting
formation, Miss Robbins! We really should make sketches of it, so we
could look up the geological facts when we get back." Everything would
have seemed normal then.

She drove slowly through the hot yellow swells, around the firm
curves; and the yellow light shone far off in the tawny valleys, where
black mares, delicate-haunched, grazed, flesh shining as the sun struck
off them. The sun beat down like a golden body about to take form on
the road ahead of her. She drove very slowly, and something began to
loosen in her, and her eyes seemed to dilate and darken as she looked
into the fold upon fold of earth flesh lying clear to the horizon. She saw
she was not making what is called "good time." In fact, she was making
very bad time.

She had been driving five hours. She looked at her wrist watch and
decided she would stop, even if it was only eleven-thirty, and have
lunch. So when she saw a little service station far down, tucked into the
great folds of dun hill, she was glad. Her car crept closer circling out of
sight of it and then circling back until her aching eyes could read the
sign — Half Way Station — and she drew up to the side and stopped. Her
skin felt as if it were shriveling on her bones. She saw a man — or was it
a boy? — with a pack, standing by the gas pump probably waiting to
catch a ride; she wouldn't pick him up, that was certain. These hills
were certainly forsaken.

She went in at the door marked Ladies. The tiny cubicle comforted
her. She opened her vanity case and took out some tissue, made little
pads and put them over her eyes. But still all she could see were those
terrifying great mounds of the earth and the sun thrusting down like ar-
rows. What a ghastly country! Why hadn't someone told her? It was
barbarous of the automobile club to let her come through this country.
She couldn't think of one tribe of Indians.

She really felt a kind of fright and stayed there a long time, and
then she got a fright for fear she had left her keys in the car, and with
that boy out there — she could see his sharp piercing glance out of his
brown face — and she had to go pouncing all through her bag, and at
last she found them, of all places, in her coin purse and she always put
them into the breast pocket of her suit. She did think people were
nuisances who had to go looking in all their pockets for keys. Habit was
an excellent thing and saved nobody knew how much time.

But at last she drew a deep breath, opened the door onto the vast
terrible bright needles of light, and there she saw through the heavy

down-pouring curtain the boy still standing there exactly as he had been standing before, half leaning, looking from under his black brows. He looked like a dark stroke in the terrible light, and he seemed to be still looking at her. She fumbled the collar at her throat, brushed off the front of her skirt, and went into the lunch room.

"My, it's certainly hot," she said to the thin man behind the counter. She felt strange hearing her voice issue from her.

"It is," said the proprietor, "but a little cooler in here." He was a thin, shrewd man.

She sat down in the booth. "Yes," she said, and saw that the boy had followed her in and sat down on the stool at the lunch counter, but he seemed to be still looking at her. He looked as if he had been roasted, slowly turned on a spit until he seemed glowing, like phosphorus, as if the sun were in him, and his black eyes were a little bloodshot as if the whites had been burned, and his broad chest fell down easily to his hips as he ground out a cigarette with his heel. The thin man brought her a glass of water. "What will you have, ma'am?" he said with respect. "I'll have a lettuce sandwich," she said. "I'm afraid we ain't got any proper lettuce, ma'am," he said, bowing a little. "We can't get it fresh out here. We have peanut butter, sliced tongue — " "All right," she said quickly, "peanut butter and, well, a glass of beer." She felt that the boy was somehow laughing at her. She felt angry.

"This the first time you been in these parts?" called out the thin man from behind the counter. "Yes," she said, and her own voice sounded small to her. "It is." The boy at the counter turned his head, still with it lowered, so that his eyes looked up at her even though she was sitting down in the booth, and a soft charge went through her, frightening. She felt herself bridling, and she said in a loud, cool voice: "This is a very interesting country. Do you know anything about the formation of these curious rocks that jut out of the hills? They are so bare and then suddenly this rock — "

Was she imagining it only, that the boy seemed to smile and shift his weight?

"No'm," said the thin man, drawing the beer, "I can't say I ever thought about it." She felt as if something passed between the two men, and it made her angry, as if they were subtly laughing at her. "I know it's hard to grow anything here, unless you got a deep well," he said.

"Oh, I can imagine," she sang out too loud; she felt her voice ringing like metal. The boy seemed not to be touched by what she was saying, but he attended curiously to every word, standing silent but alert like a horse standing at a fence waiting for something. So she began to tell the lunch room proprietor the history of the country, and he seemed amazed but not impressed. It made her feel vindicated somehow. Still the boy drooped alert on the stool, his half face turned toward her, his huge burned ear springing from his head. She stayed half an hour and so cut her time still further, but she felt much better and thought she would make up for it. She got up and paid her bill. "I'll send you a book about the Indians," she said to the thin man.

He smiled. "That will be very nice," he said. "Thank you, I'm sure," and the two men looked at each other again, and she was amazed at the anger that gushed like a sudden fountain in her breast. She sailed out and got into the car. The thin man came after her. "Oh, by the way," he said, "the lad in there has had an awful time this morning catching a ride. He's got to get up to the bridge, about fifty miles." She felt they were putting something over on her. "I'll vouch for him," the thin man said. "He lives here, and I know his folks now for eighteen years. He's been to the harvest fields, and it would be something for him to ride with an educated lady like you," he added cunningly. The boy came out and was smiling at her now very eagerly. "Now they want something," she thought, and she was suddenly amazed to find out that she despised men and always had.

"I don't like to drive with a strange man," she said, stubborn.

"Oh, this boy is harmless," the thin man said, and that look passed between the two of them again. "I can vouch for him — good as gold his family is. I thought maybe anyhow you might give him a mite of education on the way." A pure glint of malice came into the thin man's eyes that frightened her. He hates me, too, she thought. Men like that hate women with brains.

"All right," she said, "get in."

"Get right in there," the thin man said. "It's only a piece."

The boy rose toward her, and she drew away, and he sat down in a great odor of milk and hay, right beside her, stifling. Without speaking she threw the car in, and they plunged up the bald brow of the hill and began to climb slowly. The sun was in the central sky, and the heat fell vertically. She wouldn't look at him and wished she could get out her handkerchief — such a nauseating odor of sweat and something like buttermilk. She couldn't help but be conscious of the side of his overall leg beside her and his big shoes, and she felt he never took his eyes off her, like some awful bird — and that curious little smile on his mouth as if he knew something about her that she didn't know herself. She knew without looking that he was bending his head toward her with that curious awful little glimmer of a smile.

He said in a soft, cajoling voice, "It's pretty hot, and it's nice of you to take me. I had a hard time."

It disarmed her. She felt sorry for him, wanting to be helpful. She always wanted to help men, do something for them, and then really underneath she could hate them. "Oh," she said, "that was all right. You know one hates to pick up just anyone."

"Sure enough," he said. "I heard in Colorado a fellow got killed."
"Yes," she said, but she was on her guard. His words seemed to
mean nothing to him. He was like the heat, in a drowse. "My, you must
have been in the sun," she said.
"Yes," he said, "I've been as far as Kansas — looking for work."
"The conditions are pretty bad," she said.
"There ain't no work," he said simply.
"Oh," she said, "that's too bad," and felt awkward and inane. He
seemed in such a sun-warmed ease, his legs stretching down. He had his
coat in his arms and his shirtsleeves were torn off, showing his huge
roasted arms. She could see the huge turn of the muscles of his arms,
out of the corner of her eye.
They went climbing in gear up that naked mountain, and it began
to affect her curiously. The earth seemed to turn on the bone rich and
shining, the great mounds burning in the sun, the great golden body,
hard and robust, and the sun striking hot and dazzling.
"These mountains," she began to tell him, "are thousands of
years old."
"Yeah,"he said looking at her sharply, "I'll bet." He lounged down
beside her. "I'm sleepy," he said. "I slept on a bench in L.A. las' night."
She felt he was moving slowly toward her as if about to touch her leg.
She sat as far over as she could, but she felt him looking at her, taking
something for granted.
"Yes," she said, "it would be an interesting study, these mountains."
He didn't answer and threw her into confusion. He lounged down,
looking up at her. She drew her skirt sharply down over her leg.
Something became very alert in her, and she could tell what he was doing without looking at him.
They didn't stop again. The country looked the same every
minute. They rose on that vast naked curve into the blue blue sky, and
dropped into the crevasse and rose again on the same curve. Lines and
angles, and bare earth curves, tawny and rolling in the heat. She
thought she was going a little mad and longed to see a tree or a house.
"I could go on to San Francisco with you," he said, and she could
feel her heart suddenly in her.
"Why would you do that?" she said, drawing away, one hand at
her throat.
"Why shouldn't I?" he said insolently. "It would be kind of nice for
both of us." He was smiling that insolent knowing smile. She didn't
know how to answer. If she took him seriously it would implicate her,
and if she didn't it might also. "It would be kind of nice now, wouldn't
it?" he said again with his curious soft impudence. "Wouldn't it?"
"Why, of course, I'm going to San Francisco anyway," she
said evasively.

"Oh sure," he said, "I know that. But it isn't so hot going alone. And we get along, don't we?" He didn't move, but his voice drove into her.

"Why, I don't know," she said coldly, "I'm only taking you to the bridge."

He gave a little grunt and put his cap on his head, pulling the beak over his eyes, which only concentrated his awful power. She pulled her blouse up over her shoulders. She had never noticed before that it fell so low in front. She felt terrible. And to her horror he went on talking to her softly.

"You wouldn't kid me, would you? You know I like you, I like you. You're pretty."

She couldn't say a word. She felt her throat beating. He was making love to her just as if she were any common slut. She felt her throat beating and swelling.

He kept on his soft drowsy talk, "The times is sure hard." His words seemed to be very tiny falling from the enormous glow of his presence, wonderful, as if he had been turned naked, roasted in the sun. You could smell his sunburnt flesh. And you could smell the earth turning on its spit under the mighty sun. If only he were not so near; the car threw them close together, and she tried to go easy around the curves so that his big body would not lounge down upon her like a mountain. She couldn't remember when she had been so close to a man. It was as frightening as some great earth cataclysm. She prided herself on knowing men. She was their equal in every way, she knew that.

If only she could see something familiar, then she could get back her normal feelings about men. She felt as if she were in a nightmare.

"I worked when I was twenty," he went on softly. "Made good money, blew it in on Saturday night. Made big money when I was twenty—Jesus, I've got something to look forward to, haven't I?"

She sat over as far as she could. "Where did you work?" she managed to say. She prided herself on always getting information about people. They talked about Roosevelt and the New Deal. She always had strong views, but for the first time in her life she felt as if what she was saying was no good, like talking when some gigantic happening is silently going on. She didn't know what was happening, but she felt that every moment he won, was slowly overcoming her, and that her talk gave him a chance silently to overcome her. She was frightened as if they were about to crack up in a fearful accident. She relaxed on the seat, and the heat stroked down her body. She wished she wasn't driving a car. The great body of the earth seemed to touch her, and she began looking where the shadows were beginning to stroke down the sides of the mounds as if she might sleep there for a little while. An awful desire to sleep drugged her, as if she hadn't slept for years and years. She felt warm and furred and dangerously drugged.

It was as if a little rocket exploded in front of her face when he said, "Let's don't talk about that," and he leaned closer than he had. "Let's talk about you." She could see suddenly his whole face thrust to her, the gleaming strong teeth, the roasted young cheeks, and he had long single whiskers growing out like a mandarin. She laughed a little. "Who do you think I am?" she asked nervously. "Why, I guess you're a pretty good-looking girl," he said. "You look pretty good to me." She bridled at this common language, as if she were nothing but any girl you pick up anywhere.

"Why, I'm a school teacher," she cried.

He didn't seem surprised. "O.K.," he said, laughing into her face.

"Why, I could almost be your mother," she cried.

"Aw, that's a new one," he said, and he put his great hand straight on her arm. "Never heard of a girl wanting to make out she was old before."

She had an awful desire to make him say more; she was frightened. Swift thoughts, habitual thoughts, came into her head, and they seemed like frail things that the heat pounded down. Was it because they were so far out in these strange, rising, mounded hills?

"Are those cigarettes?" he said pointing to the pocket beside her. "Let's stop and have a smoke."

"Oh no," she cried, "I haven't time. I'm behind now. I've got to make up a lot of time."

"O.K.," he said. "We can smoke here."

"All right," she said, handing him the package. "You keep the package."

"All right," he said and took one out and put the package into his pocket.

The sun moved to her side and fell on her shoulder and breast and arm. It was as if all her blood sprang warm out of her. The sun moved slowly and fell along her whole side.

"Oh," he said, "I know you like me."

"How do you know?" she said, offended, trying to see the road. She felt fatuous indulging in this adolescent conversation. She let her skirt slip up a little. She knew she had good legs, tapering down swiftly to her ankles. But he didn't seem actually to be looking at her; a heat came out of his great lax body and enveloped her. He seemed warmly to include her, close to himself.

"What kind of a wheel is that?" he said and put his large thick hand beside her own small one on the wheel. "Oh, it turns easy," he said. "I haven't driven a car since I left home. A good car is a pretty sweet thing," he said, and leaned over and began to fondle the gadgets on the front, and she looked fascinated at his huge wrist joint covered with

golden hair bleached in the sun. She had to look and saw that his hair
was black on his skull but also burnt around the edges. Looking at him
she met his gaze and felt her face flush.

They fell down the valley, yellow as a dream. The hills lifted
themselves out on the edge of the light. The great animal-flesh-jointed
mountains wrought a craving in her. There was not a tree, not a
growth, just the bare swelling rondures of the mountains, the yellow
hot swells, as if they were lifting and being driven through an ossified
torrent.

The Tehachapis rolled before them, with only their sharp primeval
glint, warm and fierce. They didn't say anything about that in the
books. She felt suddenly as if she had missed everything. She should
say something more to her classes. Suppose she should say — "The
Tehachapi Mountains have warmed and bloomed for a thousand
years." After all, why not? This was the true information.

She stopped the car. She turned and looked directly at him. "What
is your name?" she asked.

Puzzled, he leaned toward her, that tender warm glint on his face.
"Thom Beason," he said. The hot light seemed to fall around them
like rain.

"Listen," he said, gripping her hands, twisting them a little, "let's get
out. Wouldn't it be swell to lie down over there in the hills? Look,
there's a shadow just over there. It's cool in those shadows if you dig
down a little — "

She saw his wrists, his giant breast, his knees, and behind him the
tawny form and heat of the great earth woman, basking yellow and
plump in the sun, her cliffs, her joints gleaming yellow rock, her ribs,
her sides warm and full. The rocks that skirted the road glistened like
bone, a sheer precipice and dazzle of rock, frightening and splendid,
like the sheer precipice of his breast looming toward her so that she
could feel the heat come from him and envelop her like fire, and she felt
she was falling swiftly down the sides of him, and for the first time in
her life she felt the sheer sides of her own body dropping swift and fleet
down to her dreaming feet, and an ache, like lightning piercing stone,
struck into her between her breasts.

She let her head fall over their hands and pulled back from him in
hard resistance. She could not go to his breast that welcomed her — All
my delicacy, my purity, she thought. He will not see me. I must not
change. I must not change. The tears came to her eyes, and at the same
time a canker of self-loathing, terrible, festered in her.

The moment had passed. He withdrew from her. "O.K.," he said.
"You don't need to be scared. Only if you wanted to. O.K. Let's go. You
can make up your time. We're only about a half hour from the bridge
where I blow."

She began driving very fast, very well. He withdrew completely from her, just waiting to get out. It hurt her, as if there had been before her some sumptuous feast she had been unable to partake of, the lush passional day, the wheaty boy, some wonderful, wonderful fruit.

"I'll swan," he said. "There's old Magill going with a load of melons. Hi!" he shouted.

She wished he were gone already. She wildly began thinking what she could say to him. She thought she would say, casually — "Well, good luck." She felt easier knowing what she was going to say. She stopped the car. He got out and stood by the car. She wanted to do something for him. She really would have liked to give him something. She thought she would buy him a melon. "How much are they?" she said, nodding toward the melons and hunting for her pocketbook. He ran over. "You pick out a good one," she called after him.

He came back with a large one with yellow crevasses. His strong talons curved around it, and he kept pressing it, leaving a dent which swelled out after his fingers. He held up the great melon with its half-moon partitions, grading golden toward the sun. She fumbled with her purse to pay for it, and suddenly she saw that he was holding it toward her, that he was giving it to her, and she was ashamed and held the quarter she had taken out, in her hand. He was smiling at her as if he felt sad for her. She smiled foolishly and sat pressing her wet hands together.

"Well, good-bye," he said. "And good luck."

"Good-bye," she said. Now she could not say good luck. He had beat her to it. Why should he wish her good luck when she had it? . . .

He turned and ran toward the wagon, climbed in and did not look back. She drove around the curve, stopped, turned down the mirror and looked at her face. She felt like a stick and looked like a witch. Now she was safe — safe. She would never never change, pure and inviolate forever; and she began to cry.

After five minutes she saw a car rounding the mountain to her right. It would pass her soon. She got out her whiskbroom, brushed her suit, brushed off the seat where he had sat, opened the back window to air out the smell of buttermilk and hay, started the car and drove to San Francisco because that was where she was going.

GONE HOME

"Now the season's over, the fishing's gettin' good," Gottschalk said, but Jonathan Hank only nodded, and through the fall haze he could scarcely see his friend, tipped beside him, against the tavern wall, but he could see the shining river and the fishermen coming in with the last catch of the season before freezing time. He tipped the bottle of corn liquor to his mouth — warmth, that's what he wanted; the liquor felt like a hot ingot, startling to his fingertips. He saw the village rising to the cemetery where his wife was buried, and he heard Old Lady Thrumbull's turkeys and a wood-cutting machine he had heard all morning. "The summer is over, harvest time is rich, fat as wild grapes, Gottschalk. There was plenty of game when we were tadpoles and it's all gone now. I can remember when they was so many berries, stained the hooves of the horses, yes sir, the goose hung high then. Time to die now."

"Don't be stingy with the bottle," Gottschalk said. "There's old lady Thrumbull come down to see the fish."

And Jonathan realized, with the late sun moving like a bee's sting over his knee, that he had not said a word, had not even said, "Now the season's over, the fishing's gettin' good." And a wild pang of regret swarmed inside him and, watching Old Lady Thrumbull fly down the hill like a ghost, it seemed to him that he had never spoken to anyone, to his poor wife Erda, to his dead son; and all the lost men of his time seemed to stand in the frosty air, closer to him than Gottschalk; all the lumberjacks, whistle punks, landsmen, seamen, some who lay upon the hill like Erda his wife, under a stone tree, with a finger pointing "Gone Home," like a sign on an empty house. Others had gone to far places and he saw them too; for banks had closed, lumber had gone, land speculation had lost them their farms, there was panic and prosperity; all the legions of lost men, absorbed, fled, forgotten in the crashing riot of building America.

"Saving at the spigot, losing at the bung," Gottschalk said, and he took the bottle, an eye on Old Lady Thrumbull, watching her through the nostalgic haze of the liquor as it poured through his rope-like veins and he thought — poor old lady, poor poor thing, just like Erda. He saw her in her long black clothes, age like hoar frost limning her delicate bones, and she seemed, like Erda, vengefully alone, a kind of outraged dignity to her, as if she already prepared herself decently and alone for a burial that would bother no one. She would gradually grow cold, he thought, she would not die, poor thing, a delicate chill would come creeping up her legs now buried in the long black skirt, and he smiled to think of death so bold to ravish these women, just like Erda; "Now Jonathan Hank," she had called him by his full name even in the dark of night, "Now Jonathan Hank, you leave me be." His mouth formed to say a word to Old Lady Thrumbull as she went by, for it was their last day upon this earth and shouldn't they speak? He saw her coming toward him in the spectral light with all the dead, past, present, and the coming dead, and he saw that she, too, walked, bemused by her coming death, as she skittered past them and he had a quick warm impulse, like the touch of the last sun on his knees, to speak to her, put his hand on her arm, but he was frightened by the cavernous eye turned toward him, as she veered and flew past and with some old coquetry patted the bun on her skull, like a flying corpse. When she faded into the bright rivergleam he had not even said a word to her and her name was a little dust poufing in his mouth and all the dead leaves turned in the wind like the soles of the feet of flying women.

"It looks like every time Old Lady Thrumbull thinks her old man is dead she says to herself, 'Glory be to God!' Let's have a beer. The devil must be after her. One beer!" he yelled, and someone far off answered, "One comin' up."

"What happened to us, Gottschalk?" Jonathan said, and then he rose crying and swearing, "I tell you I wouldn't of lost my land in Wild Cat valley that time if my wife hadn't up and died on me." All the split seconds when he might have made it, sugared off timber, made a haul, a catch, badgered him now, the fortune that stood in the wind between one man and the next, the fall of the cards, the lay of the land, the breaks. "My son aimed to clean up that time he tooken that load of pine to Wisconsin. Yes sir, but all he done was come back with my mule lookin' like bags o' bones — anyway you look at it, anyway you keep the score — "

Gottschalk was guzzling his bottle of beer and it drooled down his white beard, which stuck like straw from his chin.

"We been here a long time, Gottschalk," Jonathan said, knowing keenly now the river shining below him, the boats coming in, and next year he wouldn't be there to see it and wanting to say — It's good to think of our long life in this village, Gottschalk — history exists — we are real. Who shuts us up, lies about what happened? Who made it something different? Let us talk now of the log jams, the masts cut, the barns we've built, the houses that are here. Where is that great sound of our hammers, the riot of our mills? Where are the people who rode to town on Saturdays in sleighs full of straw; the dandy dressers, those that kept fast horses, the wanderers to Alaska, the sashayers? Were they lost? Or poor? Or dead and buried? He thought he said, "There's a history, Gottschalk, that is not in books." But what he said was, "It's your turn to pay for the beer, Gottschalk." Then he mumbled, "Grief and sorrow . . . by the sweat o' your brow and the sparks fly upwards," and seemed to drowse and sleep on the last word like some monstrous tomcat purring through his whiskers that struck fierce into the sun, out of his nostrils, sniffing now the frosty odor of death.

In his drowse it all turned gleaming and mixing in him, his whole life, like the river gleaming taut between the trees. And everything that had ever happened to him tawnied over by the voluptuous light of the last fall, and his mouth watered for it all. That Indian girl tawny and furry as the river cliffs, and was it ever better than she made it, coming eager to him. And far back the face of his mother laughing in his flesh; and the needle of death, drawing the memories through every pore and corpuscle, with a fine precise and cutting pain.

Then he dreamed that in his mouth there was a hot ingot that turned into a fabulous word, useful and glowing as a rivet, a word that would hold everything together, a workman's word, that was true, that would stand, that would be there when he was gone when another wind would stir the October dust and frost rose from the river hills and he would not be there. He thought — we've got to say it now — we got something to do yet, something to say now. He felt the most awful hunger in his life, the things he had not said, or had never been said, all bayed in his belly like a bunch of hound dogs in hunting time.

"What did you say there?" It was Gottschalk talking and he opened his eyes and the wind struck him frostily as if someone had just walked past, as if a rider rode full tilt, without clatter of hoof, or a pack of hound dogs had beaten by, invisibly, seven ways for Sunday.

"I said," Jonathan took another swig, "I said that anyway I don't have to cut any wood this year."

"Got enough?"

"Ain't nobody going to tell me this year to salt down a hog, or bury the cabbages, or get those wild grapes in the ravine ahead of you, Gottschalk."

"You'll do it. You'll wake up one morning and Erda will be telling you to do it and you'll do it."

"I won't do it," and he felt a stick of anger thrust up his blood, "I'll set here a-drinkin'."

"Old Anson Weeks was a powerful sight better drinker than you, Jonathan Hank."

"He was not, they ain't never been anybody in this village I couldn't drink under the table. Why, I remember —"

"No sir, Anson Weeks not only did that but he made money from his drinkin'. He drank all day and never did a tap and went home with more money than he came with. That's somethin' — "

"Anything Anson Weeks could do I could do with one hand tied behind me."

"Why, you old idiot. You couldn't drive a bargain like Anson even when you're sober. You was always gettin' rooked — "

This was so true Jonathan's anger was a flaming sword in his hand. "Why, you old coot, you befouler of your own mess kit — "

"Yes, sir, when everybody was losin' his head like you're a doin' this minute, old Anson was just hittin' his stride real easy like. You remember the time — "

Jonathan began to strike the air, lost his balance, got out of his chair before it toppled, and both old men sawed the air. Nobody paid any attention. Everyone was looking at the catch. Then Jonathan saw Gottschalk getting smaller and realized he was not going to fight, he was leaving, and he wanted to yell after him — Wait — wait — his last friend, but he only stood there with his hand raised and his words fell back upon him like spitting in the wind. Then he began to cry softly.

After a while he started slowly up the hill, going home, talking to himself. When night came he was lonely and wished even for the sharp tongue of Erda to flay him. Passing the white church with its tiny steeple he thought of her now and himself on Sunday, his boots creaking, and a stiff collar, following the old ladies' hips into church and thinking thoughts that would blast down the steeple. When Erda rebuked him, for she knew his carnal thoughts without words or deeds, he whispered that old David was like that and didn't the Lord love him? And what a good time he had on that roof, Lord be praised. And he could hear her snort of wrath, and the stiff toss of her head as he came through the acacias that led to her grave on the hill. Erda — he began talking to her, Erda, pardon me, excuse me, would you put up a fuss if I was buried alongside you? Being it's the only cemetery in these parts and the only lot I'm likely to afford, carpentering being what it is now — No, it ain't likely I'll snare me another lot before Gabriel blows his horn.

But when he got to her grave there was a chill silence and he felt rebuffed, like getting into bed with her. Fifteen years buried now on the curve of the hill in the dark earth that would be the grave of them all.

And he looked up the hill to Old Lady Thrumbull's house, rooted with lilac and ash, and he started slowly toward it and women could look up from the warm houses in the village and see him slowly walking along the rim, with the evening star so close it seemed he could have reached up and picked it. "Poor Jonathan," they would say, quickly turning to the cries of their living children, to the warm confusion of their cottages.

He tired and sat down in the tall plantain, and the long litany of his failure went on in him. Why didn't he get that sugared-off timber that would have made him rich and then maybe Erda wouldn't have died? If he had been there an hour earlier, or gone the day before. He could have bought a farm then with good soil, and maybe his son wouldn't have died that time when he drove to Wisconsin and brought the mules back thin as Lazarus. You bawled him out fierce, Jonathan, you old son of a seacook, beat him with a buggy whip. Why did I strike him and him so soon dead? What did he do to bring them mules back so lean and why did the mules up and die when he was only trying to haul some stuff up there and make a little dough for himself?

If he had had a team of mules that time when wheat was so high—must have been during the war—then he could have got his crop out before the storm that came from the west, with hail that laid it flatter than a pancake.

He began to cry softly, squatting in the plantain, and a mule leaned its head down from the sky above him blowing his hair up on the top of his head, nibbling his ears. He was so moved by the touch of the long dark face he began to swear and laugh. He stroked the long ears, looking into the dark mouth, saw the strong tongue and great biting teeth — a fine one — a fine one — he said with pleasure, feeling the warm solid coat, and the mule rolled back its eyes, blew a fine blast from his drawn-back snout, and Jonathan pulled himself up along the black shaft of the body and filled his lungs and yelled with the broken bray of the mule.

But nobody came out on the village streets. Even two children, far off, going to the store for the evening bread, did not look up toward the crest where he held to the shafted neck and felt the good swell of his corn-liquored blood filling his throat, for the last time, and from the village he imagined that all the voices of the dead rose with his; from the dead sockets of the deserted houses voices crept, swelled, brayed; all old conversations in doorways, from the porches where women gathered their long skirts, from the gardens, crying voices of another year, as if all were harvested now in memory, dropping down like apples, cries of *timber*; voices of women laughing; cries of birth and of death; sound of apples falling, wheat threshing, of sheep and goats that used to entrain in the early morning.

The mule stopped, shied sharply, veered away into the darkness. He stood smelling the night, his nose tickling, odors of hay, hunting dogs, polecats, the snuff of old houses, full of time, and the smell of old wood he himself had logged and cut, and as he passed the Pratt house he went up and put his hands on the best timber to be made by God and man; that kind of wood, he said to himself, never wears out, just settles. If they wanted to tear that house down they would have to blast, tear it right out by the roots.

His feet began to lift him with the earth up the path to Old Lady Thrumbull's, lifting him slowly through the cold and yellow sky. A thin thread of smoke was coming out of her chimney.

He hurried now, some dream quickening and warming his joints, a warm room, woman sight and smell again, a cup of tea with corn in it, the wonderful fidgety nerves of a woman again. He hobbled up the path that rose alongside the house with the door facing away from the village in a sudden quiet with two fir trees. There was the stoop and the door was closed. An old wagon wheel was propped beside it, and the yard was a jumble of old tools, canned beef cans the relief handed out, and he stood in the dark of the path thinking—how had she lived? How did anyone live? Maybe she was hungry, the poor poor thing, up here on this hill without chick nor child. It wasn't natural for a woman to be without man or beast to care for or feed. The poor poor thing.

And he saw her clearly again as she had stood alone like a person who has not spoken to or touched a living thing day in day out, loneliness around her as secure as her shroud would ever be, as if every living thing had receded from her, leaving her flat, like a paper doll, cut out from everything. A good woman was part and parcel of the earth and everything that happens in it, a fine warm-bosomed woman, what was better and scarcer than hen's teeth for a fact.

There wasn't a sound from the house, only the thin smoke rising a little and then poufed down as if there were no currents above to take it off and the air was blue and fragrant, and yes, there was the odor of fatback frying, pork smell, nothing better than pork smell!

To his knock, a silence spaced itself, before the door slowly opened a crack to one eye of Old Lady Thrumbull, a fearful eye, and he put out his huge hand and opened the door, pushed it right open on the pulse of a large feeling in him of paternal benevolence. She looked so tiny, and that fearful eye, and then he saw the white parchment of her skin drawn over the bones which now seemed like a bird's without plumage. It rankled him to see the fine flesh of a woman thus ravaged by too many kinds of hunger. The flesh of a woman was the best part of her, fresh and firm, giving to the touch, yet springing back alive warm and odorous.

If it hadn't been for this kind of feeling he might not have done what he did, she might not have been frightened, mistaking his gesture entirely, thinking only that he was breaking into her house, into the long, distorted loneliness which had made her room and herself tiny, sensitive to any movement, panicked so suddenly by this man in her house speaking to her again in his deep warm voice, a man's voice again in her house, bringing to her all the terror and the drunkenness and the violation of her life with her husband, all the ways she never understood a man, never was taken into the bacchanalian feasts she was asked to be chief actor in — her eyes filled with tears that he saw and he wanted to give her something that he thought she had never had, the warmth of his breast, the words he had never spoken, to warm her now the awful cold was coming into their marrow, sitting like a cat at your elbow biting with sharp teeth into your flesh, coming up from the feet like stone. Only once more — and he put his great hand on her that was to her a terrifying command, a weight of memory, and she smelled the odor of whiskey also familiar to her and misread the look in his eyes and she sprang away from him with a quick shock that shook his nerves which were running warm liquor of love in all his being to tell her that he had failed — and now the great and lonely river —

She struck at him adder-tongued, her face swirling from the black of her terrible clothes, and fright giving it its last potency of feeling. He crooned to her — the poor poor thing.

She screamed — "You keep away from me, you dirty foul-smelling old man —"

He stopped and stood in the room bending over a little amidst all her woman's things of teapot and apron and picayunish spinsterhood, pondering a deep wonder — how do I look? I sleep with my boots on. I haven't changed my shirt —

"You stay away from me, Jonathan Hank, you dirty old man!"

And the words shocked him more than any words he had ever remembered hearing. He stood as if his feet were entangled by a nest of snakes.

The room was quiet after that and she crouched in the corner and when, at last, he raised his head and looked at her, he saw her poor mouth shrunken already to the teeth, one eye higher than the other, her claw hands plucking her own body, and the hair falling off her head exposing the scalp a little, and he put out his hand — you poor poor thing.

This set her off again as if he had whipped her and she bent over, flinging the words physically out of her body like a slingshot, "I am not a poor thing," they came out like rocks on the terrible whang of her voice which didn't sound human, more like a crow caw. "I'm as good as you, Jonathan Hank. I'm as good as you. Don't you be sorry for me. I'm as good as you, you dirty old man."

And the cry rang in his vitals and he wanted to straighten her limbs and see once again that glow a man can make in a woman, and he put out his hands easily drawing her to him, so easily he took hold of the fragile bones, that he did not realize the fury of her resistance. He felt her under his hands with shock, the tiny bones, the delicate and beautiful construction of a woman — in his hands like a fine bird you have shot and he sat down with her and her mouth was open as if she was screaming but he heard no sound and he saw her eyes dilate and she fell enormously toward him and he saw the round frightened eye and the broken mouth out of which nothing came, and then she was limp in his hands lying across his knees and he said, the poor poor thing, and looked at her a long time and she got cold and he laid her out on the bed smoothing down her body, sometimes singing a little bit to her.

After that he sat down at the table and poured himself a hot cup of tea she had just been making for herself. He had a moment's deep regret — they could have had tea together. He felt very good sitting at the table as if at home again. He could see her lying on the bed. He put some corn liquor in his tea.

He went outdoors after a while and it was getting dark. It was very very still and the mound of hill darkness above him and he could see the line darkening against the sky as night made of the earth a grave.

He stood at the door and lit his pipe as if he was a landowner there. He walked around the place looking at everything as if he might be going to buy it or perhaps had just made it his own. He went up the path and picked two plantain leaves, just the spike ends which were budded with tiny flowers, and he went back into the house, but if he was thinking of doing anything with them he forgot what it was and put them in his jacket pocket as if they were some treasure. He covered her up, fixed the fire, and, softly closing the door behind him, went out.

He walked slowly down the hill. It was dark when he got to the tavern and he got his bottle filled again. Gottschalk was asleep in his chair tipped back against the tavern wall. His own chair was empty, molded to his own body, scarcely any other sat in it. He tipped back. The sun was gone now, it was chilly, but he didn't feel it.

He felt very good.

He began to easily softly think with tenderness of the woman lying on the bed on the hill, as if she might be waiting for him and he kind of took her to his heart, as if he was married to her, the poor poor thing. He kept drinking steadily, a hot flood of tenderness rising in him with the darkness of the earth.

The Dark Time

INTRODUCTION

In the Cold War period of the 1950s most American literature became conservative and apolitical, and intellectual life in general was marked by timidity and conformity. Meridel Le Sueur suffered severely from the persecutions visited upon radical writers by Senator Joseph McCarthy and the House Committee on Un-American Activities. But even though her livelihood was jeopardized and many publishing outlets were closed to her, she continued to produce reportage and fiction, much of it appearing in the magazines that succeeded *New Masses: Mainstream* and *Masses and Mainstream*.

The selections here from Le Sueur's published writings between 1947 and 1958 include both reportage and fiction. "Eroded Woman" appeared in 1948 in *Masses and Mainstream*. Like much of her thirties journalism, it finds its focus in the figure of a woman, and Le Sueur's description of the gaunt, but still proud, wife and mother of the title combines the realism of observation with the poetic sensitivity of her best writing. "Used as a tool is used, discarded as a tool, worked as a tool," yet keeping "the bare and meager boundaries of her person intact," the eroded woman is another example of Le Sueur's empathy with the downtrodden and her determination to commemorate them.

Throughout the fifties Le Sueur traveled extensively. Her favorite form of travel was by bus, because on the road and in the bus stations she could talk to people and record their stories. "The Dark of the Time" represents the reportage that resulted. The essay captures the climate of the early 1950s — especially the sense of bewilderment attendant on the Korean War and the growing racial tensions as both blacks and whites began to move in large numbers out of the South. This piece, too, eventually focuses on a woman, as Le Sueur goes in search of the place where Nancy Hanks gave birth to Lincoln. At the site Le Sueur finds that Nancy Hanks is ignored in favor of her illustrious son. "The cabin of her agony" is almost lost inside the marble colonnade, the "edifice of governing man," on which are carved the thoughts of sages, all male.

Le Sueur's interest in Nancy Hanks antedated "The Dark of the Time"; in 1949 she had published a children's book, *Nancy Hanks of Wilderness Road*. A third treatment appeared in 1954 as "A Legend of Wilderness Road"; it contains a constellation of elements familiar from Le Sueur's other writings: the woman alone, neglected or abandoned by her husband; the determination to survive; the birth of a child and the image of new life emerging from the darkness. The style of this piece, as befits its title, is often richly metaphorical. Long sentences composed of participial phrases create for Nancy Hanks an inner life of thoughts, feelings, and dreams. In providing Lincoln's mother with this inner life, Le Sueur is also "returning their history to the people."

ERODED WOMAN

The sight of the shanty in the lead mine district brought back many strains of melancholy from my childhood in Oklahoma, and it was as if I had always remembered the bare duned countryside and the tough, thin herb strains of men and women, from the Indians of the Five Tribes to the lean migrants from Valley Forge. Standing before the shack, an old lean-to, pine bent and tense from the metal onslaught of sun, I was afraid to see the woman I knew would open the door.

The abandoned lead and zinc mines stand in a wasteland of ruined earth and human refuse. Ruin shows in the form of the shanty roof, in the shape of the awful knothole eye which admits chat-laden wind and light, in the loose swinging door. The insecurities of my childhood are awakened. The mine shaft openings glitter in the sunlight and the unreal day seems to shift and shatter and the old fear emanating from the land gnaws at me, fear of space, of moving, of the town, of what?

A union man in Joplin had told me to knock at this door. "The old lady is a fighter, her son is a fighter from way back! We had the blue-card company union here first. They played all the tricks, control of relief, goons, they even had armed Indians against strikers, called everybody furriner and Communist, but we got railroaders blacklisted far back as the '94 strike, and old miners from Little Egypt who knew the score. We held out. Now we got a union. You go see the old lady."

She answered my knock. She was spare, clad in a kind of flour sack with a hole cut in the middle, showing the hulk of her bones and also the peculiar shyness, tenderness, and dignity of a woman who has borne children, been much alone, and is still strong set against rebuff.

She was shy and I was shy. When I told her who sent me she let me into the rickety house which seemed only an extension of her gothic body. She wiped a chair with her skirt. "Set," she said. "It's the chat, overn everything."

"You lived here long?"

She looked at me. Her eyes seemed dusted with chat, their blueness dimmed and yet wide open and upon me, magnets of another human being. "A sight of time," she said, "too long. When we come we were always going back to the Ozarks to a farm." We both looked out of the crooked frame of the window. A chat pile rose up, there was not a tree, flower, or bush. "Nothing will ever grow," she said, fixing her gnarled, knuckled hand in the flour sack of her lap. "Seems like you're getting sludge in yore blood."

We both looked out of the crooked window. More is said in silence than in words. It is in silence that she trusts me. "The Quapaws owned this land but the big oil scared them and they signed it over for ninety-nine years. I guess that's forever as us'n goes. I wouldn't sign over green land like that to some critters I never see.

"My son will be here. He will tell you. He's thinking all the time. Sometimes when he ain't working he makes me nervous setting thar but I know now he's thinking it out. Since the CIO come here he's been thinking. Since they had that row and we was all out of work for so long and they broke up our meetings and they beat up my son. They beat him bad and my husband didn't say anything agin't. 'Ellie,' he said, 'he's fighting for his kin. He's fighting good.' And I tended him for two weeks bandaging his raw skin. His skin was peeled off'n him. Not an inch but what was pounded like a steak and I never said nothing to him. It looked like he was hurt for some reason that was not just hurt like in the mines, not just death. It makes you sore after a while, no use seem to comin' of it. Like all the babies born so hard and dying so early."

A young man came up the walk. "It's my son that was in the strike," she said. "I been widowed twice. It's the chat hemorrhage both times. You drown in your own blood, you do. Hello, son," she said.

The boy was silent and shaggy, with the same blue eyes and a tense grievance in him. He sat on the edge of the bed, his cap in his hand. "Yes, we've got a union now, right of our blood we have. They done everything to us."

"They beat him," she said softly looking at him, and he looked fiercely and briefly at her.

"Yes, the Klan, the bosses, pickhandlers beat up every man with a CIO button. The merchants give dances and prizes if you belonged to the Blue Card."

"They tried to run him out, beat him up twice," she said.

"Don't lower your voice. The Klan don't rule here now, mamma," he said.

"I don't know. The Republicans are coming back. The Republicans sent the army. The army!" she said.

"Talk right up," he said.

"We would not give up fighting for the people and the land. I'm mighty proud of him not to lick the boots of the company. Now I'll be fixing the supper if you'll all excuse me."

When he got into it he was like a man in love. "Why," he said, "I'd kill a child of mine before he'd work in the mines. Children of lead, that's all we call them. I saw my father die, his lungs turned to stone, setting in that chair there till he held his breath and let his blood choke him and then he could lie down forever." Now the union was going to send him North to a school and he was going to learn. He didn't know anything. His mother would go with him and they would go North.

"Another migration," I said.

He looked at me. "You think we should stay? Stay put, eh?" He began to walk around the room, his hands in his pockets. The Mrs. came in. "Well," he said, "I got the seeds of unionism in me. My dad carried his union card in his heart for a long time, couldn't carry it nowheres else. He was always telling us a better life was coming through the union no matter how long we had to fight, he used to tell us. You can always do whatever you have to do to win."

The mother came to the door and said, "If you can eat what we eat, I guess like we used to say if we can stand it all year you can stand it for one meal."

We went into the lean-to kitchen. You could see the earth through the cracks but the boards were scrubbed clean as a butcher's table.

"I was a weaver back in Virginia," the mother said. "Why, if Mr. Baxter, the owner of the mill, was here this minute he could tell you, I could shore weave!"

The meal was a big plate of beans the color of dry locusts and some cornmeal bread. "If'n we had ketchup it would be tasty," he said. "Set!"

We bowed our heads. "Dear Lord, make us thankful fer what we are about to receive and fer all the blessing we receive at Thy hands. In Jesus' name we ask it, amen."

The son wanted to tell what he knew. He believed at first that the blue-card union was the best because it "ain't furrin and it ain't Red" and you kept your job. Then the Blue Card had deliberately affiliated with the "furrin" union, the AF of L.

"A man don't know which way to turn. There was riot and killing in Galena. Lots of folks showed up here from all over. The Communists they help you and they ain't afeared. They call them furriners too."

"Henry," she laughed, "he says the whole darn district is getting furrin, he says he's gonna go on further west. Further west." They laughed.

She sang in a crooked voice, "*Ladies to the center, form a star, kill all furriners near and far.* We used to sing that. Don't never see how a union against the boss is always furrin. My man always was a union man and I don't always rightly understand but I am with him till the day I die and his thinking is my thinking and his way is mine. *Heigh ho, heigh ho, I joined the CIO, I give my dues to the goddamned Jews, heigh ho, heigh ho.* Not even a song like that got our boys to testify agin the CIO. They had to bring in a lot of wild boys and pay some drunk Indians to look like they was a big army agin the CIO. The pickhandle boys went around and the Klan come in."

"I got to be goin'," the boy said.

"He's always off to a meeting," she said proudly.

He stopped at the door. "It's mighty fine, writing something. I hope you do it." He stood a moment. I held out my hand and he hesitated a moment in the dusky door; then in a rush he took it.

When he had gone it was dusk and the wood darkened. I said, "Don't light a lamp. It's nice to sit in the dusk."

"It's nice," she said sitting closer to me. "I should wash the dishes."

"I'll help you after a while. Let's just sit together." She was pleased.

I could feel the clearness of the woman, the edge, the honor, the gothic simplicity of the lean struggle and the clarity and honor with which she lived. She was close to the bone, her face honest as her house with the terrible nakedness of a tool, used as a tool is used, discarded as a tool, worked as a tool, uncared for as a human being. And underneath there stirred the almost virginal delicate life of the woman, her modest delicate withdrawals, the bare and meager boundaries of her person kept intact, unviolated, with human tenderness emanating from her, like live energy. We sat close together.

"The long trek we been doin'. My children always thinkin' we are crossing a river or that the wind is on the wagon shaking and moving. We was movin' a lot. Why, we picked up everything when the mines open at Picher. Everyone was talking about a big lead and zinc vein over here, everybody was tearing out fer the new diggings jest across the line into Oklahoma, jest a hole in the road. It was a time I tell you when everybody was on the road. You see yore neighbor sticking his head outen his shack which was movin' comical right down the road and the living going on as usual, the kids hoppin' in and out shouting more'n usual. Farmers were a-coming from Arkansas and Alabama even and Tennessee scurrying like ants to a new corpse. Ozark hillbillies was comin' in on the freights, knocking on the door at night fer victuals, women even rode the blinds in with their children. Houses from Joplin carted, villages lifted right up and took on wheels, timber pulled by mules right onto the new diggings in Oklahoma.

"First we left the cotton hills, we come trying to git us'n a piece of land in Arkansas sharecropping, but we come on here in the night then when a friend comin' through in a covered wagon with his family and said he is going to Galena for to work in the zinc thar. I didn't want my man to work ever again under the earth but he telling me then he says, 'No, Elly, you kin make a stake thar, we ain't aimin' to stay thar at all. We aimin' to make a little stake and then we goin' into that new territory of Oklahoma we stayin' thar,' he says.

"We got us some of that land, that new good land and raisin' a crop

of kids and whatever they are raisin' in them parts, but it's good land.
That thar was years ago afore the twins died and layin' out thar in no
proper earth I think sometimes I hear them playing in the woodshed.
Now back in Kentucky, I recollect thar was good sweet earth with the
sweet rot of leaves and it's just I think I hear them. I know I don't really
hear them."

All of her teeth had gone, she said, by her fourth baby and her chin
grew upward around as if to protect the sunken mouth and cheeks. "My
man got as clever a turn as you want to see with everything. I got no
education at all. We got one book, a hymn book. I know the words and
I point them out to my sons a long time afore he knew I couldn't read a
scratch. I was ashamed. I never felt much like larnin' when I come from
the mill. My pa was for larnin'. He said, 'You don't know, you air shut
up.' My ma couldn't read but she knew more'n any living woman I ever
heard tell of. And when pa was kilt in the mill she worked as hard fer
her family as cunning and strong you had to be. Born in Catawba
County, her pa owned a farm there afore the rebel war. He never owned
a slave and was bitter agin it saying the white man and the black man
had to stand together, but all his sons was killed in it one way or
another and it don't seem fair.

"Funny thing, the men always dyin' early. Hard life and dangerous,
in my family the women is left with all the chilluns to raise and by that
time you sure ain't in no shape to get another man.

"I remember we had beds of white maple pa made. Then he was
one with his hands but hard times done us out of them, we sold them
for quite a fancy price, I remember. Pa worked in the field and raised a
good part of what we et. We drawed ten cents a day in the mill. Ma
drawed twenty-five. It were winter time when I begun to work. I
recollect we went to work by lantern light and the kerosene lamps
swinging away in the ceiling, I thought they was some kind of bugs
swinging away there. Then my brother went to the mill, four of us
drawing money. Hard times fer us, hard fer me. I got a fever, I
recollect, takes grit to get a body along. I just got over the typhoid and I
went to the boss and I says I'm wuth more'n ten cents a day. I was a shy
body, I just didn't think I had nothin to lose, we couldn't eat with four
of us working and he raised me to twenty cents and told me not to
tell nobody.

"Do you think I'll meet them all in heaven? Do you believe they
will be there now? I remember them all. Sadie, Goldie, Elijah, all of
them and some of the dead ones more than the living. Oh, how it goes
on and how you live through it! Claire, Kate, and the dogs and cats and
mules and cows and calves I have fed, always feeding something, day
and midnight trying to get something to eat.

"I mourned and always mourn. Here was the pasture land and

cows grazing and the green land I remember and crickets and in no time
quicker than scat the green pasture was turned over like the palm of my
hand and the mills was belching at the tailings and the gray chat begin
to drift in all the cracks and the green land was agone forever agone and
never coming back in our time."

She arose shyly. White in the gloom, the match struck sharp in her
knuckled tree-bark weaver's hands. She held it, shaking a little, to the
lamp wick. The light shook, distended like an eye, and the house
sprang in the night in the ruined land. I saw the awkward, hunted, lost,
and wild endurance of her strong odored herb body which I could smell
like night herb and I wanted to reach out and touch her but knew her
flight. The door hung crooked outward and she went to close it. I saw
the darkness, like an eye, through a knothole of the bleached skeletal
sun-wracked pine — a thin boat in the night on a vacant sea. I saw the
frail, sagging iron bed. The broken mirror held the light in a sharp rectangle. She was looking steadily at me holding me in her silence. I saw a
picture of a dead child. A picture of a bride and groom in a round
frame, a garland of paper, faded roses about it.

I felt her deep exhaustion and her sorrow, wakened and warmed
by unaccustomed talking, like soil stirred, the sorrow of its ruin
reflected in her, the human and the land interlocked like doomed
lovers.

I felt a kind of anguish as if we rode a Moby Dick of terror — as if a
great beast rode under us not of earth but of a ruthless power that we
could neither see nor call by name.

Her eyes in ambush look out at me for what I am thinking, gravely
watchful. "My son will stay with a friend, if you would not mind to
sleep with me."

I lay awake thinking of human waste, of injuries which reflect on
the indifference and callousness of us all, of the unrecorded lives of
dead children, the million-faceted darkness of their fear and sorrow like
my own of being trapped far below ground in American life.

All over mid-America now lamplight reveals the old earth, reveals
the story of water, and the sound of water in the darkness repeats the
myth and legends of old struggles. The fields lie there, the plow handles
wet, standing useless in the mud, the countless seeds, the little houses,
the big houses, the vast spider network of us all in the womb of history,
looking fearful, not knowing at this moment the strength, doubting the
strength, often fearful of giant menace, fearful of peculiar strains and
wild boar power and small eyes of the fox.

The lower continent underlying all, speaks below us, the gulf, the
black old land.

The DARK of the TIME

Does the eagle know what is in the pit?
or will you ask the mole?
—WILLIAM BLAKE

Our people in America are in deep anguish. They are in the dark of
capitalism. The assassin passes through your hands daily as the product
you make passes into the chaos of a market you never know. The people suffer under capitalism in a different way than a colonial people, for
the masks are cunning and the naked wars of aggression are hidden
under the words of democracy, and you are delivered into the death of
wars against people you do not hate, and made guilty by Nagasakis and
Hiroshimas you did not plan.

An abyss seems to have opened between the intellectual
cosmopolites of culture and the people, hungry for word and meaning.
In the city you hear the words of contempt for our people. You even
hear that our people have so many "things"—so many televisions,
bathrooms, etc. Returning to the hinterland, I told this to a man who
travels the Dakotas and he laughed bitterly. "The thing about capitalist
'things,' commodities, is that they are not permanent. They are an illusion, you never have them—not even the toilet—now in one whole section of Dakota the outhouse has returned—not that it ever left the majority of farmhouses—but now it is gone! The killing of the REA has
thrown a whole community back to oil lamps, hand milking,
outhouses! Everybody knows you never own anything under
capitalism—it passes through your hands and one month's back payment on the installment and whisk—it is gone . . . gone with the
mortgage!"

Hurt myself by the "big city" mechanical "idea" of America, the
pawn-moving feeling of some organization, I took a bus and fell down
the dark flux of all on the move, the young reluctant warriors, in the
stinking stations of the poor, the young mothers again following,
Negro and white mothers with the hanging pelvis, the torn feet, the
swollen veins, all night with the children swarming upon them, like all
of us on the dark, gutted, eroded American earth outside the windows;
and fragrant strong as that earth and as beautiful.

Wounded from the city, return—return to the dust of earth, to the

angry lean men and the risen dust of wrecked men and women, descend
among the gentle, waiters, movers; the angry boys, green down on
their lips, going to far bases they hate; the young prostitutes clubbed by
the billies of southern cops; workers going to other plants; a generation
in anxiety moving to the burst of birth; old members of the Wilson
brigade, of the First World War, half dead and crazy; dry-leaf bitter
faces of the lost and damned from depression and war, mute and terrible testimony to the splendid "working of capitalism"; peddlers of every
shoddy lust, living off the good body like maggots and lice, and all
moving underneath, all is anguish and moving and the great culture of
the underground common to our people emerging in the night like rich
herbal emanations.

2

After I had slept, looking out at the hills and the moon riding over
and the warm sense of people like myself, we stopped at a small village
and a mother got on with a young child and two older ones, a boy of
seventeen maybe and a girl heavily rouged and pockmarked. The
mother and the little girl took the seat in front of me and the child looked
out the window at the village as we pulled out and I could see the tear
magnifying the eye for the leaving of the familiar village, for the
journey and the joy of seeing her father who was on a construction job
in Chicago and whom, with a fine contempt for space, they were going
to visit. Nancy Hanks I am sure had a body like this, ill nourished, thin
yet strong, gaunt, a little tall, black hair, blue snapping eyes, the weight
and burden strained through a sharp militant humor. She drew the
child down to sleep, with utter warm authority, gentle, no coercion,
anger, or tension. I could see her large knotted hand bear the
child down.

She told me later she had ten girls and two boys, five at home, yet
she was glad — a very good life. Work is good, a very good life with
hard work, it is good not to have enough. You have to scratch. We get
by. Her body was like a great poem to read. She gave it without stint,
like the fields, fragrant, bearing you up, and the gentle emanation of
forgiveness from her, of strength, a curious signal of resistance organized in her eyes.

I returned to the haven of woman, land, the great beloved woman
of my country.

3

In the long night, plunging south, a land unfamiliar to me, but
whose aroma rises to my nostrils, whose people, invasion thin, drift out
of the night into the bus, alight in wide lonely landscapes, or little lanes
dark under the trees, and disappear taking some of me with them, a

crying ghost following their asking as they turn at the bus gate . . . I hear behind me two boys I have not seen, their voices light and terrible, emitting words of horror — one is going to Cincinnati on a book deal, forty-five a week and expenses for two weeks, he doesn't intend to sell any books, after two weeks he will skip, got the job by shining up to the boss's wife, could have had her too but he's already running from one alimony and an angry gal whose car he stole and all he wants is to keep running.

The other one is a sailor and says he would like just a plain old job. Nothing in a job, the other one says, you can work all your life and where are you? I done everything, from driving a cattle truck to a racket in Tammany. Nothin' in it. Make a haul, that's the only hope. Some kind of a haul. I'll make mine yet. The sailor says, the only thing I care about is a sweet fast car. I don't give a hoot in hell for my life. I don't even know where I'm goin' now. Just takin' off without a parachute. I want to just ride fast and straight into hell. I don't want to take no one with me, understand? I respect the lives of other people. I'll never shoot anybody. I never said this before but I'll never see you again but it's the truth, I'll never shoot at anybody. But I don't give ten cents for my own life. Not one cent. Just like to drive straight and fast in one of these new babies, straight into hell!

4

I was never in Washington, D.C., before. I looked at it from the best vantage point, from midnight, way down below, seen by mole, bat, and night owl, in rendezvous with those who have something to say, who do not speak on the podium or broadcast, or who even try for the sixty-four-dollar question or are queen for a day. Besides, after midnight there is no chance for any of this — Colgate's is not going to call your number, or the mailman bring you a message showing you are chosen from the nation to represent what? After midnight it is all over, so I was sitting in the lysol-smelling bus station, the small rest room marked "Colored," and the awful smell of antiseptic that permeates all official buildings.

I went downstairs, and outside the rest rooms there were eight telephone booths, four on each side, and from each booth there stuck out a pair of worker's legs, in work shoes bent and battered, and from the booths there came a strange talk. I had to listen a long time to catch any of it. They were all Negroes come to this rendezvous after work in the late night, or early morning. I saw no face, only the battered shoes, one white from concrete, broken battered feet of workers who work on their feet. I listened amazed, there was much laughter but no face appeared. The feet crossed or uncrossed. Someone was telling a story but it was stopped by a kind of choral laughter and repetition. It's as if they were slightly distended in the mouth into a beautiful rhythm, the rhythm I could hear but the words must be caught in the net of the beauty of the voice and this gentle chant, and reiteration of the theme on a chorale of laughter. I could see the huge brown and black hands resting on the high knobbed knees. I could not stand there and watch. There was a bench in the rest room where I could hear the strange speech. It went on rising obviously to some climax. I could catch a word here and there, the farmer . . . stealin' . . . yes sir he was sore put — and then at the end the whole was suddenly revealed and I felt a rich delight suddenly as if I could run in and speak to all of them, for the teller on a whiff of laughter, a pouf of laughter, said quite distinctly: "And then Br'r Rabbit said to the bossman — do what you like bossman, do anything you like, but don't don't don't throw me in the briar patch. . . ." And on a great descending He! he! he! the laughter joined, flew like sharp birds, the feet pounded, hands clapped. . . .

The cop descended upon them with gruff voice, drove them out. I could hear them walking out and I had the feeling I would find the booths full of dead clubbed birds.

5

Upon the earth through the vent of the cities, the people move in the dark of the American time. It is like a descent into the South through the Virginia mountains, where we see no town for a day and a sign says, Nancy Hanks was born behind that spur of mountain, and we glide into the deep tall night, into the brawny calloused hand of our mother, into her herbal, rank, and strong odors. Like the mother of twelve she leans over us, covers us, her hair of night falling over our burnt asphalt faces.

At Louisville we descended into hell. It is one a.m. and Friday night and hundreds of soldiers are trying to get back to Fort Knox. The segregated rest room is one-fifth the size of the white. It is full of soldiers, also women and children.

The large area of a lunch room is full of soldiers trying to sober up on black coffee, or trying to get another bottle from the many old men and sharpers who are bootlegging bottles at three times their price. Small fights spring up. Old men slither on the stools beside the soldiers making deals, offering them anything from heroin, girls, to a ticket for the Kentucky Derby. More circumspect bookies circulate offering sure bets, talking into the ears of the sleepy dazed soldiers. No one is allowed to sleep. The civil police come along and punch them brutally — wake up bud. . . . For professional sleepers. Old men come in to get warm. The cops search their pockets, ask them to show a ticket, and having none they are plucked up by the nape of the neck and booted out. One worker becomes confused and cries to the cop — I have a job. I have worked all my life. I can't remember. I have a job, it's just the name. You don't work now for a man any longer—it is a company and I can't remember. . . . He was thrown out.

Above on a balcony the military police looked down upon the writhing mass, pointing out every beggar below, or sleeper. There were Negro and white MP's. They came down swiftly at any ruckus and used their clubs, they were armed with every kind of weapon.

I bought a ticket for Elizabethtown, Kentucky, where Nancy Hanks gave birth to Abe Lincoln. The turmoil of the station had come to a boil. A young Negro, very severe, sat bolt upright, and a peddler of bets for the Derby, a slick thimble rig, with the sharp face of the devil himself, stood behind him, set upon him, and a crowd had gathered as he baited him. A man's a man I always say, the pitchman said—it makes no difference to me what color a man is. He winked hugely, there was laughter. Leave him alone, a white soldier said, and swore at him roundly. He kept on—my best friends—still and all—there's a place for everyone, keep their places. The Negro soldier whirled, but before he could strike, the swift movement of many people out of a prepared coil sprang at the same time to hold him back, to snatch the peddler and move him toward the door and from the balcony came the running feet of the MP's, Negro and white, who laid about them.

The poisonous boil burst with foul pus out of everyone. The sound of the police wagon, the shouts of the people in the station, the defense of the Negro soldier, the drunken curses now of the peddler, his foul racism loosed naked, as the police half jerked his clothes off, lifted him, and, along with others, threw him into the wagon. . . . The Negro soldier was taken off to the military. The bus was now stirred like a foul slimy pool, violence broke out, people became sick, the girls shouted and tried to pull soldiers with them and then the bus came and everyone was herded into it and with a jerk we started south toward Fort Knox and Elizabethtown. . . .

It took an hour to unload the buses, some had to be carried out, others cajoled to return, some were weeping. They were so young. The bus driver, a young tender fellow, helped them all, gave them fantasies to live on, held them up, whispered in their ears, slapped them on the back. The last one gave me a big wink . . . goodbye, he siad, we go to save the world! He stumbled and skidded for his balance, turned and made a derisive gesture, half despair, half in satire of himself.

6

I was going to Elizabethtown in the dawn and I was startled deeply for the earth was red, gashed, as if steeped in blood, man-red in the dawn that flooded the tipped spring moon which seemed to pour a blood light over us. I remember I heard the earth was red here but it is startling to see it, red earth out of which came Abe, from the red dawn of Nancy Hanks too.

It was before seven when I got to a tiny bus station at Elizabethtown. There was a taxi driver who had a Yankee accent. He told me Lincoln Park and Sinking Springs were about ten miles away. I walked down the village, around the square and the court house in the center of the square, a big house probably Tom Lincoln worked on, the cemetery spreading back on the hill.

It wasn't seven yet. I stopped in the morning restaurant where workers got their lunches and had breakfast. It was full of men. There was a young girl, a young boy at the counter, and a Negro woman doing the cooking back in the kitchen. Do you know anything about Nancy Hanks? I asked the young girl who was half crazy with all the young construction workers ribbing her and eyeing her. I don't think she lives here, she said. I just about know everybody here. She shouted to the Negro woman — You know Nancy Hanks? No, she shouted back. I said, She was Abraham Lincoln's mother. There was a silence. No one laughed. The boy said, She's daid. Yes, she is, I said. He said after a while — Say, on the corner of the bank there is a thing there written about how Nancy Hanks got married to Tom Lincoln right there where the bank is.

I walked up there and sure enough it was so, a plaque on the cornerstone of the bank. I went up to the cemetery and talked to the grave digger, who knew everyone buried there, and showed me the graves mostly of the merchants, the bankers, the promoters. . . . He didn't see why he had such a job, took a man's place seventeen years ago and still at it, although the price of a grave had gone up considerable. The children began to go to school. I watched the Negro children go one way and the white children another. I said — How soon will the desegregation be here? He shouted — Never. He said Elizabethtown had so many of those bastards now since the fort and construction work and there was no place for them and they would never have it. He was very cold and practically drove me out of the grave and disappeared, throwing up the dirt angrily.

I went out into the street now coming alive and I asked a number of people and they all clammed up and looked at me coldly. By the time I got back to the square a car was following me. And as I walked, in every window faces followed me and I felt a terrible animosity. I had no way of getting out of town.

I went back to the bus station and got the Yankee taxi driver to drive me out to Sinking Springs. The country looked very very poor, scraggly scrub stands, little poor farms, thickets, the earth red. There is a park well kept and on the high hill above Sinking Springs. The spring

is, as it was then, amazingly, a Greek temple with wide steps going up
to the pillars and supporting architecture of a European world, and inside, guarded, within the foreign marble, stands the original log cabin
where, in the small corner, Nancy Hanks gave birth to Abraham
Lincoln.

No word is made of her. There is the door and the leather hinge,
and the fireplace and the wood glowing, the same logs, the helve of the
axe showing in the wood, from the energy of Tom Lincoln, and the
half-open door seems to beckon you into the bare small rectangle,
within the seed shadow, the hearth, fire, the door entrance, exit, wood
and womb.

But here the woman unnamed, the cabin of her agony within the
edifice of governing man, the thoughts of sages, all male, engraved
around the solemn marble; around the wild unknown woman, hidden
in the thought of man, bitted within an old dead idea, yet wild and
strong she is yet in the body of all women. As I run down the steps I can
see Sinking Springs just as it was, still discharging from the cave wall,
still emerging fresh from the bought world, cold and fresh from
underground. I put my hand in the deep water from deep down.

7

When I came across Kansas City to the crack train going north I
felt I had entered another country. The clean, fat, groomed people had
just gotten off the California special train from their vacations in
winter; their faces bore another history and they were very annoyed
because for some reason the train was an hour late. It was hot, the dust
storms were standing below us in the sky covering Iowa, Kansas. They
had come through it, and now the dust stood in the air like a venomed
ghost. They were angry, for we did not know till later why the train
was late.

The train is full of young hot soldiers returning home for their last
furlough before going — where? They do not know. Many of them have
slept in the depot. Some have not slept. A young blond boy sits beside
me and he sleeps instantly, his fair face flushed, his big paws crossed
over his loins and his long head falls on my shoulder. I timidly stroke
his cheek. He seems hardly older than my grandson David and the same
coloring.

For some reason there is no way to cool the train. It is unbearably
hot. My soldier woke with blue eyes like David's, his cropped poll and
red mouth, and he wanted to know why it was so hot and fell instantly
into sleep again. I lay his head gently on the pillow and manage to get
by his incredible mileage of long sleeping legs to the rear of the car
where the soldiers have opened the half window in the vestibule and
brought out the rest room chairs. I do not know then why the conductor

is so tender to them, allows them privileges, looks at them like a grieving father.

It was the middle of the flushed hot afternoon, with the Iowa corn
half a foot green, the tender light on the fields. The train stopped at a
small town. It was the complaint of the tourists that the train was supposed to be a through train but it kept stopping. Only those standing in
the vestibule leaning out of the half window saw why. The train had
stopped, and in the midst of our joking we suddenly saw a young
woman, her golden hair in a pony tail, run by, but her face was
anguished, her mouth open as if screaming. We leaned out to see
toward what she was running . . . and we saw four workers lifting a
coffin from the baggage car to the waiting hearse and some friends held
the young woman, whose eyes seemed distended, and in our eyes was
reflected a coffin. One of the soldiers has dropped his hand on my
shoulder and it is gripped hard. Korea! he says. Another boy begins
to curse.

The train moves on. A woman comes out fanning herself — What
makes the train stop? I paid for a ticket on the fast train. They'll hear
from me! The boys are silent. She goes back. Now they pass around a
bottle. When the train stops they are silent; when it starts they talk too
loud. We are catching up on time, another woman says. Oh yes, the
cursing one says, don't lose any time, get all the time you pay for. May
they choke on their own fat! he curses.

We count how often the train stops — each stop a coffin, running
crying women, the afternoon darkens for us. The boy is still sleeping.
He might be the boy in the casket. So long, so heavy in sleep bolt
upright, so beautiful. Inside the coffin the rot they have returned, the
torn loins of the builders, planters, begetters. In our nostrils the dust of
the afternoon, our agony, led into slaughters we do not dream, misled
by leaders, our constant blind struggle, receiving the new dead sons
quietly, revenge born between our teeth.

We are nearing St. Paul. The last stop, the swearing soldier leaned
out and screamed — Don't open it, for God's sake, don't open it, don't
expect to find him there! We all hold him. He becomes very quiet,
stands with his back to us looking out the window. We go along the
deep mother valley of the Mississippi. One of the soldiers says, Boy, it's
Saturday night. They'll be whoopin' it up on Seven Corners, roll back
earth and take me home. This is Saturday night. Maybe the last, so let
'er go! let 'er go! The other soldier says — Home! Return, return, he says,
there's where we went on Sunday for a picnic, the fishing hole, the
orchards, the prairies, the haying . . . the green corn knee-high by
Fourth of July. Oh God's country this is, let me return. . . . Bring me
back, that's all I ask. Receive me, furrow. Plow deep for me, Indian
valley, bring me home around the world. Oh! he cries, this country! Oh my

country. There ain't nothin' better, look at that river, the crappies, the
bull heads. Oh let me come back to you, roll me back earth, around the
world, roll me backward earth and roll me home!
 He keeps his face to the darkening land for he is crying.
 At the station in St. Paul a hearse is waiting.

8

Let us all return.
 It is the people who give birth to us, to all culture, who by their
labors create all material and spiritual values.
 No art can develop until it penetrates deeply into the life of
the people.
 The source of American culture lies in the historic movement of
our people, and the artist must become voice, messenger, awakener,
sparking the inflammable silence, reflecting back the courage and the
beauty. He must return really to the people, partisan and alive, with
warmth, abundance, excess, confidence, without reservations, or cold
and merely reasonable bread, or craftiness, writing one thing, believing
another, the superior person, even superior in theoretic knowledge, an
ideological giant, but bereft of heart and humility.
 Capitalism is a world of ruins really, junk piles of machines, men,
women, bowls of dust, floods, erosions, masks to cover rapacity and in
this sling and wound the people carry their young, in the shades of their
grief, in the thin shadow of their hunger, hope and crops in their hands,
in the dark of the machine, only they have the future in their hands.
 Only they.

A LEGEND
of WILDERNESS ROAD

To look out the winter-grey log-cabin you had to open the door against the drifts of snow, to the blast of wind and the hounds' cry and the hungry beasts a-prowl, nibbling the bare winter's bough and finding the deep root lurking with juice under the snow; but the woman Nancy with her child Sarah asleep in the bear cover with the bread next to her to keep it from freezing and the gaunt hungry child inside her, his hands like fins, his knees knocking her as he heaved upward against her sides asking for something for his hunger and his thirst and his loneliness — the woman had no roots to gnaw, no beast to savor, no book nor bell nor fine talk to bring the young un' in. The unborn child heaved upward, sounding, and she rose in alarm: would he crack out now? Where is the bolt of birth, she thought, who counts the fingers, even? There was no answer but the prowling, knocking, unborn child, casting up wing or fin, gathering the substance of a tall man in the new wilderness, on such a night of howling beasts and hunger, in such an early season of a nation's growth.

Anger warmed her too when she thought of the great sea of snow rolling away to Elizabethtown where the taverns would be roaring with heat and rum, and Tom, as like as not, smoking in that awful calm he had, the warm grog down his gullet, and the laughter and talk of others who had been to far places, and his eyes on the white thighs of Millie, forgetting the seed already sowed and the harvest breaking the furrows now.

Standing in the center of the silence, with the howling of hunger outside, the eyes in the snow, in the evergreens, in all the lonely burrows of hunger, the faces arched in asking outside the door, the eyes in the frozen fur of hungry animals, and inside her the lean bony, hungry child scratching at her ribs, she heard the scratching at the door, the gnawing at the cabin roots, the popping of the frozen trees and the long belly-howl of hunger and of the chase and of one thing eating another.

In mirage came the days of her own young hunger, a fair wilderness girl running in the barrows, peering from the leaves, bathing in the sunken springs, walking the streets of Elizabethtown, bearing the pointed finger and the whisper about her mother Lucy Hanks who had brought her over Cumberland Gap with no father and singing with the sin, once posted by the city fathers with a terrible word—fornication—and given a year's probation by the man to be her husband who wore a long coat and a stern face, though now Lucy was broken to the furrow, plowed and cropped with more children than you could count, and no more singing.

Listen to the running of the gentlemen's hounds hungry for prey, they sounded now two miles to the west near the Sparrow cabin, the nearest—and what if the child should come early and be born early, then who would lean over the one-legged corner bed and say a word of comfort and cut the cord of life? Count the time again from crab-apple time, and it should be February then for sure and certain; but you never could tell with this one, not round and swimming in a fair summer like Sarah had been but strange in her like a sack of rocks—was that a knee or a hand to shake hello?—as if she nourished in her a fin from the deeps as he seemed to moan in her lonelily and made her double with laughter and anxiety as if his bones shook her, rose and turned with some questing beyond her, with a pressure of delight and urgency. She had bent over, laughing, in the fall when his knocking had started, when she and Sarah had picked the forest nuts, buried potatoes, ground the corn meal; she would bend over, laughing silently, and shake her head and know that there was a friend coming to her loneliness in the wilderness.

"Hush thee, hush thee, thy father's a gentleman," her mother had sometimes sung, and she had put ribbons brought in a caravan over her buckskin skirt and traipsed around humming the old song:

Here we come./Where from?

What's your name?/Puddn n Tame.

What's your other?/Bread n Butter.

Where do you live?/In a sieve.

She laughed now, putting her hands on the gravid center which seemed to contain its own heat and life. "Where you from?" she asked the unborn child, in a lone cabin, in the grey light, with the hounds running for sure far off over the hills. Sarah moved, and she masked her face, neatly folding away the swollen fear and loneliness. But Sarah slept again, and Nancy ground that Tom under her heel for the silence in him, with the muteness of him, being his own man since twelve, walking west alone, no higher than a grasshopper. He was a hunter, not a ploughman, quick to look down the barrel of a gun to get prey in his sight, and she knew how every little animal felt, doomed by his steady silent gaze. No dancing in him or singing or fancy tall talk, and no softness for the reading of a book or the thoughts from the minds of tall spired men. He ate, filled the pot; he came to bed.

When she shyly looked at his stocky figure bringing meat when no one else could, she had thought he would be a friend to her, lonely like herself and shy in his wooing. So the banns had been published, and the country people had come in buckboards or a-horseback from way in the back country, the swamp people, the plains hunters, even old Daniel Boone; and everything had been in Kentucky style with the guests stuffing themselves with bear meat, wild turkey, wild ducks, maple sugar lumps tied on a string to bite off, syrup in gourds, peach and honey preserves and the whiskey barrels running like spring trees. It had been right gay to mount the horse behind Tom and put your arms around his stocky waist and feel his back like a rock of ages, protecting you from the shouts and the jokes that made you blush — to ride in the blossoming of June to the one-room cabin behind the courthouse, and turn dismayed then, after that night, caught in his trap, running in the trap of a little cabin, and only then remembering the heft of a man over you, the dark head between your hands, and the will of a man not taking you in, and all the gay fixings gone, and only a terrible darkness like drowning over you, and the sound of your own weeping, like the spring she had seen Tom fire into to start it flowing, and no woman to speak of it to, each bearing her crop in silence, saying nothing, and the earth bearing in silence.

He had invaded and stupefied her mind, too. Reading, to him, was akin to wantonness. "I always suspectin' 'bout that readin'," he said, making her hide her books as something illicit. "How you larnin' to read? From sleepin' with that golden-ha'rred preacher who come hyar to bring one o' them consarned books onc't? Or runnin' out oglin' every son of a gun with a book or a mite of larnin' comes down Wilderness Road?" She had flown at him like a magpie. "You don't larn readin' in bed. Readin' is harder'n cuttin' down a tree. I'm gonna have me a son that takes to readin', who wants to know something besides the eye down the barrel of a gun — wants to know about the whole endurin' world and the time o' man upon hit."

"You talkin' mighty flighty and high-and-mighty for a plain hunter's wife." And he had taken her down on the bed by violence.

After that she lay under him like a whippet, turning her being out yonder beyond him, way in the wilderness, and she called for a friend out of the hurricane. She had a fury in her for the ways of men taking all to themselves, learning in the books, gallivanting around, hearing all the great talk, coming west now in every caravan.

She thought, "A boy now can go out in the pike where everyone from the east is passin' by, and he can get him a heap o' larnin' just that-a-way, and the blab schools is comin' in and I heard there was a library of books not fur from here, and there there would be all and sundry to come and speak to a boy in the wilderness and tell him what they know and what they brung with them. He could study everything out now and nobody tellin' him he's a woman and should be put in the stocks on courthouse day in Elizabethtown. There are men passin' by here every day of a truth-tellin' nature and they would give hit out to a boy."

She sat on the edge of the one-legged bed, waiting, her mind roving out in the windy twilight looking for food. Thoughts came to her and all were her own since it was a crime for a woman to look into a book. She felt like the smallest door in the universe through which now came a strange man — like a little cave, secret and unknown — like a pod in the frost, a center whirling inward, now full of dreams she never knew, alive in knockings and stirrings and prescience of things and times she would never live to see.

Tough and brown and enduring she was, a storm in an acorn, wrath in a nut, a woman in a cabin, and she left Tom the poor huntsman out of the circle of her cat's cradle and turned to her own creation. The wind leaned and blew against the door, and she laughed and spoke to it. "Go 'way from my door," she said, "all of you go 'way." And to the hungry child, "I'll feed you, I'll find you food, I'll born you right there without no granny woman." For she saw clearly, standing wildly and alone, her fists clenched, that she would deliver herself in February, when the snow would be deep, and nobody would come down that road through those heavy drifts, and she would wait alone the day when she would be brought to bed, nigh on February she figured it, and she would struggle alone to bring him to birth, the raw-boned hunter's spawn, this swamp baby who would be too lean, too dark, a forest thing, made of squirrel meat and paw-paws and wild nuts and loneliness. "And I'll give you warm milk, I always have big dugs for a little one, you'll trot beside me like a long-legged fawn in a bad season, lean and rangy but beautiful to me, my loneliness made tall, my hunger walking, a friend to me in the wilderness. . . ."

Hugging herself against the cold that crept like wolf-howls under the door, through the cracks, she asked of the knobs pressing against her sides, "Is that your head or your knees or the butt end of you? Are you there, Abe? Are you warm?" And the awful answer came — hunger. "I am hungry in the darkness," the knocking said, and with an awful gnawing hollowness she admitted at last the hunger that rears in flowers and beast, speaking from the bright-fanged mouth, that asks from beast's eye in darkness, from fang and fur, claw and hand. The howling wind cried hunger, and the cry of stag and dog, and even the tiny squeaking of the field mice, the tiny deer ears, as like a shadow they flitted across her vision, all cried hunger.

Death had eaten her babies — they were so tiny and unknown in the wilderness — she had left them in the hungry earth. This one should not die. Out of the air she would snatch sustenance. Beasts and berries should feed him, he would live off frozen boughs and be kin to all the hungry. She would find a way to feed him. With a blind strength she took the long unwieldy gun, loaded, rammed it, pushed with all her might against the leather-hinged door, with a gasp fell into the great space and cold of the great earth and sky, the white space and the long shadows, the frozen lyre of the grasses rasped, harped by the wind. The earth opened fanwise, stretching out in overlapping waves beyond and beyond, and the high pulsing cold struck her, and she saw it strike blue against the snow and vault in an incredible flight of light which seemed to beat her as the wintry day drifted to darkness and the frost cupped the light like a shell.

The opened door let in the baying of the hounds, and she could see within the sound their red mouths dripping. All the shadows moved, and she had the feeling of eyes looking at her from the wind, the shadow, and the hill, and she imagined she could hear the lipping of the spring still unfrozen under the snow. Above she felt the avaricious birds flying low, hawk or crow or owl, peering upon crouching catamount, mink, or deer or tiny glass-eyed mice and hungry rabbits. Who hunted her down? She had a mad predatory hunger, now keen as that of the animals, to smell the warm odor of meat cooking spicy and flavorsome for her young.

Cradling the gun, she pushed the door shut and turned into the cold, sinking to her knees, floundering down the barrows, and she felt the child clutch her and hang to the hungry cliff of her sides. She felt something following her, and looking back saw only the cabin almost dark, the windowless sides without eye. How could so small a space hold begetting and birth, the sorrow and the waiting? It seemed to her like herself, a cave's mouth opening inward to vast spaces of the earth.

She turned and went on down the snowy hill, and ahead in the tricky light she thought she saw many animals around the Sinking Spring, and she stopped to make her cabin eyes focus on them as she raised her gun and pointed it at the shadows. She stood in the frosty cold a long time, waiting to see what shadows moved, the snow to her knees; she blended with the swell of the frozen land, and she let the sense of touch of the land come back to her, as it always had, benevolent. But she felt then a shadow following her, stopping when she stopped. She felt it behind, along her back, at the hair roots, and she stood still.

It stood still also, and she thought it was only the secret life around her, the eye of bird, of fox, of rabbit, of nests of coiled snakes, even of chrysalis hanging from a tree limb.

She moved forward, her long dress wet now, but she thought she saw a lean rabbit in the scrub. A rabbit in the pot would send up a savory odor and there would be a little meat for the picking. But the shadow behind her again moved, and the feeling froze her neck and made her back ache. She stopped; the shadow stopped. Far off she could hear the baying of the dogs, now wild upon the chase and the kill. The gun hung heavy in her hand and she felt a moment of utter cold. Then against the sky she saw the head of a doe lift — . For a moment she thought it might be an Indian, but then, unmistakably, she saw the familiar sight of the deer, standing on the spring mound, its tender butt reared, looking in fright.

The shadow behind her moved, streaked like a breath past her. She stood with her mouth opened but did not know if it was herself or the lion that screamed, or the deer. It was a sharp rending of the cold air; the baying hounds seemed to swerve and stop; and then the monumental shadows struggled by the spring, silently, as in childbirth, with only grunts and strange tearings and terrible tensions of blood and bones.

She stood like a tree rooted, her arms outheld. Then silence, except for a lapping sound. To her horror the big cat dragged the doe out into the light of the snow. She could see clearly as he opened the carcass, and the bright entrails shone of warm blood spread on the snow. He crouched with his blunt nose in the meat, and as she moved he raised his eyes and looked at her with a hungry look over his bloody nose and tearing fangs as if to say, Forgive me my hunger. . . .

She saw something on the snow beside her. It was the rabbit the cat had killed and dropped when he saw the larger prey. She picked it up, still warm, and with the gun pointed at the lion she moved backward in her tracks. But the lion was glutted with warmth, and his hunger made a tearing noise; she could see the hot blood on the snow and the neck of the deer thrown back as in terror or in love.

Slowly the night fell around her, the blue shadows rose from the earth like a tide engulfing her. Slowly, afraid to make a sharp move, she reached the door and heard inside the child Sarah crying, wakened by her hungers too. She got in and shut the door. The wave of cabin warmth struck her. She dropped the gun, she waved the rabbit . . . and began a wild singing:

> Rabbit in the cooking pot
> Shoo fly shoo
> Rabbit for my Sarah
> I mean you
> Rabbit in the cooking pot
> Shoo fly shoo
> Skip to my Lou my darling.

And Sarah cried out at the gaiety of her mother.

Nancy grabbed her from the bear cover, with the small bread in her arms, swung her round the cabin, the ears of the rabbit flying, and outside the awful cry of the catamount. "Dance to keep warm, stir up the fire, skin the rabbit and pop him in our mouths." And to the knocking inside her, "Yes, yes, hungry mouth." And, skinning the coat off the gentle rabbit who said nothing and might have been her summer friend but now fed her winter's hunger: "Pardon me, friend," she thought, "for all the hunger at the ribs of all of us, baying inside and out, crying our hunger — the fox and the squirrel and the field mice and the bugs and crickets — all, all with a beast at our ribs nipping and howling. Ah, the hunger and the cry of all brothers. Is it you, boy, knocking and splintering my ribs from hunger? You'll have in you the hungers and the haunts and the hounds of this night, the little rabbit dropped for you from the mountain lion's mouth; ah, you'll have a tough juniper heartbeat. I am strong, and you be too."

"Show me, mammy, show me how you dancin'," Sarah cried. So they danced together in the crazy firelight and fell laughing and tickling each other on the bed, and Nancy rose startled, listening for other times. "I always liked it," she told Sarah, "when the folks came in winter, and the new children, born and unborn, and the fresh milk from the cow, and golden butter, and many kinds of preserves and five kinds of meat, the table groanin' and the big loaves of bread from the ovens. Bring the little bread over and let it warm with the rabbit."

"You waitin' for someone, Mammy?"

"No," she said. "No track to our door now. He'll come up no path that you'll be seein'. I'll wait till February. I'll get my own food or a catamount'll bring it. Tomorrow there'll be some of the doe left."

"You lookin' for somebody, Mammy, to come?"

"I'm lookin' for somebody, but he ain't comin' through that door. He'll come up no path you'll be seein'. Not up that path nor through that door."

"Is that a riddle, Mammy?"

"Yes; riddle me that, Sarry. Where do you live? In a sieve. Is someone walkin' in the snow? Who is leaning from the rock? Who is mangered, leashed, and staked in me now? No path, no door." She smiled, sticking her nose in the pot where the little rabbit began to blend with the heat and spices, and Nancy Hanks hugged herself and smiled, for more than man could be the hunter, and there were no lengths she would not go to find food and fur and fire and shelter.

They sat, the kind rabbit in the pot between them, and ate and sucked the little bones and licked their lips and looked at each other smiling and the child fell over full and heavy in sleep. Nancy covered her and wrapped herself beside the fire which now must die down to save wood. Tomorrow she would find the stumps under the snow, swing the ax, bring in the logs. She had only to wait till February. She settled down with the friend coming to her in the wilderness. "You goin' to be mighty thin and swampy, but living, tough and strong. I'll have plenty for you, Abe, larnin' too, and books. You goin' to be a tall rawbone hunter's swamp baby, made o' too much rabbit meat, I reckon, lean and lonesome, but sweet as a paw-paw. You goin' to be my loneliness made tall, my hunger walking, a friend to all in the wilderness, Abraham."

Renewal

INTRODUCTION

The 1960s ushered in a new period of literary and political activity for Meridel Le Sueur, and the 1970s saw her once again a writer with an audience and a reputation. In a time of new political activism — by blacks, students, American Indians, and women — she found fresh challenges and inspiration. Today, in her eighties, she is enjoying what she calls her "ripening," and she is producing work — essays, poems, and novels — in which, she says, she is writing for the first time "what is completely me."

The style of much of Le Sueur's recent work is a multilayered, multidimensional prose-poetry that communicates not so much through conventional narrative form and causal sequences as through the creation of a matrix of event, symbol, and meaning. It is a style intended as the antithesis of what she sees as the male style of linear movement toward a "target," or a conclusion to be "appropriated." Through this style she wants to convey her sense of the world as an intricate web of interrelated parts, an organic whole that is dissected and exploited only to its — and our — peril.

This view of an organic world informed much of Le Sueur's early work, most notably "Annunciation." By now, however, it has been enriched by the accumulated decades of her own experience and especially by her awareness, in a post-Hiroshima age, of the precarious ecological balance of the planet on which we all live. Women, and their special relationship to the earth, remain central to her views. Indeed, Le Sueur's recent work emphasizes even more strongly, in ways that are bound to be controversial, women's biological or reproductive capacity and their relationship through this capacity to the land.

The excerpt from "The Origins of Corn" included here demonstrates both the new style and the broadened vision. In "Origins of Corn" her treatment of the corn ranges from the chromosomal to the cosmic, fusing science and mystery, fact and vision. The essay describes the continuous cultivation of corn by the North, Central, and South American Indians for 25,000 years; its role in the white settlement of the continent, and its exploitation for profit. But these historical and economic realities are subsumed within a larger vision of the corn: in its commonness, abundance, and survival through history; as a symbol of the unity of all people; and also, through its mysterious biochemical processes of germination and growth, as a symbol of a creative and potentially transforming energy, of the "life force" that infuses all things.

This vision of a world of process, growth, and ever-renewed and renewing energy is also to be seen in the journal entry included here. Le Sueur's journals have always been a storehouse — or, in her word, a "granary" — of ideas for her finished works. This excerpt from a 1977 journal is a series of flashes of interrelated observations. It dramatically combines the movement and energies of different phenomena — glow-worms, Indian dances, Japanese mobiles, radio signals, and the journey of several women down a river — into a vision of a world in constant motion, in which "everything moves to greater intensity, not less."

Suffering — especially the sufferings of women — and death are an integral part of Le Sueur's vision. Both the poetry to which she has increasingly turned in recent years, and the cycle of experimental novels on which she is presently working, engage themselves with women whose lives are largely defined by suffering and death. But as in her earlier work, the descent into the underground leads to renewal. The story of Persephone and Demeter is fundamental to Le Sueur's recent writing. But now the voice that speaks is above all Demeter's: fierce, protective, and grieving, she is the old woman "ripened" by sorrow into wisdom.

Often, the voice in the poems is specifically that of an American Indian woman, for Le Sueur's poetry especially shows her absorption in recent decades with American Indian people and their cultures. The poems often fuse aspects of American Indian culture with her continuing interest in the Demeter-Persephone story. In "I Light Your Streets" the American Indian prostitute who has been destroyed by white culture speaks primarily in the accents of Persephone. But in "Rites of Ancient Ripening," the title poem of a volume Le Sueur published in 1975, it is the Demeter-mother-earth figure who speaks. "Luminous with age," she is anticipating death; but death will be a renewal, since her body will nourish and fertilize the earth.

"Doàn Kêt" is a more specifically political poem, which Le Sueur sent to the North Vietnamese Women's Union as her expression of solidarity with them during the Vietnam War. One of several poems she wrote about that war, it combines factuality with political rhetoric in an effort to express her persistent belief in the unity of all women and their life-giving potential.

In recent years Le Sueur has been working on a series, or "cycle" of novels. They deal with the sufferings, and specifically the sexual exploitation, of women, identified with the technological rape of the land. In the excerpt here from *Memorial*, the first novel in the planned cycle, Le Sueur presents three women who meet in a graveyard where, seeking the burial sites of fathers, mothers and children, they connect with their lost pasts and each other. Their descent, literally into an abandoned mine pit, and imaginatively into their own past lives and into a communal memory, is followed by an ascent symbolic of hope for the future. Thus Le Sueur, in her most recent writings, continues to communicate her unquenchably optimistic faith. Her terms of reference have changed since the 1930s, but her belief in the "communal sensibility" and solidarity of the people, first formally articulated in 1934 and 1935 in "I Was Marching" and "The Fetish of Being Outside," remains undiminished.

The ORIGINS of CORN

I

Hosanna! The corn reached total zenith in crested and entire August. The space of summer arched earth to autumnal fruit. Out of cold and ancient sod the split of protein, the primal thunder. In the mayanface of the tiny kernel look out the deeps of time, space, and genes. In the golden pollen, more ancient and fixed than the pyramids, is the scream of fleeing Indians, germinal mirror of endurance, reflections of mothers of different yield.

The ancient women Gatherers, free wanderers loved the tiny grass, tendered hand pollinated it, created the great cob of nutrition which cannot free itself from cob without the hand of human.

American corn did not come from Europe or Asia. It is thought and flesh of the Americas, transmutation of communal love, Indian solidarity. Bountiful yields, rich protein, small and portable it could be carried by nation-building peoples, planted grown milled on new land, in a hole in the forest, migrant up the Mississippi, builder of new cities where wanderers could stop and build because they had corn.

Protein angels of light in the Indian air guarded by Aztec tigers, granaries out of graves sprang centuries out of vanishment, ran with slaves from the conquerors, mayan strength piled as gold in our village streets, held from usurer and marauder, apex and home of contradiction.

The great Indios threw themselves forward in sacrificial green, emerged in small time to sugar and nitrogen, germinal time brought to immense protein, magic of chlorophyll, transformation of the Sun.

Given to us from brown hands, grown in democratic weather, from the place of massacre, continental coffin made by the conquistadors hid the corn for future summer, thrown like a seed ball from people to people in twenty-five thousand years of a mothering congregation of protein, of corn nuptials, cohesions, solidarity, in the face of dangers, plunderers, thieves, predators, speculators, dice throwers, dis-ease, we lay underground with corn, hoarding the endosperm, preserving inside the shuck ancestral bridal arrayment, communal goodness, and old maps of

Indian ancestors marking the Pollen Road. The road of genetic fulfillment and endurance, comrades of surge, germinal explosions in millions
of seeds.

My grandmothers were red Indian cobs pollinated by strangers. They
bore the anger and strangeness of cross-pollination and the endurance
and the rebel yell, drawing down new sugar, oxygen of new journeys,
sweet of nitrogen drawn to the chemical love, the ovum mothering new
nations and the Pollen bringing to wind and summer ambushed
chromosomes, escaping Indians going to the hills like smoke and corn.

Hidden as we hide in our corn flesh, shards in wombs, pollen ground in
ancient metates, harvest green fingers pointing to new horizons.To be
born always new in cries, shouts, enwrapped in sheaths of summer
green, to come out of ambush, tomb, and resurrection, unknown
journeys on old paths, in ancient heart, cut by the knife of sacrifice. Sur-
render us seasonally in time, salt nitrogen, in the blessed fall of autumnal seed.

O ancient corn magnetic fields from Ohio to Nebraska claiming the
polluted air, the leached soil, the raped earth.

O American corn of the Indios. O Bread. O Summer.

II

Out of the tiny cinteotl grass zia maize was created by the Indios. The
sacred seed was planted four to the mound. The pioneer would carry the
seed in a small sack, cut down a tree in the forest, let the sun light in, dig
a hole and start a corn field. In the great midvalley he could broadcast
the seed on the fertile loam and be equal to any man.

Now a magnetic sea of immense wealth grows from Ohio, Indiana, Illinois to Nebraska, greater wealth than was ever mined. The root goes
down to water, the stalk to the sun producing the photosynthesis still a
mystery to scientists, the chemical miracle unknown. This chemical factory transforms the sun to beast and human flesh.

The Ancient American myths say a woman came over the prairie opened
her breast and saved man from starvation giving him corn.

The chromosomes of corn divide themselves into two sexes. The mother
cell contains ten chromosomes, divides equally between two new cells,
five and five alike, the new cells then divide forming four immature

pollen grains, a second division follows another pattern forming twenty out of original ten grouping in fives making four male pollen grains. Mysteriously each receives message to divide into separate functions. The last two nuclei now divide to form sperm nucleus and move upward to the tassels of pollen. The other moves to the female cob. Four female nuclei die off, four virgins are left to be August brides, each embryo containing eight nuclei genetically identical, bearing the hereditary genes. One is corn germ rich in oil, two others from starch and glutinous endosperm which is the stored food to nourish the baby kernel. This is what we also eat.

The mystery is deep. On a hot still day in August the high yellow tassels of the male plume break joyfully in the air and release the golden pollen. Down below the cob inside the shuck, the bride waits, a silken road issues from each kernel to outside the shuck, drawing in the invisible pollen.

Impatient and ardent as the bee the wind carries the pollen. The mid-valley is alive and golden with pollen abundance promised, delivered.

The silken hairs tremble out of the cob of green and moisture. The great female magnetic field draws in the eager pollen. The anthers quicken and burst the golden sheath. Millions of lovers take to the earth, the journey greater than that of Ulysses. Travels the pollen road into paradise or Hades. The pollen containing the alchemical mystery, one oil rich germ the other starchy into the waiting commune of the nutritional mother.

This proliferating corn made cities and continents of germinating people. The Gatherers took one hundred years to increase their tribe by one person. They created their brother and sister corn, which must live with them to be harvested. It cannot husk itself as the Gatherers could not be husked without corn.

In the golden edge of love we are brothers and sisters of the corn. Solidarity of the ovum and pollen, massive fusion and fission more immense than manmade atomic energy. Immense magnetism of the female earth drawing down the lover sun to pollinate to engender amino acid from corn fire, from august wedding, enormous journey of the sun into the small dark ovum of a tiny indentured kernel.

It is the green blaze of the promise and deliverance of abundance. Miles and miles of singing protein, green of thunder wedding, connubial pollination, seasonally purification of oxygen, green arousement of abundant love.

Something enters the corn at the moment of fusion of the male and female that is unknown to scientists. From some star, a cosmic quickening, some light, movement-fast chemical that engenders illuminates quickens the conception, lights the fuse.

An indefinite presence in the pollinated moment is witness to multiplicity of time and space, announcement from private to multitude, threat to scarcity pollution, dangerous to criminals and thieves, some message of the proliferation of love, spherical returns of prophetic corn.

It shouts hosannas of abundance, seed light of democratic races, magnetism of the great circular dances, green immense native light of the continents alive in the nutrient cob, brothers and sisters saved and wrapped in abundance.

Sugar in the corn. Honey in the horn.

Horn of green ovum sounding to ripe blast.

Ecstasy of doubling of being Numerous.

Women of great prosperities and generosities rising green from maize.

Fulfillment from breast out of deep root, leaven of water and oxygen, smelter of chemical combustion.

Blaze and strike of sun equilibrium, ancestral faces before Asia, proclamations of millions, of the grace of protein and the blessing of nourishment.

III

Coronado saw corn and he thought he saw cities of gold. It was the light of the corn which has produced more wealth than mines, and slaves, since Columbus noted its richness along with the beauty of the native people.

The fracture and grief of conquistadors, the genocide since the Mound Builders, the massacre of Indians, the suffering of black slaves, the cries of Apaches, Zapatecs, Ojibways, all move out of the mass grave in the season of corn.

Corn has been kidnaped, raped, stolen, overproduced, hoarded, robbed, the protein invaded for profit. Hoarders, world eaters have stolen out nitrogen. The Chicago Grain Market speculates in bodies it never sees or touches. The throw of the dice, grain futures, raises the price, robs starving children, destroys small farms,

The life-giving protein is invaded. Plunderers, desecrators, gamblers, burglars, speculators, human weevils, hoarders, thieves, world eaters enemies invade the root with the cold insolence of buying and selling what they never loved.

The world market rapes the grain and cob, object without intercourse. The delusion of money and property as theft.

Brothers and sisters of the corn are held for ransom, our flesh on the slave block, loot for dice, our flesh and blood bet upon by world maggots.

They even in their greed artificially pollinate the crops.

Hybrid corn has twenty percent less protein and five times the money value and creation of plastic cobs.

Our lives have been rented at high interest. Our magnetic fields sold like daughters, high interest and international bankers. Leaching and pollution of the soil, light diminishing in air pollution poison dust upon the delicate culms manipulated gunned down sucked dry glutton, the loving abundance turned into global greed.

I speak to you from the shuck. I send messages down the pollen road. From the great vigil of protein, from the wounded corn lying prone. Let us all speak from enzymed thunder, the bonding of the kernel. Speak from the horizon of murder and the dead corn creators alive in the pollened wind, the greedy think there is scarcity. Snipers, atomic bomb droppers divide the seed of love. It is they announce a crisis of energy. The crisis is their robbery. The crisis of predators, condors, fear of scarcity of corpses.

Hear the councils of the corn around the atomic blast. Hear the hosannas of the communal green. October message we are secure in the seed corn. Guard the democratic corn.

IV

Come myriads to the true protein.

Cry hosanna to the multitudinous congregations of millions the zenith the symmetry of the global people perfect in cob abundance.

Cry hosanna to the ripe corn, ripe in the silk kernel in the milk. All resurrected in the seed harvest. Eat the golden abundance. Save the holy seed corn for the resurrection.

Cobbing in the world vortexes, journey of the Pollen annihilates death, mathematical unity in the abundant harvest.

My hungered people come home to the cob, to the stalk, home root to the great council of cyclonic love, defying Strontium winds, purifying poisons in the ovarian grace and the joyful benediction of sperm.

The earth is not feeble and submitting. It has its directions. We have our directions. We are also fierce defenders and devourers. The seed piled in granaries and on our village streets is not for barter. It is armed corn to feed the multitudes.

It is thrust and maximum hope of synthesis, solidarity of seasons and genes.

O the dentured corn the message holographs in sacred medicine power reflecting dimensions missed strengths, gathering thunders of thousands of summers, chorales, orchestrations, riotous convictions of solidarity.

It is horn blowers of simultaneity.

Let us move inside the shuck of communal good in the congregation of cob wrapped in green carbohydrates, ancestral robes of nitrogen we can survive under the horses of the conquerors under steel hoofs of torture.

Meet me in the hub center of ovum endurance, human conceptions unarmed gunless corn.

Germinal explosions of our ancestral strength in the green tidal stem, into the live male tassel leaping from root to sun, the only rocket that contains the moon. You don't have to land on her.

Ransom the hostage cob, seed us in joy and sorrow, after alarm of winter hunger, the woman cob arises from sleep from cadavers dead ash below zero rises in the split chromosomes of sugar and starch, from caches of winter storage from the glow of mother Abyss, herbal engendering, speaking Nahautl and Lakota. We claim and ransom each other with the corn.

We will live the winter out sitting underground in all solstices, in the
nuclear seed where the mother endosperm waits for future egress.
See we will feed you while you mutate beyond the clench of power.

We counter all moves to murder and move to grace redemption of the
act of growing. The holy wafer of conception we enter each other in the
wilderness of no surveyed country, where nothing is owed, nothing is
lost, nothing spent.

Hosanna! Open the cell cry of shuck need cry to ovum, speak to corn
desire out of no wound, no slavery, no sin or murder, the fierce root into
the abyss, the staunch sugared stalk and the fiery pollen and the
magnetic cob, in the real arrangement of chromosomes.
Let us go to the mating.
Turn air into hosannas
O corn of love. . . .
                    O thunder of protein
        In the burning blaze in the autumnal air of sulphuric light
                        The green corn
                        The seed Corn
                        Rebellion.

THREE POEMS

I am luminous with age
In my lap I hold the valley.
I see on the horizon what has been taken
What is gone   lies prone   fleshless.
In my breast I hold the middle valley
The corn kernels cry to me in the fields
               Take us home.
Like corn I cry in the last sunset
Gleam like plums.
               My bones shine in fever
Smoked with the fires of age.
Herbal, I contain the final juice,
Shadow, I crouch in the ash
               never breaking to fire.
Winter iron bough
               unseen my buds,
Hanging close I live in the beloved bone
Speaking in the marrow
               alive in green memory.
The light was brighter then.
Now spiders creep at my eyes' edge.
I peek between my fingers
               at my fathers' dust.
The old stones have been taken away
               there is no path.
The fathering fields are gone.
The wind is stronger than it used to be.
My stone feet far below me grip the dust.
I run and crouch in corners with thin dogs.

I tie myself to the children like a kite.
I fall and burst beneath the sacred human tree.
Release my seed and let me fall.
Toward the shadow of the great earth
                    let me fall.
Without child or man
                    I turn   I fall.
Into shadows,
          the dancers are gone.
My salted pelt stirs at the final warmth
Pound me death
          stretch and tan me death
Hang me up, ancestral shield
          against the dark.
Burn and bright and take me quick.
Pod and light me into dark.

Are those flies or bats or mother eagles?
I shrink   I cringe
Trees tilt upon me like young men.
The bowl I made I cannot lift.
All is running past me.
The earth tilts and turns over me.
I am shrinking
          and lean against the warm walls of old summers.
With knees and chin I grip the dark
Swim out the shores of night in old meadows.
Remember   buffalo hunts
Great hunters returning
Councils of the fathers to be fed
Round sacred fires.
The faces of profound deer who
                    gave themselves for food.
We faced the east the golden pollened
                    sacrifice of brothers.
The little seeds of my children
          with faces of mothers and fathers

Fold in my flesh
        in future summers.
My body a canoe turning to stone
Moves among the bursting flowers of men.
Through the meadows of flowers and food,
I float and wave to my grandchildren in the
Tepis of many fires
            In the winter of the many slain
I hear the moaning.
I ground my corn daily
In my pestle many children
Summer grasses in my daughters
Strength and fathers in my sons
All was ground in the bodies bowl
        corn died to bread
            woman to child
                deer to the hunters.
Sires of our people
Wombs of mothering night
Guardian mothers of the corn
Hill borne torrents of the plains
Sing all grinding songs
        of healing herbs
Many tasselled summers
            Flower in my old bones
            Now.
Ceremonials of water and fire
Lodge me in the deep earth
        grind my harvested seed.
The rites of ancient ripening
Make my flesh plume
And summer winds stir in my smoked bowl.
Do not look for me till I return
            rot of greater summers
Struck from fire and dark,
Mother struck to future child.

Unbud me now
Unfurl me now
Flesh and fire
            burn
               requicken
                  Death.

I Light Your Streets

I am a crazy woman with a painted face
On the streets of Gallup
I invite men into my grave
                    for a little wine.
I am a painted grave
Owl woman   hooting for callers in the night.
Black bats over the sun sing to me
The horned toad sleeps in my thighs,
My grandmothers gave me songs to heal
But the white man buys me cheap without song
      or word.
My dead children appear and I play with them.
Ridge of time in my grief — remembering
Who will claim the ruins?
                  and the graves?
                  the corn maiden violated
As the land?
I am a child in my eroded dust.
I remember feathers of the hummingbird
And the virgin corn laughing on the cob.
Maize defend me
Prairie wheel around me
I run beneath the guns
                  and the greedy eye
And hurricanes of white faces knife me.
But like fox and smoke I gleam among the thrushes
And light your streets.

DOÀN KÊT*

I

How can we touch each other, my sisters?
How can we hear each other over the criminal space?
How can we touch each other over the agony of bloody roses?
I always feel you near, your sorrow like a wind in the
great legend of your resistance, your strong and delicate strength.

It was the bumble bee and the butterfly who survived, not the dinosaur.

None of my sons or grandsons took up guns against you.

And all the time the predators were poisoning the humus, polluting
the water, the hooves of empire passing over us all. White
hunters were aiming down the gunsights; villages wrecked,
mine and yours. Defoliated trees, gnawed earth, blasted embryos.

We also live in a captive country, in the belly of the shark.
The horrible faces of our predators, gloating, leering,
the bloody Ford and Rockefeller and Kissinger presiding over
the violation of Asia.

Mortgaging, blasting, claiming earth and women in the chorale
of flayed flesh and hunger, the air crying of carbon and thievery.

Our mutual flesh lights the sulphur emanation of centuries of
exploitation. Amidst the ruins we shine forth in holy mutual
cry, revealing the plainest cruelties and human equation,
the deprivations of power and the strength of numbers and
endurance and the holy light from the immortal wound.

---

*Doàn Kêt means "solidarity" in Vietnamese. This poem was sent to the
North Vietnamese Women's Union, where it was translated into Vietnamese
and warmly received. The poet received a letter of thanks from the women.

The only knowledge now is the knowledge of the dispossessed.
Our earth itself screams like a bandaged, roaring giant about
to rise in all its wounds and bear upon the conqueror.

Lock your doors in the cities.

There are no quiet dead — and no quiet deed.
Everything you touch now is ticking to its explosion.
The scab is about to infect.
The ruined land is dynamite. Cadmus teeth of dead guerrillas
gnaw the air. Nature returns all wounds as warriors.
The Earth plans resistance and cries, "Live."

What strikes you, my sisters, strikes us all. The global earth
is resonant, communicative.
Conception is instant solidarity of the child.
Simultaneity of the root drives the green sap of the flower.
In the broken, the dispossessed is the holy cry.

We keep our tenderness alive and the nourishment of the earth green.
The heart is central as lava.
We burn in each other. We burn and burn.
    We shout in choruses of millions.
    We appear armed as mothers, grandmothers, sisters, warriors,
      We burn.

II

Sisters, the predators plan to live within our bodies.
They plan to wring out of us unpaid labor.
Wrench their wealth from our bodies.
Like the earth they intend to bore inside the woman host,
open the artery like weasels, use, consume, devour, drill for
oil, eat the flesh of the earth mother.
Like the earth they will consume all woman flesh and the
commodities of her being.
The harbors of the world will be for the sale of her body.
The sweat shops will multiply stolen wealth of her living skin.

They slaver at the cheap labor of women around the world.
They will grind us on the metate, like living corn.
We will be gutted and used by the Companies to make wealth.
General Motors, Ma Bell, Anaconda, pickers of cotton and
coffee, hanging our babies on our backs, producers of hand
and brain and womb.
The world eaters sharpen their teeth.
Out of the unpaid labor of women they will triple their wealth.
Women far down under are trashed, pressed into darkness,
humiliated, exploited.
Half the women of Puerto Rico sterilized, the salt savor of
our sweat tiding like an ocean.
Brothels called meat markets in all the ports of the conqueror.

We are the wine cask struck to the ground, spilled.
We are a great granary of seed smashed, burned.
We are a garroted flight of doves.
We are face out of bone. Years of labor bend the bone and back.
Down the root of conquest our bodies receive the insult.
Receive a thousand blows, thefts of ovum and child.
Meadows of dead and ruined women. There is no slight death.
After the first death there is no other.
The Body trashed, dies.
There is no abstract death or death at a distance.
Our bodies extend into the body of all.
Every moment is significant in our solidarity.

In solidarity I stood at the gates of Honeywell where the "Mother
Bomb" is timed and triggered. I hid my grandsons from the gun.
I crouched under the terrible planes of Johnson, Nixon and
Kissinger.
I felt the boots on your throats as my own.
I saw the guns pointed at us all.
It was the gun used on my sister.

Now in the "white house" another mask of white criminals
turn upon us, on our native people at Wounded Knee, cut food for

our children and promise us a bigger army. Children are shot
down, I hear mothers crying from the black belt.

Women of the earth, bear the weight of the oppressor,
bearing us down into deep to glow upward from the dark,
from the womb, from the abyss of blood, from the injured
scream, from below we glow and rise singing.

III

I saw the women of the earth rising on horizons of nitrogen.
I saw the women of the earth coming toward each other
                with praise and heat
                without reservations of space.
All shining and alight in solidarity.
Transforming the wound into bread and children.
In a new abundance, a global summer.
Tall and crying out in song we arise
                in mass meadows.
We will run to the living hills with our seed.
We will redeem all hostages.
We will light the bowl of life.
                We will light singing   across all seas
The resonance of the song of woman,
                lifted green, alive
                in the solidarity of the communal love.
Uncovering the illumined fruit
                the flying pollen
                in the thighs of golden bees
We bring to you our fire
                We pledge to you our guerrilla
fight against the predators of our country.
We come with thunder
                Lightning on our skin,
Roaring womb singing
                Our sisters
                        Singing.
Choruses of millions
                        Singing.

JOURNAL

May 31, 1977

3 three women   four four women

Spring   It is like the electric theory of tesla where you invoke and continue and expand the electricity charge of the earth . . . the same charge as you have by invoking it, you repeat it, discharge it like lightning . . . like a forest of glowworms I saw once on the white river in the ozarks   all seemed to be lighting at once in a thousand million places   yet one golden light repeating, multiplying, then falling into one single light, then beginning again. There are no transmission lines   the transmission is in fields like light   is instantaneous and lights up great areas at the same time   responsive as a tuning fork to electric vibrations at a certain pitch   tune in and repeat. Repeat . . . and convulse and enlarge the field of receptivity   200 lamps lighted at a distance of 23 miles.

Tesla's ideas remain in the notebooks at tesla's museum   in belgrade museum radio signals from russia on this beam   the earth   the flesh   the woman is beaming these signals   is continuously vibrating and everything answers   vibrates at the same time. The electric energy problem solved by the earth and woman   a half hour later signals returned from the west at greater intensity   everything moves to greater intensity, not less . . . nothing can be spent, all is generated. Also come from many locations at the same time   like sound everything starts vibrating.

We all seem to be full of surprises   these are partly because we enlarge each other's perceptions, pick them up, immediately reflect them. We are like those japanese glass mobiles breaking the light, returning it in sound, breaking against each other in an outside wind.

As in the indian dances everything begins to move, the hills begin to dance, the light falls like a great torrent, the flesh jangles moves reflects the singing comes from the dancers and the dancers from the singing . . . all is plowed furrowed up planted. Bursting what does a planted field do shake like a gourd sings every inch alive . . . shaking so the light passes between us the four women the passage down the waterway between the green thighs seems to press us together in the heat and the silent slow movement over the water.

Attempt at portrait.

Power without the use of wires.

MEMORIAL

This is the first part of one of the short novels, five in all,
which will be a large symphony of five movements with the
circular structure and tonal quality of the resonance of
women. We will journey into a spoke leading to the vortex
toward the central energy of a global form, away from the
linear narrative form so highly developed by the male scien-
tific aggressive orientation of the past.
It is a story of three women: mother, whore, and intellectual,
searching for their dead and their past. They all go to the
tavern where they come together in a communal memory and
illumination of their mutual history and suffering. The three
women leave together, fall into the dead mine as into hell,
find each other in their terrible and illumined past, draw
together melded by suffering, and find the great Iowa Sow in
the night and sleep in the true and mythical identity and
cyclic return of all female nature.

Meridel Le Sueur

1

The spring flowered women and children with their picnic baskets
passing under the cemetery arch   abandon hope all ye who enter
here   O hold out my empty bowl   my salted hide tanned by
vinegar and gall   like papa used to beat and tan the pelts of dead
beaver caught in his trap
So I won't lay you out papa   perfume your beard   fold
down the limp genitals of lost fathers   burn a candle foot and
head   shake the holy water over your rotting corpses   take your
sperm tears   squeezed out of the juices of your body's sorrow
The bones lie under   could you fit them together
Could these bones rise in the month of lilacs   shake like dice on
the hills of our breast   howling squatters' rights to abandoned mine
and meadow   green hair from my mined body   death from my
mouth   I have been filled with earth murderers   criminals have
topped me
Strange and mutilated fathers buried in the pit   blood sperm
and egg   lying in the dynamited seams and arteries of the excavated
pit   fifty miles below Iowa dirt

Goodbye to the faithless and fatherless feet hanging from my
mother's bed   would you come to the hungry heart and empty
womb   take fire in the bloody and abandoned pit
I hold you papa in my mined and marauded breasts   in the
emptiness of the devourer   whore and sterile monster I have returned
among the picnickers   dank spores of the betrayed rotting in the spring
airs   they won't know me   leper matted with blood   empty
cavity of belly
It's nothing they said mining me   take it out   take it
all   knife it out   blast it out   don't let them see the mined
hole   the blasted womb

Mama said, when you were born I was glad. They took you out,
laid you on my stomach and I saw your dark hair.

Was that good, mama, was that good for you?

O it was very good but I didn't want you to live the life I lived. I
wanted it nice for you, not in this terrible mining town with the black
people across the ravine.

It was a joke, mama, we all got to be black, equal from the mines.

Go away, child, go far away, mama said, better yourself. Don't
have children. Be something.

What, mama, what can I be?

Be away from the mines, the black dirt, the terrible pit. Get out,
go! Remember me as you go.

I am here mama   I have come back abandoned   emp-
ty   hear me   I bleed empty as the mine mouth gutted   en-
tombed   torn mine pit of my belly closed   come back where our
fathers are entombed   torn closed emptied   womb of earth a
salted bowl   like the big mine machines they suction out the
uterus   mama like the coal a million years of prodded sun-
shine   taken   stolen   sold

Look at me, mama.

I see you, daughter, no eggs to ripen, no nine months to count.

You know where papa was buried?

O you know your father, girl. On pay days rowdying with the
boys, talking on street corners, whooping it up at the tavern.

I remember, mama, when we waited at the tavern door for
his check.

And him coming drunk, banging at the door, at all hours.

And us crouched in the prairie night, waiting for his drunken roar.

Yes, your papa was a carouser, that's for sure. I was glad to let him
in, great hawk flying down on us all. I lost many children from him and

buried them free as we traveled or wherever we were.

O mama, he beat you. He tore the children out of you. I held you, bleeding in the night, little wren, ravished and planted with all those blasted babies.

O your papa was a pretty man, a charmer, everyone said. Remember the circus? We waited at dawn for the trains to come in and the parade down Main Street, and we waited for your papa to buy the tickets, and he went off with a crony and we waited and he didn't come. The circus started and we waited and we were tired and the long shadows came and the circus was over and he came as if nothing had happened. O, he was a card! Merry as a cricket with his drunk cronies, all three sheets in the wind, him doing his imitation of Fields — how's my little chicadees!

Remember, mama, the wild ride home, and him singing and whipping the horses. O he was a careless man, beautiful, singing Skip to My Lou My Darling, and I always rubbed against his great legs, laughing at his jokes. O mama, he was a careless man.

Don't say anything against your father. He was a good man, went to the pits day in and day out, from can't see to can't see. O never forget, girl, his fine body down in the dark pits digging coal, and they closed the mines down and threw us out like dirt, shoveled us out. You won't find him, daughter, smelling of corn liquor and sen-sen.

Mama, laughing, beckons me across the graves, spectral in the spring green, past the buxom women in bright gingham, with their little children, spreading out the picnic cloths in the bright gold air. They come bright from the torn villages, the gutted earth. How did they make flesh from destruction? They won't know me, my sunken cheeks, my body grave of the mined womb, pit of the gutted seed.

O papa, I know where you are beneath the slag or lurking in the tavern waiting for your ruined little girl as you used to call me. Has your yearly pig fattened now, farrowed, yielded us the sweet bacon? O papa, I remember your hilarious story, rocking the tavern, about the famous flying sow. You saw her laughing, flying past you, all her heavy meat caught up in a big wind. Twice, you said, she was lifted into the air, flew throught the air, piglets and all, and landed in a farmer's field, where she first was filled by the prize boar and never eaten, honored in the village and the countryside, great goddess, full and pregnant sow, sacred winged sow, impregnated by the wind. O, you were a card, like mama said.

I'll sing you a cracked song. This is a hard song and I will sing it!

Coming from Des Moines to the phantom dead mining town, evacuated like a bombed village, after the companies took billions out of our bodies and the earth, leaving nothing but the dead after the big explosion. The company left the dead inside the earth, saved funeral expenses.

I came on the bus and the old land seemed to pour into me like mother and child after a long separation. The little thickets of plum beginning to froth looked like old women in shawls still waiting at the mine mouth for the return of the men.

I saw the one street left of the village abandoned and our old house half fallen in, slanting as if being sucked under. I could hear our cries of conception, birth, and hunger. We were being slowly killed by an enemy we never saw. Like a ghoul it sucked our blood, left us with black lung, stone lung, same for black or white.

This was a rich country, meadows and rivers and animals. The Indians who were also evacuated, stolen from, left to die, didn't have to even plant anything. The bus stopped at an old service station. Some people stayed on the slag heaps, planting corn, raising pigs.

Around the empty houses the faithful lilac and iris still remembered us among the dead earth and the ghosts. Even the slag with wind and offal of dead animals sprang out with green weeds and I cried to see the torn earth, and the brave appearance of buxom women, the rise of old meadows, the breasts of our mothers furrowing green in lilacs and burdock and thistle.

Papa! Mama! I am looking for you! I am holding out my empty womb, bowl of salt, of emptiness and begging.

Mama, you washed and dressed his dead body after the explosion.

Yes, papa had a wonderful body, and a silver tongue. Remember, he could stand swaying a little before us all and say Bryan's speech of gold by heart. O he was a wasted man, too tall to crawl in the mines the live long day.

And the Haymarket speech, mama—Let the voice of the people be heard!

Sometimes he would tell the whole story of the Haymarket martyrs and how they put sacks over their faces as they hanged them and tears would be on his cheeks.

Remember, girl, how we used to pick lambs' tongues, dandelion greens in the spring, and dock and summer berries.

And you made us whistle as we picked wild strawberries so you'd know we weren't eating them.

O we had good times too. It wasn't papa's fault we got no place, only deeper in debt and children. There was something we didn't know against us.

Why did I go away? You had something real, mama. The way you scrubbed his back when he came home and the children coming bloody between your legs and you suckled them, even the cave-ins, the dangers

were real. You said, climb the ladder of success. But you could stand at
the tipple and wait for a live man, and weep for real and terrible death.
    I thought it was best, daughter.
    Papa said, your mother is crazy. Your people are here. Who's go-
ing to defend you, if not your kith and kin, the people who know the
same suffering as you? But, papa, you knew they take it all out of you,
you are gutted for their profits, you knew that. I heard papa say to
mama, I got no cock for you. I put it into that bitch mine. I am empty. I
have to sleep. She washed his body, swathed his dead limbs. She touched
him so tenderly, saying it was none of his fault that he didn't make it.
He worked down in the dark and gave me good children, she said.

*I was mined papa like you   I was suctioned scraped torn
violated and emptied   mined robbed stolen   as they stole you
papa   spectral city rising out of the pits   out of our bodies for
wages   I thought it was for love but I sold my body there   I was
hunted by armed hunters and criminals   slave catchers   buyers
of bodies*
    *He told me they could take it out   scrape it out   blast it
out   doctor of death   he said the uterus was filthy useless   you
don't need it   hazardous to your sale on the auction block   in the
mines they have suction machines   blasting tools   and cutting*
    *He said I would be free   and men would swarm at me like a
honey pot   I am free in the grave   in the gutted seed   spectral
village of our begetting now the dead ruins of wasted workers   papa
said you cannot bury the unjustly dead   they will howl forever and
haunt you and shake the earth*
    *O regal women   mothers below the sod in proud sleep   faith-
ful women lilacs budding in rape   arms folded waiting at the tipple
for us all to come home   green embryo children I must cover with
sod as you did mama*
    *Earth skin covering us   corpse return to mother land   wash
us clean of coal dust   as mama washed you papa   folding your
hands over your genitals   wash us whiter than snow   put our
mother hands over the torn bodies   pitiful in their torn muscles and
the great black curls of your breast naked pitiful and dead*

wait   for me mama
buried alive   my salt bowl of sorrow
run   run   before the old soldiers shoot
over the unknown graves
and the old Judas preacher
shows us the glory of the company death

phantoms are running over the graves
see through my hollow flesh
phantom
let me go down   rot
cover me with sod soil
explosions   burning bushes
eyeless   ashes and fecal drop
run run between sire and mare
run from the murderer I slept with
fork and crotch of kill
float in the Iowa air with the spectral
smashed amputated flesh unknown
most frail most human most dear most lost
father in spring melting of dung
of another year's rotting and rutting
of flying sows and sperm
sprung from bud bursting wombs
festering wounds
arms
and legs rotting and howling
fathers I look down on your fierce dirty beards
nest for turds of rats socket eyes looking up for rescue
gouged and abandoned in torn bowels
in the cave of old summers
memories crawl like maggots
summers exploited exploded gouged screwed eroded looted
killed
mothers sorrowing grass out of your knees   peony bushes
and lilacs breaking to bud from wild green wombs
buried in earth   light me   keep with owls' light
and greening hair upright from frightened skulls
O papa   O mama come   come
leap out of rape into scream
in ruin and wrath let the waters down
in ruin   and rot
gangrened wound   pus lighted in
ruined land as if all slag and ruin

rose to flower some bright flesh
breasts of milk leaning over the
smoking abyss
shades of ruined flesh turn to ripe
great udders to the torn mouth
enormous sows   opened to sweet flesh
graves curling like the lips of roses
in the flight of prophetic owls
groan and quake of opening egg
lips of earth
swelling
and a wilderness of ova

2

Descend down the throats of lilacs   shrubs do bud and shake to
moisture   do you smell sorrow   old shawled women ghosts   at
the tipple of disaster   stone me in the ruined village   howling
witch at the cemetery gates   lambs will not take away the sins of the
world   mother clay salted like hides   let the fertile women spread
their corn shuck skirts upon the new green   put down chicken salad
and fried chicken for the children   with dandelions in their
fists   arouse fragrant matrons and old virgins from Dachau   old
soldiers on cane and crutch   and after the rusted oratory of the old
preacher   young men blowing taps for the bomb that will kill them
And I will be gone   I will not sing the song

Then I saw her running from grave to grave, disheveled, one eye
higher than the other, crazy, stooping, her thin face in her wild straw
hair, peering at the stone slabs. She flew toward me, crying, Missus,
can you read? Can you see good? Can you read these here sayings cut
in stone that tell who lies here dead and gone? Suddenly she was close
upon me. I put my hands out to fend her off like the dread flight of an
anguished bird. She took my hands in her dry claws. I could smell her
terrible life like a starving animal's.

Air you lookin' fer a body?

I don't know, I said. I had a father I thought was buried here. I'm
going now.

Why not stay till you find yore pore daddy and give him a flower
and a howdy and remembrance.

I forget now, I said, where my father was buried. Maybe he's just
down at the tavern.

O fathers! She laughed like a young girl, O fathers! You never sure
they're put down or when they will rise and claw out of the grave to

swear bloody murder at you. Shore enough it's them whistlin' up their buddies on moonlight nights, gatherin' up the rascals to whoop it up at the tavern, primin' they selves to get a human woman down for seeding. We gotta have fathers.

Yes, the lovely fathers.

Why, the fathers, yes, the great seed fathers. Yes, the roving rascals. My mama used to say, my daddy just had to hang his pants on the bed post and she'd get knocked up. What did your daddy do?

He was a miner mostly. I don't remember him much, I lied. She was leading me back into the cemetery, past the graves. Why, Missus, O remember them all, every one. My daddy is buried inside the mine. You remember the big explosion and they sealed them in. The mine is his tomb. The company just sealed up the mine and left them down there in the dark they was used to. I don't have no tombstone to read for my daddy. He always said not a sparrow falls. Missus, see if you can read it on a board here about my little baby. We dug the grave ourselves and she lay in her father's tool box and I tried to remember the tree she was near and we left her never to come this way again. I come here on a bus thinkin' I might find her place of burial in the earth.

For some reason I followed her now in her anxiety, leaning down to read old inscriptions. No no, she would cry, her name was Heather. I always liked the word Heather. I never seen any as I know of. Yes, it was that year, what year was it now, two after mama died. Over here, Missus, over here, what does it say now? Yes, the dead hanker to be remembered. Those in their prime hate to leave us, blown sudden like, to kingdom come. He was a dynamiter and the earth blew up on him and buried him forever. We cried for him, honey, we all surely did cry for him. And I am cryin' now. Same earth tooken my babies, and we folded them down, and patted the earth over them like a blanket. How many little 'uns you had?

None I said, and never will.

Oh it's sad to have them and sad not to. It's a hard hard road picken in the fields, know nothin' but stoop labor. Sometimes I cain't remember where they are all laid to rest. I had four men and three women livin' not countin' those tooken out of me by hook or crook, on account I couldn't feed no more. When you push 'em out, the head out of the furrow, it's always spring, and when they die you become a grave. Sure enough, I remember now, we brought her in the wagon, and sure enough, I remember now, it was in the pauper's place. We couldn't buy no grave ground. The earth got no price and gives eternal care. I guess the grass stands high.

She had my hand now and I gripped hers. We entered a corner of the cemetery with wooden decayed signs and naked mounds, with old tin cans and dead flowers.

I'll try to read the signs, I said. They are washed out by rain and time.

It's no use, she said, never you mind. My body is her grave. Little Heather, she was a bonny baby, until the day she choked with the croup. We was workin' on the corn canning, I remember. Never mind, it's in here, rememberin'. The dead are hungry to be remembered. They cry in the night. Sometimes I rise up, hearin' my mama callin' me. Mama, I answer her. I can feel her right sweet in my breast, breathin' heavenly breath, without corruption, as the Bible says. Sometimes she is holdin' the dead, my little sparrow, my little mama, hunted down, wrung out, trapped, famished, carryin' a heavy load, screwed down in the furrow, hungerin' and thirstin', a crucified Jesus woman.

I was afraid now I was going to cry. All right, let my lost laying father lay, let him alone, his beard thrust up into the dark.

O the poor fathers, leaping like goats over the target, into the winning and the losing.

She turned and touched me so kindly. I never had anyone grasp me like a root, lean into me and seem to draw me out of the dark of anguish. She moved through the tangled arteries of loneliness, her quick sorrow strong, torn like bone of the terrified, running from hunters, running curved in the spring strong light. And I touched in her the terrible land and the explosion of all the violence, insult, blows, neglect, sorrow under the aimed gun of the assassin, and mourned with her the tiny corpses of our children, without name, long rotted.

We began to run from grave to grave, breathless, laughing. We fell together on the grass. Are the dead chasing us? Are they calling us, playing hide and seek?

She began to roll with laughter. We're sittin' on the front porch of old stinker the banker. He'll charge us interest.

She got up and began a curious dance, waving her thin arms, laughing, bending, running wild, quick among the swollen buds of the peonies, curled outward, breaking, stretched open in heat for the outflow of flower. I looked at her queer dance in wonder. She was entering me like the roots mama pulled out of the ground for healing, the long roots out of the dark that healed us. I couldn't leave now.

A tiny, wiry old man, bright and alive, ran to her, catching her in her mad gyro, cried out to her, Yore the daughter of Shaemus I knowed. I'da knowed you anywhere, his quick way and hawk nose.

You remember Daddy, she cried.

There ain't nobody gonna ferget him, how we dug fer seven days to git him out, and the Company said, hit's enough, seal them in and he's down there still. They closed the mine off and left them down there ferever.

Yes, they done that. She sprang to him and wound her thin arms around him and they stood embracing, heads close in communal memory. Why yes, she cried, you might remember. You was here when we come in that buckboard with those two old mares with my little dead girl in the summer. She was my fifth, the first to die and that's a hard thing. We was singin', Swing Low Sweet Chariot, comin' fer to carry me home and you helped us dig the grave. My daddy always said you was the best union man in these here mines.

They began running and I ran with them and we read on the faded wood, Little Alice. Seemed to be a whole lot of little children lived a couple of months. Written out in black paint, Suffer Little Children To Come Unto Me, and little carved lambs, and hands intertwined.

Looks like she ain't got no name merked anywhere in this world, the old man said, wiping his head, folding his crooked legs to rest.

Sign probably rotted or somebody taken it. Well it's all right. She's buried in me and I got a sign fer her.

Missus, the old man said, I want to tell you there's places laid out by the company to be buried where they say. Not a black person buried here. Never. Had to send the dead black to Des Moines. Now ain't that somethin'? Good enough to die in the mines like flies but not to be buried where their kin folk can visit them.

He took a bottle of redeye out of his pocket and took a swig and she took a swig and I took a swig and it went down like a hot ingot.

He put his root tree hand on her knee. Well, how are ye, old girl?

Well, I'm alive and kickin' and that's something. How are you, Paddy, old IWW, old hobo?

Well, I escaped old king coal that merry old soul. I never even got the black lung. When they closed the mine I went west, helped organize the Western Federation of Miners. I'm a hardy toad, come out of the holy beak, too mean to die. Kept alive just to spite 'em. You lookin' to put a flower on the mine mouth fer yore daddy?

Yes, I given him remembrance on this memorial day. I don't like it he's sleepin' in Company earth.

Fiddlesticks, the Company don't own it, they just stole it.

Well, that's the truth. You a good keen old man, Paddy. I'm mighty glad you alive. You outfoxed them, you did. What you doin' here, Paddy, mournin' fer us all?

I come to bear witness. I try to come every year. I'll never let them ferget. I got to speak for the wounded and the dead. Come down to the joint tonight. The old boys will be there. Come bend the elbow with the livin', wet yur whistles and speak with devils and angels.

Then a big fellow with one arm came up and slapped her on the back. Well, well, he said, the good old girl herself. And she quickened

and bridled and the color came into her and she sprang with challenge
and a touch of derision. Well, it's good to see you, Matt, the crowin'
cock of them times!

And you was the best lay in the country, they said.

O you old cock of the roost, she laughed, you never knew who
you had in the hay.

Glad to see you got your vixen tongue on you still, you good old
girl. Bring your fancy friend and come to the tavern tonight and give us
a whirl.

She held out her hand, timid and shy, caught up her stringy hair
like a young girl, as if terribly burnt in some fire, and the old man
seemed to catch some electric charge and began to laugh and hum in a
high voice.

*All the wizards of ruin burnt in the raw green   leaped out
screaming   the awful and lost sybils of prophecies sat over the burning pit of ruin and despair   out of the lilac's fire sybil   ovarian
pods   the hinged seed   sword edge   cutting peony light   we
burned together flesh now   in the dying day   cry out of
tomb   tipple dark opening*

shaking flesh
descend
go down   go down
open the maws of dark
descend through the vaginal
entrance of lilacs
sod of dead flesh
remembered green loins
struck to flesh
dark old summer womb of green and rot and worm
dung struck to radial
skeleton to kernel
memorial with others greening
hot ingot
old man's red eye
struck to fire

5

You all fixin' to do me wrong, you all hatin' me and pointin' a
finger at me for comin' back to your dirty town from the houses of
Oklahoma City. I been sold in Omaha, Des Moines, and Kansas City,

and other places I cain't remember.

Ain't you Rose? You lookin' mighty familiar.

No, I ain't. You got me mixed up with someone else.

But the woman turned a terrible face to look back, and I knowed she remembered my pretty face before the gang took me over yonder by the old banker's stone, six of 'em. Why'd I come back here where my poor mama cringed down when every boy in town thought they could throw me down anywheres and even the banker and the preacher and railroad agent would pay me to meet them in secret above the grocery store.

Why hello, girl, ain't I seen you before?

They look like the good old boys who got me down in the cemetery when I was a girl my mama called the Rose of Sharon, the lily of the valley. But my papa already set me on his knee and made me think I owed him to let him put his hand up my skirt. And when he heard he lay me down in the woodshed and took me and then beat me.

They was singin' out — Iowa girl, the devil made you mouth, you burnin' up the south.

Get away from me, I hissed, and hit at them with my pocket book.

You got a creamy skin, gal, you just made for sin.

I knowed you. I remember you. My pappy said he saw you on the streets of Oklahoma City.

Ashes to ashes and dust to dust, go away, girl, you smell of lust.

Get away from me. I got me a pistol. I'll shoot you full of holes and I know where to shoot too.

I'm not a girl, I'm a scythe. I'm a deep hole and you pigs will fall in and never be seen again. You pigs, you're worse than any pig. Get away from me.

What's the matter here, one of the old soldiers said. On such a day ain't seemly for the young to be fightin'. Why, ain't you Rose of Sharon? My, you was a pretty gal and you look all right to me now, baby. Don't think you're looking at an old wreck. Why, I'm full of the old dander.

Get away from me, I said, you dirty old soldier, get away.

The boys hummed at my back, Come out tonight, buffalo girl, come out by the light of the moon.

And the old man said under his breath, spitting, whore, bitch.

I felt like crying. I wanted to leave, but I saw Yoni, that good old woman, friend of mama's, with another woman I didn't know, kind of dressed different than around here, and I knew she'd think of mama with me, and I ran over to them.

Why, Rose of Sharon, Yoni cried. Why, girl, it's good to put my arms around you.

I could hardly keep from crying. She smelled like mama. Nobody put their arms around me for so long. I hung to her. I didn't ever want to look up from her thin neck, her breast against me.

Why, you're mighty thin but pretty as a picture. Ain't you eaten? Why, Rose, this is my lady friend here come to find her pappy's grave and help me lookin' for my little babies. You don't remember my baby Clara do you? How's it goin' with you, darlin'?

No use to hide anything. It's going going gone with me, pickled and soused, takin' the leavens now, the hoboes bums winoes with a dollar. All they want now is baby dolls. O you beautiful doll, you great big beautiful doll, let me put my arms around you, I just can't live without you. Yes, the little girls. If you're fifteen, yes, they pay for young meat, lamb. I been just turned out because I couldn't make it, not even a good pimp for me. I need a hundred fixes and I'm fixed.

Why did I come back to this stinking hole?

Why, you come to see us old friends who remember you, how pretty you was. O mama used to say it did your bones good to see you, like a wild rose in the meadow.

O yeah, that ain't worth anything in the brothels of Kansas City.

Well it ain't worth anything in the world, Rose of Sharon, but if'n you see it once you never forget it and if you have it you don't lose it.

O bullshit, I said, angry. Who's your fancy friend?

Why, I don't think you remember her. She's been to New York up among 'em. She's come back to honor the grave of her pappy.

No such thing, the woman said, kind of angry, but she took my hand and she seemed a kind of sorrowing woman in her good clothes and her smell of the city.

I best be goin' back to Des Moines.

Why no, Yoni says, you come all this way and now we'll find the grave of your mama.

But all these people, I said. They remember. . . .

They don't remember the bad. Now they come and put flowers on the dead in the wars. O they have a long time to remember what is true, who took the bloom and the blest, who tore the wound open. My mama knew the enemy and she and your mama made up for the corpses by crops of good flesh.

O yes, I said, flesh opening like the earth to be gouged and broken. Great tractors gouged the earth and brought up the jewels and sold them. They blinded me. I fell into the pit a golden girl to come up a hag.

No, we ain't no hags, Rose of Sharon. We are good bright shining women like them lilacs of the sweetest memory and giving. Now ain't we lilacs burst out for our mamas.

I felt some awful scab fall off my wounds and the pus ran out and my skin was golden. I followed them two women looking for my mama's grave or my grave.

I got the cops after me, I said to Yoni. They havin a clean up in Des Moines and we got to get out of town for a spell. It'll pass over.

Why good, she said, we goin' to have a get together of old timers at the tavern in the evening. You come along, you be with us.

I kept close to her. I followed her.

I remembered when I had no fears, went running like this to trees of fruits not graves. Split open, ripe, I was ready for whatever happened to me. I was glowing, a persimmon at ripe, on my breast and belly alight in the sun little golden hairs, like a peach, and to my surprise a bush of great golden curls way up my belly.

They followed me like I was taffy, and I thought it was just the gold warmth and the light and the hearth flesh burning, smelling, tasting, like bees around petals opening.

They used to say in the coal dust town with the Negroes across the ravine and everyone with coal ground into them that I was the only white person, or golden person, and the men coming home at dusk like gnomes called out, hello Goldilocks, hello baby, hello light of the earth, give us some light. And I was a young girl skipping with pleasure, thinking they saw me as light, as flower, as gold.

What can you do with the singing   and the wandering   the running slight virginal girls of the wilderness   spindly-legged   breasts like hanging globes   and god help you the hounds follow   whistling at you   grabbing you from behind at picnics   throwing you under them in the thickets   and you fighting them   holding the cleft of your thighs shut

And the words of mama   telling how they came across the Appalachians   and the great revivals in the forests   where you had to run from the horny men   and thousands fell down speaking in tongues and gave entrance to each other in god's ecstasy   thrown down like the earth   seeded by passing bucks going nowhere you would never see again   and digging it out with spoons   for they aimed at no tenderness or child   but only jock and jut   and ran leaving for other gold fields

Look out mama said   you'll be robbed and drouthed and torn by the teeth of renders

Prairies   like my mama's blankets pulled around us while we bled aborted birthed and died   a stick across our mouths to bite on   keep from screaming

I followed these two women away from the street, the lousy pimps and the Johns bargaining. How much? How long? How big?

I can jump a man quicker than a cat smiling and catch him in the bad place to make him holler, but something naked cowered inside me, scared. I had to jack-roll a poor horny John. Got the terrible blues. Don't feel like picking them up anymore. Think of lying straight out under the earth like we put Mama. Maybe I came to lie beside her now. O let me. Let me now.

She said, come with me, you all come to the tavern now.
Where, I said.
O no, Rose said, I don't want to see those good old boys of long ago. O no, not me.
O the good old boys are now old men, honey, and they will all be turnin' and dancin' and the memories will heat us all and we will sing and the juke box will be roarin' out for the dancin'. Let's leave the old ancestors turnin' their faces up into the dark of the great spring sow's belly of corn Iowa.
Now let us walk together. Come, Rose, and walk into this night. We are walkin' with the dead and wounded and the sun is going down.
I am shy, she said, I am wounded and shy.
Yes, Yoni said, we are walkin' on the hard roads. Yes, we will bend the elbow and drink with those who live on and remember.

The roads were darkening and the bright fat mothers were calling their children in, and calling goodbyes, calling into the moist darkening of each other cries high in human flights through the dusky damp of memory. The air felt dark and cool and the slag ruins opened like druid mouths. I gave up forever looking for the lost grave of my mad-clown father.

Come, Yoni said, taking our hands on each side of her. And we went through the arch and into the slag hills that now took no light, gave back no resonance, cinders and earth turned inside out. The earth opened in great pits yawning like beasts, but Yoni knew the way. We rose and fell through these dead heaps, the only light now around the horizon where the furze of trees made a thicket of light.
I fell down and Yoni dragged me behind her and Rose was running on and laughing, I know these pits of hell, I'll never forget them. This was the space of ruin for me.
I have to pee, Rose said.
Yoni stopped and raised her skirt.
Oh, it's good to piss in the dark on the beating earth.
The only better thing is pissing in the snow when it steams up and hisses.
They were standing with their legs apart, their dresses lifted, and I could hear the stream on the slag.
What's the matter, woman, she said to me.

I don't know how, I said, I can't do it.

Why, there's nothing to it. You direct it down so it won't wet your legs. Just let the waters of Lethe down.

I laughed, you'll have to teach me.

Now, look at my belly, flat as a girl's. They tell you children ruin your body. It isn't children, it's work and fear. Look at my nipples rosy as buds, and I nursed six children. Come on, feel.

She guided my hand and I was surprised by the firm belly and the great bush of hair that sprang out like some burning secret under her cotton shift, lively as a red fox springing out.

Let's go, Yoni cried, letting down her skirt. And we ran.

AFTERWORD
TO THE SECOND EDITION

Now that I am older it is even more wonderful to look at the gathering of this anthology, like some excavation of lost testaments, the transformation of silence into language. Now, looking back, it seems even more an act of courage than it was at the time, a great gamble to bear witness to reality in the face of patriarchal enemies who maintained the silence of the oppressed as a fortress of death.

My work was buried like that of an anti-fascist writer who buried his writing in his garden. When he dug it up it was too late. You are buried with your work.

But now I am beset with many terrors and fears. Did I bear witness truly to the terrible times through which I lived? Was I intimidated, injured, mute? Was I vague, filled with old ideas, romanticism, illusion, and fear? I had a duty to bear witness. I spoke out of the disasters of the world wars, depressions, slavery, conquest. Even women did not always want me to speak out. My grandmother hated my writing. She said she had spent her life concealing her life now I wanted to tell about it. You were figuratively burned as a witch for revealment.

Looking back, I feel I did not reveal enough. I didn't know how to do more. There was no precedent for telling the truth about the life of women. Did I betray my grandmothers, the lost and muted women? Did I make my stories too decorative, too pleasant, even too lyrical? I often felt myself on the edge of despair. I did try to commit suicide. Writing down what happened was often secret, written under the quilt at night, hidden in diaries.

Sometimes writing was like sinking down into a deep well, dangerous. You who now have begun to tell it cannot imagine the anguish, the terrible struggle of becoming visible, the dangers of old images, of country sorcerers and voodoo culture. Like Van Gogh I went out in the village at night with ten candles fastened to my hat to surprise the truth from every object and being. Compared to the anguish and the delusion of our lives these are meager pictographs on the cave wall, suggesting merely the dimensions of our struggle.

Like all witnesses, I am dissatisfied, guilty, fearful I have in some way betrayed those whose voice I was. We did not emerge from the past unhurt. I sometimes feel ravaged, root blasted, injured, scarred. Out of our mutilation and silence, you can hear our scream. These fragments of reality are wrested with pain, from a half-seen reality. We made the drawings in the stirred dust. You must decipher, illuminate, and translate them.

We do not appear suddenly as by miracle. Our heads are excavated from prairie soil. Many of us died in concentration camps, even after we were rescued. We could never eat again. You will have to expose us cruelly and love us.

Yes, like all witnesses of holocaust, I am dissatisfied. Yet it is a miracle that these tiny portions of reality survived, like the Dead Sea Scrolls, preserved in huge vessels in a dry country. I was not only blinded by sinister illusions, but by the form and substance of the patriarchal language. Did I fall into the pit of romanticism, lyricism, the trough of pleasant, feminine conclusions?

Now you can look for the necessary and living word, the word of nourishment and relationship. Now we can deny the patriarchal world of betrayal of the object, of seizure and exploitation. Now we can find the revolutionary, revolving, and circular word, and the structure that leads to action and synthesis.

Yes words can be stolen, shrouds of reality, seducers, a bell ram leading you to slaughter, forming fake structures of mandarin patriarchal brutality. I have felt sometimes like not speaking, like being mute. But now I feel we must take words back, warm them and make them glow again, and allow them to lead us to relationships and tenderness and illumination. We must give them flight again and milk and juice.

This book is not just a book to consume and throw away. It is part of a pattern of creative work and understanding. It is not strange that the book should be published by The Feminist Press. Never before have I had a woman editor. The Feminist Press respected the work as a reality not an entertainment. The gathering of this book took a number of years—from the time that Tillie Olsen suggested it, and her daughter Laurie and other editors of The Feminist Press came to my daughter's basement in St. Paul, where my unpublished work is stored, and where they spent a week collecting out of the tombs my writing of the past. It seemed to me that they looked at these scribblings as fertilizer, as new images, as shards dug from the past, as occasions for learning and history. Several editors shaped and reshaped the book in those years. They also created a new form—not a volume of success, or ego, but a book of learning, of growth. Pears cannot ripen alone. So we ripened together. Florence Howe and Elaine Hedges held it in focus and Elaine Hedges made of the growth and chaos of my life work a learning tree, a map, a light. She brought the fragments together in a synthesis so that we all might learn.

A great tide has carried this ripening to us. Our audiences nourish—the women who ask for and draw the images in great collective congregations. Other publishers and friends and passionate believers at great sacrifice and care give us visibility: a group called Villages and Voices—of creators, not consumers so we all become part of writing, editing, typesetting, distribution; John Crawford, who came to the basement and found *The Girl* written in 1939 and never published; Mary McAnally and her celebration of women's song, *We Sing Our Struggle*.

Perhaps women like me of another generation are a bridge. Pass over, use the energy of the root in our witness and our singing. So we will never be gone. You have more tools now. The fog is lifting over the illusions. You have begun to tell it. You will bear sharper witness. Be bold. Tell it all. Don't spare the horses. The earth is waiting to hear you. All the children and the ancients are waiting. We shall come home together.

BIBLIOGRAPHY

ORIGINAL BOOK PUBLICATIONS

The Girl (Cambridge, Mass.: West End Press, 1978)
Rites of Ancient Ripening (Minneapolis, Minn.: Vanilla Press,1975)
The Mound Builders (New York: Franklin Watts, 1974)
Conquistadores (New York: Franklin Watts, 1973)
Crusaders (New York: Blue Heron Press, 1955)
The River Road: A Story of Abraham Lincoln (New York: Alfred A. Knopf, 1954)
Chanticleer of Wilderness Road (New York: Alfred A. Knopf, 1951)
Sparrow Hawk (New York: Alfred A Knopf, 1950)
Nancy Hanks of Wilderness Road (New York: Alfred A. Knopf, 1949)
Little Brother of the Wilderness: The Story of Johnny Appleseed (New York: Alfred A. Knopf, 1947)
North Star Country (New York: Duell, Sloan, & Pearce, 1945)
Annunciation (Los Angeles: Platen Press, 1935)

RECENT REPRINTS

"Persephone," *Lady-Unique-Inclination-of-the-Night* (Autumn 1977)
Song for My Time (Cambridge, Mass.: West End Press, 1977)
Women on the Breadlines (Cambridge, Mass.: West End Press, 1977)
Harvest (Cambridge, Mass.: West End Press, 1977)
Corn Village (Sauk City, Wisc.: Stanton and Lee, 1970)
Salute to Spring (New York: International Publishers, 1940, 1977, 1981)

OTHER RECENT PUBLICATIONS

"Struck to Ash. Struck to Fire," *Great River Review* 21, 1 (1979): 31-43.
"Excerpt from 'The Origins of Corn,'" *New America: A Review* 2, 3 (Summer-Fall 1976): 20-23
"Excerpts from Meridel Le Sueur's Unpublished Journal, Summer 1964," *Ms.* 4, 2 (Aug. 1975): 64.
"Journal Excerpts," *The Lamp in the Spine* (Summer-Fall 1974): 94-126.

Selected criticism, Reviews, And Interviews

Clausen, Jan, "The Girl," Motheroot Journal (Spring 1980): 3.
Clausen, Jan, "Review of Women on the Breadlines, Harvest, Song
    for My Time, Rites of Ancient Ripening," Conditions: Three
    (1978). (Available from Box 56, Van Brunt Station, Brooklyn,
    N.Y. 11215)
Hale, Dorinda, "Le Sueur: Living, Writing from Within," Sojourner
    3, 3 (Nov. 1977): 9,21.
Hampl, Patricia, "Meridel Le Sueur — Voice of the Prairie," Ms. 4, 2
    (Aug. 1975): 62-6, 96.
Hampl, Patricia, "My People Are My Home — A Profile of Meridel
    Le Sueur," Preview (Nov. 1973). (Available from Minnesota
    Public Radio,45 E. 8th Street, Saint Paul, Minn. 55101)
"Interview," West End Magazine 5, 1 (Summer 1978): 8-14. (Available
    from West End Press, Box 7232, Minneapolis, Minn. 55407)
"Le Sueur. Woman Writer, Political Activist," Worker Writer 1,5:
    1-2, 7.
". . . on the far edge of the circle. . .," Lady-Unique-Inclination-of-the-
    Night (Autumn 1977): 14-15.
[Schleuning], Neala Young, "'America — Song We Sang Without
    Knowing' — Meridel Le Sueur's America" (Ph.D. diss, University
    of Minnesota, 1978).
Smith, Mara, "Meridel Le Sueur: A Bio-Bibliography" (Mimeo-
    graphed, University of Minnesota, 1973).

Original Publication of Selections in this Volume

I. Origins
    From North Star Country (New York: Duell, Sloan, & Pearce,
        1945).
    "The Ancient People and the Newly Come," in Growing Up in
        Minnesota, ed. Chester G. Anderson (Minneapolis, Minn.:
        Univ. of Minnesota Press, 1976).
    From Crusaders (New York: Blue Heron Press, 1955).

II. The Emergence of the Writer
    "Persephone," Dial 82 (May 1927): 371-80.
    "Spring Story," Scribner's Magazine (May 1931): 553-62.
    "Wind," Windsor Quarterly (1935): 1, 3.
    "Laundress," American Mercury (Sept. 1927): 98-101.
    "Our Fathers," Intermountain Review of English and Speech
        (Feb. 1, 1937).
    Annunciation (Los Angeles, Calif.: Platen Press, 1935).

III.· The Thirties
"Women on the Breadlines," *New Masses* (Jan. 1932): 5-7.
"Women Are Hungry," *American Mercury* (March 1934):
    316-26.
"I Was Marching," *New Masses* (Sept. 18, 1934): 16-18.
"Cows and Horses Are Hungry," *American Mercury* (Sept.
    1934): 53-56.
"Women Know a Lot of Things," *The Worker* (March 1937).
"O Prairie Girl, Be Lonely," *New Caravan* (1945).
"The Girl," *Yale Review* 26 (Dec. 1936): 369-81.
"Gone Home," *Kenyon Review* 7 (Spring 1945): 235-45.

IV. The Dark Time
"Eroded Woman," *Masses and Mainstream* 1, 7 (Sept. 1948):
    32-39.
"The Dark of the Time" *Masses and Mainstream* 2(Aug. 1956):
    12-21.
"A Legend of Wilderness Road," *California Quarterly* 3
    (Winter 1954): 3-9.

V. Renewal
"Excerpt from The Origins of Corn,'" *New America: A Review*
    2, 3 (Summer-Fall 1976): 20-23.
"Rites of Ancient Ripening," *Corn Village* (Sauk City, Wisc.:
    Stanton and Lee, 1970).
"I Light Your Streets," and "Doàn Kêt," in *Rites of Ancient
    Ripening* (Minneapolis, Minn.: Vanilla Press, 1975).
"Excerpt from *Memorial*," adapted from "Struck to Ash.
    Struck to Fire," *Great River Review* 21, 1 (1979): 31-43.

The Feminist Press at The City University of New York offers alternatives in education and in literature. Founded in 1970, this nonprofit, tax-exempt educational and publishing organization works to eliminate sexual stereotypes in books and schools and to provide literature with a broad vision of human potential. The publishing program includes reprints of important works by women, feminist biographies of women, and nonsexist children's books. Curricular materials, bibliographies, directories, and a quarterly journal provide information and support for students and teachers of women's studies. Through publications and projects, The Feminist Press contributes to the rediscovery of the history of women and the emergence of a more humane society.

NEW AND FORTHCOMING BOOKS

Always a Sister: The Feminism of Lillian D. Wald, a biography by Doris Groshen Daniels. $24.95 cloth.

Bamboo Shoots after the Rain: Contemporary Stories by Women Writers of Taiwan, edited by Ann C. Carver and Sung-sheng Yvonne Chang. $29.95 cloth, $12.95 paper.

A Brighter Coming Day: A Frances Ellen Watkins Harper Reader, edited by Frances Smith Foster. $29.95 cloth, $13.95 paper.

The Daughters of Danaus, a novel by Mona Caird. Afterword by Margaret Morganroth Gullette. $29.95 cloth, $11.95 paper.

The End of This Day's Business, a novel by Katharine Burdekin. Afterword by Daphne Patai. $24.95 cloth, $8.95 paper.

Families in Flux (formerly *Household and Kin*), by Amy Swerdlow, Renate Bridenthal, Joan Kelly, and Phyllis Vine. $9.95 paper.

How I Wrote Jubilee *and Other Essays on Life and Literature,* by Margaret Walker. Edited by Maryemma Graham. $29.95 cloth, $9.95 paper.

Lillian D. Wald: Progressive Activist, a sourcebook edited by Clare Coss. $7.95 paper.

Lone Voyagers: Academic Women in Coeducational Universities, 1870–1937, edited by Geraldine J. Clifford. $29.95 cloth, $12.95 paper.

Not So Quiet: Stepdaughters of War, a novel by Helen Zenna Smith. Afterword by Jane Marcus. $26.95 cloth, $9.95 paper.

Seeds: Supporting Women's Work in the Third World, edited by Ann Leonard. Introduction by Adrienne Germain. Afterwords by Marguerite Berger, Vina Mazumdar, Kathleen Staudt, and Aminata Traore. $29.95 cloth, $12.95 paper.

Sister Gin, a novel by June Arnold. Afterword by Jane Marcus. $8.95 paper.

These Modern Women: Autobiographical Essays from the Twenties, edited and with a revised introduction by Elaine Showalter. $8.95 paper.

Truth Tales: Contemporary Stories by Women Writers of India, selected by Kali for Women. Introduction by Meena Alexander. $22.95 cloth, $8.95 paper.

We That Were Young, a novel by Irene Rathbone. Introduction by Lynn Knight. Afterword by Jane Marcus. $29.95 cloth, $10.95 paper.

What Did Miss Darrington See? An Anthology of Feminist Supernatural Fiction, edited by Jessica Amanda Salmonson. Introduction by Rosemary Jackson. $29.95 cloth, $10.95 paper.

Women Composers: The Lost Tradition Found, by Diane Peacock Jezic. $29.95 cloth, $12.95 paper.

For a free catalog, write to The Feminist Press at The City University of New York, 311 East 94 Street, New York, NY 10128. Send individual book orders to The Talman Company, Inc., 150 Fifth Avenue, New York, NY 10011. Please include $2.00 for postage and handling for the first book, $.75 for each additional.